What others are saying...

"This lively fictionalized account of the life of Makikele Malatji, a key figure in the nineteenth-century history of Phalaborwa, is based on the author's extensive collection of oral traditions supplemented by a deep knowledge of the archaeology and anthropology of the area. Dr. Scully traces this ruler's astute leadership during a time when his kingdom faced internal divisions exacerbated by encroaching European settlers, traders, and travelers; he also highlights the political influence exercised by royal women. Appropriate for readers of all ages, the book will be of interest to anyone seeking to understand and preserve South Africa's rich local and regional heritage."

Iris Berger, Ph.D., Vincent O'Leary Professor of History, University at Albany, State University of New York. Author of **South Africa in World History**

"*The King History Forgot* is a remarkable story, and a valuable piece of the complex picture of nineteenth Century Southern Africa history. Scully listened to accounts from elders of the Ba-Phalaborwa tribe, mining details from a rich oral history to reconstruct the life and changing times of the Northern Sotho king, Makikele Malatji. Makikele's defense of his copper-rich kingdom against Swazi, Zulu and European incursion preserved the integrity of his people and infused a sense of pride continuing to modern times. I became aware of the wealth of African oral tradition passed down by elders while a Peace Corps Volunteer in rural South Africa in the late 1990s. Sadly modern events, urbanization and need to migrate for work have interrupted this unwritten flow of stories. Scully's book, written by someone who understands the ethnography and archaeology of Phalaborwa, is thus an engrossing read, and an important gift to future generations"

Jason Carter, J.D., 42nd District, Georgia State Senate, Decatur, Georgia. Author of **Power Lines, Two Years on South Africa's Borders**

"Too many of history's fascinating characters and important events are lost forever because no one cared enough to find, understand and share them. Each one that is lost takes with it lessons that can teach us about our own world today. In bringing to life the story of Makikele Malatji and his people, Robert Scully has given the rest of us a chance to learn from their fascinating lives, culture and exploits. By using the technique of historical fiction, Scully takes us into the world of the Phalaborwa people in a way that is both engaging and entertaining. History may have forgotten this king. But Scully did not. I, for one, am grateful."

Michael Nyenhuis, CEO, Medical Assistance Programs (MAP) International, Atlanta, Georgia

"A powerful story which needs to be told and now is being told. Traditional wisdom and experience, such as that passed down from earlier times among the Ba-Phalaborwa, can lead us down a positive path for the benefit of today's generation and especially for those confronted with the challenges of improving their overall state of well-being."

Neil Shulman, M.D., Emory University Department of Medicine, Atlanta, Georgia. Author of **The Corporate Kid** *and* **The Backyard Tribe***; Author and Associate Producer of the film* **Doc Hollywood** *starring Michael J. Fox.*

"Dr Robert Scully was introduced to African history and culture in 1965 when he came to St. Mary's Kibabii Secondary School as a Peace Corps Volunteer teacher. His interest in oral traditions and ethnography eventually led him to pursue a degree in Cultural Anthropology. At the time African history was supposed to be non-existent because there were no written records which were the basis of Eurocentric historical discourse. This was of course a real injustice to African history and culture which is passed on through oral traditions.

Fortunately, since the 1960s, oral traditions have become the hallmark of the reconstruction of African history and culture. Unfortunately, oral traditions can only go as far as the 15th century. To fill the gap before then African scholars turned to archaeology, which provides them with information on the origins of humanity, both from the biological as well as the cultural aspects. Being a student of cultural anthropology, Dr Scully has used the Ba-Phalaborwa to demonstrate how the rich traditions of that community can be used to illustrate not only the African past but also the present and the future. Dr Scully has also demonstrated how an actual situation can be used to inform a literary piece of work in the same way students of literature do. This work is certainly a must read for professionals in history, cultural anthropology, literature as well as any general reader interested in African history and culture."

Simiyu Wandibba, Ph.D., Former Director and current Professor of Anthropology, Institute of African Studies, University of Nairobi, Kenya

THE KING
HISTORY
FORGOT

To Jeff Roll
With Thanks for all
you do in The arts
Bob Sully
07/17

THE KING HISTORY FORGOT

MAKIKELE,
THE 19TH-CENTURY
LEGEND OF PHALABORWA,
SOUTH AFRICA

A NOVEL BY ROBERT T.K. SCULLY

Two Harbors Press
322 First Avenue N, 5th floor
Minneapolis, MN 55401
612.455.2293
www.TwoHarborsPress.com

Some of the settings, events and names in this novel are real, however, the
characters and story are fiction and the author intends no inferences regarding
names or places mentioned.

ISBN-13: 978-1-62652-391-3
LCCN: 2013918944

Distributed by Itasca Books

Cover Design by Mary Ross
Typeset by James Arneson
Edited by Sarah Kolb-Williams

Printed in the United States of America

This book is dedicated in memory

of

LEPATO II BROWN MALATJI
Late KGOSHI of Makhushane Tribal Authority

and

Lebowa Government Minister
With gratitude for his hospitality and encouragement
during my tenure in his domain.
May his aspirations for the Ba-Phalaborwa
be one day realized.

COVER ILLUSTRATION

The cover illustration shows *Kgoshi* Makikele Malatji, king of the Copper Throne, standing resplendent in his leopard-skin robe and jackal-skin headdress. In his left hand, he holds a crescent-shaped copper ceremonial axe, and in his right, an iron stabbing spear. Around his neck, he wears a copper disc in the shape of a crescent moon, ceremonially given to him by his father, *Kgoshi* Meele Malatji, at the time of his coming-of-age ceremony. He stands majestically on the skin of a lion, the one he had presented to his father following his first kill.

Nearby, Makikele's mother, the Queen Mother Mokadi, now elderly and bent, sits on a woven reed mat, proudly watching her son as the king's trumpeter sounds the ceremonial *phalaphala*, a long arched sable antelope horn, announcing a meeting of his royal council. She wears a bead necklace, and her extended legs are lavishly adorned with countless copper rings and beaded bands. Her prized possession is a bracelet of copper and red beads. One large glass bead, the central stone of the piece, had been brought by Makikele from the ruins of Dzata, ancient capital of the Venda, one of his northern allies.

They wait in the cattle enclosure of Makikele's capital at Sealene, surrounded by palings of the fortified village. Between them burns the sacred fire and surrounding them are ceremonial poles crowned with sacrificial animal skulls.

The backdrop shows Sealene Hill, the royal burial hill and ritual center of Phalaborwa. Here are situated the graves of previous kings, nobles, and famous historic personages, and a place where Makikele offers prayer libations and animal sacrifice to his ancestors.

FOREWORD

This book by Robert Scully, which includes a great deal of accurate historical information about nineteenth-century events in the Phalaborwa area, has been written as a fiction. This has made it possible to avoid sensitivities among modern Ba-Phalaborwa concerning nineteenth-century feuding between families about positions of leadership and power. It has also made it possible to provide dramatic descriptions of personal events among members of Makikele's family. Of particular interest to me are the descriptions of metal mining, smelting, and trade at Phalaborwa during this period.

Makikele occupied the Copper Throne of Phalaborwa during a major segment of the nineteenth century, which was a period of considerable strife. This was the time of the *Difaqane*, with warfare between the conquering Zulu army and other groups in Southern Africa. It was also the period during which the Swazi invaded the Lowveld. Makikele managed to save his chiefdom from these ravages.

On the positive side, the importance of Phalaborwa's production of copper and iron became particularly influential during the period of Makikele's rule. Metals, particularly copper, were traded from Phalaborwa across the region from the Drakensberg to the coast of Mozambique. Thus the Ba-Phalaborwa were involved with various surrounding African groups and with the Portuguese on the East Coast.

In our youth, I was a beginning archaeology teacher at Binghamton University in New York and Scully was a graduate student there. In 1970, I obtained a grant from the National Science Foundation and launched a nine-month exploration of the archaeology of Phalaborwa. This involved residential and metal-producing sites, extending over more than 1500 years. I recruited Scully to study the oral history of the Ba-Phalaborwa, most of who were then living in the segregated township of Makushane. While he interviewed people, the archaeology team investigated the archaeological sites at Kgopolwe, Sealene, Lolwe, and areas nearby in the Kruger Park. These had, in fact, also been residences and metal-producing areas during the reign of Makikele.

From June 1974 to June 1976, Scully did intensive doctoral thesis research at Phalaborwa, learned Northern Sotho, and acquired a valuable knowledge of the oral history of the Ba-Phalaborwa. His thesis was completed in 1978, but he maintained an interest in Phalaborwa and has helped the Ba-Phalaborwa with their land claims.

Scully has now produced this book for people who read historical fiction, but particularly for the descendants of Makikele and his tribe, with special emphasis on high school learners. It contains not only an account of historical events of the nineteenth century, but also accurate descriptions of the mining and metal production that took place at the time. I gather that the book may yet be translated into Sotho, which is a plan I support most heartily.

Nikolaas J. van der Merwe Ph.D., Archaeologist retired from the faculty of Harvard University and Professor Emeritus of Natural History for the University of Cape Town, South Africa. Author of The Carbon-14 Dating of Iron.

PRINCIPAL CHARACTERS

Joao Albasini, called "Jiwawa," a Portuguese elephant hunter

Lepato, son of Makikele

Lesibi, favorite wife of Makikele

Maboyana, sister of Makikele

Majaji, son of Makikele

Makikele (pronounced "ma-gi-gay-lay"), son of King Meele

Masalani, Venda witch doctor

Masetla, Makikele's brother and warrior leader

Meele, Phalaborwa king and father of Makikele

Mokadi, mother of Makikele

Molonyo, Swazi war leader

Ntlabede, paternal grandmother of Makikele

Paane, half-brother of Makikele

Phatladi, maternal uncle of Makikele

Ramatladi, half-brother of Makikele

Setakgale, mother of Ramatladi

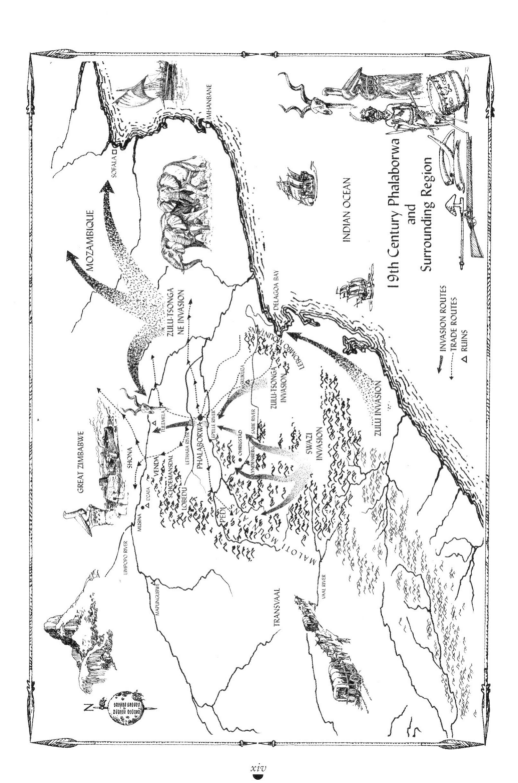

19th Century Phalaborwa
and
Surrounding Region

MOZAMBIQUE

SOFALA

MHANBANE

INDIAN OCEAN

DELAGOA BAY

ZULU-TSONGA
NE INVASION

GREAT ZIMBABWE

SHONA

VENDA

DZATA

MUSINA

LIMPOPO RIVER

MAPUNGUBWE

LOBEDU

SCHOEMANSDAL

LETHABA RIVER

TILEMELA

PHALABORWA

LEPELLE RIVER

SELUKLIZA

OHRIGSTAD

LYDENBURG

SABIE RIVER

PEDI

ZULU-TSONGA
INVASION

LEBOMBO MOUNTAINS

SWAZI
INVASION

ZULU INVASION

MALOTI MOUNTAINS

TRANSVAAL

VAAL RIVER

→ INVASION ROUTES
···· TRADE ROUTES
△ RUINS

N

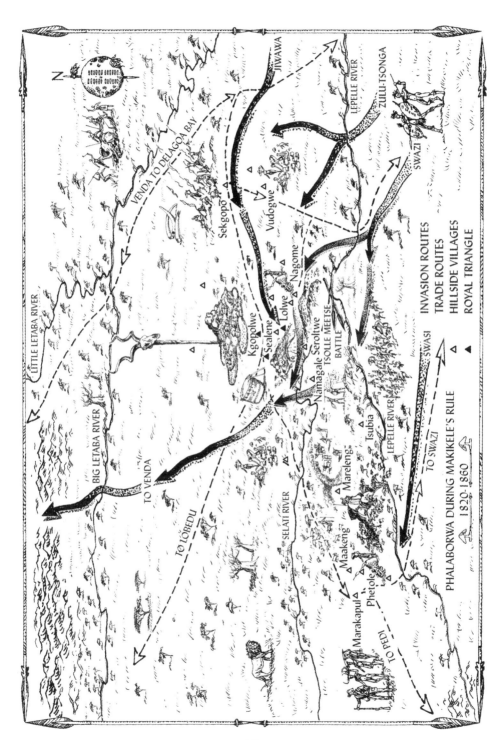

LITTLE LETABA RIVER

BIG LETABA RIVER

VENDA TO DELAGOA BAY

TO VENDA

TO LOBEDU

TO PEDI

SELATI RIVER

Marakapul

Phetole

Maakeng

Mareleng

Tsubia

LEPELLE RIVER

TO SWAZI

SWASI

Kgopolwe

Sealene

Lolwe

Nagome

Namagale Seroltwe

TSOLLE MEETSE

BATTLE

Sekgopo

Vudogwe

JIWAWA

LEPELLE RIVER

ZULU-TSONGA

SWAZI

INVASION ROUTES

TRADE ROUTES

HILLSIDE VILLAGES △

ROYAL TRIANGLE ▲

PHALABORWA DURING MAKIKELE'S RULE

1820-1860

N

CHAPTER ONE

Mokadi's Son

Mokadi was a daughter of privilege, born in the 1700s to a noble family of the Mathipa lineage near Sekgopo Hill in Phalaborwa, South Africa. History only whispers her name in Makhushane, a tribal center in Phalaborwa, where her descendants live today. The stones and abandoned terraces of Modimolle Hill, where her bones lie, and at Sekgopo, where she grew up, keep their silence. The noise of modern life distracts. It steals attention away from a woman whose memory has faded too deeply into African history.

In another village, not far from Mokadi's childhood home at Sekgopo, lived her cousin, Setakgale Mathipa. She was many years older than Mokadi, and they were not good friends; a bitter rivalry existed between the two villages. Both families were tied in wife-giving relationships to the ruling Malatji family, whereby it was prescribed that the king should marry his mother's brother's daughter. The term "mother's brother" was a flexible usage applying to many different maternal male relatives, including halfbrothers, stepbrothers, and cousins on the mother's side. This practice was known as *malome* marriage in Mokadi's Northern Sotho language and culture.

When Mokadi was still a young girl, she learned that her cousin had been chosen to marry Mosholwane, who then occupied Phalaborwa's Copper Throne, the recognized hereditary ruler, or *kgoshi*, and the patron and overlord of their families.

Mokadi remembered well the day the king's men came to take Setakgale to the royal enclosure at Kgopolwe Hill. She was just seven at that time, but Setakgale had already reached puberty and participated in the *bjale,* or girls' coming-of-age ceremony.

"I am to be a queen, cousin, and one day my son will be king of the people," Setakgale said boastfully with a tone of condescension to her little kinswoman. "This brings great honor to my family."

Mokadi had accompanied her mother and others of her village to Setakgale's father's settlement where a group of traders camped. This was along a well-defined foot trail leading north to where the neighboring Venda people had their villages. It was a meeting place where locals could safely exchange goods with groups passing through the region. Her mother carried a large basket of metal objects produced near their home and several beaded calabashes and finely worked animal pelts. She sought cotton fabric, a scarce commodity brought by traders from the coast, to embroider with ostrich shell beads.

Mokadi's task was to carry her newborn brother, Poponono. She was excited to accompany the adults. Poponono was small and light, no burden at all tied to her back swaddled in a goat skin. She could easily keep pace with her mother, handing Poponono over for breastfeeding when needed. Men and boys accompanying them sang traveling songs, the women and girls softly joining in, laughing when inappropriate words were playfully shouted by jokesters to add a funny twist to well-known verses. "Which animal goes zig and then zag and then zig and zag across the open bushland?" one tune went. The proper reply all knew to be "the guinea fowl!" However, nonsensical answers were shouted out or a lewd word, a play on actions of the bird or its name. All would laugh. For Mokadi, the journey became a game. She would remember these childhood times with a smile.

At about age twelve, Mokadi experienced her first vaginal bleeding. As the monthly menstrual cycles started, in the village, several of the other girls her age also began their first bleeding. It had been anticipated and whispered about over the past months as the girls gathered out of sight in a close-knit circle of friends to talk.

Since the beginning of planting season, Mokadi's mother and grandmother had watched for signs of her onset of puberty. "You must watch for the bleeding to begin," her mother instructed. "Other girls your age have already begun their monthly period, and you will start soon too."

Her grandmother joined the discussion to reassure her and to make certain she would be informed when Mokadi did indeed begin her menstruation. "It will certainly be in the next monthly cycle," the old woman counseled with a reassuring smile, "and when this does happen, you will come to my house so I can care for you and keep you clean and away from others until it stops." She pointed a wooden mixing stick at her and cautioned, "It is not good to mix with others, especially with men, when you have your period. It is particularly so when you have your first period. That is why you are taken into seclusion." The old woman smiled to herself as she left the child to tend to her kitchen. She remembered how frightened she had been when her first period started, and how she ran and hid from her mother until found by a girl of the village and taken to the girls' seclusion hut.

When Mokadi's bleeding did begin, she was taken and hidden in a small house behind the one where her grandmother lived. Three other village girls her age also beginning their menstruation joined her in hiding.

Fed and cared for by the old woman and two others, all beyond childbearing age, the four girls were taken out each morning before sunrise, hidden from view beneath blankets, and secretly led to bathe in a nearby watering place. The oldest of the care-giving women, the grandmother of her playmate from an adjoining family compound, spoke to the girls on this first morning of their seclusion. "The cold morning water removes the heat caused by your bleeding. It makes you clean and less likely to cause danger to others." The three girls obediently squatted at the stream's edge, giggling and squealing as the first cold water touched their feet and hands. Each lifted up the leather apron worn by every girl and splashed themselves with the cold liquid. "Clean away all the residue of the night's bleeding. Make sure it is all gone and you are clean inside." The girls continued to laugh as they followed the old woman's instructions. "You will come here every morning until the bleeding stops; only then can you return to your mothers' houses."

Although they returned to their families after the first period ended, the girls kept at a distance from most others in the village until the next harvest came and went. As the last millet was stored in above-ground granaries, all the village girls newly menstruating that year were taken to a secret lodge constructed in the bush for the *bjale,* a female initiation rite.

The secret ceremony, presided over by a senior woman of the king's household, marked the girls' transition from childhood to sexual maturity.

Mokadi was surprised to discover upon arriving at the isolated ceremonial lodge that she was accorded the highest rank among the initiates. She had been aware of the importance of her family and the respect shown to her father in the men's gathering place and to her mother, but it was nonetheless a surprise to be placed at the front of the line of girls and to be addressed with deference by her fellow initiates and the women conducting the rites they would undergo.

Here, deep in the bush in a place made sacred and taboo to men, she and her fellow initiates were taught the secrets of their gender, the rules of proper behavior as women and future wives, and the ways by which they might make themselves sexually attractive to their future partners.

As highest-ranked member of her bjale, Mokadi was expected to lead the group of seven initiated girls when it came time to return to Sekgopo Hill, the central village of her Mathipa lineage. Here, after many weeks of seclusion and training and ritual ordeals, the initiates were welcomed home with happy shouts and songs and dancing accompanied by drumming.

As custom required, Mokadi was given new clothing by her parents. Her ornately beaded leather pubic apron, worn by all girls and women, now included a long leather back apron reaching down to her knees. To all she would now be seen as a mature, initiated woman, eligible for courtship and marriage.

She would continue to live in the care of her father and mother until an appropriate family was chosen into which she might marry.

During the following harvest season, Mokadi was called to her father's house. Gathered in the courtyard seated near the fire were her father and mother, her grandmother, and several of her uncles. They greeted her as she appeared from around the reed privacy wall. Lowering her eyes as she entered, she quietly returned their greeting and made a silent clapping gesture while bowing her head, a sign of respect to her parents and family.

"A marriage has been arranged for you, Mokadi," said her father with a stern voice. She noticed that her mother and grandmother and several of the uncles were smiling, despite her father's somber demeanor. Discussions of her need to soon marry and who might be chosen for her had circulated in the village and in women's gossip during the harvest. A recent visitor to her father from Makwibidung, a settlement to the north of Sekgopo, had started a rumor that someone from there would be chosen for her husband—but this proved to be false. She had also heard that inquiries had been made by local families about marriage but had been courteously declined. And so she quietly waited, trusting that her family would make a good choice for her.

"We have consented to a man in Lobedu," he continued, "a betrothal cow was sent from his parents to confirm the agreement. We have agreed on a bridewealth for you and have closed the gate to any other inquiries. These marriage goods, your *motheko*, have been collected by his family. They will bring them here to us soon." With this announcement, Mokadi's mother broke the formal tone of her father with a joyful ululation, causing all to laugh. A relaxed atmosphere set in as her father described the next steps to be taken.

"You and your mother must begin to grind millet to take on your first journey to meet your future mother-in-law. When you reach her village, this will be cooked into porridge and fermented into beer so that she knows you will be a good wife and properly care for her."

"Yes, Father. This will be done," she replied, lowering her head in respect. With this said, her mother immediately added, "The Lobedu will see what fine millet we grow when the rains have been good. When they watch you grind and pound millet they will see how well brought up and hardworking the women from here can be."

Her father then explained, "The man is our cousin. Both families are pleased about the marriage. It will strengthen a long-standing trade connection between us. You should prepare to leave soon, when the next group sets out with goods for barter in the kingdom of Lobedu."

In the quiet of her mother's kitchen house later that day, while freshly pounded millet was boiling in pots for an evening meal, Mokadi was counseled about her forthcoming trip and marriage.

"As you know, Daughter, my family is local and they mostly live near Sekgopo. But your grandmother came here from Lobedu and knows about these people. You must listen to what she has to say as you prepare for the trip."

It was the grandmother, her *gogo*, who now quietly talked about the region and the girl's future in-laws. Mokadi was excited she would soon marry like so many of her friends.

Although thoughts of leaving her home and family for a strange country over five days' journey away troubled her, she dismissed those thoughts. To refuse this choice of a husband was impossible, anyway. Better to trust in their judgment and make the best of the situation. She sensed that things would work out well for her.

While her *gogo* spoke of the arable Lobedu farm country, the abundant herds of livestock, and the kinswomen she would work with and grow to know, Mokadi wondered about the man she would soon marry and live with. *Will I please him? Will he be kind to me?* But she dared not raise these questions.

Instead, she listened to her grandmother's recollections about Lobedu, the family ties and friends she had known there, and to the stories about the eternal Queen Modjadji, who controlled lightning and the rain that blew east to water Phalaborwa. She learned that her future husband had been settled, with others from his age-group regiment, in a hillside village, a border village and trading center leading to the queen's capital. She also learned that other young couples were building and thatching new houses there and that water was plentiful and sweet. Mokadi attentively followed her grandmother's account, responding "good" and nodding with each new detail.

Then, smiling at her daughter-in-law now busy with cooking pots, the old woman moved closer to Mokadi and spoke to her in a reassuring tone. "He is still young, and you will be his first wife. They tell us he is tall and a strong and fleet hunter, and has hunted lion and elephant. They also say his father brings trade goods to Modjadji's village and has a large herd. I am told the queen's brother knows this young man who will take you."

Seeing from her posture and eye avoidance that her granddaughter was embarrassed by this shift in topic, the old woman shook her by the shoulder and chuckled as she continued, "Yes, they say he is tall, one of the tallest in his regiment. You should find him pleasing." She watched amused as Mokadi bit her lips in embarrassment.

"I knew his father when I was young." The old woman continued, "He was a good man. You treat the father and mother well and they will treat you well." Chuckling again, she rose to depart the kitchen hut, but then turned with a smile. "I knew when that Lobedu messenger came to my son and asked for a meeting that it would be about this family, that they wanted our little puppy here." Both mother and grandmother laughed at this traditional reference to a bride as a "little dog," and so did Mokadi as her *gogo* again playfully poked her, this time in the belly.

The marriage delegation taking her to her future home stopped along the way to visit relatives at Kgopolwe. This was the residence of *Kgoshi* Mosholwane, who had married her cousin Setakgale. Mokadi and the kinsmen accompanying her stayed on the outskirts of the royal compound, and much was made of her journey as a bride to Lobedu by the local women. In the evening they were taken to the King's residence, where she briefly saw Mosholwane and several of his sons as she sat close by them in a circle of women.

Little was later said about this long-ago journey of the young bride, Mokadi, and the marriage to a man she did not know. Some whispered about her husband's death a few years later, although the circumstances remained masked under a shadow of mystery. Later rumors hinted that a new occupant of the

Copper Throne, *Kgoshi* Meele, had Mokadi's husband poisoned because he wanted Mokadi for himself. Other stories suggest her husband was killed in a skirmish between *Kgoshi* Meele and warriors of the Lobedu queen near Makhutso Hill, which marked a disputed boundary between the two kingdoms.

After her husband's death, Mokadi returned home to Sekgopo Hill but then received a summons to Kgopolwe, where the new king lived. When she arrived at the king's enclosure, *Kgoshi* Mosholwane was dead and buried a long time.

Mosholwane's son and heir, Meele Malatji, had many wives. Two were Mathipa family unions, *malome* marriages, and sons had been born of these wives and recognized as heirs apparent to the throne. Paane, the son of Meele's great wife, the first of his Mathipa marriages, was senior in rank to the others.

As a royal widow of the late *Kgoshi* Mosholwane, Setakgale had been inherited by Meele and was now a member of the successor king's household at Kgopolwe. She had produced for him another son and potential heir, Ramatladi. This ancient custom of reallocating a widow to brothers and sons of the deceased functioned to care for the royal children of her marriage and to retain the wealth, kinship relations, and alliances they embodied. When *Kgoshi* Meele sent for Mokadi, she too became a wife and, like Setakgale, one of the numerous women of his extended family.

After Meele married Mokadi and she became pregnant, the king sent her home to be assisted with the birth by the women of her family at Sekgopo. Adhering to the custom for new wives, Mokadi and her newborn remained at her home village until weaning of the child took place.

Mokadi had been taught as a royal bride that her husband's family was of great antiquity. His genealogy, recited on official occasions, contained names of many rulers and allied lineages that had provided wives to the ruling Malatji family for generations. She learned that Meele had succeeded his father, Mosholwane, a powerful but tragic figure in the tribe's recent history, and that before Mosholwane, the warrior king Kgashane Malatji had ruled Phalaborwa for many years.

In the late eighteenth century, when Meele ascended the Copper Throne, the extensive kingdom was bordered on the east by the Tsonga, a loosely associated network of small localized kingdoms. These Tsonga people were slowly expanding into the eastern Phalaborwa region where they sometimes raided for cattle and poached game, particularly elephants. However, small groups of Tsonga, mostly displaced families, were permitted to settle at the eastern border villages controlled by Malatji and Mathipa headmen living in and around Sekgopo Hill. These newcomers lived with the Sotho-speaking Ba-Phalaborwa as client families. Some served as herbalists and healers; most were taught to work smelters and forges in their host villages.

To the southeast of Meele's kingdom, there was an expanding Swazi presence. For long periods of time, Swazi interaction with the rulers of Phalaborwa was peaceful and involved trade for local iron products, particularly iron spears fashioned to Swazi specification. However, the harmony between these two trading groups was disrupted from time to time by disputes. One such hostile encounter occurred a generation before Meele became king, when Phalaborwa was invaded by a Swazi army.

This resulted in the death of his father, Mosholwane.

Mokadi discovered, as she quietly listened to talk in the royal family compound, that the history of her husband's family was complicated and rife with disputes and fighting. She learned that Mosholwane had been made *kgoshi* with the help of powerful Swazi interest groups that infiltrated and for a time came to dominate the royal court at Kgopolwe Hill. According to these stories, a marriage alliance then followed with a Swazi noblewoman, Ntlabidi, a kinswoman of Mswati, the Swazi king. The marriage was part of a peace pact, creating a kinship bond between the two royal families.

Later in his rule, as Swazi influence became oppressive, Mosholwane and his family allies staged a revolt against the invaders. During the fighting that resulted in the capital, Mosholwane was killed by a Swazi war leader, Magadima, who then became regent. This Magadima was later replaced by another Swazi regent called Ngwane, who ruled until Meele was recognized as *kgoshi*.

While accounts of the past differed in detail depending on the skill of different storytellers and the extent of their memory, it was clear to Mokadi that succession to Phalaborwa's copper- and iron-rich throne had been strongly contested. Wars had been fought and people killed in disputes to control her husband's iron weapon production and access to his ore sources. However, when she arrived to live at Kgopolwe, the Swazi had been expelled for a long time. Only those Swazi married to locals were permitted in the capital and surrounding villages. All other foreigners were forbidden access to Lolwe Hill, where copper and iron was mined, and other royal precincts.

To the south, in the mountainous regions overlooking Phalaborwa's lowlands, lived another large neighboring kingdom:

the Pedi. From time to time during the eighteenth century, the two kingdoms waged war over territory along the southern borderlands. For the most part, however, the Pedi maintained good relations with Meele and his predecessors. These two peoples spoke closely related dialects of the Northern Sotho language, sharing many cultural characteristics, farming and husbandry technology, and religious beliefs. Like other neighboring areas, the Pedi traded agricultural products with the Ba-Phalaborwa for iron and copper. They also respected the magical powers believed to emanate from Sealene Hill, the royal family's revered ancestral burial site. Over time, the Pedi adopted some of Phalaborwa's ritual practices, most noticeably their sacred drum cult. These cultural ties and trade alliances between the Pedi and Phalaborwa were long-standing and mutually beneficial.

At the time of Mokadi's marriage, her husband Meele had been ruler of Phalaborwa for a number of years and had established a political unity between east and west. The eastern regions were governed from Sekgopo Hill, a fortified stronghold and extensive village which had earlier been independent and ruled by various families. Control of the western portion of the region was based at Sealene and Kgopolwe Hills. Meele's political center at Kgopolwe proved a good strategic location, giving him control of vital copper and iron ore sources at nearby Lolwe Hill. Metals traded were his primary source of wealth and power.

Several months after Mokadi returned to Sekgopo Hill, as the eighteenth century drew to a close, her first son, Makikele, was born—another prince and potential heir for *Kgoshi* Meele. The birth was kept secret, a custom in the case of male children fathered by a ruler. Only Mokadi's immediate family, the king, and the queen mother, Ntlabidi, knew of the birth.

This son, initially given the childhood name Modupe, which described a downpour of rain at the time of his birth, would one day be called Makikele. The name Makikele was a derivative of the Sotho verb *go ikele*, and in his case taken to mean "he who goes about the land meeting people." From an early age, Makikele was a curious, inquisitive, and gregarious boy.

When Makikele was four years old, *Kgoshi* Meele sent for the mother and child, giving gifts to his Mathipa in-laws at Sekgopo Hill. Makikele was brought to live at Kgopolwe, the royal village of his father, where he and his mother became part of the king's large polygamous household.

When they reached Kgopolwe, the mother and son were received into the royal family enclave and lived in a new house that Meele had ordered to be built for them.

There was tension in King Meele's household when this new wife and child arrived at the royal enclosure. The principal wife of the king at this time was the mother of Paane, and her son was regarded as the likely heir to his father. Not all in the royal family accepted this, however, and Setakgale, considered by many to be a higher-ranking royal wife, soon displaced this earlier wife in ritual prerogative and become the great wife of Meele. With this turn of events, Paane and his mother were sent away to live elsewhere.

This, however, could not have been anticipated as Mokadi and Makikele arrived as newcomers to the well-established domestic setting of the royal extended family and its retainers. The first indications that bad blood existed between the two royal women and their respective branches of the Mathipa family came shortly after Mokadi had settled into the pace of life in Meele's capital. The altercation occurred while Mokadi and other women pounded millet cobs on the open-air threshing floors near the queen mother's granaries. As she swept newly separated grain into collection piles, her cousin and co-wife leisurely approached her accompanied by her son, Ramatladi.

"So, cousin," Setakgale said with a sneer at Mokadi, "you are also called to be a wife of the king and do his work. But remember, I am of higher rank than you, and it is my son, Ramatladi, who is favored by the king. You are a junior wife with little status, and your son will have no power."

Mokadi humbly accepted her place as a junior wife, one of many co-wives in a large patriarchal royal family. She loyally performed all the tasks that a good wife was required to do, including accepting her turn on the king's sleeping mat and receiving his visits to her own house.

As the months passed, Mokadi noticed that the king called for her more often to serve him and was taking a greater interest in Makikele. The king already had many children, but was especially fond of his newly arrived son.

One day, while the king was resting, Setakgale stormed into the king's hut. Mokadi sat silently in one corner spinning cotton thread.

"What is she doing here?" Setakgale demanded. "I am of higher rank than she is. I am custodian of the medicines which protect you against witchcraft and make rain. I am the one who should be sitting at your feet, not her."

The king stood and glowered at Setakgale. He was a tall man and an imposing figure. He towered over the diminutive woman.

Setakgale immediately knew that she had made a mistake and flinched as she felt the king's eyes boring into hers.

"Woman, do you forget who I am? You do not question my authority, or my choices. Leave my hut. I will only call upon you when I need you. Go. . . now."

As Mokadi's favor with the king increased, so did that of her family and child. Setakgale's privileged status, on the other hand, became increasingly threatened, and her son's paramount position among Malatji princes questioned. The two women and their sons were destined for further confrontation.

Sometime later, Mokadi was carrying water to the king's hut when Setakgale accosted her.

"You have already given the king a son, haven't you? And you are young and seductive—that is why he favors you over me. My son, Ramatladi, may not be powerful now, but he will grow up to be a great warrior. Your son will be weak."

Mokadi quietly responded, "If the king favors me over you, it is his decision which of his wives he prefers. It is the ancestors who determine strength and character in our children. No one can know which of them will be strong, which weak."

Setakgale rushed at the unsuspecting Mokadi, her arms flailing. She scratched her long nails into the soft skin of Mokadi's face and tore at the multiple strings of beads and jewelry she wore around her neck. As copper and ceramic beads spilled to the ground from their cotton strands, Mokadi responded with kicks and pounded Setakgale in the chest with her fists. When Setakgale released her grip, Mokadi shoved her away, and she landed in the mud. Setakgale pushed herself to her feet and charged again.

"Stop!" The king's eyes flashed. "What is going on?" The king and his mother had been returning to the royal residence from a meeting of court elders when they came upon the incident.

"She attacked me." Blood dripped from the scratches to Mokadi's face.

The king turned toward Setakgale. "Is this true?"

Setakgale bowed her head in shame and whispered, "Yes."

"Speak up, woman."

"Yes, it's true." She lowered herself to her knees and looked down at the ground. "Please, forgive me."

"Leave my sight, woman. Such behavior is unbecoming for a woman of your rank."

Setakgale scrambled to her feet and ran from the king's presence.

Later in the evening, under cover of darkness, she sent a servant girl to steal an article of clothing from Mokadi's house. She instructed the girl to choose something intimate to her body that might be used at a later date to do her harm through witchcraft. She would stop at nothing to maintain her position as great wife, and to safeguard the rank of prince heir to Meele's legacy for her son, Ramatladi.

This was the beginning of bad blood between the women, which would lead one day to further confrontation and nefarious consequences.

There was much sympathy for her son Ramatladi among the elders and leaders of the tribe. Later in life, he would be regarded as an honorable man, but his pathway to kingship had been crossed by Mokadi and her son. Little did they realize at the time that this early feud would become a festering sore with no cure for many years to come.

CHAPTER TWO

Gogo's Domain

When he was about four years old and had been fully weaned, Makikele joined the other young boys of Kgopolwe in herding livestock. He and other young children first learned to care for the lambs and newborn calves. These defenseless small animals remained in the village enclosures when the herds were taken to morning pasture.

As Makikele grew older, he joined the bigger boys handling first the goats, and then the cattle of the royal village. This was a time when young boys, under the guidance of senior men, competed with their peers in games such as wrestling, running, and hunting and learned how to use weapons, particularly throwing the spear and shooting the bow and arrow.

During this time, Mokadi's older brother, Phatladi Mathipa, a member of the king's inner circle of advisors, took Makikele under his wing, teaching him the customs of his people and the virtues and proper behavior expected of a son of the royal house.

"The first virtue is courage," said Phatladi. "What can you tell me about courage?"

"It means being brave."

"That is right. Which animal is the most courageous?"

"The lion?"

"Wrong—the lion is a courageous animal, but the most courageous is the leopard. That is why your father, King of the Copper Throne, who is the most courageous man in the whole of Phalaborwa, wears a leopard-skin robe."

"How can I prove my courage?" asked Makikele.

"When you are older, you will be expected to hunt and kill a lion. When you make your first kill and present the lion's skin at the royal enclosure, the king's *kgoro*, your father and the men of the village will celebrate, and your mother and all the women will ululate.

"The next virtue is caution. Unless you are cautious in the bush, you will never make your first kill. You must learn to outsmart the lion. But do not just be cautious of the lion—he is not your most dangerous adversary—be cautious of your enemy; the one you trust may sometimes be your most dangerous enemy.

"The next virtue is endurance," Phatladi continued.

"What's endurance?" replied Makikele.

"It means not giving up. Endurance is needed by those who extract copper and iron from the mines at Lolwe and by those who travel the difficult trade routes, which bring prosperity and renown to Phalaborwa. You are not considered a true Ba-Phalaborwa man without such ability to endure hardship."

"Are there any more virtues I should know about?"

"Be generous. It is important for a young person, and especially a royal child, to be generous with friends and to respect and listen to elders, doing their bidding quietly and swiftly. As a Ba-Phalaborwa prince, you must acquire understanding of social ranking in this complex world of relationships and the ritual protocol necessary in much of daily life. As a royal

Prince Makikele hunts with bow and arrow

child, you are expected to know that you are different from the children of slave, common, and even noble families."

The doting uncle paused to smile at Makikele, as he always did when concluding their dialogues, and he quoted a much-repeated household proverb: "You must work hard and struggle in life before you can sit and enjoy yourself."

As Makikele grew older and his play groups became work groups, he came to recognize that there were social differences that were important to maintain. For example, on a hunting trip, a prince or noble boy learned to expect a slave boy to do the more menial tasks, such as fetching firewood and retrieving game shot with arrows or brought back by hunting dogs. Boys of higher status, on the other hand, were expected to be the spokesmen for the group when passing through villages, encountering passersby while herding animals, or seeking food and drink.

Like many boys of his age, Makikele learned to play the flute. These simple musical instruments were carved from reeds or bone and used both in play and in entertainment. He learned many traditional songs and ritual praises and proverbs used both in everyday life and on special occasions when people greeted visitors or attended ceremonies.

Makikele proved himself to be a natural leader of his play group. He could wrestle and was a swift runner and bowman. His many talents were praised by his mother and the women of his family, and increasingly the men of the village and his peers recognized his excellent character and praiseworthy abilities. This reached the ears of his father and was a source of endearment to him.

Makikele was also a keen observer of the work of the village herbalists and shamans, who produced medicines and magical formulas used in rainmaking and many other rituals performed during the yearly agricultural cycle. They also provided medicines when family members and villagers fell ill, feared bewitchment, or were troubled by the many challenges of everyday life and work.

The queen mother, Makikele's paternal grandmother, Ntlabidi, and her retinue of royal women and attendants played a key role in these cyclical rituals. Makikele enjoyed standing with other children in the fields outside the village watching the annual performance of planting and harvest rites.

One of the most important of these ceremonies was the First-Foods Ceremony held annually to celebrate the harvest, when the new crops ripened at the end of spring in late December or early January. The whole village gathered in the presence of the king and presented the first produce of their harvest. Then the queen mother, assisted by her court shaman and other herbalists, used special medicines, including parts of a freshly killed *klipbuck*, in a formal ritual designed to imbue the crop with the blessings of the ancestors. Once this was done, the king was invited by his mother to be the first person to sample the new harvest. If anyone else sampled the harvest before the king, this was considered a sin against the ancestors, and the perpetrators would be heavily fined. After the king had eaten, the various regional royal *ntona* and elders would sample the harvest, then village headmen, and finally the common men and their families.

When he was older, Makikele joined the royal family in processions to nearby Sealene Hill, the royal burial ground, for ancestral propitiation ceremonies conducted by the king. Joining them were the queen mother, the king's eldest sister, and trusted members of the royal patriarchy. These rites, performed during the tribe's complex annual ritual cycle, were believed integral to successful farming, hunting, trade, and metalwork. It was at Sealene Hill that he saw the graves of previous kings, nobles, and famous historic personages. There he witnessed prayer libations and animal sacrifices offered to the ancestors by his father, his father's brothers, his elder brothers, and high-ranking members of the royal court.

At other times, young Makikele and some of the other boys would join his grandmother, his *gogo*, at her residence, or in the kitchen in her enclosed courtyard, to listen to stories and discussions among the older women she attracted around her. This was the setting in which folklore was transmitted from one generation to the next. His grandmother used to tell many stories from the past about treasures of the ancients, heroic battles and individual feats, tribal origins, wanderings, and wars. He particularly enjoyed hearing about his family's origins in places far away to the north, where the Shona and Venda live, and about their migration south before settling in Phalaborwa. Some stories were related over and over again. One of Makikele's favorites was the story of the *noko*, the Malatji lineage's porcupine totem.

"The porcupine is a very special animal. Does anyone know why?" asked the queen mother.

"Because he has sharp quills," said one of the boys. There was a ripple of laughter in the hut.

"You laugh," said the old woman, "but he is right. If you try to interfere with a porcupine, you will be the one who comes off the worst. You cannot get close to a porcupine unless he lets you. If a porcupine takes up residence near your courtyard, you can learn a lot from him. He will find a quiet place to make his den, and then all he needs is a source of food. Porcupines do not have good eyesight and may not see the enemy coming. They have no fear, but they do not like confrontation and do not travel far beyond their den. Very little disturbs a porcupine from his uncomplicated lifestyle. In fact, a porcupine is full of trust and powerful medicine."

"Like the medicine the shaman prepares for the sick people, *gogo*?" asked Makikele.

Makikele's question made the old woman smile. "Yes," she said, "something like that. You are a very intelligent boy, Makikele. Your father will be proud of you."

Hearing the old woman's praise, Makikele felt a surge of warmth pass through his body that added to the warmth he felt from the kitchen fire.

Before she continued her story, the grandmother passed around a plate of salted marula nuts, freshly roasted on the fire.

"*Gogo*," said Makikele, "what can we learn from the porcupine?" He had heard the story many times and knew the answer by heart, but nevertheless he was anxious to hear it again.

"You are a clever boy," said the ancient *gogo*. "It was in the time before the Malatji lineage ruled Phalaborwa, before they drove away the Shokane from Lolwe Hill with the magic *tshekga* fire. It was the time of Kulwana and Selematsela, the first ancestors to come from the north with millet, peas, and sweet potatoes. Their totem animals were the impala and the baboon. When the first Malatji came here, he was chased by local people who wanted to kill him. He ran swiftly through the bush, but they circled widely to surround him and tried to kill him with their spears. Aahuah! They ran after him and it seemed he would die."

"Did they catch him, *gogo*?" Makikele had heard the story many times before and knew the answer but enjoyed goading his grandmother with such questions.

"No, Grandson! Goodness no!" she exclaimed. The children laughed. "This is where the porcupine comes into the story."

She grew very serious as she continued. "You see, surrounded by those who would kill him, Malatji found himself near a large marula tree where a porcupine had dug a hole. It was a big hole going deep into the ground. Malatji crawled into the hole to hide. While he was crouched down inside the hole, the porcupine returned and followed him inside, exposing its quills to the entrance of its den. When the men reached the hole, all they could see were the quills of the porcupine sticking out, and they passed by. The porcupine had saved the life of the first Malatji. From that time onward, because the porcupine had saved Malatji's life, Malatji and those who came after him adopted the porcupine as their totem. That is why the praise singers say, 'Aaahey, Malatji! Aaahey, big porcupine who was saved from the enemy!'"

Makikele and the other children all smiled at this story of their origin. Their grandmother then imparted a further message from the porcupine story.

"Remember this, children." She pointed a mixing stick at them to hold their attention for a few more seconds. "The porcupine totem teaches us not to poke our noses into other people's business, and not to be fearful or greedy. Do not let other people or events interfere with your life. Sometimes you need to just stop and think. Just as the porcupine does not use his sharp prickly quills unless he is attacked, so you should not be unkind to other people unless they hurt you first."

A porcupine protects Malatji

As the children ran off from the old woman's kitchen house to play, she called out after them with a well-known ancient proverb: "May you grow to be bigger than an elephant; may the rhinoceros be a toy to you. May you be greatly blessed."

CHAPTER THREE

Manly Ordeals

For boys of Kgopolwe, the time eventually came to transition from boyhood to manhood. During the winter months of Makikele's sixteenth year, *Kgoshi* Meele called for the organization of a Phalaborwa-wide male initiation ceremony. This important rite of passage for boys was called *Koma,* and it also included *Dikomathuku*, the rite of forming a new regiment of warriors comprised of these initiates.

Makikele, who was now a tall, lean youth with a thin growth of facial hair, looked forward to the ceremony with a mixture of anticipation and fear. He understood the importance and relevance of the ceremony as an initiation into manhood and his right to be a warrior, but he feared the unknown. What was going to happen at this coming-of-age ceremony was a closely guarded secret, and Makikele knew better than to ask the older boys what to expect.

In advance of the arrival of the new initiates, young warriors who had previously gone through *Koma* had been sent, under the supervision of selected tribal elders and specialized shaman, to construct a secret ceremonial lodge. It was built on a hillside a short distance from the royal capital located in uninhabited bush beyond the Selati River.

When preparations were ready at the *Koma* lodge, senior male relatives brought all uncircumcised males of Makikele's age to this encampment, for it was required that every boy participate in order to be admitted into adult male status.

Removed from the comfortable fires and kitchens of their mothers' homes, the boys began a long period of isolated training, controlled and disciplined by selected warriors and tribal elders. No initiate was permitted to leave the camp under any circumstance, not even sickness. It was understood by all that some initiates could die while in *Koma*, never to return to their village, their names never mentioned again. Access to the lodge was forbidden to all women and the uncircumcised, under penalty of death. Women could bring food and provisions for sons and brothers to a designated area out of sight of the lodge. From there, guards carried it to the lodge to feed and care for the men.

As a prince of the ruling house, Makikele occupied the position of honor in the age group being formed during the initiation *Koma*. This position would remain with him for the rest of his life, and his fellow initiates were expected to retain a lifelong bond and loyalty to Makikele. They would become his personal regiment.

The group that *Kgoshi* Meele brought together on this occasion was a significant group because it was the first to involve all of Phalaborwa's young men together in a single large ceremonial center. Previous generations had conducted separate regional *Koma* ceremonies, with the approval of the king, in many lodges built near the larger villages. This kingdom-wide *Koma* ordered by Meele introduced Makikele to all young men of his age group from families living in different parts of his father's kingdom, and from all social ranks.

As son of the king, he was the highest-ranked participant, and as such he was ritually recognized as leader of this large age group and head of the army regiment that these men would form. The bonds of friendship and loyalty forged during Makikele's *Koma* would provide a kingdom-wide cohesiveness among these youths that would be the foundation stone for a political unity essential to the future survival of Phalaborwa.

When recruits arrived at the initiation lodge, accompanied by the men of their families, each was washed and coated with white clay. Naked except for a small piece of cord around the waist, they were led through a massive throng of armed warriors and elders. The tightly clustered tribesmen chanted warrior dirges to the accompaniment of drums hidden from view by the sheer mass of sweating bodies pressed together encircling a low stone outcropping. Here dignitaries of the initiation lodge and a witchdoctor, robed in monkeyskins, awaited their arrival.

Lined up according to rank, the young men were led through the pressing crowd of spectators to the stone. Here, the seated witchdoctor cut away their penis foreskins with a ceremonial knife to the cheers of onlookers. As each was pushed forward to confront the surgeon, surrounding spectators shouted out threats and warnings not to show fear or pain, which would disgrace the honor of family and lineage at this moment of manhood.

Following their ordeal, the young men were lead into seclusion inside the initiation lodge to be treated with special medicines applied to their wounds to stop bleeding and prevent infection. Here they remained for several weeks until their wounds healed and the active training program of the initiation *Koma* could begin.

During those winter months in the *Koma* lodge, lineage elders, led by a brother of the king, taught the initiates about the rules and laws of social rank, correct protocol, proper behavior, and the secret sacred traditions of their kingdom and people. Excursions into the surrounding bush to perform group tasks and to hunt provided practical exercises intended to teach manly virtues such as loyalty, bravery, and fortitude. Those boys initiated together became circumcision brothers, an age group for life. As they matured, they were expected to form a warrior regiment, ready to fight together when called on to do so by the king.

One day, when the initiates had been at the lodge for several weeks and were in the forest undergoing training in the stealth required for hunting lion, a leopard was spotted on the hill behind the camp. All remained silent, as they had been taught, but all eyes were fixed on the animal when it turned, bared its fangs, and stared directly at Makikele. Then, in an instant, the leopard vanished, melting into the undergrowth.

When they returned to the bush lodge, there was much talk about the leopard. When some suggested hunting the beast for its spotted skin, the *Koma* leader cautioned restraint. "*Kgoshi* Meele must be informed," he said. "The leopard is not like the lion, to be hunted and its organs used in the production of medicines. The king wears a leopard-skin robe as a symbol that he is ruler of the the Ba-Phalaborwa. Only he may decide whether or not to kill the animal."

When Meele heard the story of the leopard and its fixed penetrating stare at Prince Makikele, he recognized the significance. The leopard was a spirit apparition and a good omen that Makikele would one day achieve prominence. The king kept this knowledge to himself, not wishing to cause division between his other sons and Makikele. He knew the vision of the leopard was a sign that something great would befall Makikele following *Koma.*

"The hunting of this leopard is forbidden," he said. "Any man who attempts to kill or harm this leopard will be executed."

During the concluding days of *Koma* training, the elders presented each initiate with a ceremonial club, carved medicated sticks, and other ritual objects. The young men then covered their bodies in red ochre and, when ordered to do so, set fire to the lodge. With the roar of the burning lodge to their backs, they marched in procession to Kgopolwe, keeping their heads and shoulders bent in a posture of submission and deference, carrying their clubs and ritual sticks pressed to their foreheads, and with eyes downcast.

Kgoshi Meele received his new regiment at Kgopolwe Hill with a great reentry ceremony, the *Dikomathuku*, to be acknowledged as men and warriors and their new regiment named.

The royal drums, including the great carved drum, *Boretsho*, and the smallest and most sacred of the drums, *Tlanka*, oiled down with red ochre, sounded the arrival of the king and his wives and family.

The new regiment was led into the royal cattle enclosure and marched through an arcade of ceremonial entry poles to stand before the king and the king's council. An assembly of all the warriors from the vicinity, many visiting relatives of the participants, and the whole village watched on.

The king, clothed in a leopard-skin robe and a jackal-skin headdress decorated with feathers and carrying the crescent-shaped copper ceremonial ax, sat in quiet dignity on his stool behind the drums. Alongside him sat his mother, wives, and other members of the royal family. He waited for the young men to assemble before him.

The initiates were ranked according to the status of their family and village and lined up in columns, seven men in each column, before approaching the king.

Then the brother of the king, who had been leader at the initiation lodge, formally announced their successful completion of *Koma* and commanded the regiment to prostrate themselves before the king and the royal regalia drums. They fell to their knees and bent forward with heads touching the ground. All waited in complete silence as an aged spokesman of the king entered the enclosure, consulted with the king, and then slowly stepped forward from behind the drums to address the assembly. Welcoming the initiates and the large tribal gathering, he pronounced blessings on Makikele's regiment.

During the ceremony, Makikele received a copper disc in the shape of a crescent moon. It was ceremonially placed around his neck by his father as a symbol of his regimental leadership. This emblem would be incorporated into his regalia, recognized and respected by all his age group.

Then, a group of warriors carried the head of a large black bull with widely curved horns into the enclosure and placed it at the top of a newly-cut ceremonial pole. This would stand with dignity among the cluster of other poles to commemorate the successful *Koma* and serve as a sign to all visitors.

Once the address was completed, drumming resumed, and the newly initiated men were led away to isolated family compounds or lineage rest areas to meet with family and friends and to be fed. They remained in partial seclusion, with their bodies painted in red ochre, until they were ready to return to their home villages.

Dikomathuku ceremony at Kgopolwe Hill

This dismissal was a signal for the king's feast to begin. It was launched by a large circle of men dressed in skins and feathered headdresses, blowing whistles and flutes and dancing the popular charging bull dance. A cloud of dust rose up when women and other villagers joined the dance, many stomping feet and kicking up dirt as a bull would when pawing in agitation. As the circle of spectators grew, the royal drums were supplemented with sounds of lesser drums brought into the clearing by onlookers.

Three bulls had been killed, skinned, butchered, and roasted nearby. Large quantities of millet were also cooked and a special brew of beer prepared for the occasion.

Feasting continued late into the night, and large quantities of meat and beer were consumed. The newly initiated greedily ate portions of meat and other food brought to them by their family members at the celebration. Sisters and male relatives of the young men visited them in their separate groups, sitting or standing in circles on the periphery of the festivity.

At sunrise the following day, most groups departed for their homes, the young men to be received again with much ceremony, this time by their individual village elders. Once welcomed back home, they removed the ochre from their bodies. This marked the end of their ritual separation and beginning of their new lives as village men and warriors of the king.

CHAPTER FOUR

Mokadi Hatches Her Plan

Mokadi had grown accustomed to life in the royal polygamous family. Each of the wives had her own circular house, the more senior wives being housed closest to that of the king himself. They also each had their own herds of livestock and fields.

The higher the rank of the male in the village hierarchy, the more wives he was expected to have. As king, Meele had many wives.

It was common for the ruler to have one or more wives from each of the powerful families in important villages and in the borderlands where loyalty was needed to protect the boundaries of his kingdom. Children of these women were Malatji by lineage and therefore loyal to Meele at Kgopolwe. They also maintained close and valuable links with their kinsmen in their mother's villages. This system of marriage alliances built political and economic ties that included elaborate gift-giving relationships flowing to and from Kgopolwe, as well as a steady flow of tribute to the capital.

The sizeable bride-price, the *motheko*, that passed to these subject villages began a complex patron-client relationship that was lucrative and increased the stature and power of those families that had royal connections. The family of a royal wife incurred responsibilities as in-laws to the king, and their stature grew as children of the marriage, and particularly royal sons, brought their maternal relatives into privileged access to the king and his council.

From his stronghold at Kgopolwe, Meele, like those who ruled before him, was able to control much of the extensive lowlands between the surrounding Lepelle and Letaba Rivers. Councilors from each subsection of the Malatji kingdom reported to the capital, brought tribute from trade and the annual harvest, and provided labor when called on to do so.

Sekgopo Hill, the eastern border village, was a center of several influential families who had histories of providing wives to past rulers. Most prestigious were the Mathipa, an ancient family that once ruled and retained some ritual functions from their time as leaders. Although separate male initiation rites, the signature ceremonial prerogative of kingship, had been removed from them by Meele, the Mathipa remained a powerful interest group. This power came through their role as an important wife-giving family to the Malatji, one from which kingship might derive. Although wealthy and influential, the Mathipa were divided among themselves and often at odds, a weakness which the king used at times for his own political advantage.

The wealthy Mathipa lineage provided several wives to Meele; Setakgale, the mother of Ramatladi, and Mokadi, the mother of Makikele, were highest in rank. Both of their sons and several other sons born of prestigious royal wives would be seen as candidates to succeed Meele as king. The Mathipa, in turn, were connected by kinship and were patrons to client groups throughout the Sekgopo region and in the many neighboring kingdoms and cheifdoms where they maintained trade partnerships. They were powerful and influenced decisions at Kgopolwe, particularly those related to trade and territorial disputes on the eastern border of Phalaborwa. Meele relied on them to maintain his control of the east.

Mokadi had joined the royal family as a junior wife, but in the months that followed her son's *Koma*, the pecking order in the royal household began to change. At the *Koma*, Makikele had proved himself to be an outstanding warrior as well as possessing leadership qualities required of a future king. As Meele began to show favor to this son, he also elevated the rank of the young man's mother, Mokadi.

But this was also part of Mokadi's plan. The most powerful women—the great wife, the king's paternal aunts, and the queen mother—were influential in the running of the royal household. As a young royal wife, Mokadi decided to ally herself with her mother-in-law, Ntlabidi, the queen mother, and with her husband's senior sister, who was then the spiritual guardian of the royal family and custodian of the many harvest and planting rituals. Mentored by the queen mother, who had herself been an outsider—a Swazi noblewoman given as an alliance bride to guarantee peaceful trade ties—and by her sister-in-law, the three formed a political unity and supportive friendship within the royal family. Over time, this bond elevated Mokadi to a position of influence, giving advantage and power to her family and her children. Later, as royal succession came into question, this female royal triumvirate facilitated a shift in power which made Mokadi's son, Makikele, a favored candidate for her husband's throne.

Mokadi was a critical thinker, able to navigate the complex relationships of her husband's political world. She knew the importance of having well-placed allies. Her own close kinsmen—her brothers, uncles, and nephews—became influential and wealthy as counselors to the king and his family, and as appointed leaders of villages strategic to the king's power. Royal patronage was the reward for loyalty, giving Mokadi's people access to those closest to the king. As envoys to surrounding rulers and trade partners, this importance grew. However, their influence and power was fragile, dependent on Mokadi's position in the royal family and that of her children.

Rival competing factions in the court of *Kgoshi* Meele, different lineages, families, outside groups allied through marriage and tribute, and other branches of Mokadi's own extended family all vied for influence. As the king grew old, political factions at court and in the villages of the realm became increasingly suspicious, tense, and at times hostile.

While due to complex rules of etiquette and protocol, social interaction between these groups might have appeared quite formal and civil, beneath the cordial surface, resentment, envy, and jealousy festered. This was particularly the case among the king's wives, mothers of scores of royal sons. Each had family interests and sons they hoped to advance into greater prominence.

CHAPTER FIVE

Copper

Following Makikele's *Koma* and *Dikomathuku* ceremonies, the young initiated men returned to their villages and began a period of transition in their lives before they would be allowed to marry. During this time they lived apart as a regiment, participated with adult men and their dogs in hunting groups, assumed more responsibility for animal husbandry, honed their fighting skills, and developed expertise in crafts, mining, and metalwork. This new regiment served as a labor force for tribal leaders in their home regions, and on special occasions, for the king himself at Kgopolwe. They would also now join the older warrior regiments to fight whenever war drums sounded.

Some of the young men apprenticed themselves to shamans and herbalists to learn the arts of healing, protective magic, and witchcraft for the benefit of their families and society. Others became hunters or livestock herders or joined family members on trading journeys. Most became engaged, in one form or another, in the mines and at local village smelters and forges.

Makikele used this period of transition to develop leadership skills, build friendships, and to acquire the expertise needed as a future leader of his people. It was during this period in his life that he first traveled extensively with adult men of the royal household.

On occasions during this time, Makikele represented his father on trade trips across the territory and visited political centers with the king's representatives. He visited his maternal kin in many parts of the realm, and was received by uncles and cousins with great distinction and deference as a son of the king.

Trade was controlled by *Kgoshi* Meele and by his representatives, his *ntona* or headmen, in every region. The *ntona* were eyes and ears throughout the kingdom and along the ancient trade routes that passed across Phalaborwa's borders. The king received a portion of all trade goods as his tribute. These were carried to the *mashate*, his residence at Kgopolwe, or distributed to political allies and family members in other locations. This enabled him to amass wealth and enrich leaders loyal to him throughout his domain.

Probably the most coveted of trade imports were guns. These were initially of Portuguese make and brought to the African coast in the 1400s. A slow trickle of guns found their way to the southern African interior during the early 1600s. Africans from the coastal areas acquired them and traded them with villages further inland. In time, guns passed along by trading groups reached the mountainous Venda kingdoms and came into the hands of its various rulers. Trade with these metal-producing kingdoms to the north of Phalaborwa first came indirectly from the Portuguese port towns of Sofala and Inhambane. The guns and other trade goods passed from village to village and from one chiefdom to another along the Limpopo River.

There were also trade routes along ancient footpaths to Phalaborwa, running south from the Limpopo and north from the Lepelle River. These were used by hunters and groups carrying valuable commodities such as salt, red ochre, copper ingots, and iron products for barter in neighboring regions. On rare occasions, trading groups from the port towns, including Delagoa Bay further south, ventured deep into the interior in an effort to bypass middlemen. Well-armed caravans sometimes succeeded, through bartering goods and establishing gift-giving relationships, in negotiating passage with local rulers who carefully guarded access to trade routes passing through their villages.

It was during one of these trade trips, three years after his initiation, that Makikele had the opportunity to visit and observe the metalworking villages in Phalaborwa's western border region. Some of the villages were large-scale foundry sites, continually producing the metals demanded by traders.

Phalaborwa was renowned for the rich iron and copper ores found at Lolwe Hill. The Malatji, who owned these ores, mined, smelted, and forged them into valuable tools, weapons, and other products. The mining and metal-producing culture in Phalaborwa existed long before *Kgoshi* Meele or his father, and even before the first Malatji ancestors reached Lolwe Hill. Indeed, oral traditions associated with the history of Phalaborwa and the royal hill forts of Sealene and Kgopolwe spoke of more than twenty rulers of this iron- and copper-producing region.

Traders came to barter for the Lolwe Hill metal from as far away as the Indian Ocean, where the Tsonga-speaking people lived, and from the highland Venda kingdoms to the north, who in turn bartered goods and ore with great Zimbabwe further north in Shonaland. Phalaborwa also traded with their western neighbors in the realm of the mysterious and feared rain queen, Modjadji, of the Lobedu, and with Sekhukhune, a powerful farming kingdom overlooking Phalaborwa in the Maloti Mountains. Traders even came from the distant cattle kingdom of

Sobhuza in Swaziland looking for iron hoes, spear points, and the distinctive Phalaborwa copper ingot called *marale*.

The rainy season had passed, and a lush millet crop ripened along the Selati riverside as Prince Makikele and Masalani, the court shaman and rainmaker, departed from *Kgoshi* Meele's royal enclosure en route to Nagome Hill, where Maphalakanye was headman and *ntona*. Placed at Nagome by Meele to govern and defend this gateway to his capital at Kgopolwe Hill, Maphalakanye served as the king's liaison with trade groups from Swazi and from the Pedi rulers in Mapulaneng and Thabina who were middlemen for more distant western groups.

Makikele noticed that the largest residential areas at Nagome were situated on the southern and eastern sides of the hill. Farmhouses with livestock pens, and granaries spread out at the foot of the hill and were perched on numerous stone-walled terraces that climbed the talus slopes beneath Nagome's tall granite outcroppings. Metalworkers, on the other hand, were concentrated along the northern side of the hill in the direction of Lolwe and the royal villages several miles further north.

When the royal party arrived, they noticed metalsmiths and forgers already busy preparing smelters for production.

"What are they doing?" a young warrior in the party asked Masalani.

"Those large rocks have been carried here from Lolwe Hill. They contain a very strong iron ore only found at Lolwe, but in demand everywhere. The workers are breaking down the large rocks into smaller stones. They will then heat the smaller stones with charcoal to extract the iron."

"What will they use the iron for?" the youth again inquired of Masalani.

"Iron is much harder than stone or bone. The smiths use it to make spear blades and arrow points, as well as hoes and other tools."

A large trading party had been granted entry to Phalaborwa by way of an ancient trading route called the Maloti escarpment trail, which led to Nagome. The group had crossed the Lepelle River border near a hill village named after Mashale, one of the king's headmen, and were camped there, awaiting permission from Meele to proceed to Nagome. They had brought grain and livestock to barter, and a selection of cotton cloth and glass beads which were popular but rarely reached this far inland from the Portuguese fort on the Indian Ocean coast. Messengers from Mashale to the king would bring details about the trading party, valuable information for use when trading negotiations began.

In Makikele's entourage was a small contingent of warriors, including several archers, and forty porters carrying ore to their final destination at Phetole Hill. He also brought his four hunting dogs with him, as he expected to have time to track animals on the higher grasslands west of Nagome.

A number of women also accompanied the caravan. Some came along to prepare food and others carried goods for trade. One young mother and her small child traveled with them to Phetole, and from there were to continue on to the Kingdom of Lobedu to join her husband and his family. She was newly married, had given birth to a daughter at her father's village, and would now permanently reside at her husband's Lobedu farm. The Lobedu were closely affiliated with the Ba-Phalaborwa and shared a common language, many marriage ties, and the same religious beliefs. The two groups had been at peace for many years.

When Makikele learned of the young woman's journey, he thought of his own mother, who as a young woman had made the same journey to Lobedu from far-away Sekgopo village. It was her widowhood that had brought her back to Phalaborwa and to the royal enclosure at Kgopolwe. Many times she had told him the story about her days as a bride in the court of the hidden rain queen, Modjadji, who was feared and said to be immortal.

Masalani, the king's shaman, carried with him bundles of special leather pouches holding small amulets, about three inches square. These were to be placed in the floors of newly-built smelters. They had been purchased by Meele and brought from Masalani's home in Venda. They were believed to contain strong magic that would ensure the quality of iron and copper products emerging from the fire and their appeal to incoming traders. The shaman, who was well into his fifth decade of life and had been employed by Meele for almost twenty years, would bless each production station and its workers so that everyone would benefit from the tasks ahead.

As they approached Nagome Hill, Makikele ordered Masalani and the caravan to proceed to the main village. He had decided to remain behind with several companions to observe the smelting and smithing in this smaller artisan settlement near the northern fringe of the hill.

After accepting formal greetings and words of welcome by the metalworkers and their families, he sat in the shade of a

cluster of marula and acacia trees observing two new smelters under construction and the repair of several others. While
Makikele had observed metal production underway in surrounding villages near his home at Kgopolwe, and was accustomed
to hearing the sound of heated ingots being hammered into
implements on anvils by their smiths, he had not previously
witnessed the construction of a smelter.

Makikele sat under an acacia tree chewing on marula nuts
served to him by an old woman, a member of the smelter's
family.

"Many people, both men and women, work on the forges
and smelters which are scattered throughout Nagome," the old
woman said. "See those women there?" She pointed to a group
of women working on large piles of rock near the construction
sites.

"Yes, my grandmother." He addressed her in a respectful,
soothing voice, warmly smiling at her as she became more
comfortable in his presence.

"That is iron ore. Women from the village have carried it
from Lolwe Hill, with the permission of the king, your father.
They are now breaking it up into smaller stones," she said.

While they talked, a party of five men armed with spears
entered the compound from an acacia grove to the east. They
escorted an equal number of women carrying large baskets.

"What is in the baskets, my grandmother?" Makikele asked.

"That is charcoal. They make it from hard woods felled in
the bush," responded the old woman.

"And what are those women doing?" Makikele pointed to
a group of women who appeared to be digging and pulverizing red clay from a cluster of small mounds close to the
workplace.

"That is the soil from abandoned termite mounds. The clay contains termite secretions, a sticky substance that tightly glues the particles together. It forms a hard, durable material used to construct the smelter walls. When the material is heated during smelting, it becomes even harder and nearly indestructible. Other women carry water to the site in pots from wells dug into the dry riverbed," described the old woman.

All these tasks were being completed close by the future smelter sites, where circular holes had been dug as footings for the structures about to be built.

"That is an unusual breastplate," the old woman observed. As she pointed toward his chest, he studied her wrinkled hand attached to a still-strong arm, which was weighted with copper and iron bangles and bracelets consisting of iron beads interspersed with pieces of shell and a few fragments of blue glass. Around her neck, suspended from cotton string, hung a small iron pick, the trademark of every Ba-Phalaborwa housewife. Alongside it hung a tooth. Makikele thought it was possibly the tooth of a calf, or perhaps it came from a sable antelope, an animal renowned for its healing powers.

Makikele fingered the crescent-shaped copper disc given to him by his father at the *Dikomathuku*. He turned it so that it caught the sun's rays and reflected them into the woman's smiling face.

"It was a gift from my father at *Koma*. Now, grandmother, it is your turn, so tell me about copper smelting and how these beautiful discs are made."

"Copper ore consists of smaller stones than iron ore. It is dug out of the mine shafts beneath Lolwe Hill, but is rare in comparison with the darker iron ore that can be found everywhere above the ground surrounding and on the hill. Copper ore is green and must be handled more carefully than iron ore. It is stored in leather bags kept near the chief smelter's house. The women of the smelter's family hammer the ore into finer particles before it is distributed for melting and molding into ingots.

"An ingot of copper, called a *marale*, usually takes the shape of a rod with a bulbous head at one end featuring whisker-like projections. Copper is an extremely precious metal, a highly prized commodity which must be guarded and controlled. These *serale* ingots are used to purchase cattle or even serve as bride-wealth in marriage negotiations. They are later fashioned into bracelets and beads, which are sold or given as valuable gifts," she continued.

Makikele held his crescent-shaped copper breastplate once again and felt awe that such beauty and value could emerge from the coarse green stones. *Truly, fire was a powerful force,* he thought, *magical in what it could create.*

The old woman excused herself and left Makikele alone. He turned his attention back to the construction of the smelter. He marveled at how the women breaking the rocks into smaller stones, those bringing the charcoal, those pulverizing the red clay from the termite mounds, and those carrying water all performed their tasks quickly, simultaneously, and at several locations and various elevations on the hillside.

Makikele left the shade of the marula tree and ambled down to inspect the smelters more closely. He approached a man who seemed to be supervising the operation, gave the traditional greeting of respect, and asked him to explain what they were doing.

"First we plaster a floor for the smelter using the termite dirt. It sets quickly, so this must be done while it is still moist and before it hardens. In the middle of the floor we make a small hole about this size." He held out his clenched fist. "This hole will hold the strong magic Masalani brought in the leather pouches.

"We are building two different types of structure," the man explained. "The copper smelters are circular and domed, about this thick at the base and thinner at the top." He held his hands separated by about eight to ten inches to indicate the thickness of the base. He went on to describe that the smelter was about two and a half feet high with the same diameter at the base, and that a twelve-inch opening at the top would serve as a flue. "There is an opening at its base," he said. "A clay pipe is placed in the opening to direct air that we pump in using a bellows made from impala skin.

"The iron smelter is quite different. It is about the same size as the copper furnace, but it is in the shape of a triangle with three clay walls supporting one another. These walls are connected at the base and taper toward the top, where they meet to form a small chimney opening. Three bellows pipes are fitted into these wall openings close to the ground and likewise attached to double bellows made of impala skins. Impala horns are fitted to the bellows and used to pump the air that heats up the fire until it is hot enough to melt the ore.

"Both copper and iron smelters are buttressed along the outer walls with dirt, which serves to support the walls as well as provide insulation and heat retention," he explained.

"And what are those men doing?" Makikele pointed to the nearby terraces.

"They are the smiths. They are making smaller dual-bellowed forges lined with clay," the man replied.

A flat square-shaped granite anvil stood alongside each forge. "The anvils are used to fashion the iron and copper drawn from the fire," the man added.

Copper smelters, air bellows, copper bangle, and *marale* ingot

That afternoon, following a meal and shortly before the caravan was scheduled to leave, several of the clay ovens were fired up. Pump men straddling their bellows pots forced air into the clay vent pipes. Makikele heard one of the smelter-men calling to his assistant to add charcoal to build up the heat, and the first ore was placed onto the coals to be turned into iron. These artisans would work throughout the night and into the morning processing ore, which would then be handed over to smiths, who would fashion it into finished marketable objects.

CHAPTER SIX

Hospitality

Prince Makikele's caravan formed a long line as it left Nagome to begin the thirty-mile trek, following the Selati River and its tributaries to Phetole Hill village. The porters and women who already comprised part of the caravan were joined by a guard of archers and spearmen. No gun bearers were available because *Kgoshi* Meele had deployed his artillery for elephant hunting in the eastern territories.

The southern borderland had been quiet for a number of years and the road they traveled was isolated, only passing through several hunting areas and cattle stations and two or three lookout villages. Otherwise, they crossed through game-filled grasslands known for their predatory felines, in particular fierce lions.

The caravan got off to a fast-paced start, the cattle enjoying their freedom after being fenced in all night. The herdsmen began singing a cattle song, which seemed to keep the livestock moving at a good pace despite the morning heat. By the first hour, they passed between Seroltwe and the Mabokha Hills. Seroltwe was a well-guarded lookout post protecting the king's capital on the west side.

As they approached the pass, Makikele's trumpeter sounded several blasts on the *phalaphala*, bringing a group of fully-armed warriors and much of the village down to watch them pass by. An elderly man danced and sang as the cattle passed and the royal entourage briefly stopped for greetings.

"Aaahey, Malatji!" shouted the elderly man, calling out the praise for the royal Malatji family. "Aaahey, Makikele, son of Meele, son of Mothatewaleopeng of the distant watering hole at the place called Makwibidung. Aaahey, porcupine totem! Aaahey, Malatji of Lolwe the iron mountain, ruler of Phalaborwa, where pounding of the forgers' hammers never ceases!"

This was followed by a chant of ancestral names recited by the commanding ancient voice, accompanied by the ululation of village women.

Many onlookers joined in, shouting, "Aaahey, Malatji! Aaahey, son of the royal porcupine totem!"

As Makikele passed, each one lowered their head while repeatedly placing their right hand on their left hand in the traditional sign of greeting and respect.

As in each of the western villages passed through on the journey, Makikele met several young men of his circumcision regiment. He stopped and greeted each one of them happily, identifying some by name. Those from Seroltwe, and a few who joined them from the Mabokha Hills, walked with the entourage as far as the ford of the Selati. Some waded across the shallow expanse with Makikele before saying good-bye. It was an easy crossing, the river being low from lack of rain.

From the far bank of the Selati, Makikele looked east to see the lofty granite cliffs of Sealene Hill bathed in full sunlight. He said a short prayer to this hill where so many of the royal family lay buried: "Protect us on this trip; may no evil befall us."

He thought about Kgopolwe, his home, which was now even further away. He wondered about his mother, Mokadi, and remembered her laughing face when she brought him his morning meal the previous day. She had placed a small woven packet in his hand. "Carry this with you," she had said. "It will keep you safe." She gestured for him to place it in the leather pouch secured to his belt. She had probably gotten it the previous day from old Sekedi, the herbalist and witch who had provided her with healing potions and remedies for sickness for as long as he could remember.

Mokadi was a good mother and a strong woman. His father trusted her and occasionally would allow her to serve the traditional millet beer to him and his counselors when they met to deliberate government matters. His father trusted her with secrets, such as his uncertainty about Masalani's continued service to him and her family's involvement on the council, and his fears about the credence of some of its more outspoken members. She had an aptitude for analyzing the real motivations behind the things people would say to the king. She even cautioned her son to look beyond the words people said to discover the real reasons for their speech and actions.

"I know, mother," he had said. "I have heard *gogo*'s story about the porcupine totem many times."

Mokadi had instilled in him a fear of evil intentions and bad magic that could be used against him. His father and his mother had enemies who would do him harm as a way of harming them. His gregarious inclination was checked by a reserve which was recently reinforced during his initiation rite. At the *Koma*, while ritually isolated, he had been shown deference by all in his regiment based on their family's rank and influence. In such settings, bloodline and proximity to the royal line by way of wealth and influence were the determining criteria. He was cautious of contact with people who were not part of the royal family or who might fail to follow protocol when addressing him.

About two miles to the north stood the stronghold of Namagale Hill, where Monyaela, a member of Meele's inner council of advisors, was headman. It held quite a few of the king's cattle in its fortified enclosure. A number of the cows being transported that day were descended from those that Monyaela held as a client to his king, including several from cattle transacted during royal wedding negotiations. Makikele reflected that some of them might one day come to him when he was permitted to marry.

He could see Marumushi Hill south of the trail they were following. Each of these hill villages had active iron and copper smelting operations like the one at Nagome. Each made a contribution to the kingdom's trade. Although metalwork was a year-round activity, the time of Makikele's trip coincided with the prime smelting season. Soon, with the arrival of harvest, the major trade season would begin. Then people would focus attention on marketing the many and varied metal objects they produced.

When the distinct sound of stone pounding metal on stone anvils reached Makikele's ears from the worksites in these distant villages, he repeated to himself the well-known phrase, "Phalaborwa, the place of the crying anvil, where the sound never ceases throughout the land." It was true, he thought, the metalwork never ceases in his father's kingdom. And he felt a kindly sense of pride in his homeland.

By late afternoon it was hot, their pace had slowed, and the cattle had to be goaded to move faster. The caravan eventually reached the almost-dry bed of the Motlemorula Stream, a tributary of the Selati River. This would lead them to Morelang, where they would spend the night.

Thick vegetation covered both banks of the Motlemorula. They followed the south contour of the stream, which passed through open grassland with very little tree growth but was interrupted every quarter mile or so by termite mounds that projected out of the ground, red and stark.

Impala grazed in small herds, with smaller groups of three or four kudu, and at one juncture they spotted several zebra. Scouts returned to caution that lions had been seen in some low-lying rocky configurations. These were unlikely to be a problem until nightfall; however, they guarded the cattle more carefully while several archers moved ahead to hunt impala for the evening meal.

Apart from lions, leopard had also been reported to hunt in this region. One of the guides had seen them many times while on hunting trips in the area. Leopards, too, could be troublesome for the cattle.

The route took them along an ancient trail, which passed by a large singular baobab tree stranding on high ground. It was close to a curve in the watercourse and about two miles from Morelang, their destination for the night. As they approached, it appeared silhouetted against the sky and the distant hills of the Pedi escarpment and Maloti Mountains. The entire caravan stopped at the tree while a messenger was dispatched to alert Morelang of their arrival. The shade of the tree made this a pleasant place to stop. Women, accompanied by spearmen, went to collect water in a shady grove where surface pools remained year-round because of their depth.

After drawing water for the travelers, cattle were allowed to descend to the stream bed to drink.

It was dusk when the *phalaphala* trumpet was blown to announce their arrival at the Morelang cattle post. The isolated settlement consisted of a cluster of houses and several large cattle pens interspersed among a stony low hill complex. The village itself was small and heavily fenced in with thornbushes and poles. In some parts of the village, low stone walls strengthened the barriers and separated the cattle pens from other areas of domestic activity.

They were met by the headman, Nareng.

"Welcome to Morelang," he said. "Please pen your cattle within the thorn enclosures. The lion have been quite troublesome in recent weeks, but we did manage to kill one large female."

The headman showed Makikele its skin, which was staked out to be tanned, and also a large leopard pelt, hunted during the rainy season. "The leopard skin is for your father, *Kgoshi* Meele," Nareng said to Makikele. "You can take it with you when you leave."

While the pelts of other spotted cats were used and worn by witchdoctors, healers, and some headmen, the leopard was exclusively a part of the royal regalia.

"With the king's permission, I hope to trade the other pelts when the Pedi come to Phetole," said Nareng.

The travelers settled in for the night. The hunters had killed two impala for meat. Cooking fires were started, and by nightfall a meal had been prepared. While the entire party would sleep in the open, senior members of the entourage ate with the headman and village counselors in a fenced-off compound reserved for private meetings and men's work. Fresh beer had been made by women of the headman's compound, and a good meal was shared over discussion about their trip, condition of the local livestock, expectations for the coming trade season, and the security of the region.

"The livestock at Morelang are healthy and our cattle herd is expanding," said Nareng. "It has been a generation since the last cattle epidemic decimated most of the herds in the low country."

One elder commented on the decline of tsetse following that rinderpest epidemic, while also giving lurid details of the difficulties faced by cattle owners in those days. An accounting of stock belonging to the king was given with enthusiasm.

"Lions are becoming an increasing threat," said Nareng. "This forces us to heavily fence the village with the flesh-tearing, hooked thornbushes that grow everywhere in this place. It has been hard work, but once the entryways are closed off at night, the village is impenetrable to lions. Leopards, on the other hand, pose a different problem. Two got into the enclosure on a dark night only a week ago and made off with a goat and a calf. They managed to jump over a section of the barricade, which was lower than the rest, and carried their kill out of the compound the same way they had entered. We all marveled at their strength. They are dangerous cats, and we fear they may attack and eat people next."

Makikele listened intently when one of the village hunters, a young man in his twenties, told of a harrowing encounter with two lionesses while stalking kudu. He was one of the Pilusa lineage and had been in Makikele's *Koma* regiment, and Makikele knew he was an entertaining storyteller.

"The lionesses were hidden only a few feet in front of us on a hillside," he said, "and attacked the kudu just before we prepared to walk by them. Though we were vulnerable as we slowly, stealthily approached the kudu, we were totally unaware of the crouching lions. They ignored us when the kudu bolted and they took off after them. But for the kudu, we would have had a bad time of it."

As the group prepared to sleep, Makikele wondered if lion would be a problem for them the next morning. They would be crossing the last miles of grassland to Phetole, where they would discharge the herd they had brought with them. It would be exciting to watch his spearmen drive off the big cats. Perhaps they would kill one and retrieve the skin and body parts. Masalani would appreciate having lion ingredients for his magic potions. Lion fat, he knew, was a much-sought-after component for war medicines, and the claw and some internal organs had healing values.

The next morning, the group woke up before dawn and ate a quick meal before assembling to leave. Nareng, the headman, thanked Makikele, Masalani, and others of high rank in the party for their stay and presented Makikele with two yearling calves. They would be taken to Phetole to be added to the royal herd, and their increase monitored over the years. This gift would become part of a complex patron-client livestock network, linking Makikele and his father to Nareng of Morelang and his family. Offspring of the two calves would be recognized as part of this gift and knowledge of them tracked for generations. The gift provided an important tie for Morelang with the royal family, and a bond that might be useful to both donor and recipient at some later time.

At sunrise, Nareng ordered the large, tight clusters of thorn-bushes that served as barricades to the village to be opened, and the party exited Morelang for the last leg of their journey.

Five young men, including the storyteller from the previous evening, lined up to say good-bye to the prince. Each spoke briefly with Makikele, each one paying his respects to the leader of their *Koma* regiment. The prince in turn acknowledged each by name.

Maintaining ties with his regiment was an important role Makikele played as a prince of the royal household. Their loyalty to Makikele and the Malatji ruling family was important for the future well-being and security of the kingdom. Makikele knew he served his father well by strengthening these ties. Strong, loyal fighting regiments had been essential in earlier times for defending the nation's borders and serving as a police force, deployed by the king and his council in times of need. The kingdom would not be safe without the vigilance and loyalty of its men of fighting age and their families. This new regiment, national in nature for the first time, would require maintenance if it were to be a strong and unified force. Makikele understood that time spent with these fellow age-mates had a strategic function, one his father insisted he maintain and develop while he traveled as his representative.

CHAPTER SEVEN

Lesibe

The final leg of the journey to Phetole was hot and slow. By late afternoon, the three peaks surrounding the large border village complex could be seen due west. These were the hills known as Phetole, Maakeng, and Marakapula, each towering above the grassy plains. The settlement, which was their destination, was saddled between Phetole Hill and a cluster of low-lying hills and rock formations on its eastern side.

Phetole was a large village complex located close to a curve in the Selati River. It was a sentinel village and trading stop. A much-traveled pathway from the Lepelle River entered Phetole from the south. To its west, a low-lying range of hills extended from the Lepelle to the Letaba River. The largest of these was Makhotso Hill, which marked a much-disputed border region dividing Meele's kingdom and Lobedu, the highland stronghold of Queen Modjadji.

Standing between the several granite hills and lesser stone outcroppings, Phetole was well-fortified with a large population, which had been reinforced with young men from the new regiments formed over the last decade. Several of them were from Makikele's circumcision regiment, sons of noble families, whom he had befriended during *Koma*, and he looked forward to seeing these men again. Most of the young men came from eastern villages, relocated by Meele to strengthen the western border. Many were related to him by blood and through marriage ties. Some were sons of newer groups who had assimilated into the kingdom, people displaced from the highlands during the time of Makikele's grandfather. They were now loyal to Meele and to Sealene Hill, his ritual center.

Two messengers were sent forward to announce their approach and the travelers quickened their pace. The calves gifted to Makikele by the Morelang headman moved in step with the herd, but lowed occasionally as if protesting their removal and forced drive in the heat. They both drank greedily at the water stop and looked in good health.

Left with the royal herd at Phetole, the calves would begin producing calves themselves in two years, and he calculated their potential increase over five years and more. With his father's permission, these could constitute the base of his own holding of cattle at Phetole. Some of his mother's herd at Kgopolwe, and those she shared with her brothers at her home village, would also one day become available to him. As a rule, his father and his mother's brothers dispersed their livestock to many different locations. This made for healthier stock and reduced the danger of decimation from theft or disease. There had been cattle raids on the eastern borders by the Tsonga, and retaliatory raids which added stock to all of Meele's herds. Some of the stock being driven to Phetole was of Tsonga origin. They would be bred with stock traded from the Pedi and Lobedu. A portion of the Phetole herd was available for trade, and some were reserved for breeding purposes to improve lines and for other transactions deemed important by the king and his counselors.

When the party was within a mile and a half of Phetole, the trumpeter sounded their approach. Makikele could see people walking toward the village gates, children running and shouting, and dogs barking. Makikele's four hunting dogs, curbed with rope now, barked in reply and wagged their tails. The women in the group began chattering among themselves and smiling, glad to be at the end of the long, hot, dry trip.

When they entered the village through the thorn and pole gate, a woman from the village recognized a family member in Makikele's entourage and began ululating. The village headman, Makikele's young uncle, Bangeni Malatji, a kinsman to his father by one of his grandfather's wives of the Pilusa iron-working family, greeted him, praising their porcupine totem, the name of the king, and their common ancestor, *Kgoshi* Mothupi Malatji.

Bangeni was accompanied by one of his own sons, Lukoba, who had been an initiate with Makikele at the circumcision rites three years earlier. Bangeni had been an official at the circumcision camp, had joined with other leaders in teaching the initiates about Phalabowa lore and proper behavior, and had helped transmit secret information and songs performed during the ceremonies.

Although of the royal line, Lukoba had not been included in the separate quarters of the circumcision lodge reserved for high ranking princes and noble sons. But on this occasion Makikele greeted him as a kinsman, while the citizens of Phetole watched with curiosity. Formal greetings were exchanged between the caravan members and village leadership followed by discussion of many practical matters, such as allocating and apportioning out the new livestock into pens and where goods brought from Kgopolwe and Lolwe would be stored.

Then the royal guests were led through the main village to the lower level of the settlement. As they passed through the village, Makikele saw women and men beginning to barter food and other items. Members of the caravan party quickly dispersed among the villagers, some being led to a far cluster of huts where freshly brewed millet beer could be found.

The leaders of the visiting group then ascended the lower slopes of Phetole to a stone-circled compound where Bangeni and his several wives, children, and other relatives lived. In an adjacent and separate stone enclosure were several neat clay-walled cottages, one of which was allocated for Makikele's use. Masalani first entered the house, inspected the interior, sprinkled a black powder possessing protective magic, and emerged, nodding to Makikele and his young uncle that it would be suitable for the prince.

Before nightfall and after the guests had been made comfortable, Makikele, Masalani, and some of their men joined Bangeni Malatji and a party of senior village men to visit the smelters and forges in operation at Phetole. Descending the hill, they headed north through neat garden patches and alongside thatched houses, passing over several low-lying stone formations and low elevations of rock clusters. When they descended into a more secluded part of Phetole, they lost sight of the main village and entrance gate.

The sound of stone hammers drew Makikele's eyes toward a worksite northeast of Phetole Hill.

"What is going on there?" he asked.

"We are expanding," said Bangeni Malatji. "What you see is a new secondary settlement. We have been working in that area for several years, but recently it has expanded rapidly. We now have an extensive grid of working smelting furnaces."

"I am very impressed," said Makikele. "Tell me more."

"There are two main smelting centers in the complex, with furnaces lined up in rows of four and five workstations already in operation or in the process of being made ready for firing."

"Are they for iron or copper?"

"There are smelters for both. Look over there." Bangeni pointed to a row of conical-shaped smelters. "They are the copper smelters. And over there—" he pointed in a different direction, "—those larger more triangular-shaped furnaces are for iron."

Each furnace was surrounded by heaps of stone, non-ore-bearing rock discarded during the smelting process. The size of these heaps indicated the sites had been used for a long time.

On the periphery of the broad expanse of furnaces were the houses, with gardens and stone-lined livestock pens belonging to the families of the metalworkers.

"Are those new furnaces under construction?" Makikele pointed to two flat areas on the westernmost line of smelters.

"Yes, my prince."

"I have seen smelting and forging work in most sizeable villages in Phalaborwa, but this is the most extensive metal smelting worksite I have ever seen. The number of furnaces and the extent of the operation surprise me and also impress me."

As he walked through the village, he noted several different lineages at work, each serving the interests of different trade partner groups. There were also several Lobedu families who he assumed had married into the local population. Several families of the Mathipa lineage, to which Makikele's mother belonged, had trading ties with the Lobedu on the western border. Makikele guessed that this link accounted for the presence of so many Lobedu having settled here in Phetole.

He heard greetings shouted to men of the Ngwane lineage, who maintained ties with trading groups from Swaziland. The Ngwane, who were specialists in forging and crafting the large Swazi stabbing spear now being adopted by warriors in the younger Phalaborwa regiments, could be found working in many border villages frequented by Swazi traders. Wherever the Ngwane were found, one could usually also find members of the Hlame lineage, middlemen who traded directly with the Swazi.

The Hlame traded at these domestic sites and also traveled into the far reaches beyond Phalaborwa, wherever the expanding Swazi were settled. These Hlame, like the Mathipa, were some of the earliest known peoples in Phalaborwa, living in the region long before the Malatji arrived. Both groups were tied to the royal Malatji lineage through multiple marriage alliances, of which the venerable Queen Mother Ntlabidi was the most prestigious. They could speak various Nguni languages, such as Swazi, Zulu, and Tsonga, and were important go-betweens as diplomats to the various Nguni-speaking kingdoms, as well as being effective traders.

The Ngwane metalworking specialists had their largest residential base closer to the king's main settlement at Kgopolwe, where they provided weapons for Meele's armory. The Hlame, on the other hand, retained their political and trade base near Sekgopo Hill, the kingdom's eastern border stronghold. Other families at Phetole traded as well with the highland tribes, such as the Pedi, the Kgatla, and many others seeking prized Phalaborwa goods.

Bangeni Malatji escorted the group east of the main worksite onto a boulder-strewn knoll where Tlagolo of the Selepe family had his compound and livestock pens. The knoll provided an excellent vantage point to observe most of the village below.

Tlagolo Selepe was the headman of the smelting village. As such, he was responsible, with his sons, for overseeing the distribution of ore brought from Lolwe and the smelting of iron for onsite weapons production. Tlagolo was very old, enfeebled, and nearly blind. He was greatly respected as a tribal elder, had been a counselor to *Kgoshi* Meele, and was said to have known both King Mosholwane and his predecessor, King Kgashane, when they controlled Phalaborwa's iron and copper. Born in the Selepe metal working village near Nagome Hill, he had worked as a youth at the weapons-making forges and had been apprenticed to Tshentshe Selepe, one of the early gun makers brought by *Kgoshi* Kgashane from Venda, their northern neighbors.

"When they were very young, Tlagolo Selepe, his brother, and two of his sisters worked in the Lolwe Hill mine shafts," Bangeni explained to Makikele. "Being small in stature, their size was well-suited to descending the narrow causeways into the underground caves where copper ore was hammered loose and brought to the surface. When he outgrew this work, he was taught how to work the iron smelters, and then later he was allowed to work the gun maker's forges.

"Like his father before him, Tlagolo was a counselor to the king on metal production and matters of defense. A trusted advisor and a good manager, he was sent here to Phetole by *Kgoshi* Meele to oversee the metalworks and maintain the quality of workmanship," continued Bangeni.

Phetole, like several other strategic border villages at various corners of the kingdom, was a major contact point for the lucrative metal commodities which distinguished Phalaborwa. The trade brought in much-needed food and consumables, as well as technology and additional livestock, which was never sufficiently available in the low country. These commodities enriched the royal and noble families who controlled the flow of goods. Tlagolo Selepe was a member of one of the well-placed artisan families providing the expertise, and in his case the security and control, which was needed to keep the system working effectively to everyone's benefit.

Old Tlagolo expectantly awaited Makikele's arrival. Although diminutive, as were most of the members of these specialist mining families, when greeting Makikele he bowed and applauded in the traditional sign of deference. His aged voice was not loud, but was one that commanded attention.

"Aaahey, Malatji!" he said. "Aaahey, Makikele, son of Meele of the porcupine totem!"

"I bring greetings to you and to all the Selepe living at Phetole," Makikele replied with a smile to this aged client of his father.

"I am honored to have *Kgoshi* Meele's young son in my home. I have observed you many times over the years, and most recently when I had the privilege of assisting with the higher-ranking royals and nobles in the circumcision lodge. I was impressed by your quickness to learn, and by the way you conducted yourself as a leader. You have all the qualities of a worthy son and representative of your father."

Other inhabitants of the compound gathered outside the reed wall barrier surrounding the entrance to Tlagolo's house. Tlagolo knew how important it was that this young royal report back positively to his father on what he had observed. With Bangeni Malatji beside him, he described the work of this village to Makikele, and arranged for him to tour the smelting sites the following day.

Children mine copper at Lolwe Hill

Makikele's porters, seated on a flat section of ground below Headman Selepe's house, were ordered to bring the substantial quantities of ore they had carried from Lolwe. This was allocated to various piles of the green and black stone already stored near the compound, and then inspected by the family. Makikele, Bangeni, and old Selepe would each report back to the king's council at Kgopolwe on this new consignment and give an account of the finished ore it would produce, the range of objects emerging from the forge, and the value they would bring at market.

Bangeni, as *ntona* of the village and king's counselor, would finalize the margin of profit from sale of goods produced from the ore. With the greatest detail, he would report on the portion reserved for royal entitlement and the form this would take in grain, livestock in various locations, and trade goods from the coast and surrounding highland tribes. He would as well allocate profit shares to other stakeholders involved in the complex network of middlemen, artisans, and leaders. Following the highland harvest season, everyone anticipated a prosperous trade season.

With formalities completed, the guests returned to the main village to be accommodated for the night. Fresh millet beer had been brewed that day, and Bangeni gave orders to butcher a goat and a Pedi sheep with fattened tail for the royal group. An additional goat, several hares, and an antelope brought in by hunters were butchered for the porters and regimental guard accompanying Makikele.

That evening, Bangeni Malatji, in his capacity as a king's counselor, hosted a lavish dinner for Makikele, his immediate entourage, and special guests from the village. The meal was served inside his fenced enclosure away from the view of ordinary villagers. A drummer and flute player provided music, accompanied by the village bard and his sister, who performed praise songs and recited popular odes.

In addition to the ordinary millet beer available throughout the year, Bangeni had also arranged for a special brew of a marula beer, made from green early-harvest fruit pulp. Having fermented in brew pots for more than a week, it had a higher-than-usual alcohol content and was sweet as well as intoxicating.

From early morning, women of Bangeni's compound had been busy preparing the large meal in a closed-off cooking pavilion near the main house. The largest clay cooking pots had been brought in from village kitchens, some for brewing beer, and others to boil food.

The carcasses of the goats, the sheep, and the much-liked springbok were hung from the shelter's posts and crossbeams to cure. Large numbers of cattle flies, attracted by the dried blood, crawled over the meat as it awaited processing. Occasionally, when disturbed by passing workers busy with the fires and other preparations, they formed small swarms. Unharmed by the insects, the meat was then grilled over coals, and some small portions added to the vegetable dishes.

Bangeni's mother, a Hlame from Sekgopo, and his great wife, a daughter of old Selepe and the mother of Lukoba, oversaw the food preparations. They monitored the work of younger women of the household as they ground grain in the large permanent stone mortars and then pounded it into even finer flour in upright wooden mortars. The women used smaller stone mortars and pestles to grind dried marula nuts from the previous year's harvest, which were added to starch and vegetable dishes. Wild peppers, onions, and garlic were also added to some of these dishes, along with the most important flavoring of all: salt.

The women pounded several long strips of dried game meat into a fine powder with wooden pestles. This would also be added as a relish to some dishes. They cut the portions of larger dried pieces, the ones made from game steaks, into thin chunks to be passed among the guests, along with salted dried marula nuts and roasted mopane worms as appetizers before the main dishes were served. When the larger cuttings of meat were completely cooked, they were removed from the fires and brought into Bangeni's reception area to be eaten.

The diners sat on low stools and benches in a circle, facing toward the center of the enclosure. Makikele remained at the back of his entourage, his messenger relaying greetings, good wishes, and questions to him from those attending. Makikele had invited Lukoba to join his circle and spoke to him directly during the evening. This distinction was much appreciated by Lukoba, and his mother and father were pleased that their son had found favor.

They greeted the prince when he arrived with applause, and shouted out one of the proverbs used on such occasions when greeting dinner guests: "The forefathers said, 'When an honored visitor comes to our house, we should eat with him and make happy noises.'"

All joined in with laughter, affirming the host's ceremonial greeting by pounding their feet on the freshly dung-smeared clay floors.

Among the guests bringing greetings to Makikele that evening was a distant male cousin of his mother's, also of the Mathipa lineage from Sekgopo. He had with him two daughters, one still a child, the other having completed the *bjale* rite of maturity. The latter was an attractive young woman who would soon be found a husband. As was proper, both girls avoided eye contact with the men and seated themselves on the floor with other women in the gathering while their father gave greetings.

When the father's tie to Makikele's family had been properly established as in the *malome* category, Makikele sent a messenger to convey his good wishes to the father, saying, "Prince Malatji gives greetings to his mother's brother." He also enquired about the names of the young women.

The older girl was called Lesibe, the younger Seakati.

This done, Makikele requested that a goat from the royal herd be given as a gift to this *malome* and his family to thank them for the visit.

Makikele's messenger reported the gift to them as they left the compound. As head of a poor family with few livestock and appended to the wealthier Selepe family living in Phetole, it pleased the distant relative to be so honored. He promised the prince's messenger he would return with a gift before the prince left Phetole.

That night while Makikele slept intermittently, sometimes awoken by the snoring of his messenger and attendant, both curled up in skin blankets in front of the house door, he thought about the young woman Lesibe's visit, her comely posture and fine features.

He had noted her quiet discussion with several women guests. He had also observed the coy smiles and glances toward him by some of the older women, and the occasional laughter that interspersed their conversation.

While he tried to sleep, he thought of Lesibe. When she and her father were about to leave Bangeni's compound, while returning a greeting to one of the diners, she had briefly looked in Makikele's direction and their eyes had met. He had stared at her until she turned to leave. Thoughts of the brief exchange when their eyes had met excited him, and the image of her comely figure and disposition stayed with him throughout the night.

The girl's father would be classed as a mother's brother, a *malome*, even though remotely so. This accorded him the eligibility to provide a wife to the prince. However distant the actual tie might be, this suitability applied and had not gone unnoticed either by the dinner guests or by Makikele. He decided that he would ask his mother about the girl when he returned home to Kgopolwe.

CHAPTER EIGHT

The Hunt

Early the following morning, Makikele was up before dawn to go hunting with his bowmen and dogs. Wild pig had been spotted that week and one killed by watchmen. With an early start and helped by the dogs, Makikele hoped they might locate several wild pigs during the hunt. The meat was well liked, and the hunt offered a challenge. The boars could be quite dangerous to man and hunting dog and could swiftly eviscerate a careless dog when cornered. The quality of grass in this valley was good and attracted migratory antelope, zebra, and occasionally the enormous eland. Makikele brought a hunting spear and his long knife for possible close encounters with game. He expected, however, that his bowmen would bring down fast-footed impala and the larger more desirable grazing animals abundant in this sector of the kingdom. If luck was with them, they might encounter lion, in which case he intended to play a primary role in a kill.

To the west of Phetole village, the land descended into a stretch of stream beds and water courses fed by catchment from the three peaks surrounding the village, and from Marapong Hill about two miles to the west. The banks of these streams and waterways, some with year-round surface water, were used for millet cultivation and also for grazing. As the grain ripened before harvest, the fields were guarded by young men to keep animals and birds away.

Four dogs on leashes sniffed the trail. The hunting party strode down the rock-strewn talus slopes that extended westward from Maakeng Hill to a meandering stream bed, which bisected the plane separating them from the distant Marapong Hill. They followed the stream, but avoided the thicker trees and scrub bush rooted in the moister soil of the water plain. This route took them through acacia-dotted grassland where game grazed.

On each side of the stream, millet and maize grew in patches tended by villagers. They guarded the fields, now that the grain was ripening, to keep game, baboons, monkeys, and even elephants from destroying the crops. They herded their livestock away from the bushy waterline, keeping them on higher ground to protect them from the bite of the tsetse fly, which caused sickness and death. Only certain open areas free of bush were considered suitable for watering livestock. Even then the herders had to be vigilant, protecting their cattle from the dangerous disease-carrying flies. The game animals also preferred these more open-standing water spots, coming to drink at sunset and into the night.

A small herd of giraffe watched the men making their way along an elevated trail running parallel to the water course. The animals galloped away to a more distant acacia grove and began browsing among the thorny leaves. They remained vigilant, but appeared unconcerned by the stealthy line of intruders with their dogs. The giraffe were accustomed to humans passing through their grazing territory, as herders often brought cattle through the region in the wet season. Only rarely were the giraffe hunted, and on this occasion they sensed that the focus of this hunting band lay elsewhere.

One of the village hunters knew of a pride of lions in the vicinity. He thought they might locate a mature male to stalk. Scouts were sent out. One soon returned from the south, where the grassy stretch opened out onto a broader expanse of rolling flatland interspersed with low overgrown rocky outcroppings. In one of these rock clusters, the scouts had spotted two lone male lions. They were separated from the local pride of females and cubs, dominated by older males.

"This is what we will do," said Tchwene, the senior hunter. "We will split into two groups. The wind is blowing from the west, so one group will move ahead south of the lions with the dogs, and the other will approach from the northeast. Both groups will attempt to get close to the lair without detection and release the dogs to distract the lions when they pick up our scent."

"You are a shrewd hunter, Tchwene; we will follow your plan," said Makikele with a reassuring grin. He knew the dogs, which were from the king's kennel, were trained to hold game at bay and would give both groups time to close in on the lions without detection. "When we are close enough, release the dogs to distract the lions. That will give us time to close in and attempt to spear both animals."

The lions crouched low in the grass, their tails twitching as they picked up the scent of the approaching hunters. They snarled with fear as they spotted three men appear fifty feet upwind, moving slowly in crouched stature toward them. This was Makikele, one of his archers, and his spear carrier. The larger of the two beasts made a short, quick charge at the three figures, baring his large canines.

Makikele shouted to him, "Come, lion! I am ready for you. Come to my spear."

The lion stopped short in his tracks, raised his dark mane in a threatening display of power, and glared at Makikele with his dark yellow eyes. Then, with swift, determined steps, he charged again, this time directly toward the three men who tantalized him with wild roars and loud shouts. The angry beast, seeing his three adversaries aggressively challenging him, slowed his gait, turned to his right, and again roared savagely, his black-tipped tail slapping against his haunches.

The second lion, seeing his comrade threatened, stood up from his low grassy perch and roared at the three intruders but kept his distance, studying the encounter with trepidation and pacing in a circle. Sensing a great danger, he sniffed the air in the direction of the second hunting party when it emerged from a clump of thornbushes a short distance to his left.

At that instant, when the charging lion hesitated and the other beast sighted the second party, Makikele signaled Tchwene to release the hunting dogs.

It seemed only a matter of seconds, although ten minutes must have passed, and the hunt was in full assault with the agile, snarling dogs holding the now-alert felines at bay. Both cats roared their displeasure, attempting to maul the lunging dogs as the hunting groups closed ranks to prevent either animal from escaping.

The larger of the two cats, the one closest to Makikele's party, became the prime target for a kill. Makikele and his spear-wielding companion, backed by the archer, approached the now-enraged cat. Makikele respected and feared the big cat but knew that he should appear unafraid in front of his men. In a heightened state of excitement and aggression, he threw his spear. Instinctively, he bolted backward to escape the lunge of the angry cat. The spear hit the lion's side but was deflected by the animal's fast movement and failed to penetrate the hide. The second band of spearmen approached aggressively from behind, targeting the larger male. Makikele snatched another spear and approached to make a second thrust while three of the dogs attacked the lion's hindquarters, diverting his attention.

"Kill, kill!" he shouted, sinking the razor-sharp spear blade into the lion's upper chest. This second attempt was effective in thwarting the cat's charge but did not reduce the power of his vicious attack. Concentrating his effort on his closest assailant, the ferocious cat reared on his hind legs, lashed at Makikele with both front paws, and then spun around quickly when one of the dogs sunk its teeth into a hind leg and another savagely attacked his underside.

"He's hit, watch out!" Makikele hollered, pulling back to run from the attacking lion. At that moment, two other spears found their targets. The angry cat screamed viciously, bit at one of the spears, and then lunged at his assailants. In a rage, the lion grabbed one of the dogs as it greedily attacked the bleeding cat. Tearing with giant canines and hooked claws, the lion ripped a hole in the dog's shoulder and neck, crushing its bones. It yelped away, dragging its lacerated side. Two more spears, thrown by the backup group, penetrated the flank of the large cat. The animal was seriously injured, but remained aggressive when the men and dogs closed in for the kill.

"Leave him for me!" Makikele shouted. Wiping sweat from his face, he stepped forward, arm and leg muscles tightened, to thrust a well-aimed stabbing spear into the lion's chest and heart. As he lashed out in desperation, the black-maned giant's heart pounded one last time. His frame trembled, his muscles tightening before he collapsed with a final futile snarl and died.

The second smaller cat, frightened and sensing danger, fled toward a thicket of scrub bush, quickly outpacing the dogs. One of the hunters whistled and they gave up the chase.

Makikele's kill was a magnificent sight. His men shouted and hooted as they congratulated him on making the first hit and then the coup de grace. All talked at once, recounting the excitement of the kill.

"I was ready to fire," said one of the bowmen, "when I saw it lunging at Prince Makikele, but then I held off when I saw he had the better of the lion."

The carcass of the dead lion was cut open, and all of the major organs—heart, liver, lungs, stomach—were removed and put in leather bags. These would be given to Masalani and the other medicine men serving the royal family. Certain lion parts, including bone, sinew, and fatty tissue, were much coveted for local healing pharmacology and as ingredients in magic potions and amulets. The skull and claws were left attached to the skin, which Makikele wished to present to his father.

All game belonged to the king, and particularly in the case of the larger animals—cats, rhinoceros, elephant, hippopotamus, and crocodile—only designated portions could be retained by the hunters. But this was a special hunt; it was Makikele's first direct kill. His father and the men of his village would celebrate and his mother would ululate when he presented the skin at the royal enclosure. The king would reward all those who had participated in the kill, but not with portions of this royal trophy.

First lion kill

While some of the hunters prepared the lion's remains for the return journey to Phetole, the party's guide took Makikele and his archers to a cluster of rocks where the wounded hunting dog had dragged itself and lay panting on its right side. The injury was severe. The lion's claws and teeth had caused irreparable damage to the dog's bones and blood vessels, and it was certain the animal would die. The royal hunting dogs were a distinct breed of a local hunting hound kept in all villages. This Malatji breed was light brown in color, with black spots on the rump and hindquarters and speckles around the face and chest. Well-muscled and slightly longer than they were tall, they possessed a ridgeback which rose in a hackle when excited or threatened. Slender in build, agile and supple, the breed was capable of great speed. The dogs were intelligent and could be trained for stalking large game. They were also used in war and as guard dogs to protect the villages.

"Give the dog some water, Tchwene," Makikele instructed the chief hunter, who stood at his side with one of the archers, and then he addressed the dog. "Thank you, brave friend. You have served us well. May your spirit carry you swiftly on your journey to the world of the dead. I will sing your praises in the king's meeting place whenever I tell the story of this lion hunt."

Then he put the dog out of its suffering.

It was mid-morning when they set off for Phetole. Part of the hunting group, hoping to bring back meat to the village, continued further south where kudu and gazelle grazed. But Makikele and most of his men returned to Phetole with the royal hunting dogs.

Members of the hunting party led the way, chanting and carrying the lion skin above their heads. Makikele and the others marched behind with the dogs. Most of the village came out for the victory parade, enthusiastically cheering Makikele and his men.

The remaining lion parts, even more valuable than the beautiful skin on display, were handed over to Masalani to inspect. When they reached Kgopolwe, the court shaman and other guardians of royal medicines and regalia, including the queen mother, would decide how the body parts should be distributed.

The parts were used to make powerful remedies and magical ingredients in the village, but were also valuable as trade commodities. Although the Phalaborwa district was best known for the high-quality metals it produced, its ivory, rhino horn, hippopotami skins, and ingredients from other animals, particularly the great cats, were much-coveted trade items. Makikele had heard that certain medicines made from Phalaborwa game were used by the Tsonga, their eastern neighbors. Ivory and medicines were traded from one group to another until, on reaching the Tsonga coast, they were traded with the white-skinned Portuguese operating from large ocean-going boats and from their fortified village near King Maphuto's capital.

CHAPTER NINE

Phetole Foundry

Three days earlier, several of Makikele's circumcision age-mates living in Phetole had been invited to join his group at the dinner hosted by Bangeni Malatji. The following morning he sent a messenger, inviting them to join him on his tour of the smelters and inspection of the cattle pens.

To protect the cattle from tsetse flies, they were not taken out to graze before the morning dew evaporated, but on this occasion Phetole's herders delayed their departure even longer until mid-morning to accommodate the royal inspection. They separated portions of the herd belonging wholly or in part to the king into pens, for closer examination and discussion.

Following a morning bath and a breakfast of porridge washed down with warm millet beer brewed the previous night, Makikele received Bangeni Malatji in the guesthouse court-yard. After formally exchanging greetings, the headman invited Makikele to accompany him to inspect the cattle pens and the permanent herd. The headman wished to discuss how the newly delivered cattle and other livestock would be integrated into the stock pens. Makikele's age-mates were already there waiting for him when he entered the network of congested dung-filled cattle enclosures.

"You are aware that all cattle are in some way related to the royal herd?" the headman asked Makikele.

"Yes, they either belong to the royal family outright or as progeny of stock distributed throughout the kingdom over the generations."

The headman nodded. "They have either been given as bridewealth or as gifts for service and to build alliances."

Makikele knew that one day, when his time came to marry, some of this livestock could well go toward the bridewealth gifts he would need to acquire wives. He thought that the two heifers given to him by the headman of Morelang might also one day be used for this purpose.

Cattle were highly prized for their social and religious significance, particularly in marriage negotiations and ritual sacrifice on special royal occasions. Vulnerable to disease, especially that caused by tsetse flies, they had little value as a trade commodity and were rarely slaughtered except for sacrifice.

"Do you think my role in acquiring these cows for the royal herd might be factored in when later allocations are made?" Makikele asked.

"As an unmarried man, you cannot acquire cattle for yourself," the headman said. "However, this acquisition on behalf of the king may be taken into consideration."

Makikele smiled. "They are twins and thus more likely to have twins as well when bred. Can we see the bulls?"

"Of course. We have several strong breeding bulls."

Bangeni signaled for the herd boys to open the pen holding the brood bulls for Makikele's inspection.

"These will be freely bred with all the cows in grazing herds to ensure a good annual increase," he said. "See those completely black bulls over there?"

Makikele looked in the direction the headman pointed, and nodded.

"They are reserved for royal use. They will probably be used for sacrifice."

Makikele knew very well, as did all the people, that it is the black bull which is killed and its skin used for royal burials, especially for that of the king. They were also prescribed at certain times for ancestral prayer and propitiation.

Makikele observed the royal earmark, a distinct lopping off of the right ear tip, on all of the bulls and most of the other stock.

They moved on to another enclosure containing several cows and their offspring, most of them red with spotted white backs, or red with white side markings.

"These cattle can be traced to your mother's bridewealth," the headman said. "They were given by *Kgoshi* Meele and his family to her Mathipa relatives. The king ordered them to be sent here from Kgopolwe rather than driven east to Sekgopo, your mother's home village. *Kgoshi* Meele wants his herds to be widely distributed in different locations. These cattle are placed in the care of Mathipa family members and other royal allies in this corner of the kingdom."

As they moved from one stock pen to another, they continued discussing the complex ownership and caretaking relationships connected with cattle and other livestock distribution and breeding.

Following the inspection, the herds were released and driven from the village enclosure to grazing grounds on the upper grassy levels. These were now free of the early morning tsetse, which retreat to the moist shade of bushy stream beds as the grasslands dry out during the morning.

The royal party walked to the village's northern extension where smelting work was being conducted. As they walked through a cluster of houses on a ridge of boulder-strewn talus between two of the hills, Makikele got his first close-up look at a lower-lying metalworker's village.

"This is huge!" Makikele said to the headman. "I have seen nothing as extensive as this near the royal villages—not even near Lolwe, where the ore is mined."

Extending outward along the flats were contiguous rows of smelters, each with five or six furnaces. The rows were interrupted at times by rocky intrusions in the topography, and therefore some of the furnaces were not in an exact line, but were placed to the front or the back or onto stone formations using the irregular terrain as natural windbreaks.

Makikele's overall impression was one of a well-organized and highly specialized worksite on a scale he had never seen before.

"We are located near a main trade route," said Bangeni. "So the scale of our operations very much reflects the scale of trade entering the region from the western highlands as well as from Swazi, and occasionally from the coastal groups passing though the Lebombo Mountains and along the river courses that run eastward."

Surrounding the artisan quarter were homes and livestock pens. Scanning the quarter, Makikele could easily distinguish the conical copper smelters from the larger three-walled, triple-vented, iron smelting furnaces. They were much the same as the ones he had observed under construction at Nagome village, but their number and the volume of work going on in this village was quite overwhelming to take in.

Judging by the deep, spread-out banks of slag piled on all sides, most of smelters appeared to have been used for many years. Most were of the iron-making type. Copper furnaces, much fewer in number, clustered along the western side of the complex where the terrain was steeper, although one occasionally stood in line with the rows of iron smelters.

In this western section, three new furnaces were being constructed, along with what was apparently a newer line of worksites. They appeared less congested with slag piles and other rubble than the ones that had been in continuous use over many years.

By the time the royal party arrived, many of the furnaces were being cleaned, fueled with charcoal, and activated. Four or more men worked at each site, three of whom sat at the corners of the iron furnaces straddling double bellows, their hands methodically lifting and lowering the skin pumps forcing air through clay vent pipes and onto the fire in the clay-walled heating chambers.

Makikele's porters had delivered the copper and iron ore brought from Lolwe to the metalworking quarter, and they presented the ore to the headman for storage and distribution. He spotted large stockpiles of charcoal beside some of the houses and at points along the working lines of furnaces. Men and women carried fuel to individual worksites, and women balanced clay water pots on their heads, negotiating their way among workers ladling liquid into drinking gourds. As the party walked between the furnace lines, they were greeted by workers continuing their steady, unbroken, rhythmic labor. A drummer pounded out a familiar beat, and the people on one work line joined in the beat with songs.

It was midday by the time they reached the new furnace construction sites. After receiving greetings from the various headmen, Masalani proceeded to discuss religious matters with shamans and village leaders. They in turn directed the masons to prepare holes centered in the floors of the smelters. In these were placed the magic elements Masalani had brought from Kgopolwe to fortify and protect each worksite.

As he had done at Nagome, Masalani placed finely woven packets into the holes in the floor of each new smelter. Masalani had placed a number of objects inside these magic medicine pouches, including herbs he had collected, small stones he had gathered at the sacred burial hill of the kings at Sealene, and fragments of human and animal bones from sources known only to Masalani and the keepers of such secret knowledge in the king's village.

It was said that the powerful medicines used to strengthen iron came from Masalani's home in Venda and from Bokgalaka, north of the Limpopo River, where the greatest of all the metal workers lived. It was from this region that the royal Malatji family were believed to have originated before they adopted the porcupine as their totem in Phalaborwa. Masalani's magic was an important part of the preparation of these smelters, something that would ensure the success of the villages, the new worksites, and those who worked there.

Although Makikele did not address the forge workers directly, he learned from his messenger and in discussions with his hosts that those constructing the new sites were of the Pilusa family. One of the oldest Phalaborwa metalworking groups, they had lived among the Phalaborwa people for a very long time. Some claimed they had been metalworkers in Phalaborwa even before the earliest Malatji arrived following their migration from kingdoms north of the Limpopo River. These Pilusa families were scattered throughout Phalaborwa in many villages. They were trusted vassals of the royal family, and had been given a place of honor according to their rank at important ceremonial events and council meetings.

Copper and iron smelting and forging

The messenger greeted them on behalf of the prince with well-known praises for the Pilusa family name. "Aaahey! Aaahey, Pilusa people who know the ways of the rain clouds, you Pilusa who make iron ore look like drops of rain. You grow strong by pumping the bellows. You grow by melting iron. Aaahey! Aaahey, Pilusa from the place where red oxide is found. Aaahey! Aaahey, the people who followed Malatji from the north, the ones who lit the *tshekga* fire that drove away the Shokane. Aaahey, Pilusa, the men of iron!"

They in turn praised the Malatji, and their praise was acknowledged with smiles and nods and handclapping, both by the prince's delegation and by those invited to accompany them.

When Masalani had finished depositing the magic packets in each furnace and blessed the new smelters, workmen covered each hole with clay and proceeded to complete the construction of the smelters.

Bangeni Malatji then led the visitors back to the main village. The *ntona*'s family compound stretched upward along the western slopes of Phetole's towering megalith.

The headman pointed to a building on one of the highest terraces. "A new house is being constructed up there," he said. "We will attend the blessing ceremony."

Passing a cluster of eight houses and a large stone-lined livestock pen at the foot of the hill, they climbed a walkway leading through a maze of terraced house sites. The highest terrace, a large leveled space bordered by stone retaining walls, backed directly onto the granite walls of the summit.

From this prominent location, Makikele could view the entire village and much of the surrounding countryside. In the distance, he could see Marapong Hill which housed a small clustered settlement on its talus slopes. He could also trace the route they had taken when hunting the previous morning. Small herds of cattle and goats grazed in the higher, drier areas. Along the contours of the water course, on the Phetole side of the river, he observed sizeable strips of cultivated land. These darker, greener patches defined clearly where the open savannah blended with the efforts of the villagers to maintain a domestic hold near water.

A sentry sat atop the granite peak above him. As at Kgopolwe, Makikele knew the advantage of these lofty lookout points, where all the surrounding territory could be surveyed. A sentry's vigilant eye could prevent a surprise attack from enemies and protect livestock from cattle thieves. Makikele remembered many stories of the wars during the time of his grandfather, Mosholwane. Warning calls from atop all the surrounding hills had safeguarded his people from warring rival villages and from outside incursion by eastern Tsonga cattle raiders, the expansionist Pedi, and Lobedu to the south and west. He wondered if Phalaborwa was as secure now as it had been in those troubled times.

Looking toward the north, he had a bird's-eye view of Phetole's metalworking settlements and the extensive line of working furnaces. Viewed from this altitude and distance, the huge scale of the operation became even more apparent than it had been at ground level. By this time, most of the furnaces were fueled and fired up, their heat being stoked with numerous bellows. Makikele counted about twenty active furnaces. They were emitting columns of smoke, and an army of workers was moving around and between workstations doing the many tasks required to produce the metals needed for trade and daily livelihood.

Sounds from anvils picked up momentum as pieces of molten metal, extracted from the furnaces, were transferred to forges and hammered into tools. In one family compound, hoes were being crafted; in other locations, spears, adzes, chisels, arrows, and axes were shaped and finished with precision. Makikele had noticed on his tour earlier in the morning that one small forging site took scrap iron from other locations and produced the small metal nut picks, the *modukulo*, which every woman wore around her neck to extract marula nuts from their pips. He could not guess how many of these multipurpose picks, forged from Lolwe iron, were being used throughout the kingdom and far beyond Phalaborwa's borders.

At specialized copper worksites, metal was being drawn into wire to be later used to make jewelry and beads, and most importantly in the manufacture of copper trade ingots. This was one of the more intriguing and complicated activities Makikele had witnessed close-up on his tour.

The process involved removing molten copper from furnaces with iron scoops while still liquid and pouring it into the folds of freshly-butchered and wetted animal skins. The skins were then rolled using up-and-down movements to shape thin rods about half to one inch in diameter. The head of the ingot was formed separately by pouring molten copper into clay molds dug into the ground. When cool, they were later attached to one end of the rod at forges away from the smelting site. Makikele had observed that, while the mold was being dug, a thin iron awl was poked repeatedly into it, puncturing its wall in several places, creating narrow outlets through which some of the molten orange ore could seep. The appendages created by this seepage gave the ingots their distinctive whiskered look when cooled and removed from the clay.

The finished ingot, known widely as the Phalaborwa *marale*, was valuable and widely used in trade. In most cases, the ingots were later melted down by craftsmen and re-crafted to produce ornaments and other prized objects. Makikele was reminded of a recent bridewealth exchange he had observed at his father's house that involved the transfer of several of these *serale* used as substitutes for cattle. He could think of nothing else as highly prized in these negotiations as cattle and *serale*. He would carry a number of these freshly forged ingots back with him to Kgopolwe as royal tribute from Phetole's *ntona*.

As Makikele continued his ascent up the hill, he discovered a large circular clay-walled house already standing on the terrace. Leaning against the house wall, shaded by its thatched eaves, he contemplated the world beneath and beyond. Alongside this structure was the nearly completed wall of a new circular structure about ten feet in diameter. Roof poles had been set in place to receive freshly cut thatch piled in bundles around the construction site. When Masalani and several of the village's herbalists and witchdoctors joined him and members of Bangeni's family on the terrace, he inspected the interior of the new house.

Directly in the center, a sizeable hole had been excavated into the floor. This would be the receptacle for a pot containing protective magical ingredients and objects to be buried and sealed when the floor and walls were plastered by women, after the men completed the thatching. As in the case of the smelting sites, and particularly because the house would be occupied by members of the Malatji family, special items had been brought from the royal village and combined in secret with local medicines to safeguard the new structure.

Bangeni's elder and widowed sister, who lived near him in Phetole, joined the group to offer prayers of blessing for the house. Standing outside the house, surrounded by kneeling and prostrate kinsmen, in a high-pitched voice she called on the ancestors to hear their voices and to protect the family and those who would use the house. As she made her invocation, magic ingredients were placed into a clay pot which was encased beneath the house floor. To conclude the rite, a young goat was then butchered and allowed to bleed over the site. Later, the carcass would be grilled and eaten by those participating in the ritual.

After the ritual ended, women prepared clay for plastering the walls while men climbed the roof, quickly tying down bundles of long river grass used as thatch. Construction would be completed the next day. It would then be used by the family and special visitors, the protective pot-burial making it a sanctuary from evil.

CHAPTER TEN

Lolwe Mines

The following morning, awakened early before the first roosters crowed, Makikele made ready to lead his convoy on its return journey to Kgopolwe.

As the sun rose, the party prepared to leave Phetole. Porters sorted items to be carried. Along with iron tools, spear points, and a quantity of adzes and chisels, they carried copper *marale* ingots and bundles of animal skins destined for the king's village.

They were packed and almost ready to leave when Bangeni spoke with Makikele. "I have two requests," the *ntona* said.

"Yes?" said Makikele.

"The first request is to ask if you could take some boys to Lolwe. These five young boys from our village have been selected from the metalworking families to go to Lolwe Hill to work in the mine shafts and to learn forging. Later, once they are fully grown and no longer suited for work in the mines, some of them will train to be smiths. Could they accompany you and your party on your return trip?"

"Of course," said Makikele. "I will be pleased to take them with us. Who are these boys? What is their lineage?"

"Two of them are from an ironworking Pilusa family, another is a child of a resident Ngwane family that makes spears and hoes for the village. One of the others is related through your mother to the Selepe metal workers who live in the metal working village near Lolwe."

Makikele thought of the many stories he had heard about the Selepe gun makers. The praise poems of one of his most famous ancestors, Mothatewaleopeng, described him as the first king to own guns. He wondered if perhaps it was this royal ancestor who had brought the Selepe people to Phalaborwa. King Meele had many times commissioned the smiths of Selepe village to make him a new gun with their forges, or repair an old or broken one. The Selepe people were long-time vassals of the royal family and no longer considered foreigners.

"And what is your second request?" Makikele asked Bangeni Malatji.

"I apologize for the last-minute request, but I have four ivory tusks for the king. Could your porters carry them?"

Makikele knew that carrying the tusks would slow down the party's progress, but he didn't want to offend the *ntona* and the ivory would please his father. "On behalf of my father, thank you," he said. "The tusks will be stored at Kgopolwe with others recently hunted. The king's annual stockpile of ivory from hunts in the western part of his kingdom and near the capital will soon be sent to his Tsonga trade partners living east of Phalaborwa."

The smell of morning cooking fires permeated the village as Makikele made ready to depart. He accepted thanks from the *ntona*, Bangeni, and his family. Greetings were given to his age-mates through a spokesman. In some cases he personally said good-bye to men of his age group who were of noble rank as they stood beside the village stockade and assisted in opening the gates. Many village women and children watched as porters lifted their bundles, and more crowded at the village exit as a trumpeter blew his *phalaphala*, announcing the party's departure.

As they departed, Makikele noticed his Mathipa kinsman standing with his family near the gate. As they bowed, making the traditional clapping gesture and nodding good-bye, he acknowledged them. The young woman, Lesibe, who had caught his eye at the *ntona*'s banquet, approached him with her father. She knelt before Makikele and presented him with a finely tanned rock hyrax pelt, which she held up to him with both hands. When he accepted this parting gift, he looked at her downcast face and his own hands briefly touched the girl's fingers. As he took the pelt he held onto the girl's fingers, giving her a slight tug. Glancing up at him in confusion, she quickly looked away in modesty to evade his stare.

Makikele studied the girl's comely figure and the curve of her back and buttocks, and felt a surge of excitement. Her humble demeanor also pleased him. She had caught his curiosity at the *ntona*'s dinner, and on each of the nights since their encounter, she had remained in his thoughts as he passed into sleep. Instead of handing over the gift to his attendant, he tucked the hyrax skin into his knife belt, positioning it to cover his momentary arousal from public view. Both actions were noted by the girl's father, who would mention it to his wife that evening. Makikele renewed his determination to ask his mother about this provocative daughter of her relative and made a mental note to do so. Perhaps Mokadi would arrange a meeting.

The return trip to Kgopolwe followed a different route. They took a more northeasterly trail, passing through several small villages until they reached Dithobe Hill, a sentinel village on the banks of the Selati River. From Dithobe they followed the river due east to Namagale Hill, where the river widened and could be easily forded. They made good time reaching Namagale Hill, despite taking a detour to avoid grazing hippo along one deep river bend. Without livestock, women, or children to slow down the group, only the elephant tusks weighing down some of the porters impeded their travel time. They expected to reach Lolwe before nightfall.

As on their outward journey, they made brief stops to greet villagers who assembled at their passing. In each case, Makikele addressed village leaders and spent a short time with age-mates he found among the residents. He noticed a laxity in security in many of the smaller villages and the absence of lookouts or sentries where settlements surrounded larger granite hills. In most cases, it was only the approaching sound of the *phala-phala* that made villagers aware of their proximity. He made a mental note to mention this to his father's counselors when he reached Kgopolwe. It seemed to him that although the southern chain of villages they visited on the outward journey had good alert systems, the villages along this northeastern route were less vigilant to possible hostile incursions, should such threats emerge. This buffer of villages, responsible for the early warning of trouble from the west, did not seem reliable.

By late afternoon they forded the river, reaching Lolwe Hill well before dark. Alerted by the trumpeter, Lolwe's residents and workers gathered to greet the arriving caravan. Boys emerged from the mine shafts and a large group soon gathered to observe the royal entourage arriving along the Selati River trail.

After formal greetings from village leaders, the caravan porters rested in Lolwe village. The five boys brought from Phetole were introduced to the village headman and then joined family members and villagers who had agreed to accommodate them.

Makikele was accorded the hospitality of the headman of the Selepe people of Lolwe Hill and discovered that one of the boys he had brought from Phetole, the one who was related through his mother to the Selepe metalworkers, would be housed with the headman's family.

After he had rested for a few minutes, Makikele noticed that the Selepe boy, not understanding the proper etiquette, had approached him and stood before him.

"What do you want, boy?" he asked.

The boy remained silent, but Makikele warmed to this curious youngster.

"Lost your tongue, have you? Let me tell you a story."

The boy's eyes lit up, and he nodded slowly.

"When I was a boy, about your age, I was hunting guinea hens and rabbits with some friends here in Lowe Hill when we came across one of the mine shafts. We decided to explore. I remember squeezing myself down a narrow shaft, clinging to a rope, and dropping into a large dark cave. It was very cool down there, and I remember seeing several young boys of about your age working by the light of a lamp, chipping stone away from the walls with dolomite hammers and iron chisels, looking for the veins of copper ore running through the hill. They hauled the green-specked copper chippings to the surface in baskets attached to ropes, the same ones we had used to climb down the vertical shaft."

"How old is the mine?" the boy asked.

"Let me see." Makikele tried to estimate the age of the site by counting the names of Malatji rulers in the much-recited royal genealogy. "I do not have enough fingers to count," he said with a laugh. "The names of my ancestors exceed the fingers on both my hands."

The boy laughed also. "The mines must be very old. Please tell me more."

"Before the Malatji arrived to rule Phalaborwa, the Shogwe people controlled Lolwe and mined it for many generations. The Shogwe are now scattered families living in many villages, but even today some live in a settlement at the foot of Sealene, the sacred royal mortuary hill. They are called the Seale people now, and they continue to bury their dead in a section apart from the Malatji kings. Some say it was the copper that attracted the Malatji here when they left their ancient northern homeland along the Limpopo River. This was in the days when the now mostly abandoned Dzata, Mapungubwe, and Thulamela were centers of power and wealth. Mining at Lolwe must date back hundreds of years."

"Please, honorable prince, tell me about the iron. Is it really used to make guns?"

"Yes, it is used to make guns. Although Lolwe's underground mines contain iron ore as well, it is not mined like copper. Instead, the ore is collected from easily accessible surface deposits found throughout the hill and on the surrounding plain."

"It looks like the hills must have cast these stones from beneath and thrown them to the surface," the boy said.

Makikele laughed again. "It might seem like that, but the origin stories of the arrival of our people at Lolwe tell that they engulfed the hill with fire to drive away the primitive Shogwe,

Extracting Lolwe copper ore

who were without fire and ate their food raw. Perhaps this ancient conflagration exposed and spread the iron stones they now collect to make iron."

"Please good prince, tell me more about the guns."

"The Selepe are the king's gun makers who were brought to Lolwe Hill from the northern kingdoms by Mothatewaleopeng many generations before my father and even my grandfather were born. The village of the Selepe gunsmiths lies close to the capital, Kgopolwe. They settled there during the time of my ancestor, *Kgoshi* Kgashane Malatji, who had built Kgopolwe Hill into a large, well-defended, and highly productive community."

"But where did the Selepe gun makers come from?" the boy asked, then waited expectantly for an answer.

"The Selepe people came from Venda in the north, and the guns they made were like those used in Venda, short-barreled weapons with loading rods, the most accurate for close-up hunting and defense. Earlier people had to purchase guns from the Venda, or from trading parties traveling inland from the Portuguese-controlled coast. The presence of the Selepe at Lolwe and Kgopolwe meant that Phalaborwa no longer needed to get guns from others to hunt elephants and for defense. They could make their own. Guns had become highly desirable and were even used in bridewealth exchanges by families arranging marriages. Previously iron hoes and copper *serale*, our distinct local ingots, had been used in trade, as well as some livestock. From the time of my grandfather, guns began to play a greater role in trade negotiations and became the pride of headmen and hunters."

"But, good prince, guns are not just for trade, are they?"

"No, it is true my father, *Kgoshi* Meele, used guns for trading goods with communities and the neighboring Sotho kingdoms, but he also used them to defend his capital town at Kgopolwe against attack. Guns have helped make Phalaborwa strong and its hunters famous. Did you see those four ivory tusks my porters are carrying?"

"Yes, they are huge!"

"They are a gift from the *ntona*, Bangeni Malatji, to my father. He killed the elephants with guns."

"Does your father have lots of ivory? Where does it come from? I have not seen many elephants around here," the excited young boy exclaimed.

"You will find large herds of elephants near all the rivers and permanent water holes, but the larger elephant herds are found in the eastern parts of the kingdom. The eastern hunting grounds provide the bulk of our annual ivory harvest and this is stored in Sekgopo village, where many of my mother's relatives live."

"Is your mother the king's great wife, sir?"

"She is one of his wives, but he has many."

"What happens to the ivory?"

"The ivory is traded with the Tsonga. They carry it from Kgopolwe and Sekgopo to the coast. There it is again traded. This time it is stored on large sailing ships which have brought valuable goods from distant lands and tribes to exchange for the tusks. On rare occasions, coastal caravans bypass the Tsonga middlemen and enter Phalaborwa territory to trade directly with Kgopolwe at one of *Kgoshi* Meele's trading posts near surrounding sentry villages. However, no foreigners have been permitted entry to the royal center.

"Coastal caravans have become more frequent during my father's lifetime. Most of them enter the kingdom from across the Limpopo in the north; less frequently, trade groups enter

Phalaborwa from the southeast, passing through Swazi and Tsonga territory while coming or going further west to trade in Lobedu and Venda."

"What else do they trade in exchange for the ivory?"

"An ivory tusk could at times be traded for Portuguese guns, flintlocks that are superior to those made locally. Most sought after, but rarely traded, are guns owned by a few caravan leaders and used for hunting and protection. These, however, are hard to find this far inland. They also bring cloth and beads, but they don't trade only for ivory. The most highly prized commodities are the locally produced iron and copper."

The boy's eyes widened. "The iron and copper from here?"

"That is right. But that is enough storytelling for one day. You had better run along. The headman will be wondering where you are."

"Thank you, Prince Makikele, good-night."

After Makikele had rested, the headman took him to inspect the copper mines.

Lolwe Hill actually consisted of two broad rounded hills of about equal size. These were linked by a natural land bridge strewn with boulders and rocks, giving them a near-symmetrical appearance. At their base on the south side, in the cleavage between the hills, was an open semi-circular trench about one hundred feet long and seventy feet deep at its center. Further up the hillsides were open mine pits. These working shafts ran seventy feet or more down into the hillside, where they broadened out into subterranean galleries carved out by generations of miners seeking copper ore from veins running through the hill's core.

From the south side of Lolwe, Makikele observed a number of mine shafts being worked in both hillsides. While taken on tour, he passed several groups of mine boys standing by their worksites. These small figures, still diminutive and agile enough to negotiate the narrow tunnels and underground passageways, greeted him respectfully and with curiosity. As he passed by them, he heard the mine overseers directing them back to work. It would soon be sunset, time for the boys to return to the village for their meal and to rest. Since they were children, they would get some playtime before dark.

Makikele observed a large opening dug into the eastern hillside. Here hot coals smoldered against exposed stone, heating them to facilitate ore removal.

"This large adit is the horizontal entrance to an underground mine," the headman explained. "From the opening, it quickly narrows, becoming a horizontal shaft leading into the hill. This in turn opens into a wide circular underground chamber. Work along the passage concentrates on the veins of copper. Sections of the rock are hammered loose; in some cases, iron gads and chisels are used to loosen hard sections where cracking has occurred. When the rock is brought out from the mine, it is further broken down on the ground outside. The copper ore is separated from the rock and taken away, leaving mounds of waste rock."

Makikele noticed that there were heaps of rubble everywhere, some quite large, attesting to the site's long duration as a mine.

The village headman explained the ore-sorting process to Makikele. "There are two types of stone that can be melted into copper. One is green and the other is bright blue. They both produce copper and can be mixed together in smelting. I think the copper disc you wear was made from the blue stone to make it shine in the light."

The headman then bent to pick up a piece of dark magnetite from under the cover of grass and stubble. "This is iron ore. Although iron ore is widely found in the vicinity, I assure you that ore of this quality is unique, and found only at Lolwe in Phalaborwa. Once melted out of the rock, it produces the very strongest iron tools and weapons. This quality, distinct to Lolwe, attracts the surrounding mountain peoples and the eastern coastal tribes to the Phalaborwa lowlands. Here they trade for pieces of the ore and its products."

Makikele understood how valuable these ore deposits were and the need to seclude and carefully guard this mineral wealth from the outside world. He thought about the much-sung praise poem which proclaimed that Phalaborwa, the land of his Malatji family, "is truly better than the South and all other lands." But he also sensed that vigilance would be required if Phalaborwa was to remain wealthy and strong and the Malatji were to retain their monopoly and control. From discussions he had heard at the king's council meetings, there was internal dissent and jealousy in the kingdom, and powerful forces threatened along Phalaborwa's borders.

Completing his inspection of the mines, he joined his waiting escort and left Lolwe for his father's village. As he walked the remaining miles to his home at Kgopolwe that evening, he thought about the foreign trade groups passing across Phalaborwa's borders. Some groups entering were as large as the sentry village populations through which they had passed. He also pondered the slow response of these villages to approaching groups, and their lack of vigilance.

Had his father's kingdom become too relaxed and confident? he wondered. A hostile army could easily reach the Selati River crossing leading to the royal citadel at Kgopolwe Hill. Did this

Deep mine shaft in Lolwe Hill

laxity exist along the northern Limpopo River passage and in the east near the Lebombo Hills, which demarcated the Tsonga frontier? This was Phalaborwa's prime elephant hunting reserve, supplying stockpiles of tusks for the coastal caravan trade. He would speak of this to counselors at the king's gathering place. Perhaps his mother's brother, Phatladi, a member of the king's inner circle of advisors, might bring his observations to his father's attention.

CHAPTER ELEVEN

Sealene Hill Burial

When Makikele reached Kgopolwe that evening, the royal village was noticeably subdued and quiet. He entered through a gate alongside the main cattle enclosure before ascending the hill to his mother's quarters midway up the path to the king's residence. His mother, Mokadi, awaited him with the news that his Great Uncle Phirimela Malatji, a younger brother of his late grandfather, *Kgoshi* Mosholwane Malatji, had died.

"I have reserved a selection of foods for you to eat," she said while uncovering a still-steaming pot of vegetables and another of ground millet and maize cooked together into a thick, sweet-smelling porridge. "You must eat quickly and accompany me to your uncle's house."

To this staple local dish, she had added boiled greens and a handful of roasted and salted marula nuts. The marula harvest had been bountiful and the salt, an expensive condiment procured from the banks of the nearby Selati River, would enhance her son's appetite. Mokadi enjoyed feeding her children and adding special culinary touches to this otherwise bland starchy dish.

Makikele was hungry. After washing his hands and mouth, he greedily helped himself to the food, combining the marula as a relish with the porridge dish and vegetables.

Mokadi continued talking while her son ate. "The widows and his children are gathering. The correct ritual must be observed for Phirimela's internment at Sealene. He has left us and must be properly laid to rest with the dead."

The old man had also been a trusted councilor to *Kgoshi* Meele, serving his nephew loyally just as he had previously been loyal to his brother, Mosholwane. As a Malatji prince, he would be buried at Sealene Hill with other prominent men of the royal family.

This was the first burial Makikele would attend on the royal burial hill, which was reserved for immediate family of the king and certain noblemen who had served the family. Makikele welcomed this new role as an initiated prince. He had been instructed since childhood about the significance of Sealene Hill, the ancestral spirits that resided there, and their continuing role protecting his family and the tribe as a whole. As yet he was inexperienced in the practices surrounding the customs of the hill's mortuary and knew that he would be under the scrutiny of the senior men and women of his lineage. He was reassured with the knowledge that several of the older royal men who had attended him at his circumcision would certainly guide him in the correct protocol for the burial rites that evening.

"It will be important for you to assist in the burial," Mokadi said, watching him satisfy his appetite and wash down the food with two cups of millet beer. "Your father has been notified of the death, and Phirimela's sister, your elder paternal aunt, will select the location for his grave when we go to Sealene after dark."

Makikele quickly finished his meal before again washing his hands and mouth.

The two emerged from Mokadi's house. They walked single file, son ahead of mother, quickening their pace when they reached the far side of Kgopolwe Hill where the dead man's compound was located.

Kgopolwe was a large village dispersed among many hillside terraces. Entrance to the ancient leader's enclosed private quarters was at the base of the hill, demarcated by livestock pens. The house was surrounded by those of the deceased's four wives and their sons' family dwellings. These were encircled by an assortment of small pens for fowl and livestock and a plethora of outbuildings for cooking and food storage. By the time Makikele and Mokadi reached the dead man's house, all of the widows and many of Phirimela's sons and male relatives had already gathered.

Mokadi washed her hands with water from a large pot beside the entrance, and then quietly seated herself on the women's side of the courtyard. Makikele also washed his hands and face before stepping into the courtyard to join the male relatives seated near the king. All were being served freshly brewed millet beer. This mildly alcoholic beverage was the mainstay of all social gatherings and was mandatory at important rituals, and particularly at funerals.

A black bull had been killed and carefully butchered, keeping the skin intact so that it could be used as a sack in which to place the dead man's corpse.

After a few minutes, the door of Phirimela's house opened and his wives and aged sister emerged from the poorly-lit interior. The youngest wife emerged whimpering, stifling her sobs with her hands as she joined the other women in the dead man's courtyard.

The women of his household had been preparing his body for burial, removing clothing and jewelry and cleaning the corpse.

They had cut his leg and arm sinews to facilitate arranging his body in a fetal position. The corpse was then secured with rawhide ropes in preparation of placing it in the bull hide prior to burial. This arranging in the fetal position symbolized his passing from life, which had begun as a fetus. Into eternal rest, he would once again lay like a fetus. It would also discourage witches or sorcerers from later attempting to exhume the body.

Once the women had completed their task and exited the house, Phirimela's sons entered and placed his body inside the bull skin, closing the opening securely so it could be carried by the men of the funeral cortege.

As they were making the final preparations, Makikele's brother, Ramatladi, arrived with his mother, his sons, and other members of his household. After ritually cleansing themselves at the water pot, they entered the compound, joining *Kgoshi* Meele and others comprising the funeral entourage.

Makikele had observed many village burials during his lifetime. Ordinarily a head of household and his wives were buried beneath the cattle enclosures shared by his lineage. Younger men and women of lesser importance were buried in the yard near their houses. Babies and stillborn fetuses were placed beneath the floor inside the mother's house, while older children were buried under the thatched eaves of the houses. This, however, was the first death he had witnessed of a royal male of high enough rank to be taken to Sealene, dwelling place of royal ancestral spirits. The burial this night would have additional sacred significance.

The funeral entourage, moving in silence, began the two-mile walk to Sealene for burial. Approaching Sealene village from the north, the procession of mourners skirted the quarters of the Seale people residing at the hill's base. Reaching the western side, they began climbing a pathway leading up to the cemetery. Residents emerged from houses and walled enclosures to silently watch the advancing mourners. Slowly, people clustered at a respectful distance on either side, keeping quiet vigil in the still night air.

At the foot of the hill, the men and women removed their clothing. Led by Phirimela's aged sister, Mmamatchwene, they began climbing the footpath to the cemetery terraces. It was Mmamatchwene's role to select a burial site. The widows and other senior women related to Phirimela followed the men. They were also naked, except for the copper and beaded leg, arm, and neck bangles which never left their bodies until they too, died.

In the still night, everyone could hear Mmamatchwene's frail, high-pitched voice as she called to the spirits of the mountain: "Aaahey, ancestors of the Malatji! Aaahey, Malatji of the little porcupine totem who came from across the great river! Aaahey, the little porcupine who ran away from Mmakao of the baboon totem! Aaahey, you who chased away the Shogwe with fire! We bring Phirimela to a safe place, to be with you our ancestral spirits. Aaahey, Mothatewaleopeng, the great Malatji ancestor! Aaahey, Mosholwane who was king! Hear us Kgashane and Sekhutusemmoto, who rest here at Sealene! It is I, your grand-daughter of the porcupine totem. We bring you your grandson. We are giving him a proper burial. We have done the right things. We follow the customs correctly. He is leaving us. He is now part of your world."

The old woman's frail voice began to weaken. Attempting to navigate a turn in the stony upward path, she stumbled to one knee. Several of her kinsmen took hold of her, steadying her as she continued the climb.

She continued reciting her frail litany. "We give Phirimela to you. Aaahey, ancestors of the Malatji! Aaahey, Kgashane! Remember us who remain among the living!"

While Makikele climbed the hill, he kept his eyes focused on the silhouette of his dead great-uncle's body, shrouded in the black bull skin and carried on the shoulders of Phirimela's sons and other closely related men. Makikele could see from the number of stone terraces they passed that the hill was populated with many gravesites. At one juncture along the way, torchlight illuminated a long, narrow terrace containing stone cairns and potsherds indicating numerous burials scattered throughout its flattened terrain.

"This is where the Seale people continue to place their dead," an elderly relative, assigned to him as a guide by his mother, whispered in his ear.

Makikele recollected that the Seale were the earlier rulers of the mountain, and remained its guardians.

"The Seale were buried here before the Malatji arrived in Phalaborwa and took control," the old man added. "There are others buried here as well, people of the Pilusa lineage who have the lion as totem, over there on the left; some others too. The Malatji are placed in holes higher up." Gesturing upward with his head, the man indicated a large conglomerate of stone walls. "That is where she will have them bury the old man."

The reflection of moonlight from the massive granite walls of the sacred hill gave these burial terraces a luminous appearance. Even though it was night, Makikele could easily detect the outline of rocky ledges and some substantially constructed stone retaining walls. Holding a torch above their heads, the guide pointed to an upper ledge with neatly dressed stone, some with a cross-hatched inlaid design, much like that etched on the rims of ceremonial clay pots.

"That is our ancestor Mosholwane's terrace. Kgashane and other kings are buried over there." He pointed out a particularly pronounced series of terraces jutting out from the rising granite summit about halfway up the mountain. "That is where the nobles are buried, straight ahead, where the old woman is taking us."

Mmamatchwene, who led the long line of mourners along the hillside trail, was a few years older than her brother and a dependent widow living in his family compound. As Phirimela had declined in health, she too had become quite frail in the months preceding his death. She repeatedly stumbled as she walked barefooted along the narrow, darkened pathway winding through the stone retaining walls and up into the higher terraces of the hill. One of her nieces, seeing her struggle, passed through the line of men to assist her. While she ascended, Mmamatchwene continued her call to the ancestral spirits.

She selected a flat section on a terraced slope for the burial site. It was near the base of the hill's towering granite core. One of the men handed the old woman a digging hoe, which she ceremonially pounded on the ground to indicate where her brother should be placed. She then gestured for the men to begin digging a shallow, round grave. First to dig was his eldest son, and then his other sons in order of birth. His sons were followed by the king, who stepped into the shallow hole and, with much care and respect, slowly removed several clumps of soil and stones.

When Makikele reached the gravesite to join the other royal men, King Meele stepped out of the grave and passed him the iron hoe. Makikele followed his father into the shallow burial pit and removed several clumps of dirt before handing the tool on to another. Everyone noticed Meele's gesture toward his son, and recognized it as a sign of great honor. Custom ordinarily prescribed that the king should be followed in such burial rites by his brothers and half-brothers according to their rank, then to sons and nephews and other male relatives. At this particular funeral, a ritual preference might have been given to Ramatladi, who was fathered by *Kgoshi* Meele, but also considered the "ghost son" of the late *Kgoshi* Mosholwane. This was because his mother, Setakgale, had been a widow of Mosholwane before she married Meele.

Everyone gathered at the gravesite noticed what had happened, and that Makikele had been favored over Ramatladi. This news would be discussed repeatedly when the details of Phirimela's death were passed from village to village.

Ramatladi, who had become accustomed to receiving deference as a double prince due to his special birth order, also observed the king's gesture of preference to Makikele. He glowered first in Makikele's direction, and then fixed his eyes on the king. When he eventually had his turn at the grave, he snatched the hoe from the man before him, and threw it down in disgust when he had finished digging.

His mother, Setakgale, who remained at a lower level of Sealene with the king's wives, had not observed this breech of etiquette. Word, however, quickly reached her and other members of her family, and she was greatly concerned this action might undermine her son's popularity and his much-assumed right to one day rule when Meele died.

When the grave was four feet deep, they lowered the old man's body, encased in the seamless black hide, onto the dirt floor. Care was taken to place the body so that he faced northward, in the direction of his Malatji lineage's origin. This would ensure his contact with more distant ancestors, now fellow spirits he would intercede with on behalf of the living.

Mmamatchwene then approached the edge of the pit and placed several items alongside her brother's body. These magical charms and personal possessions of the deceased would keep him safe and content in his repose.

Several of the men then gathered large stones and constructed a cairn on top of the filled grave, both to mark its location and to keep animals from digging into the burial site.

When the burial was completed, all the mourners ritually washed their hands with medicated water as they had done earlier at Phirimela's compound. Phirimela's four widows then carried the water pots to the cairn, stepped onto the site, and smashed the pots and their contents on the grave. Following this final ritual, the widows broke the silence of the night with loud screaming and wailing. Women further down the hill and in the village below heard the cries and lamentations and joined in. Some of the sons and nephews of Phirimela also began to cry out in mourning for the dead and much-respected patriarch.

In contrast to the silent beginning of the funeral journey, the return to Kgopolwe was filled with mournful cries, shouts of grief, and the loud sobbing of women. This lamentation was picked up by passersby and by the many gathered at the deceased elder's village.

On the day after the funeral, all immediate family members and the men of Phirimela's village shaved their heads as a sign that they had lost a close kinsman. The king and his immediate family also shaved their heads to show the debt owed to this great councilor of kings, who was himself the son of a king.

Mourning would continue for a week while many visitors brought their condolences to the widows and men of the family.

When condolences had been given by the royal household, Makikele was approached by one of his father's servants, the slave Notsi. He requested that Makikele join the king and men of rank in his lineage at the royal livestock enclosure the following day. This was the place where men summoned by the king met to discuss tribal and domestic issues and legal matters. Because the state of mourning was already underway when Makikele had arrived home and the need for haste in preparing for the burial, he had not had time to meet his father and present him with the skin of the lion killed during the Phetole trip. He gave instructions to his attendant to prepare the skin for his presentation to the king the next day.

When Mokadi returned home from the gathering of widows and other mourners at Phirimela's compound, she asked Makikele to join her in her house for some food.

Mokadi's house, like most of those of the king's wives and close family members, was situated on an upper terrace along the winding pathway leading from the men's meeting place, the *kgoro*. The passageway was in fact a broad corridor, wide enough for seven cattle to pass side by side. Many family compounds were clustered along this thoroughfare, their locations determined by the social rank of the occupants. Rank was determined by closeness of bloodline to the royal family, and the king's favor.

In earlier times, before Kgopolwe was fortified, the king's family had occupied the left side of the back entrance to the *kgoro*, the most frequented passageway into the open meeting place. From this location of highest rank, all other residences were linked, with the domestic units of lowest status encircling the periphery of the settlement. The lowest-ranked residents, vassal families from many lineages and slave families now integrated into the community, occupied the right of the *kgoro* entrance.

The pattern of house distribution at Kgopolwe was similar to that throughout Phalaborwa. The highest-ranked family, usually a member of the royal lineage or an appointed *ntona* of the king, occupied the place of honor at the *kgoro's* entrance. Close to these were housed retainers to the king, including members of the Mojela family, who by long tradition were the king's food tasters, and the Mmopa family, whose head traditionally announced and introduced the king when he attended meetings at the *kgoro*.

The nearest house on the right of the *kgoro*, a small circular structure with attached cooking shed, belonged to the slave Notsi, a Tsonga captured as a child during cattle raids when Meele was a young man. Notsi had lived in Meele's father's village and was a retainer to the king, serving to keep the various fires lit in the royal enclosures. He lived with a wife, acquired from a nearby village, and two children.

In the case of Kgopolwe and many other villages now relocated around more defensible hills, higher-status domiciles were often found on terraces in elevated locations built behind stone retaining walls filled with soil. This meant that, instead of living close to the *kgoro*, the powerful men of Kgopolwe, including the king, had to descend along the hillside passageway, past much of the village, to enter the meeting place. On ceremonial occasions, when summoned by the king's trumpeter or the beating of the great drum of the council, men of importance would walk in procession to the council enclosure to await the king's arrival and entry.

Makikele joined Mokadi in her residence along this royal pathway to be served a meal from her kitchen house. While a slave girl prepared the main course under his mother's supervision, Makikele nibbled freshly fried mopane worms from a small clay bowl placed near him. This was his favorite appetizer. His mother smiled when she entered the house, and then she seated herself on a mat to watch him chew the crisp delicacy. These large larvae were harvested during the late summer rains when they emerged to eat mopane tree leaves.

Makikele thought about past mopane seasons from his childhood and smiled. They were the times when all the women and children of the village roamed the bush, gathering worms. When gutted, roasted, and dried, they kept well in storage and were a source of food throughout the year. Since both the mopane and the marula nut harvest had been plentiful that year, there would be much to eat in all the villages, and possibly surplus to trade.

Mokadi waited for the simple meal of cooked chicken, sorghum, and boiled greens to be served to Makikele before giving him the reason for her summons. As she watched him savor the meat, dipping his hand into the hot millet porridge and then combining it with the vegetables as a relish, thoughts of his childhood passed through her mind. She could still see the face of a small boy in his now-maturing features. He had grown tall, strong, and intelligent. He had performed well at *Koma* as head of his regiment. It had been the largest in memory and included all uncircumcised males of age since the last ceremony more than ten years earlier.

"You made me so proud," Mokadi said, "when I heard about your prowess as a leader among the initiates at *Koma*, your success in hunting, and the dignity with which you conducted yourself. I remember one still evening during the ceremonies, when I heard the distant voices at the initiation camp singing ancient Phalaborwa songs. I imagined you enthroned as head of the large assembly when it returned from seclusion.

"And then the leopard appeared as you were hailed as head of your circumcision regiment. When this apparition was reported to me, truly it was at that moment that I understood that you were destined for greatness. I knew that you would be blessed and protected by the royal ancestral spirits and by those of my own ancient lineage. I hoped that I might live to see this greatness unfold.

"It was obvious to me that your father was also proud of your feats during your coming of age. Although the secret male ceremonies were forbidden to us women, your father often shared with me accounts of your conduct at mealtimes and during our time to sleep together. I know the king has important plans for you. I will guard your interests, perform prayers, and seek magical intervention to protect you."

Makikele ceased his eating while he listened to his mother's loving comments, and they looked at each other in quiet mutual affection; the two were held together in a bond no words could capture. Mokadi's voice broke the silence.

"The king has called you to the council," she confided in a low voice as he finished eating.

"I have been told, my mother. I will go to the *kgoro* tomorrow morning when the council meets." He paused to await her reply and, finding none forthcoming, he continued, "I will present to him the lion I killed at Phetole. Three of us attacked it with spears. The others only slowed it down, but my spear brought death. I have the skull. All of the other parts, except the hide, were taken by Masalani for use in medicines here in the king's *kgoro*."

Looking down at her sitting mat, Mokadi smiled to herself and waited for more details from her son.

Makikele recognized the power of making a dramatic appearance. "I will approach the *kgoro* through its exterior gate, leading my men bearing the lion skin for the meeting with the king. I will time this appearance to follow the release of livestock for grazing in the mid-morning. Most of the senior men will be present at this time to receive the king and the village will be fully active following the morning meal. If I am favorably received, I might be asked to join the counselors and be questioned about my findings while traveling the western region of the kingdom."

He, in turn, waited for a comment. Slowly, his mother showed her happiness with a low refrain. "My son, you must wait until the men have all gathered around the fire. Give the king your hunting spear as well, and be patient for him to speak. The women will ululate, praising you and the lion when you make your entry. I will spread word of your plans and bring people to see the lion."

"I will seek the assistance of my uncle, Phatladi," Makikele said.

Phatladi Mathipa, who resided at Kgopolwe with his family at the king's request, was Mokadi's brother. Makikele addressed him by the title *Malome* to show respect and to denote this close maternal kinship tie. He was a trusted advisor to the king and an important liaison with his kinsmen in the eastern provinces and at the Mathipa stronghold, Sekgopo Hill. Mokadi had given birth to Makikele at Phatladi's village. As was the custom, Makikele and his mother had settled permanently at Kgopolwe shortly after his weaning. It was at this time that his uncle, Phatladi, had been asked to relocate near to the king. Phatladi now lived in a place of honor, but not as a royal, on the right side of the pathway leading to the king's cattle enclosure, the royal *kgoro.*

Mokadi continued to look away as her son finished his meal, but he sensed she had more to say and added, "Will my mother come and watch me enter the *kgoro?*"

"I will join my co-wives, the queen mother, and other family women watching your entry." Now looking in his direction, but without eye contact, she added, "Your father wishes you to go on another journey soon. The council has recommended this, in particular my brother and the closest of your father's brothers and uncles. I will ask for some of the lion fat to have a protective amulet made for you to wear on the trip."

Makikele acknowledged his mother's comments with a nod, but thought it improper to question her further, knowing that her information came from the council and was confidential. He stood up to leave while the slave girl poured water for his hands and mouth.

"I will instruct my attendant to arrange for the huntsmen to carry the lion hide and skull when I make my entry," Makikele announced.

As he stooped to exit the doorway, he turned and mentioned his meeting with Mokadi's kinsman at Phetole. He showed his mother the rock hyrax pelt the girl had given him.

"It was handed to me by your cousin's older daughter. He calls her Lesibe. I find her appealing."

"I will see what I can find out about the girl, but leave the pelt with me. The gift is already talked about here, so give it to me," insisted his mother.

Knowing his mother's concern about improper gifts and the possibility of something evil coming of it, Makikele placed the skin beside her on her mat.

"Say nothing more about this," she cautioned in a low steady voice.

Continuing to look away, this time toward the exit to her house, Mokadi watched her son as he drew aside the hide door covering, observing his muscular legs, loins, and torso as he left to walk to his bachelor's quarters behind her walled enclosure and goat pen.

This was a time of mixed emotions for Makikele. So many profound things had occurred since returning from his trip: the death and burial of Phirimela, his father's gesture at the grave, preparations for his appearance at the king's *kgoro* the following day, the council's decision to send him away, and his mother's comment about Lesibe. While he walked toward his quarters, he mulled over all these events that had shaped the last few days of his life. Then he thought of Lesibe and a strong sexual excitement took hold.

As Lesibe dominated his thoughts, he looked up and saw Thalila, Ramatladi's youngest wife, approaching. She had a large pile of firewood balanced on her head that she was carrying to her home. Seeing her lithe young figure, and the breasts accentuated by the hand held above her head supporting the firewood, Makikele became even more aroused.

As she passed, Makikele said to her in a low voice in the secret speech used by lovers, "Are you ready?"

"Yes, I am ready," Thalila whispered back to him, and passed on her way without looking at Makikele, so as not to attract suspicion from curious villagers.

This signal from the girl meant that she approved of Makikele's advance and proposed to accept him to her mat that night.

Such amorous overtures were rarely spontaneous encounters, but rather the result of confidential inquiries made to a potential paramour's trusted age-mates, or to a discreet relative of the beloved. Before leaving for Phetole, Makikele had asked about Thalila to her aunt, a gregarious old woman living in the village. Gossip among the women of Kgopolwe had indicated that there was friction between the girl and Setakgali, her mother-in-law, because Thalila had not yet conceived a child after several years with Ramatladi. But rumor also had it that Ramatladi was "a man bitten by a rabbit and one who had lost his interest in women." This popular proverb, now bantered about by the women, was mostly applied to older impotent men with young wives, or to describe bachelors who preferred the company of regiment age-mates to pursuing women. Thalila's aunt had responded to Makikele's discreet overture with approval and endorsement of their involvement.

When she had dismissed her servant and was alone, Mokadi reached for an ornate medicine gourd, one of several hanging in a cluster from a roof beam in her cottage. Drinking from it, she spat the contents of her mouth onto the hyrax skin.

Lifting it with a mixing stick without touching it, she dropped it into a small basket. She decided to take it that evening to old Mother Kholene Malesa, her diviner, to find out what might be intended by the gift. She would also find out more about the girl, Lesibe, and her parents. The Mathipa lineage was large and scattered widely in many villages beyond their traditional home at Sekgopo Hill. She would keep her inquiries discreet to avoid any gossip in the royal household, particularly among the king's wives.

She knew that the king, her brother, and elders of his lineage would discuss women appropriate for her son when the time was right. However, she was determined to also make her own inquiries from the branches of her family with unmarried daughters. At the right time, and after she had gathered her own information, she intended to discuss the matter of a wife for Makikele with the king in private. There would be ample time for this, she thought to herself, once Makikele left Kgopolwe.

That night, Makikele sent his attendant to request a meeting with his uncle. He planned to tell him of what he had learned on his trip to Phetole; in particular, he wanted to report on the laxity of security he had seen in many of the sentry villages and cattle posts guarding the western approaches to the capital. He hoped this information would be conveyed to the king's council and that he might be asked to report his observations to them. Although he considered it unlikely that the king would talk directly with him on this matter, details would certainly reach his ears and be given consideration.

This initiative, and the killing of his first lion, would certainly please his father.

After he had dismissed the servant, he passed out of his hut and made his way in the darkness to the home of Thalila. There was no moon that night, so he navigated by the faint glow that came from the cooking fires around the compound, but he remained in the shadows. He entered Thalila's hut by the back door, made his way to her sleeping mat, and lay down beside her.

Thalila was Ramatladi's favorite wife, but she did not find the dour, middle-aged Ramatladi attractive. Makikele, on the other hand, was young, strong, tall, and handsome. He had a reputation of being humorous and playful with women in private and energetic when with them on their sleeping mats. She was excited by this clandestine meeting with Makikele.

During her *bjale*, Thalila had been taught the proper sexual practices when with men and was the perfect host for Makikele that night. Makikele found the woman attractive and his needs were met, but he found himself thinking about Lesibe as he embraced Thalila.

CHAPTER TWELVE

A Lion Skin and a Hyrax Pelt

Early the next morning, at the sound of the first rooster crowing, Makikele released himself from Thalila's arms and crept out by the back door of her hut. It was still dark outside. This was an important day for him, and he did not want to be seen acting inappropriately. Any rumor that might insult and discredit Ramatladi further could have troublesome consequences for Makikele.

The time had finally arrived for him to present the lion skin to his father. When the huntsmen carrying the lion skin approached the main entrance to the king's cattle kraal, they chanted: "Aaahey, Malatji! Aaahey, son of the porcupine! The porcupine that drove away the Shogwe! Malatji who said the sun emerges from the sacred water hole, the *sediba*! Aaahey, Makikele, son of the king. You have brought a lion for the king!"

The line of men, led by Makikele, carried the outstretched lion skin, its head held up with teeth exposed. Behind the lion-bearers were archers and spearmen who had been on the expedition to Phetole. Not all had accompanied Makikele on the hunt, but all in his age-group now joined in the procession to the king's enclosure, shouting praises to Makikele, the king, and the

Malatji royal family. The procession skirted the village residences to enter the main external gate through which all important court events began. It was here that the king received guests, and it was through this entrance that Makikele had led his regiment at *Dikomathuku* following their initiation into manhood.

Women and children gathered outside the heavy timber and thorn enclosure to watch the prince and his men ceremonially honor the king. Women of the royal family entered by means of a rear passageway, which led from the residential side of the village. They carried mats and would sit in a separate group on the ground across from the senior men of the royal house. All sat within a low stone-walled circle shaded by two large marula trees. While this meeting circle and its fire was customarily reserved for men, on public occasions women of stature also occupied the space, albeit in a subordinate position to the men seated on stools.

The tribal fire had been fed a few minutes earlier by Notsi, the Tsonga slave. Smoke rose in a white column as fresh wood ignited. The large carved ceremonial drum, *Boretho*, carried by six men from the palace compound, produced a deep sound which resonated throughout the village. To add dignity to the occasion, the king had requested that it be separated from its three sister drums, stored under the eaves of the regalia house, and brought to the *kgoro*. The entire village now emerged from their houses and crowded around the thorn enclosure to witness the unfolding drama.

As the somber setting began to take on a festive feel, Mokadi spread a mat on the ground beside the aged queen mother and sat among her co-wives and elders. Was it already three years ago that her son had led his initiation regiment to this very spot? It had been the largest tribal gathering she had ever seen. How time flies by like an arrow, she thought. She now waited excitedly for her son's appearance. Makikele, her firstborn son, would soon take his place among the powerful. His father intended him to receive respect; in time, he would command the attention of all Phalaborwa.

As the men bearing the trophy arranged themselves in formation, ready to make their entry, Makikele studied the ten tall poles lining the gateway like sentinels. Ornate, some colored with red oxide, most were crowned with the skulls of animals that had been ceremonially killed. Bull skulls from the two previous initiation rites stood side by side; others were from the time of royal marriages. Several of the upright posts held large game trophies. A kudu skull with serpentine horns looked down on the men as they walked through the passageway. Makikele wondered if his lion skull would be displayed in this gallery. The decision would be his father's.

Two of his age-mates joined the procession, wearing monkey-skin headdresses and playing bone flutes. They performed one of the high-pitched tunes popular at dances and drinking parties. The musicians accompanied the group, jumping and prancing in circles while they walked across the large circular cattle pen and toward the king's council, seated in the stone enclosure to the right.

Women and children and other onlookers began to laugh and shout.

"Makikele! Makikele! You bring us a lion!" some called out. "Makikele of the big porcupine! Aaahey, Malatji! Aaahey, porcupine totem of the Malatji! Aaahey, *Kgoshi* Meele, you have a brave son! Aaahey, mother of Makikele! Aaahey, daughter of the Mathipa lineage!"

Makikele carried his spear across his shoulders and a knife in his belt. The crescent-shaped copper disc, given to him by his father at the *Dikomathuku*, was polished to shine. While the assembly cheered and shouted, he and his men walked with the gravity of warriors. With deep guttural tones, they chanted a tune from their initiation regiment. When they arrived to stand before the king and the great drum, they continued their chant, but all around became quiet. The flutes were silenced. Kneeling with shoulders and heads bowed, weapons held outstretched before them, the young men waited to be acknowledged by the royal council.

When the band of men approached, Mokadi stepped forward and began a loud, high-pitched ululation. She was liked by the village women, as well as respected and sometimes feared as a royal wife. Women and girls in the surrounding crowd picked up her call with a chorus of loud ululations which filled the air.

Mokadi began to dance before the king and the entire village. Although she was now middle-aged, she was still a tall and graceful figure. Hands held high, she performed the gazelle dance popular at women's events; making small circular motions, she pranced and kicked up dust with short steps.

Observing her, the village women increased their ululation, and many also began to imitate the royal wife's steps. This loud, spontaneous outburst put smiles on the men's faces. The queen mother, who rarely showed emotion in public, shook her head and spoke with some of her aged companions, evidently pleased with her daughter-in-law's joy. Even *Kgoshi* Meele grinned broadly when he witnessed this demonstration provoked by his favored royal wife.

The king's senior counselor called forward a court bard, a man recognized for his memory of praise poetry and his singing at special events, to voice a litany of formal praises to the king. While he intoned the well-known names and praises of

Makikele presents his lion to Kgoshi Meele Malatji

past kings and princes, the crowd responded, repeating familiar names and affirming the bard's performance.

When the praise poems were completed, the king's senior councilor stepped forward as spokesman for the king. He raised his hands to silence the crowd and said, "The king welcomes his son, Prince Makikele, and his companions back from their hunting and trade trip to the western border district. The king is pleased to learn that the expedition was successful and asks Prince Makikele to tell us about his trip. Stand and tell us about your journey."

Following this announcement, the councilor waited for the prince to step forward and address the circle of men. Makikele rose to his feet, placed his spear on his right side, and spoke to the royal councilors. As was the custom, the king was addressed only indirectly.

"I give praise to my father, *Kgoshi* Meele, great leader of the Ba-Phalaborwa of the porcupine totem. Every village along my recent journey sings the praises of Meele, the great Malatji, the son of Mosholwane, the guardian of Sealene. Aahee the *Kgoshi* of Phalaborwa!

At this exclaimation of praise to his father, the entire gathering joined in, shouting out Makikele's praise, "Aahee Kgoshi Phalaborwa!"

When quite returned, he resumed his recitation by saying, "In every village, the porcupine totem is seen to be strong; the fire of Sealene and Kgopolwe burns in the hearth of the cattle enclosure of each village. The people are loyal and send their portion of the king's tribute to Kgopolwe. The men of my regiment and I bring a gift to the royal cattle enclosure of *Kgoshi* Meele Malatji."

With this he stepped aside and gestured for the lion-bearers to place the cleaned and stretched lion skin on the ground in front of the council of men. The group of men nodded and smiled in the direction of the king, who looked approvingly at the large dark lion hide. Approaching the king's spokesman, Makikele asked permission to also present his spear, explaining that it was the one which had killed the lion.

The councilor then turned to the council, announcing, "Prince Makikele wishes to present the spear used to kill the lion. Made here in Selepe village, it is returned washed with the blood of a great beast killed for the king's use."

The king gestured his acceptance, which the spokesman then announced loudly to the assembled throng. This was received enthusiastically, and sounds of approval echoed throughout the onlooking crowd.

The young men and Makikele were asked to sit in the cattle enclosure while the royal council addressed an issue of importance.

The king's spokesman rose once more and announced, "It is the command of *Kgoshi* Meele that Prince Makikele should accompany Masalani, the king's magician, on a trip to his homeland in Venda, where he will become apprenticed to a school of magicians for an amount of time needed to acquire knowledge of Venda magic and medicines. He will depart for the northern kingdom following the next millet harvest. Prince Makikele is requested to join his father at the royal compound this evening."

With this announcement made, the council disbanded, and the members of the royal entourage rose to their feet and departed through the rear exit from where they walked to their many houses scattered up the hillside.

After sunset, Makikele joined his father and members of his advisory council in the enclosure surrounding the king's residence. On the ground beside the fire pit lay Makikele's lion skin brought from Phetole. The king sat on a decorated wooden bench near the lion's head.

"My son, you are a brave man to kill this lion. I was your age when I killed my first lion. You have done well. The people are pleased to see you return safely."

He turned to one of the councilors, Pishani, the brother of one of his wives. He spoke quietly with him, and then sent him on an errand to one of the huts clustered around the king's large steeply thatched dwelling. Pishani returned shortly afterwards and handed Meele a leather armband decorated with copper and red beads.

"Come here, my son," the king beckoned to Makikele to approach. "Masalani has prepared this band for you. Wear it during your travels. It will protect you and bring you good fortune."

He pushed the band onto Makikele's left arm and then briefly held onto his son's wrist and elbow before releasing and dismissing him from the meeting.

By this time Makikele was a mature male and, as was the custom, ready to find a suitable wife and start his family. In this he sought the counsel of his mother, Mokadi. The discussion took place one evening during the growing season when the village rested following a busy work day.

"Mother, do you remember the girl, Lesibe, I told you about—the one whose father is your kinsman, the ones I met at Phetole?" he asked while joining her following the evening meal.

"Yes, I remember—the girl who gave you the rock hyrax pelt."

"I wish to marry her, mother, before I travel to Venda at harvest time."

"Old Mother Kholene Malesa has confirmed that the girl is untainted by any magic or evil forces."

"Old Mother Kholene—what does she have to do with Lesibe?"

Mokadi looked down at the palms of her hands and a smile formed on her lips. "My son, when you brought me the hyrax skin given to you by the father of Lesibe, I took it to old Pulani and asked her to perform divinations to understand the intent of the gift. Seeing that you were attracted to the child, it was important to find out as much as possible about her, and if the gift had any ill intent. I did this to protect you and to learn as much as I could about her parents and this branch of my family."

"Thank you, mother; you were right to do so. I am glad the old woman found nothing of concern."

"I also made some enquiries about Lesibe and her family in both Phetole and Sekgopo, where these people live."

Makikele, becoming excited, asked, "What did you find out, my mother?"

"The girl is indeed in a *malome* relationship to you and is suitable to marry, but there is one thing you must know."

"Yes, mother, tell me."

"I spoke with your father about this. At first he was reluctant to consider the girl as a wife for you. However, when no evidence of witchcraft or ill intent was found to be connected with the circumstances of your meeting, he agreed to the marriage; but she cannot become your great wife. The family has little strategic importance, not like my family. Your great wife must be selected from higher rank, from a family of greater stature and influence. For this reason, the king and I have first betrothed you to my niece, Mosale, the daughter of your Uncle Phatladi. It is important that this be done before you take other wives. This will ensure a suitable mother for a future heir to the throne, should you be called one day to this honor. Mosale is still a child, not yet old enough for female initiation. A bull and a pregnant cow were sent to seal the agreement. Although other marriage goods will be provided for her family in the future, the betrothal has been sealed and cannot be broken."

"I understand this, my mother, and I accept my father's wishes on these matters. I do, however, want to marry Lesibe, Mother."

"I could tell that these were your thoughts, my son. A mother's intuition enables her to sense such things, and so, once the first marriage commitment was sealed, I began discussions of a betrothal with Lesibe's family. Several of your paternal uncles approached the bride's father in Phetole. Animals, hoes, and quantities of millet have already been sent to begin bridewealth discussions. The family is favorable, and we await a final transfer of marriage goods to conclude the process. As you know, marriage discussions are very detailed and take time, especially when a Malatji prince is to wed. My brother Phatladi has provided the final betrothal bull so that no other suitor might approach the father to request her as a bride.

"Lesibe will be a welcome bride to my compound. She is well brought up, hard working and strong. She will be a helpful daughter-in-law. Now, as far as future marriage, you will have other wives in due course. Your father wishes an alliance with a relative of Queen Modjadji of Lobedu, and your grandmother has long ago sent messengers and gifts to Venda seeking a royal marriage link. It is also considered felicitous that you marry into the Hlame family at Sekgopo and that Sealene's guardians, the Seale, transfer a girl in marriage in due time."

"I will marry these women, of course, but Lesibe is the one I love now, and always will," said Makikele.

Once the king had given his consent to the marriage with Lesibe and Lesibe's family had also indicated their agreement, Mokadi made arrangements for her brother, Phatladi, and a delegation of young men to travel from Kgopolwe to Phetole to finalize nuptial transactions. Phatladi and his group brought with them a bull to make the proposed alliance irrefutable, so no other suitor could pursue Lesibe—this custom was called "closing the gate of the kraal."

Once the gate was closed and Lesibe's family had shown their commitment to the marriage by accepting the gift of the bull, representatives of the groom's family each determined what they should send as *motheko*, or bridewealth transfer, to conclude the match. This involved members of the royal family, including the king and his brothers and other close kinsmen, as well as Mokadi and her family—above all her brother, Phatladi, who was delegated as the *motseta*, or go-between.

Marriages in Phalaborwa, especially those of noble lineages and the royal Malatji family, were expected to include a communal transaction. In this case, all major families and clients of the king contributed something to the bridewealth.

Thus began a flow of goods, including token livestock which were shifted from the royal herd at Phetole to Lesibe's father's family; also hoes, copper objects, cloth, and large quantities of millet. These things were transferred over a period of months and presented to the family by representatives of the groom's family.

Shortly after the conclusion of this transfer of gifts, Lesibe and a delegation of women from Phetole traveled to Kgopolwe to visit her future mother-in-law, Mokadi. They carried with them gifts, baskets of millet, and a new beer pot.

Lesibe stayed for several days performing a number of domestic chores, including cleaning Mokadi's house, brewing beer, and grinding grain. This would be her future home, and her visit to Kgopolwe was a symbolic ceremony showing that she would be a hardworking and dutiful wife, one who would provide good care of her mother-in-law and her new family. Following this visit to get acquainted, she returned to her father in Phetole.

King Meele and his family had decided on a sizeable bride-wealth, wishing it to be impressive to the residents of Phetole, an important allied village. The king also wanted to enrich the bride's family, which had no livestock and was a modest scion of the large and widely distributed Mathipa lineage that served as clients to the wealthier Selepe forgers and trader families of Phetole. These included Tlagolo Selepe, *ntona* of Phetole, whom Makikele had met when he toured the area as a young man. The bridewealth transfer would increase Lesibe's family's material well-being and their status in the village now that they would be affiliated by marriage to the king.

This done, Phatladi, the *motseta* from the royal family, informed the bride's family that representatives of the groom's family would soon arrive in the village with the final bride-wealth goods. These representatives were young men of the royal family, including young uncles, cousins, and brothers of

Makikele. These were joined by his young Malatji kin living in Phetole and some of his circumcision age-regiment members who were also friends of noble birth.

Men from the bride's family and friends of the village met these Malatji men who slowly transferring the bulk of livestock in the bridewealth exchange, amid cheers and celebration. As each member of the groom's family presented an item, it was accepted by a member of the bride's family.

As each gift was presented, the bride's people praised the virtues of the bride with quips such as "That is not good enough for our wonderful daughter," "Keep the gifts coming," and "We expect more."

The groom's representatives, likewise, good-naturedly extolled their continual presentation of marriage gifts and their great value with comments like "Look how wonderful these marriage gifts we give you are!"; "The cows are fertile and the bull is one of the finest!"; "Look here! The quality of this hoe is of the finest, made from Lolwe iron!"; and "The millet comes from the royal granary; none could be finer!"

This ceremonial competition between the two groups delighted both sides and the onlookers, who cheered each time praise was sung out by the two groups.

When the final gifts had been presented, the bride's people invited the groom's representatives to enter the family compound, where a feast was set out in a public place near the bride's mother's house. The bride's father had slaughtered an animal for the occasion, and her mother had prepared beer and food for the visiting men. The bull given by Makikele's maternal uncle, Phatladi, was also slaughtered for the feast, as a thanksgiving offering to the bride's parents for fulfilling their part of the agreement.

On such occasions, young men and women from different villages, those who were still available for marriage had a chance to meet one another and become acquainted. During the day of feasting, girls of the village were permitted to select and seek out a favorite male guest who had caught their fancy. Each made her desires known by placing her mat beside him, and then feeding her young beau with meat from the wedding feast. This was followed by singing, dancing, and flirtation between the young revelers, now excited by the anticipation of new romance.

Later during the festive banquet Lesibe appeared, led from her mother's house, to be presented to Makikele's representatives and his uncle. Earlier in the day she had worn the short cache-sexe apron of an unmarried woman, but now, as a bride, she was dressed in the longer, ornately beaded skin apron of a married woman. She took her place, sitting with Makikele's delegation of guests at the feast. Women of the village then presented the bride with a number of items: ears of millet as a symbol that she must be a hard worker in the fields, a broom symbolizing cleanliness, a grinding mortar symbolizing food preparation, and many other items. Other villagers presented the bride with gifts of household items, and the feast continued throughout the day and night.

The following day, Lesibe, accompanied by a few women of her family, was escorted from her home to Kgopolwe, to her mother-in-law's residence. Here she would begin her life as a married woman with Makikele.

As their arrival at Kgopolwe was announced by the king's trumpeter with loud blasts from a ceremonial *phalaphala*, Lesibe entered Mokadi's walled compound. She was completely covered with skins, hidden from the view of the throngs of festive spectators waiting to see Makikele's bride. When a spokesman for the royal family formally asked her to identify herself by name and to show her face, she remained silent and hidden. To the laughter of the expectant crowd of merrymakers, Lesibe repeatedly refused to reveal her identity until coaxed to do so with a series of gifts: a carved and decorated wooden ladle, a beaded gourd dipping cup, and a brightly-woven wool shawl. Once these gifts were placed at her feet, she spoke her name for the first time in Kgopolwe.

As was the custom, while her face remained hidden, Lesibe presented Mokadi with a loin of the animal slaughtered for the feast in her village. Mokadi's acceptance of this gift was the sign for Lesibe to fully reveal her identity by removing the leather bridal mask concealing her face. This first view of the bride's face was met with cheers and shouts of approval from the smiling onlookers.

A far louder uproar began, however, when Makikele emerged from his mother's house, dressed in a hyrax skin cloak and feathered headdress, his torso shining from anointment with oils. He wore the hyrax pelt given to him by Lesibe when they had first met, suspended from his knife belt as an embellishment to his frontal waist garment. He escorted his bride to a newly built and thatched circular house prepared for them in Mokadi's compound. Lesibe's new home was close to Queen Mokadi's own house. This was where Makikele and Lesibe consummated their marriage and began life together.

Several months following Makikele's marriage to Lesibe, when it was almost time for Makikele to travel to Venda, he noticed a change in Lesibe. She suffered occasional bouts of vomiting in the mornings, and her burgeoning waistline revealed that she was with child.

Makikele regretted that he had to leave at this time, but knew that custom prevented him from being present at the birth of his first child anyway. Within days of the discovery of the pregnancy, he had to say good-bye to his wife and depart with Masalani on the road north to Venda.

Lesibe lived under her mother-in-law's supervision and guidance until well advanced in her pregnancy. When nearing the time of her delivery, Lesibe returned to her father's village for the child's birth. She remained there until it was time for weaning, at which point she returned to Mokadi's family compound at Kgopolwe with her baby. It was only with the birth of her first child that Lesibe was recognized as an adult, fully integrated into her husband's family and its communal life.

CHAPTER THIRTEEN

Venda Sorcery and Magic

It had been many years since Masalani, the king's witchdoctor, had last made a trip to his home in Venda, and he looked forward to seeing his native land and his people once more. He had married two wives in Phalaborwa and established a family village and herbal workshop a short distance from the royal residence at Kgopolwe Hill. The king had rewarded him for his services. When not performing duties at the capital, he was permitted to practice his herbalist skills in his family's compound near the farmsteads and metalworking center of the Selepe people. The Selepe also originated from Venda, but they had arrived in Phalaborwa many generations earlier. However, they recognized Masalani as kin, and this affinity had allowed him to secure his first wife from this lineage of metal experts.

He had trained his wives and children in the knowledge of local ingredients for his craft, and as a family they had built a prosperous healing village. His two sons and three daughters were all skilled in collecting and preparing the complex produce from the Phalaborwa bush countryside. The land was rich, not only in the many herbs, roots, bulbs, and tree barks that comprised the formulary for healing, but also in the abundance of game products needed for stronger medicines and magic.

Masalani's reputation was widely regarded and people, even entire families, came great distances to solicit his assistance in dealing with sickness and disease, and for remedies and amulets giving protection during crises in their lives. Magical components in medicines relating to royal matters were produced and housed in the king's village and guarded by trusted advisors and royal women of the household. Masalani had access to these coveted game products that passed through the king's domain, which was a lucrative circumstance and had helped him become wealthy in his practice.

Over the decades, he had managed to transfer some of this wealth to his home village in Ngome in Venda. Here his other wives, children, and now grandchildren operated a healing center not far from the royal enclosure. Ngome was one of many autonomous and sometimes competing Venda principalities that formed when the earlier centralized high kingdom based at Dzata Hill had splintered and dispersed along the Limpopo River.

Two of Masalani's Ngome sons had carried their craft to an eastern trading crossroads near the abandoned hilltop fortress of Thulamela. It was here that gold objects were once made and traded with Arabs, Portuguese, and Dutch on the coast. Indeed, the Lemba people, a small, secretive lineage living in many villages throughout Venda and north of the Limpopo among the Shona, were believed to be the descendants of the now long-forgotten Arab traders.

Masalani's sons, in their dealings with the Lemba and other metal specialists, had occasionally managed to obtain and trade small quantities of the shiny yellow metal, which had a value far beyond the copper and iron smelted locally in Phalaborwa and Venda. But it was now a commodity rarely found.

With family members living in the three regions, Phalaborwa, Ngome, and Thulamela, it was possible for them to procure and move valuable commodities between their villages. This enabled them to enhance their reputation as healers and traders in rare goods.

Masalani was now an old man, and wished to return permanently to his family in Venda. His sons were well established with wives and children of their own, each a useful link in the transfer of goods between the many villages of his family. Through his brothers and nephews and cousins, this trade linkage extended further north into Shona lands.

Masalani had provided an important liaison between the royal houses of Phalaborwa and Venda, as well as with the Lobedu in the mountains to the east. All claimed common origins and saw themselves as related. Even during times of warfare and disputations, which frequently complicated the normal exchanges of products and services, he and his sons and relatives managed to continue the flow of more coveted objects and trade commodities, particularly those relating to magic and healing.

The current royal delegation bringing Prince Makikele to Venda provided an opportunity for Masalani to strengthen his family's ties with both royal houses. Should Makikele one day become king, and there were indications that this might be the direction Phalaborwa would take, it boded well for Masalani and his sons in the future.

Masalani, in preparation for the trip, had mentored the young prince regarding greetings and customs appropriate for the Venda court. Although the Venda nobility and the Malatji had many customs in common, certain behavior in the Venda royal *kgoro* would seem very formal to Makikele. He would need to know the fine points of etiquette, such as the *losha*, a profound bowing to those in authority, which was not so prevalent and elaborately performed in his father's court. While Masalani remained in Ngome, he would translate for Makikele when with the royal family. An attendant would later be appointed to help him communicate and to serve him during his sojourn in Venda.

The royal Venda village at Ngome was a walled cliff-top residence, surrounded by terraced yards and residences protruding from the outer slopes and hillsides. The architectural complexity of the king's enclosed residence amazed Makikele. The entire hilltop was encompassed by massive stone walls five feet high and equally wide, forming a base for a tall timber wall embedded in the stonework. The timber stockade, made of a rock-hard wood called *musumbiri*, rose another eight feet above the stone encirclement. Within the enclosure was a maze of additional tall stone terraces leading to a honeycomb of house sites, associated domestic structures, and livestock pens. Gates to these private quarters were made of posts in stone frames. Makikele would later learn that many of these entryways were constructed with defensive trap doors to prevent intruders from entering without the permission of those living within.

Deep within the fortified enclave was an oblong stone edifice constructed flush with the eastern battlement wall. Roofless, and entered through an opening between the two sets of stone walls, the enclosure had as its focal point a stone pillar rising above the height of the surrounding walls. This impressive column of grey stone was decorated in places with pieces of bluestone inset in a crosshatched pattern. Makikele recognized the pattern of the blue inlay as similar to some set into the older retaining walls of royal burial sites at Sealene Hill. He would later learn that the stone at Ngome had been brought from Dzata Hill.

At high noon, when the sun penetrated the enclosure, this column, with its blue highlights, held the observer's eye and then lifted it upward. The effect gave an observer, standing at the column's base, a sense of linkage with the vast sky above.

Makikele was told that this impressive column and its stone embellishments were believed to possess cooling spiritual qualities, giving power to those in its presence. It served as the king's private temple, a sacrificial area for ancestral propitiation and intercession. On a colossal scale, this resembled the smaller earthen sacrificial mounds, the *dipekko*, encasing embedded upright river stones, found in many Phalaborwa headmen's compounds. He remembered watching his grandmother, the queen mother Ntlabede, praying at a *dipekko* shrine by her house at Kgopolwe. Each served a similar ritual function as this larger structure at Ngome, a place to gather for prayers, sacrifice, and libations.

A week after his arrival, Makikele was presented to Nagome's king, his queen mother, men of the king's immediate family, and his wives. A reticent figure, not unlike his own father, the king was pleased with the gifts sent by King Meele, and approved Makikele's residence near his capital where he would learn local healing skills.

Shortly after being received at court, Makikele left Masalani's homestead to reside as an apprentice to one of the court herbalists, an elderly man named Pulani. This distant relative of the king had lived for many years in the royal village as one of the keepers of regalia. In his youth Pulani had been apprenticed to various court sorcerers and herbalists and had accumulated a vast knowledge. Now in his old age, he was also considered one of the most important custodians of sacred Venda healing and magical tradition, and he was venerated for his wisdom and ability to treat the sick.

Two other young men were also apprenticed to Pulani, both from Shona country north of the Limpopo River. The three of them would train together under old Pulani and his assistants. They shared a sleeping house in his compound, which was located a short distance down from the hilltop which accommodated the fortified royal enclosure.

Life in Pulani's village was simple compared with that of Kgopolwe Hill. While the royal residence and village surrounding the king's sacred cattle enclosure were heavily populated, the site of Pulani's home was more isolated and sparse. In most respects Pulani's compound resembled all others in the surrounding countryside, having a central cluster of circular houses bordering a livestock enclosure. Each of these units in turn had an assortment of smaller domestic structures in which food was stored and prepared. It differed from other family compounds in one distinct way: each domestic subunit in Pulani's village also had specialized storage facilities and workspace for processing herbs and materials needed for the healing arts. These were littered with what seemed like an endless inventory of herbs, roots, leaves, bones, and stones of every size and color.

It seemed to Makikele as if everyone in the village was part of Pulani's herbal medicine production workforce. Even the children worked, gathering materials from the surrounding forest and bush, or using grinding stones to pulverize bones or roots.

On the first day of his arrival, Makikele observed a group of small boys returning along a forest trail carrying baskets of old bone fragments and the feathered remains of bird carcasses. All these objects would be processed by village residents for Pulani's use.

During his apprenticeship, Makikele observed and learned many things that he would use when he returned to Phalaborwa. But there were two skills that he intended to acquire as a matter of priority: knowledge of rain and war medicines. His tenure with Pulani was an opportunity to learn about powerful Venda magic, something respected and sought after throughout the region.

Before her son's departure from Kgopolwe, Mokadi, who had once lived in the culturally related kingdom of Lobedu, was able to teach him some words which resembled those of Venda. His grasp of the language quickly improved during his apprenticeship with this old court sorcerer. Makikele was soon able to communicate with the people of Venda, and he eventually became fluent in their dialect.

But his greatest enjoyment was sharing stories with his two fellow apprentices from Shona, while the three of them learned the language together. The names of these two young men were Ngunzi and Shumba.

"What is the meaning of your names?" Makikele asked his fellow students as they became acquainted.

"Ngunzi means 'the bull,'" the first replied, smiling.

Makikele returned the smile. "Bulls are very important to us," he said. "We use the skin of a black bull for royal burials. Recently, one of my uncles, Phirimela Malatji, died. He was buried in the skin of a black bull. We also sacrifice and eat the flesh of the black bull at important ceremonial occasions. And when my age group successfully completed *Koma,* the head of a bull was placed at the top of a ceremonial pole as a sign to all the visitors. We even have a charging bull dance."

"Is it true you are a prince?" Ngunzi asked.

"Yes, my father is *Kgoshi* Meele, king of all of Phalaborwa. He has sent me here to study with Pulani. I have accompanied my father's magician, Masalani, who comes from Ngome."

Makikele paused before asking his next question. "And what does the name Shumba mean?"

"My name means 'the lion,'" replied the second youth.

"What a strong name. The lion is also very important to my people."

Makikele went on to tell them about the fierce lions roaming the lowlands of Phalaborwa, and about his lion hunt and first kill. "My father was very proud when I presented him with the skin," he concluded.

"What is the meaning of your name, Makikele?" asked Ngunzi.

"It means 'one who travels about the land meeting people.'"

"Certainly that's a fitting name for you, Makikele," responded Ngunzi.

In time the three youths became inseparable friends, fellow workers, and quick studies of the knowledge they encountered as apprentices to Pulane. Together they explored the farmland and forests surrounding Ngome, made friends, and became known among the local residents.

Makikele learned that many separate Venda kingdoms were located along the long, meandering Limpopo River and that they had trade and kinship ties with the Shona people north of the river. This river route also linked Venda with coastal trade centers controlled by Tsonga rulers and with the Sotho- and Nguni-speaking worlds. He quickly discovered that encounters with trading groups were common occurrences for residents of Ngome as caravans traversed the main east–west trail that roughly paralleled the Limpopo.

His two Shona companions explained to him that many coastal caravans passed through Ngome on their way north to Dzata and then across the river into Shona, and that these could be quite large. He soon observed on his own that many consisted of long lines of hundreds of porters, gun bearers, and traders. He also noticed that Coastal Tsonga traders wore cotton cloths around their waists and cloth shirts and hats.

"I have now seen many traders in this region," said Makikele on one occasion when the three men sat eating their evening meal. "Today I saw some pass through who wore colored cotton cloths around their waists and across their shoulders and chests. This apparel seems to distinguish them from their porters and bearers, who carry only a cloth or skin blanket and shoulder pouch as personal items, but otherwise traveled naked."

"Yes," said Shumba. "They are a different group of men from the coastal towns. They hire the porters from inland villages to work for them. These traders in turn work for others living in coastal settlements, who supply them with goods from the boats passing by from other lands. They bring many bolts of fabric for trade and also bring shells and glass beads. These things were once scarce commodities inland, but are becoming more plentiful as trade objects sought after by villagers for ornamentation. Such items are also incorporated into ritual objects and decorative chains and bracelets."

"We trade for the same coastal products in exchange for our iron and copper mined at Lolwe Hill, or for ivory taken from elephants we kill with guns and axes. I saw one of the traders with a gun," remarked Makikele.

"But guns are rarely traded," Shumba pointed out to Makikele. "These men carry guns made by the Portuguese in their homeland and bring them on their ships. They need them for defense and hunting while traveling."

"We, too, have both foreign and locally made guns in Phalaborwa. My father has some. I suspect that the king here at Ngome has some Portuguese guns in his armory also. I have seen some of his warriors and hunters with the cruder, more bulky local guns. I also heard that one of the king's brothers, a man known for his marksmanship, owns a particularly beautiful gun purchased from a coastal trader. They say this firing piece can hit a target one hundred paces away with far greater accuracy and force than locally made guns."

"Shona travelers rarely possess guns," said Shumba, "but if they do, they are of local production. Our people are usually armed with only spears and clubs."

"I saw one group from the eastern village of Thulamela," said Makikele. "The caravan leader stopped and talked with Pulani. They carried ornate beaded gourds, leather, and cloth. We learned they were heading west from Dzata to trade in villages near Mapungubwe Hill. There were a number of women in the group. One was a bride being taken to her new home. Another was seeking medicines and ancient objects to incorporate into amulets for use in curing and ancestor prayers. The group leaders showed Pulani a small object and several beads made from gold at Thulamela."

"No doubt the gold was mined in Shona country and carried to Thulamela," said Shumba. "It is a rare artisan work these days. The metal is scarce and mostly traded in northern port towns from where it is taken on the large ocean-going boats to Arab and Portuguese villages, which are far away. This rare yellow metal has great value. Did Pulani trade for the gold objects?"

"Pulani tried bartering, but without success."

On another occasion, Shona traders from a northern village passed by Pulani's settlement in search of cattle. They were heavily armed with spears and carried leather shields. They shouted greetings to Shumba and Ngunzi as they made their way to the capital to ask permission to proceed on to the livestock grazing regions further west from Ngome.

Although mostly restricted to Pulani's family circle and his two friends, Makikele occasionally visited members of Masalani's family living in a more distant village, two days' journey northeast of Ngome. Masalani's son was particularly hospitable to him, welcoming him to his family compound and, on one occasion, allowing him to accompany a group that was tracking and capturing deadly venomous black cobra and puff adders.

While many snakes could be found in the Venda highlands, a particularly large selection, including the aggressive black cobra, inhabited a rocky dry terrain north of the village along the route to Thulamela. This ancient hilltop trading center, now mostly abandoned, preceded the Venda settlement of Dzata and was once a powerful metal trading kingdom at the time when Makikele's Malatji ancestors and their followers migrated south to live in Phalaborwa.

The hotter, drier region bred many kinds of snake desired as ingredients in medicines and magical potions. The hunters trapped many of them alive, and then killed, gutted, and dried them wherever the party was camped. Others, captured alive, were placed in leather bags and brought back to Masalani's village. Makikele was given a share of the hunt to take back to Pulani. This included two live puff adders, which would be milked for their poison, as would a large black cobra and several green cobras he himself had captured.

Pulani was very happy to accept these snakes, and incorporated them into his complex pharmaceutical formulary. A number of the larger snakes, some as much as four and five feet long, were dried for display and hung with the many others in his collection, head downward from the roof poles of Pulani's divining house. This forest of serpents could be quite intimidating to visitors and patients entering the dimly lit, strangely sweet-smelling space for consultations, divinations, or treatment.

Pulani's regime of study was demanding. During the early months of their stay, the three students acquired practical knowledge by joining gathering expeditions into the countryside and the high mountains. They learned how to identity herbs, roots, bulbs, grasses, and minerals that made up the raw materials required for the large inventory of medicines and potions used in Pulani's craft.

The mountainous region in which the Venda lived was much colder than the hot, dry Phalaborwa lowlands, and Makikele found the change invigorating. He noticed that the moist Venda

Ivory traders from Delagoa Bay

climate produced a more varied flora and fauna than the drier Phalaborwa. There was an abundance of baboon and vervet and colobus monkeys; the latter's black and white pelts were highly sought after. Varieties of spotted cats seen only rarely in the south were also abundant in this country.

In their work under Pulani's careful scrutiny, the three apprentices were expected to locate, procure, and process from local sources most of what Pulani required to do his work as a master of the healing sciences. This hands-on approach enabled them to identify and categorize an extensive inventory of healing ingredients available from the surrounding forest and bush environment.

In some cases, such as when digging roots and tubers from the ground, they learned that the manner of excavation could impact the efficacy of the crop when later used in treatment. For example, if the hole out of which the fever root was extracted is then filled with dirt after its removal, the root's effectiveness would be diminished. The fever root was a woody shrub, easily identified by its white flower and strongly scented leaves, and had many functions in combination with other ingredients. When chewed, it could remedy certain intestinal ailments; when combined into a tea with the blueberries and crushed bulbs of the baboon grape, a dark-leaved climbing shrub, it could remedy bad blood ailments, which were a common occurrence.

The three apprentices also began to understand how this complicated pharmacology combined in various ways and could be used to diagnose, treat, and protect patients in need of help. While many remedies were administered internally to treat an ailment—ingested, inhaled as vapors, smoked in pipes, rubbed into incisions, or inserted anally—others were used externally as a prophylactic to prevent illness or evil.

Some medications were employed to heal illnesses caused by witchcraft; others, if properly prepared, would protect against attempted witchcraft. A number of black powders, collectively called *ditshidi*, were of particular value when witchcraft was diagnosed. Pulani would determine the necessary ingredients through divination; then, under his direction, an assortment of tree roots, barks, and carefully selected perennial flower seeds were burnt into charcoal, ground into powders, and mixed with fats of animals of the same gender as the victim being treated. These compounds were then rubbed onto sticks, which were taken and placed across openings to the sick person's house. Such approaches afforded strong protection until a patient recovered.

Preventive measures of this sort were particularly important because a person in a weakened state, whether from malaria, intestinal worms, various poxes, respiratory diseases, or other debilitating illnesses, was also more vulnerable to bewitching and harmful sorcery.

As the months progressed, the three apprentices were allowed to observe and assist their teacher in diagnosing illnesses. They received Pulani's clients, arranged for consultations with the medicine man, interviewed patients, and conducted physical examinations. While observing and studying the many divining techniques Pulani used to identify causes of sickness, they were able to determine appropriate remedies for treatment. Pulani employed many techniques. Choosing the right treatment was the craft of his specialization.

By the end of the year, the three young apprentices had begun to acquire the ornamentation and regalia of diviners that would set them apart from others. They were also directly involved with attending to selected patients who visited the healer's village.

Because of his status as the son of a royal family, Makikele was also permitted to accompany Pulani to the king's compound. While in the royal enclosure, he observed the ritual application of medications to the sacred drums and the use of rain medicines. Drum rituals were a primary component of the art of war magic, and Makikele meticulously set about studying their preparation, use, and the doctoring which enhanced their power. These secret activities took place deep within the king's domestic enclosure. Pulani, while having a major role to play, was not always involved in the more secretive activities surrounding sacred regalia, rain, and war magic. These were the prerogative of the queen mother, her son, and certain closer family members.

Pulani was, however, exceptionally well informed about these matters, and Makikele hoped to master Venda powers by combining the experience he gained by his privileged access to the royal family together with the knowledge he was acquiring from Pulani.

CHAPTER FOURTEEN

Sacred Forest, Dark Water

During the second year of their apprenticeship, the three men underwent a series of rituals and tests to confirm their acquired status as medicine men. When Pulani and several of his colleagues were satisfied the men had learned how to identify, collect, and process the full herbalist inventory and perform divination, they were taken into a sacred forest to a remote grove of trees alongside a lake. Here they underwent a rite of passage confirming them as medicine men and healers.

The first part of the ceremony was a time of ritual cleansing and symbolic trials. They were shaven of all hair, bathed in cold mountain lake water, fed purgatives to cleanse their bodies, and then anointed with medicated hippopotamus fat for protection.

This culminated in a ceremonial submersion in a deep lake pool, the dwelling place of crocodiles, but ruled over by an ancient giant serpent embodying powerful forces.

Before they entered the sacred pool, Pulani treated the water with black powders to protect the initiates from dangers that might lurk in the dark depths beneath the green, algae-rich surface.

When Makikele lowered himself into the pool, the numbing water made him gasp. By the time his shoulders were submerged, the mud beneath his feet caused him to slip. He felt himself fall, and was then pulled into a deep hole in the lake floor as if being dragged into an underworld. Looking upward, he could see the morning sun and the splashing of the other young apprentices. Then he turned to his left and found himself facing a crocodile that lay in repose beneath a submerged stone on a clay ledge, which was illuminated by a shaft of light. The enormous dark reptile had her eyes fixed on the helpless visitor as he sank downward. Despite his training as a warrior and his close encounters with poisonous snakes and an enraged lion, Makikele was terrified by this close encounter with the giant reptile. He turned away, attempting unsuccessfully to float upward to escape the monster.

"Wait, Makikele, son of the porcupine, you do not need to fear me." The beast slid from its dark sanctuary and came alongside the frightened prince before continuing to speak through its parted teeth: "Take hold of my back and come with me."

"Yes, Great Mother," replied Makikele. He took hold of the creature's massive shoulder and felt himself pulled deeper into the dark, watery recesses, stopping abruptly with a jolt when the great crocodile reached the pool floor. The collision thrust Makikele forward and away from the cold, hard-skinned beast, until he landed on a bed of dark stones.

When his eyes adjusted to the darkness, he saw an enormous snake, its pale body entwined among the dark, irregular contours of its murky abode. Large dark eyes followed the young prince's descent; soft scales embraced Makikele's body as the serpent coiled itself, first around his legs, then his torso, and finally his neck and head. Caressing and probing with its agile tongue, the smooth-skinned giant stared into Makikele's face, seeming to find pleasure in the shared warmth of their embrace while its hold on the youth tightened.

Then, as if satiated with this intimacy, the serpent released its grip on Makikele, unwinding itself to support him with its graceful body, while they floated slowly upward together. Their eyes remained locked in a curious bond. Small fish of many colors emerged from every direction, surrounding Makikele's body, pulling at his skin as if grooming for lice. Hundreds of them invaded every crevice and corner of his now-limp frame, slowly lifting him, feet first, toward the light on the surface.

Makikele rose toward the sunlight, his eyes still drawn to those of the great reptile, which emitted a high-pitched whistling sound from its throat.

Then the serpent sang, its voice getting louder as the two separated: "You will not drown like your uncle, Labado, who caused dissent among the people. Be brave, little porcupine. All will gather around you as you ascend to the light, like the preening fish that will raise you up and caress you."

While the figure retreated from the light to return to its rocky bed, its voice became higher-pitched. "Fire, not water, is your destiny, Makikele. Look to the light, little porcupine of Malatji. Do not curl up in your den; do not hide among the rocks of Kgopolwe."

Makikele reached the water's surface, gasping for breath, and screamed, "Yes, my mother!"

He emerged in a far corner of the pool, a distance away from the group who now searched for him. One of Pulani's attendants heard his cry and spotted him on the distant shore. He and several of the other men ran to the place where Makikele's limp body floated. They jumped into the water and pulled him to safety.

One of the men assisted the tall, lanky prince from the water, saying, "We thought you were dead when you disappeared."

The men helped him as he staggered to the ritual encampment where Pulani sat near the main cooking fire. Balanced on three stones above the fire, a cauldron of herbal liquids boiled, tended by the aged sorcerer herbalist.

They placed Makikele prostrate on the ground near the fire, where he vomited repeatedly with great force. Between each bout of retching, he gasped for air. A greenish discharge emerged from his mouth and nostrils. Pulani caught as much of the liquid as he could in a gourd cup and poured the rancid-smelling residue into the boiling pot. While Pulani performed this libation, he droned words that were strange to Makikele's ears—maybe Shona language from the north, he thought, gasping for air between bouts of retching. Gradually, as the unfamiliar litany faded into a humming chant, his vomiting ceased, and he was wrapped in warm furs. Now, shaking with cold, Makilele sat between the other initiates for warmth, and watched with them as Pulani concluded his preparations. Smiling and nodding with approval at Makikele, Pulani assured him and the others that a great magic had been done.

A portion of the herbal potion was cooled in a gourd and passed to each of the initiates in turn. When they took a draught of the bitter ingredients and swallowed, they coughed.

Pulani's assistants then painted the three men's bodies with red ochre and led them back to Ngome. There, in the presence of the king, his council, and court sorcerers, the initiates were accorded the status of medicine men, or *dingaka*.

Makikele encounters a spirit serpent

Even before they arrived from the forest and entered the gate of the king's cattle enclosure, word of Makikele's mysterious disappearance underwater and his conversation with the Great Spirit Snake living in the sacred pool spread throughout the capital. That evening, around every cooking fire and men's gathering, the people discussed the story of Makikele's death and rebirth, his descent and encounter with the spirit world, and the messages transmitted to him.

They pressed Pulani's staff and family members for more details. The story of this mystical encounter gained embellishment as it was passed from mouth to mouth throughout the capital, and then on to other villages. Before long, everyone was talking about Makikele and a certain charisma surrounded him, especially among the common villagers who lived beyond the capital.

In a private audience with the king and the queen mother, Pulani related the sequence of events and the messages believed to have transpired in the spirit world of the sacred pool.

Later, they sacrificed a goat kid and a hen at a shrine located on the right side of the doorway of the queen mother's house. They consulted with an oracle to help interpret this encounter with the supernatural.

The oracle suggested to the queen mother, without being specific about its source, that ancestral forces guided this young man's destiny, emanating from supernatural sources shared by both royal families. The ambiguity vexed her. Interrogating the ancient court seer only resulted in further vagaries, but hints of an answer lay in the direction of Dzata, where both lineages traced common ancestral ties.

Recalling Masalani's family links with the distant hilltop city, she persuaded the king to send an entourage from her court to Dzata so that prayers and spirit offerings might be given in the old royal burial ground. This ancient resting place was venerated by both the people of Venda and by their southern cousins, the Malatji.

Shortly after Makikele's initiation experience, the queen mother dispatched a messenger to accompany a group of traders who were on their way to Phalaborwa.

"Take word to the royal family at Kgopolwe and other centers along the way that are related to Ngome," she instructed the messenger. *Such news will add to our reputation as a center for sorcery and magic*, she thought as she dispatched her emissary. *It will also enhance the reputation of Prince Makikele.*

The queen mother knew that the young prince from Phalaborwa was being groomed for an important role in service to his father, and that these mysterious encounters could raise his estimation among his people. She also knew that Ngome needed close allies if it was to remain strong. Recognizing Makikele's presence in Ngome to be an advantage to them and his capabilities to be significant, the queen mother summoned a trusted retainer to travel along with the group heading to Kgopolwe.

"Here is a powerful amulet I want carried to *Kgoshi* Meele's mother, the venerable queen mother, Ntlabidi. She has a reputation as a faith keeper and must hear the account of Makikele's wondrous spiritual encounter."

After the servant had accepted the amulet from the queen, she handed him a leather bag containing a collection of rare pieces of glass strung with cotton into a wristband.

"Then, I want you to go on to Lobedu to take this gift of six-sided blue beads to Modjadji, the rain queen," she said. "Make sure she also hears the story of Makikele's exploits."

Queen Modjadji occupied the position of son-in-law to the aged Venda queen, having exchanged a bridewealth to marry a wife from her branch of the Venda royal family. It was the custom among these two peoples for powerful women with cattle and other wealth to assume the status of a senior male through the acquisition of wives. As such, she could assume a role in decision-making councils ordinarily not available to a woman. This Venda wife had been assigned to a close kinsman of the rain queen, and they had produced several children. One of the girls would soon reach puberty and receive her *bjale* initiation. The Venda queen mother wished to suggest possible marriage ties for the girl. One consideration was an alliance with Ntlabidi's household at Kgopolwe by marrying her to Makikele. She pondered the implications of such a tie compared with advocating selection of a girl from her son's patrilineage resident in Ngome. Perhaps, in time, she thought, both would be possible.

CHAPTER FIFTEEN

Apparition on Dzata Hill

Toward the end of his second year of indenture to Pulani, Makikele became a frequent and familiar presence in the royal court at Ngome. Although the queen mother was an elusive figure who lived in seclusion with several ancient female relatives, her slaves, and attendants, she took a keen interest in Makikele. On many occasions she permitted him an audience in her private walled quarters attached to the king's residence. Here he became acquainted with women of the king's immediate family and lineage, and he observed the everyday interaction of these powerful figures who guarded the authority and sacred personage of the king.

Much of their lives revolved around prescribed rituals relating to the annual agricultural cycle, just like those of royal women in his homeland. The extraordinary events in life, such as human and cattle disease, illness and death, infertility, drought, feuding, and war, were addressed through more secretive and occult solutions. Makikele set about learning these secret Venda sciences. He did this through close observation and discussions within the royal enclosure and by seeking Pulani's counsel and his interpretations derived from a long life serving the royal family.

Following one of these audiences with the queen mother, Makikele was approached by two councilors while drinking beer with a group of men in the royal cattle enclosure.

"*Trobela*! Prince Malatji, son of the porcupine lineage which rules in the southland," the senior of the two greeted him, bowing down and performing the ritual handclapping required when addressing nobility and royalty in court.

"*Trobela* Makikele, apprentice to Pulani the witch doctor," the second man added while they seated themselves near him beside a secondary fire lit for warmth at a distance from the sacred fire of the king.

Makikele stood and also performed the ritual greeting, the *losha*, returning their compliments. "Greetings, councilors of the king, the great ruler of Ngome, descendant of the illustrious kings of Dzata, Thovhele, and Thohoyandou, the great elephants of the Venda. I am honored to have you join me on this cold morning. I hope you are both feeling well, and that the king is strong and receiving your good counsel today."

"We are both well," the first one replied. "How are you getting on at the village of Pulani, good prince?"

"All is well with Pulani; he is a wise and good man. I am fortunate to enjoy his hospitality and to be his student." He paused to receive their response, knowing that they likely carried information from the king's council for Pulani or possibly for him.

Women attendants served the men gourds filled with warm millet beer. After refreshing themselves, the two men waited in silence for an invitation from the prince to speak.

Soon the ritual salutations ended and casual conversation began with Makikele commenting, "The beer is very refreshing. It is of a high quality, very much like that served in my father's cattle enclosure in Phalaborwa. It reminds me of my home."

Now, having entered into a less formal discourse, the older of the two asked, "There is wonder by many about whether the Malatji prince might be available to join a group traveling to Dzata, the hill sacred to all Venda. Would this be a possibility, kind prince?"

"Can you tell me more, good man?"

"The entourage will include several members of the royal family. They wish to offer prayers to the spirits of dead kings, ancestors of Ngome's royal family. Some in the group will also meet with Masalani's family members to trade. They live near the hill."

Although excited by the thought of travel to this sacred center, Makikele recognized that the invitation was of royal origin and required a formal reply to the messengers, expressing gratitude for the invitation and his willingness to accompany the group. He knew from Pulani that artifacts from such revered places as Dzata, Thulamela, and even distant Mapungubwe were kept as part of the royal regalia at Ngome and other royal centers of the more than thirty autonomous but interconnected Venda principalities. Makikele thought the trip might provide an opportunity to obtain such relics for his own family, as well as to see and learn about this distant land and its sacred hill shrine.

Makikele had heard talk of other sacred hills located east and west of Dzata, along the Limpopo, and of the distant Zimbabwe of the Shona kings. Relics from these sanctuaries sometimes reached Ngome, carried by pilgrims and traveling shamans—such objects as a discarded grinding stone, wood from an abandoned dwelling on a burial hill, bones, and scraps of rusted iron. All these objects had meaning and power because of their links with distant ancestral spirits believed to still dwell in such places. Although the more recently departed royal family spirits resting closer by had a more direct impact on the day-to-day issues of family and community concern, these remoter heroic spirits also had a special place and function in prayer and royal intercession for all the people.

Such relics provided the families' priestesses, the king's great sister and his paternal aunts, the vehicles through which intermediation with more ancient ancestors, those of legendary accounts and songs, might be reached in times of great need. It was common practice to incorporate a piece of bone, wood, or metal into an amulet or piece of jewelry to bring good luck or to protect from evil forces. Makikele's mother had, for example, given him a small amulet containing beads made from ostrich shell and red glass from her Sekgopo ancestors.

"As you know, the Malatji lineage that rules Phalaborwa came from the northlands, much as your Venda ancestors did," Makikele commented. "This was before we adopted the porcupine as our totem. When the first Malatji came from here to settle in Phalaborwa, we were known as 'people of the baboon.' It was an ancient northern lineage, the old totem still found among some living at Dzata," explained Makikele.

The councilors nodded in agreement. "You might wish to accompany a group of the king's relatives to pray on Dzata hill," one of them said.

"It would be an honor and would symbolize the unity between our two peoples," Makikele replied, knowing that his words would reach the inner walls of the king's enclosure.

Masalani and his son, who lived near Dzata, had spoken of this place respected by all Venda, and Makikele looked forward to visiting and observing the people along this well-traveled interior trade route. He decided to consult with Pulani about possible trade goods for the trip, and to offer to procure medicines that Pulani might wish to acquire from this distant mountain region steeped in legend and mystery.

He wondered if he would meet people of the baboon totem still living there, and even discover Malatji people. He knew from tribal tradition that the name had been carried with them from a place called *Bokgalaka*, somewhere north of the Limpopo River, before they migrated south to settle in Phalaborwa.

Two weeks later, the delegation from Ngome set off for Dzata along a well-defined trail. After three days they reached Dzanani, a well-watered lowland region between highland ranges. The party proceeded at a slow pace, accommodating the needs of several older members of Ngome's royal family, including a sister of the king.

Unbeknownst to Makikele and the other members of the party, they were being followed. A man, hidden from their sight, shadowed their every move.

The man was a Ba-Laudzi, one of the non-Venda peoples living in villages throughout the region. He was an itinerant trader known as Sabasa, who traveled between Venda, Lobedu, Phalaborwa, and Pedi trading skins and animal parts. In addition, he often carried a type of soft graphite stone popular with women for use in decorating pots and other objects. He also traded herbs for medicines and carved wooden amulets believed to have magic properties. The man was known in some Phalaborwa villages and often traded with members of Setakgale's family, including her son Ramatladi.

When he was last permitted to visit Kgopolwe, Sabasa had completed a transaction of lion skins and rhinoceros horns with Ramatladi in exchange for a copper *marale*. As he prepared to leave, he was summoned again to meet with Ramatladi, who approached him with a proposition.

"You are traveling to Venda soon?"

"Yes, good prince," the man replied, smiling broadly and performing the *losha* in a deep bow, while softly clapping his hands to show the greatest of respect. He was grateful to be once again inside the royal precincts of Phalaborwa's capital, and in the presence of one of its most prominent princes. "I will take the salt trail to Lobedu, and then head north to Venda."

"Do you stop in Ngome, where Masalani's people live, and do you know the village of Pulani the herbalist?" Ramatladi studied the man's face and his fawning posture with some distaste. Unlike the Ba-Lemba, who were well-known and respected itinerate traders from the north, these Ba-Laudzi were disliked by many. They were seen as crude and demanding in their manner of bartering.

"Yes, good prince, I have business in the village of Pulani. I know him well, and often stay nearby on my way north."

"Excellent," said Ramatladi. "Would you like to acquire for yourself additional copper *serale*?"

"A single *marale* is a valuable item, my prince. To obtain additional *serale* would be a great good fortune. I am very interested, good prince." Hesitating for a moment, Sabasa raised his eyes to study the arrogant figure standing before him with arms crossed. He sensed condescension and distaste in the prince's tone as he spoke and that his every movement was being studied. Lowering his head to avoid direct eye contact, he then added, "How might I come by these copper items? What do you wish to trade?"

"This is not an offer of trade. I have another proposition for you, if you are willing." Ramatladi softened his tone to await a reply from the despised Ba-Laudzi.

"Oh! I listen with great interest, my prince. What kind of proposition do you offer?"

"What I am about to tell you is between you and me only. No one else must know of it." His voice grew severe, almost sinister. "Word of this discussion must never leave these walls." Ramatladi played with a flute made of a porcupine quill as he spoke, tossing it from one hand to the other then placing it to his lips and pointing the ornate feather-tipped end toward Sabasa's face and body. "Do you understand what I am telling you?"

The Ba-Laudzi's smiling expression of submission shifted to one of concern, and fear entered his eyes. The trader had seen the effect of magically treated reed and bone flutes before. He knew the porcupine quill was used for witchcraft and understood that Ramatladi would bring him harm if betrayed.

Ramatladi raised the flute to his lips and pretended to play it. The man held his breath for several seconds before he replied.

"Yes, I understand, my prince; no one shall ever know of our arrangement."

"Good, then this is your assignment. You will go to the house of Pulani. There you will find my brother, Makikele. You will gain his trust before slipping this into his beer." Ramatladi placed a small leather pouch of yellow powder on the ground between them.

"Is this . . . is it a medication, my prince?"

"No, Sabasa, the powder contains a magic ingredient, a potion to prevent him from returning here to Phalaborwa. You must see that he drinks it. You must then disappear undetected, and never mention it to anyone." An evil grin crossed Ramatladi's face as he continued to watch the frightened trader. He then blew several high-pitched flute notes into the now terrified trader's face.

"But, my prince." Sabasa swallowed hard to clear his throat, now dry from fear and to steady his voice. "But why should you want him killed?"

"It is not for you to ask why, you stupid man, but simply to do as I tell you."

Having angrily silenced Sabasa, who had foolishly mentioned the true purpose of the task, Ramatladi nonetheless proceeded to explain the reason for the risky deed expected of the Ba-Laudzi trader.

"He is a threat to the succession. My father, *Kgoshi* Meele, wishes him dead. If he returns to Phalaborwa trained in the art of Venda sorcery and magic, he will bring harm to the royal family. We cannot allow this to happen. He must be removed." Ramatladi laid out five *serale* on the floor next to the bag of poison. These copper ingots are each worth several head of cattle. They will be yours. Will you do it?"

"Yes, my prince, I will do it."

"You understand the consequences of failure?"

"Yes, my prince." Sabasa lowered his eyes away from Ramatladi's stare.

The crafty trader listened to all the gossip around beer pots in the many villages where he was welcome. He knew the prince's words were lies. It was commonly accepted that Makikele was loved by the king, and that his mother, Mokadi, was favored by the old ruler.

"You must also take these with you." Ramatladi passed him a bow and a quiver of arrows tipped with poison. "If you cannot put the powder in his drink, the bow will provide an alternative means. Either way, he will be removed."

Bowing to the prince, he glanced at the wealth in *serale* ingots placed at his feet. *With such treasure,* he thought, *a younger wife would be possible and much more livestock for his family.* To kill was a dangerous matter to be avoided, but his fear of what would befall him if he failed was strong and he knew the prince's flute had already bewitched him. At Ramatladi's gesture he gathered up the copper ingots, hid them in his leather sack, and stealthily left Kgopolwe.

Sabasa arrived at Pulani's house a few weeks later, only to discover that Makikele had left for Dzata. Hence he now followed the royal entourage, waiting for the opportunity to carry out his mission.

In Dzanani, the party from Ngome rested for two days before making the final two-day uphill trip to Dzata. The stop gave Makikele a chance to explore the countryside. Joining a hunting party of young men of Dzanani's royal house, he traveled on the open bushland on both sides of the river dividing the picturesque valley. The large herds of antelope and dryer grasslands resembled Phalaborwa's terrain, and he enjoyed stalking spoor and animal trails as they hunted with bow, spear, and dogs.

Cattle-herding communities occupied this territory. Herds were similar in size to those in highland Ngome. This was of interest to Makikele, who had assumed that at the lower altitudes, husbandry would resemble that of Phalaborwa. Drought and tsetse fly, which kept herds in Phalaborwa small, did not exist in this region. He was told that wide tsetse-free corridors existed in lower riverside localities, and that several of these zones extended southeast in the direction of the Tsonga herding peoples. Another stretched due south toward Phalaborwa at a river juncture many miles east of Dzanani. He wondered if this passageway was the route his own Malatji ancestors might have taken while migrating with their herds.

On the sixth night of their seven-day journey, they encountered a coastal caravan enroute to Shona country. The two groups camped beside one another, and in the evening the men met around a central fire to talk.

"Where are you headed?" Makikele asked.

"We are traveling north to trade for gold and ivory," said the caravan leader. "Metal sources have become scarcer in recent years, requiring more extensive trade trips inland."

Makikele noticed that the man had a dignified bearing, spoke fluent Venda, and could use a Sotho dialect from the highlands similar to that spoken in Phalaborwa.

"We have deposits of iron and copper ore in Phalaborwa," Makikele replied.

"We know of the copper source in Phalaborwa, and of the southern trail leading from the coast to the escarpment and then across the Sabie and Lepelle Rivers." Pleased to discuss a familiar topic, the young traders enthusiastically shared stores of their experiences crossing the countryside surrounding Venda.

Makikele listened with particular interest to their descriptions of his homeland and his family, and how it was perceived by the youthful travelers as a wealthy, carefully guarded mining culture which, like Queen Modjadji's Lobedu, was protected by powerful witchcraft.

"Phalaborwa also has many elephants, rhinoceroses, and hippopotamuses, and the people there trade the lucrative products from their hunting such as tusks, horns, skins, and oils."

"You are correct," said Makikele.

Most of the men in the other group were coastal Tsonga, but two of them were of a mixed population from the coast which lived by trading and farming near the Portuguese fort in King Maphuto's realm. Makikele wanted to learn more about the distant coastal settlements and the strange lands beyond the seas.

The first of the two men took up the challenge. "Many ships anchor in the fort's port," he said. "It is called Delagoa by the white men. Further north is another port called Inhambane, and there are others up the coast beyond that. They come to trade and to collect and transport goods long distances, sometimes crossing the deep waters to reach lands belonging to Arabs, Portuguese, and others from very different peoples living beyond the great water."

"What kind of people are they?" Makikele asked. "Why do they come to our lands?"

"The lands of these people are wealthy with much to trade, but they lack metals, ivory, game, and domestic livestock. From

Inhambane, ivory and other products, such as iron, copper, and cured and raw hides from game, are shipped to faraway places with strange names like Olan, Yema, Arabya, and Zanj. Most of all they want gold, which has great value and is scarce."

"Tell me more about the coastal forts."

"They are places where slaves, men, women, and children are bartered in exchange for the many things brought to land in the great boats."

"You mean slaves captured in war?"

"No, many people are captured from villages by slave hunters and taken to the Portuguese fort where they are sold, traded just like livestock. It is a big business which is supplied mostly by the coastal Tsonga people, although inland caravans regularly bring slaves down to the coast as well. These slaves are sent away on ships, and never return."

"This does not seem right to me," said Makikele. "While slaves captured during war are common in many communities, and certainly needed, they are of local origin, captives or individuals sold during famine and hard times. Our slaves are absorbed into village life and become like other common people, living orderly lives, following our traditions and customs. With some exceptions, children of slaves marry freely and out of bondage."

"This is different," said the second man. "These slaves are badly treated. Captured men sent north to Arab and Portuguese lands are castrated before being traded at markets. Women are taken into the families who buy them; however, the children remain slaves even when fathered by the men who own their mothers. A slave remains a slave forever, without family or ancestors."

Makikele tried to control his emotions. "This is a grim fate which greatly troubles me. I cannot comprehend this form of bondage, the separation from ancestral land and ties of lineage. Slaves of this sort must be cursed. Separated permanently from the land of their origins by the sea, they would have no tie with the world of their ancestors, which is so crucial for the well-being of individuals and families. They would be like abandoned calves left unprotected in the bush. Tell me more about these Portuguese people. I am intrigued to learn more about them and their habits. Do they have many guns?"

The first man answered, "The fort they inhabit is strong, made of stone, earth, and timbers. It has withstood a series of attacks, which they have defended with powerful guns and iron-tipped arrows shot with great force from atop its high walls. Their iron weapons and tools are of high quality. Away from their fort, however, they are no match for the physically superior Tsonga and Shona. They are heavily bearded, and their hygiene is of low standard. Their clothing and footwear are well-made, but heavy."

"Nonetheless, these Portuguese men are brave and vicious fighters," said the other. "They are persistent when bartering and enjoy sleeping with Tsonga women, since they have none of their own with them in their settlements. The children of these relationships are not claimed by them. This has resulted in a mixing with the population living near the fort and along the River Sabie. They farm, hunt, speak Tsonga, and serve as liaison with inland tribes. Some of these mixed-race people make trading trips among the coastal villages, but, as a rule, they do not gain entry into the kingdoms and chiefdoms further upcountry. They have greater access to Portuguese goods than others, and many are armed with guns."

The following morning, the two groups parted. The caravan continued on its way northwest, intending to cross the Limpopo and enter into Shonaland. Makikele and the royal entourage also made their way north, following a well-traveled mountain passage toward Dzata.

They had not traveled far when they saw another group approaching from the east. While they were still some distance away, Makikele noticed that some of them wore strange clothing, boots, and wide-brimmed hats.

When they were just a hundred yards away, Makikele was shocked when he saw the color of their skin.

"Who are these strange men with the flesh of an albino and facial hair that looks like the horns of an ox?" he asked.

"They are white men from the kingdom over the sea that is called Portugal," said Ndwambi, one of the queen sister's attendants, who had encountered white traders before and had a poor opinion of them.

"They look so ugly and uncouth," he continued. "They are haughty, and the guns they carry over their shoulders make them appear fearless, yet they are clumsy and encumbered by their clothing. They are in fact weak and fragile."

When the two groups met, one of the white men extended his hand toward the king's brother, Thavhane, who was leading the royal expedition north.

"What is the meaning of this gesture?" asked Makikele. "Why do they not show deference to noblemen by bowing and performing the *losha* greeting?"

"The white man is ignorant of the customs of Venda," said Ndwambi. "They are ignorant of your customs and those of the Shona from where they have just come. The outstretching of the hand is their way of offering friendship. By so doing, they are requesting that Prince Thavhane extend his hand as well, and that they should grasp their hands together and shake them."

"The Portuguese have very strange customs." Makikele laughed along with others in the royal entourage while they watched Thavhane slap and swing hands with the strange white-skinned traveler.

One of the white men removed a square piece of cotton cloth from inside his garment and wiped the sweat from his forehead; then he spoke in a strange language.

The Tsonga spokesman, who accompanied them, then translated: "The white man, who says his name is Ignatsio, gives his greetings to the Venda. He wishes to present the royal *ntona* with a gift."

The man named Ignatsio handed the king's brother a bead necklace. Thavhane grinned, snatched the gift, and placed it over his neck.

The Tsonga interpreter spoke again. This time he was not translating, and knew that the Portuguese would not understand his words. "The white men are troublesome, but necessary," he said. "They bring us beads and fine cloth, as well as the best guns."

Makikele had listened for long enough. He felt uncomfortable in the presence of the Portuguese. "Are these the white men who make slaves of our people, castrate our men, steal our women, and send our children to faraway places where they will never again learn about their families?"

"No," the Tsonga spokesman replied. "These are good men who just want to trade with us. It is true that such evil men do exist, but I have not met them."

"What is it like living on the coast and mixing with these people?" asked Makikele.

"The sea is like a lake which extends further than any eye can see and takes many days to cross. The Portuguese travel from their homeland on huge wooden boats they call *nau*. Instead of using oars, they use the wind to power these boats. They catch the wind with huge pieces of strong cloth they call *vela*. On their *nau*, they bring many goods to trade and sell. They have built large villages with houses made from stone, and they construct stone walls in the sea where they tie up their boats."

The Tsonga trader laughed as Makikele exclaimed, "Could this be possible?"

"Indeed it is possible," he replied, "and the Portuguese and Arabs have taught us that there are many kinds of people in the world, with strange customs and traditions. Many of the things they have taught us and provided for us are good, but some are bad. Through trade with the white man, we get things that we need to make us strong."

"I would like to visit these places," said Makikele, "to see the stone villages built by the white men and the great boats that come from far away across the vast lake you describe. One day I hope to travel to see these things for myself."

The following day, the royal party arrived at a cluster of villages located on the southern slopes of Dzata Hill and extending out into the Njalele Valley along which the northern trade route passed. The region was inhabited by a mixed group of Venda lineages, including a small group of Lemba potters and iron-workers. There were also herbalists, beer makers, and traders in skins and farm goods, as well as farmers and herders.

Inside the wooden and reed-walled gardens surrounding houses were numerous food storage facilities, including above-ground granary baskets and large clay pots. The region around Dzata Hill was a passageway along the southern Limpopo, a stopping off place for trading parties and travelers coming and going in every direction. Local people, it appeared to Makikele, maintained a profitable trade in food and many other items needed by travelers.

It took a day for the Ngome royal party to settle into various guest quarters in the village. On the second day, gifts were exchanged with their hosts, and arrangements made for them to be taken up the steep Dzata hillside the following morning. There they would visit the ancient royal enclosure on the mountain top to perform ancestral prayer libations.

Their hosts claimed distant kinship to them from the time of the dissolution of an original centralized Venda kingdom. This had taken place many generations previously, during the reign of Thohoyandou and following the death of his father, King Thovhele. The Venda believed that their ancestor Thohoyandou had magically disappeared, that he continued to roam the country, and that he would one day return to restore Dzata. The many Venda kingdoms, now separated and independent from one another, extending along the Limpopo and in the Venda Highlands, claimed descent from these earlier kings. All looked to Dzata as their sacred mountain.

Makikele was accommodated by a younger brother of his father's magician, Masalani. He and his extended family lived in a large village on a terraced hillside close to the main settlement. The village was enclosed by a wall of timbers and, judging by the number of houses it contained, was home to many.

Makikele extended greetings and presented gifts to his hosts before settling into the guesthouse made available to him. He felt at home in this working settlement of herbalists and healing practitioners, which was similar to those of Masalani and Pulani. He was immediately comfortable with the familiar trappings of the healing business providing the village's livelihood.

Accompanied by Senganga, Masalani's son, he set about exploring the local area to learn as much as he could. Makikele observed local iron smelting and forging worksites, noting that the structure of the furnaces differed from those found at Lolwe, Phetole, and most other smelting locations in Phalaborwa.

In a small clearing in the trees close to a neighboring village, he saw a large number of pots piled together under a mound of ashes. He watched as several Lemba women removed the different-sized pots from the still smoldering remains of a wood fire, and brushed them off to cool. The clay pots had been fired the previous night. Examining them, he saw they were almost identical in shape and decoration to those made in villages near the Selati River clay deposits in Phalaborwa.

Seeing that Makikele was interested, Senganga explained, "The Lemba people make most of our pots as well as doing iron smelting. Their workmanship is very good and preferred. They bring clay from the Limpopo River. Only certain places have the right quality clay needed for such work."

"How do they make the pots?"

"Come, I'll show you." Senganga led Makikele further into the village where a woman sat inside a windbreak preparing river clay for molding into pots.

"*Trobela*, Mmammola! We have come to watch you work."

"Welcome, Senganga," the woman responded with a smile.

"Don't let us interrupt you. Prince Malatji, our visitor, wishes to see you build a pot from clay."

"Please, do watch," she cheerfully welcomed them and gestured for them to approach.

"First of all," Senganga explained as they stood outside the low, mudded reed fence observing her work, "she breaks the dry clay into small pieces using a stone grinding slab and a stone hammer. She then works water into the clay using her hand. When the clay is softened, she pounds it once again on the grinding block. This time she uses a wooden rolling stick to remove large impurities. As she flattens and rolls the clay with her hands, she detects and removes smaller stones."

Pleased to have an admiring audience for her otherwise quiet routine, Mmammola worked intensely, steadily, and with quick precision to create a pot for her visitors, molding it with her hands from a single lump of the moist clay. When the pot was fully shaped, she carefully smoothed the surface, first using her hands to test for uniform thickness, then using a mussel shell to scrape the inner and outer surfaces. This action produced a noticeable scratching sound whenever the shell contacted pebbles still in the clay. She also used the shell as a knife to remove the rough clay rim. Splashing the inside and outside surfaces with water and rubbing them with her hand, she worked the freshly cut rim into a smooth lip using her thumbs.

"You will notice that designs are incised on the pot rim while the clay is still wet," said Senganga. "She does this with a small pointed metal tool attached to a piece of leather, which she wears as a pendant around her neck. The finished pot is then placed inside her cool thatch-roofed house so it can slowly dry without cracking and be free from dust, which could spoil its surface. The drying process takes about a week. The pot is then ready to be fired.

"When hardened by the fire, additional decoration can be added. She can apply red pigment, imported from Sekgopo in your father's domain, or local graphite. She will rub them onto the surface, which can then be polished. Mostly it's the women who make pots."

They thanked Mmammola, gave her a gift of tobacco snuff, and left to continue their tour.

As roosters crowed in the many farmyards at sunrise on the third day following their arrival, the party from Ngome assembled at the Dzata Hill caretaker's village and began their ascent to the abandoned Venda capital.

It was a gradual climb, the party following a narrow over-grown trail single file, led by the hill's caretaker and several of his children. The three elderly royal women with their attendants, an archer and a spearman, were in the rear. Some members of the party balanced pots of freshly-brewed beer on their heads; others carried baskets of millet, tobacco, and sweet-smelling dagga leaves. All these things would be employed ritually to please the ghostly occupants on the hill summit.

Hidden but also treading the rocky pathway was Sabasa, the Ba-Laudzi assassin, who had followed Makikele's party from Ngome. He shadowed them at a distance, never allowing himself to be seen.

Unlike Sealene and Phalaborwa's many large hillside vil-lages, Dzata had no dramatic granite outcropping crowning its upper level. Instead, the upper reaches were flat, extending out a great distance, its surface interspersed with low-lying rocky formations and the stone rubble of fallen walls and house ruins. At a distance to the northeast, the sacred hill was dwarfed by a much larger and steeply inclined mountain. But Dzata was a massive hill, and Makikele speculated it had been chosen by the ancients as a more defensible royal domicile.

The passageway upward was strewn with loose, flat stones similar to those incorporated into terraced garden retaining walls, houses, and livestock pens of residents on its lower levels.

When they reached higher ground the path became steeper, and at several turns they passed carefully built rock cairns. The workmanship of these structures was quite refined, using a layering technique made easy by abundant flat, smooth stones carefully stacked horizontally by the masons. Makikele presumed these to be markers built to guide visitors.

Approaching the summit of Dzata Hill, they passed through a large opening between tall, thick stone walls. These were more massive than those Makikele had observed at Ngome's royal enclosure, although the workmanship bore a resemblance. Entering the walled summit, they were confronted by tall rock battlements which, despite the thick growth of trees, cacti, and scrub bush, could be seen throughout the length and breadth of the extensive abandoned occupation site. Within this massive battlement, a honeycomb of walled passageways and interlocking terraced enclosures led in every direction. Ruined house structures, now fallen to the ground, were visible everywhere. This had been the capital and royal residence of Venda rulers, dating to a time before Thohoyandou.

Makikele was struck by a sense of great antiquity, and he speculated that these now-quiet precincts had once also hosted his Malatji ancestors before they left for Phalaborwa.

As mid-morning sun illuminated the extensive ruins, the color of the stone caught Makikele's eye like nothing he had seen before in his travels. In the exposed cross veins was a dark blue hue, creating the illusion of stripes where the flat horizontally layered masonry followed the contours of the wall. In the days when it was occupied, Dzata must have been a wonder to behold, something visitors could not forget. Even in its present abandoned and overgrown state, the impact of this distinct coloring was astonishing.

While the royal party was taken through the labyrinth of overgrown rubble to the burial grounds to prepare their intercessions, Makikele remained near the entrance with others of the group, including servants and bodyguards, who would not participate in the ceremony.

Exploring parts of the rubble walls and derelict buildings, his eye caught the glint of a blue bead and several pieces of broken pottery in a section of disturbed subsoil where an animal had been digging. The six-sided glass ornament and etched clay fragments resembled those found in his homeland. Probing further with his walking stick, he uncovered a fragment of rusted iron, the end point of a broken hoe. It too resembled those made by Phalaborwa forges. While he continued probing along passageways, he found other artifacts. Placing these objects in a leather pouch for later use, he reflected that these ancient Venda and his Malatji lineage were indeed of one stock.

While still exploring, he was summoned by the royal women and obediently followed an attendant, who led him into a central part of the ruins.

Here he observed the three crones crouched together in a clearing bordered by clusters of fallen rocks. They were surrounded by their fellow worshipers. The senior women were performing prayers and libations, the oldest of them calling out the names of ancestors, both male and female, in praises.

They had removed their cotton outer clothing and sat naked except for their beaded leather aprons, multiple strings of neck beads, and bangles on their wrists and ankles. The men had also removed their clothing.

Makikele stayed in the shadows and watched as the three old women took turns puffing on a pipe. They appeared to be in a semi-trance, which he guessed was induced by the sweet-smelling dagga smoke reaching his nostrils. The plant had been grown in the Swazi and Pedi highlands since ancient times and traded in Phalaborwa. It was also abundant in the Venda highlands and selectively used, he had learned, as one ingredient in a number of treatments in Pulani's pharmacy.

His suspicions were confirmed when the three women rose to their feet, and started swaying together to the soft rhythms of a small drum and a high-pitched flute. Makikele knew that the ostrich feathers attached to the flute were medicated with powerful magic and the sound it made carried to distant places far beyond their Dzata sanctuary.

The pace of the chant and the dance quickened and continued to accelerate for several minutes, the old women oblivious to those observing their ritual. Suddenly, as Makikele stepped out from the shadows toward their ritual space, the music stopped and the women turned to gaze in his direction. The sun reflected off the copper and red beads that decorated the leather armband Makikele wore on his left arm, the armband his father had given him before he left Phalaborwa, to provide him protection and good fortune.

"Bring him here," called the most ancient of the three.

"We present this man to you," she called out in a frail chant to the spirit world, echoed by the other celebrants of the ritual. "He comes from the south to learn from us. His people departed from Venda long ago, but are part of us. He has come back to you, his ancestral spirits. Make him strong and brave."

While the group affirmed the chant of the wizened old princess, a younger member of the party yelled out and pointed toward a far wall partially hidden by trees. All eyes turned and stared in that direction. An animal briefly emerged from the underbrush, its spotted fur unmistakable as it traversed an exposed section of wall. Glancing over muscular hunched shoulders and looking in their direction, the animal bared its fangs, lifted its tail in a salute, and then quickly vanished.

"*Nkwe*, the spirit leopard," they all whispered simultaneously, then froze in silence, staring at the now-empty precipice framed by the larger distant hill. All paid attention as a sudden breeze rustled leaves and grass, and then vanished into silence. Everyone knew an ancestral spirit had appeared, embodied in the form of a leopard.

Makikele recalled the leopard he and his fellow initiates had seen in the forest near his *Koma* lodge and wondered if these two apparitions were connected. He was not the only member of the party who had noticed the animal had saluted him.

There was much chatter and speculation among the servants and other attendants as the small group of pilgrims excitedly descended Dzata Hill into the surrounding Njalele valley.

"Perhaps it was Thobela, or Dzembanyaka, ancient ones who crossed the Limpopo to Dzata," said one.

Leopard spirit at Dzata Hill

"Or Thiendelu, from whom all the royal families of Venda and those of Phalaborwa and Lobedu are descended," said another.

As the group turned a bend leading down from the hill they were confronted by a horrific scene. A man lay dead beside the trail. The foliage adjacent to the path was covered with blood, and there was a large ghastly hole in the lower torso of the fallen man where his entrails and large organs had been torn out.

While they were still considering the circumstances of this man's demise, they heard the sound of a large animal charging through the undergrowth. For a moment the group stood motionless in fear. Then the spearmen and archer accompanying them positioned themselves to guard for animal attack.

"The leopard," one attendant whispered.

Near the mutilated and partially eaten body lay a bow and quiver of arrows.

"The bow has the mark of Phalaborwa," said another in the party. "What can this mean?"

The first to reach the body picked up one of the arrows and examined the tip.

"Poison," he said.

The oldest of the three royal women approached the scene of carnage, studied the opened eyes and mouth of the savaged corpse, and announced, "This man meant to kill Prince Makikele, but the leopard saved the prince from harm by killing the would-be assassin. Makikele truly is a man possessing powerful magic."

The old women and the shamans knew a great blessing had come to Makikele on Dzata Hill. The spirit leopard apparition and the would be murder's mutilated corps confirmed it. Word of this wonder, and of the power of Dzata, passed among villagers along the return route and then throughout Ngome, and, in a short time, reached distant Kgopolwe.

CHAPTER SIXTEEN

Phalaborwa Redux

A few days after Makikele returned to Pulani's compound, he received a surprise visitor. His mother's brother, Phatladi, having joined a trade caravan on its way from Phalaborwa to Venda, had arrived unexpectedly, bringing news from Phalaborwa.

It had been a long journey for the aging man. The dry season had begun, and his ten-day trip by foot through grasslands and scrub bush had been hot and dusty. While such a journey could be made at a steady pace in six days, the long line of porters, merchants, and women with children had stopped at a number of larger villages along the way to barter and exchange goods and news, which delayed their arrival. However, it had been an opportunity for Phatladi to talk with old acquaintances and relatives who lived in villages along the way.

As the caravan wound its way through the northern lowland bush and began to ascend into hillier terrain leading to the Venda highlands, Phatladi had reviewed in his mind the details and events leading to his being delegated to bring the young prince home to Phalaborwa.

The reunion with his nephew was a happy one. After going through the formalities of greeting one another and sharing an early morning meal together, they sat under the eaves of Makikele's house in the herbalist Pulani's village.

"Uncle, how good to see you," said Makikele. "Is everyone at Kgopolwe and Sekgopo well? Although traders and travelers regularly bring news from Phalaborwa, I have not talked with a close family member since my departure more than two years ago. But your presence does not bode well. What news do you bring, Uncle?"

Phatladi enjoyed the cool moist air, but had a blanket draped over his shoulders for warmth. A shade tree cast a cool shadow over the reed privacy fence that separated them from the busy daily activities of the rest of the village and masked the surrounding domestic noise.

"Listen, my nephew," said Phatladi, "I have some disturbing news. Your father summoned me to Kgopolwe, where I consulted with him and your mother, Mokadi. He entrusted me to bring you this news." He spoke quietly, methodically, as he began to explain the series of recent events at Kgopolwe. "Mokgoropong, your half-brother, is dead."

"I have already heard this news, uncle. It reached me from passing traders and by way of a messenger sent by my grandmother to the royal family here in Ngome." He spoke in a solemn tone, while studying his uncle's face for signs of grief, but saw none. "Tell me, Uncle, how did this sad event come about?"

"Mokgoropong challenged the king's leadership."

There was a stunned silence as Makikele took in the implications of this news.

"As you know, your father was already in declining health when he sent you to Venda. He has continued to weaken, and medicines do not bring back his vigor. Many believe his blood is bad and that he will never recover."

The words of his uncle made Makikele angry. He wondered who had bewitched his father and evaded the detection of royal divination to bring the king into so bad a decline.

"After you left," his uncle continued, "your father's health deteriorated to such an extent that he was no longer presiding at ceremonial events and religious rites, nor giving audiences to important visitors. He was no longer even making rulings on the arbitrations that take up so much time at the capital. The senior members of the council, those of us who have the king's ear, met and made the decision that your brother Ramatladi should be the one to take over some of the king's duties. He seemed the best one to do these things. After all, he has for a long time been the king's representative, hearing daily court cases, receiving petitioners coming to the royal enclosure, determining which among them deserved higher consultation and decision-making, and those the king alone could pronounce on."

Phatladi reached over and touched his nephew's knee for emphasis. "But Ramatladi's growing power and influence has upset many. The king's household is now isolated and separated from important decision-making. Ramatladi has even taken control of some of the king's regalia, including *Tlanka*, the smallest and most sacred drum. Setakgale, his mother, has taken charge of the rain medicines, keeping them in her house. A number of her male relatives now live near her compound. They are guarding her. They are also influencing the king's thinking. Some suspect they have brought sorcery from Sekgopo and from the Tsonga, brought it into the king's household. Many whisper that this evil magic escapes detection, that court diviners cannot overcome its impact on the king or find the cause.

"This is why Mokgoropong, as an elder Malatji prince, openly challenged Ramatladi. He did this with the blessing of many in the royal family and among the noble lineages and powerful families. But the king himself was displeased with this confrontation, not wishing his older son to gain tacit control of power should he succeed in displacing Ramatladi."

While the elderly man spoke, his eyes wandered around the enclosure, noticing the many items relating to Makikele's life as an herbalist. He then studied the copper crescent suspended from Makikele's neck and resting on his muscular upper chest. It looked as new and bright as the day his father had presented it to him, the day when Makikele returned from the initiation lodge leading his newly formed regiment. Phatladi had been present at the secret circumcision camp and had participated in the concluding trials and questioning of the newly initiated.

Phatladi's eyes moved from the finely forged copper ornament to his nephew's clear dark eyes. *He is very much the son of Meele Malatji*, he thought, as he continued to explain the troubles besetting the royal village at Kgopolwe.

"The king, your father, objected to Mokgoropong trying to usurp Ramatladi's position because he wishes you, Makikele, to one day rule."

Makikele broke the eye contact between them, and nodded, remaining silent in his thoughts.

"But, when Mokgoropong was found dead a short distance from his house at Kgopolwe, the king was very angry."

At the mention of his half-brother's death, Makikele interrupted his uncle to say, "Mokgoropong, son of Malatji of the porcupine, may your walk in death be a good one."

Makikele looked at his uncle sadly, grasped a handful of ashes from near the fire pit, and threw them across the ground to his right side. "He was a strong man, a brave man."

Although he had heard of the death months before from a group of travelers from Lobedu staying overnight near Pulani's village, he followed custom by expressing reverence for his dead sibling to his uncle. Making a clicking sound with his tongue followed by a deep sigh, he looked away from his uncle, and then nodded to him to continue his story.

"It was poison. Divination pointed to Ramatladi and his mother, Setakgale, as responsible. Men closest to the king confronted them angrily, but in secrecy. They were ordered to the small meeting yard adjoining Mokadi's house. This is where the king mostly lives now. Your mother and sister entered by way of a back door and listened. Ramatladi and Setakgale denounced these accusations against them. Setakgale spoke out with anger, asserting their innocence of any evildoing and insisting they would both submit to trial by poison to prove they were guiltless. Ramatladi then responded by accusing the family of Maphalakanye Malatji and your brother Paane, and others living with them at Nagome Hill, as culpable in the prince's death. They were ordered to be silent and to keep this accusation secret. Nothing came of the confrontation at the time. There was no trial by ordeal of poison."

Makikele had heard earlier from the Lobedu account that his mother had been insulted by Setakgale at the time of this confrontation in the presence of the king and his close council of relatives. He sensed that the enmity that was smoldering between the two women and that the competing branches of the Mathipa family these royal wives represented had become open and hostile.

Makikele knew that his next comment would add more weight to his uncle's conviction that the conflict was escalating.

"An attempt was also made on my life a few days ago, Uncle."

Phatladi rose to his feet and exclaimed angrily, "No, tell me this is not true, my nephew. How could this happen? I thought you were safe from harm here in Venda. Who tried to kill you? Why would someone do this?"

Makikele related the story of his trip to Dzata, concluding with the apparition of the leopard and the dead man found by the servants on the trail on their way down the hill.

"The man had a Phalaborwa bow, and a quiver of arrows tipped with poison," he said.

Phatladi remained silent for a few moments before pronouncing his conclusion. "Ramatladi! It was Ramatladi who arranged this. He must have recruited this man to kill you. Will he stop at nothing to gain the throne for himself?"

"Uncle, we have no proof that my brother was behind this."

"You are right, but this is too much of a coincidence after the death of Mokgoropong, also by poison. How did the man die?"

"It was the leopard that killed the assassin."

Phatladi was triumphant in his pronouncement. "The leopard appeared to you at *Koma*; the leopard appeared to you again on sacred Dzata Hill, home of your Malatji ancestors; and the leopard saved your life. These are signs. You will one day wear the leopard-skin regalia. The Copper Throne of Phalaborwa shall one day be yours."

There was a brief pause, as they both pondered this possibility, before Phatladi returned to the story of Mokgoropong.

"Mokgoropong was buried among the royal graves on Sealene Hill. The king then ordered all residents, royal and common, to shave off their hair in mourning. Following the mourning period, the dead man's two widows were distributed as wives. One went to Ramatladi, the other to your half-brother, Mabu, so he can raise a son for Mokgoropong by this woman."

Phatladi paused to assess his nephew's reaction to this information. Finding him quiet and deep in thought, apparently moved by the account of his brother's murder, the old man continued, "You should know that some of the king's advisors, mostly those in the immediate family, wanted you to inherit Mokgoropong's widows—both of them." He raised his voice to make a point of this. "But your mother counseled against this. You already have one wife, Lesibe, whom Mokadi highly favors. Your betrothal to my daughter, Mosale, as your future great wife is also sealed, and your mother and grandmother are planning other marriages to strengthen alliances."

Makikele was anxious for news about Lesibe's birthing, but he knew protocol required that he first inquire about Phatladi's daughter.

"How is my cousin Mosale, Uncle? It will soon be time for her to join me at Kgopolwe. If what you tell me is true, then I must begin a family and take my place in the king's council with other heads of royal households."

"My daughter will soon complete her *bjale* and, when you return to Phalaborwa, it will not be long before she is brought to Kgopolwe to join you to begin married life."

Makikele nodded his approval. "Do you have any news of Lesibe, uncle?"

"She has already born you a son. She will soon wean the child and return to Phalaborwa."

Makikele smiled. "This news gives me great joy. I look forward to her return from Phetole. Lesibe and Mosale will get along well together and give me many children."

The uncle realized he was losing focus in his discourse and returned to the specific topic of the dead prince's murder and its aftermath.

"When the period of mourning for Mokgoropong ended, the king surprised many in Phalaborwa by holding a new wedding feast to establish the status of your mother, Mokadi, as his principal wife. He commanded the extinguishing of all fires in every village, and had a new ceremonial fire drilled with sticks at your mother's hearth. The fresh embers were then taken out to rekindle all the headmen's hearths and village fires throughout Phalaborwa. The head of every extended family then contributed to the royal bridewealth. They were required to give animals or the equivalent value in ivory or metal goods, so that all lineages and groups were represented in the marriage transaction."

Makikele looked pleased at this tribal-wide tribute. "Did all the regions participate?"

"Indeed they did. Even Ramatladi's kinsmen were compelled to give something." The old man chuckled at this detail of his story. "Yuuuu!" He snapped the fingers of his right hand in his left palm making a clapping sound. "One must assume they were not pleased. And so my sister, Mokadi, is now great wife and is praised as 'keeper of the nation's fire' and as 'she for whom the nation's cattle are gathered.' By this ceremonial act, the king has validated the rank of your mother as his great wife, the mother elephant of Phalaborwa, the *Mmamatlou.*"

To avoid any reference to the possible imminent death of the king and Makikele's succession to his father, the old man merely said, "Your status has, as a result of these changes, also changed. That's why I am here, nephew. You must return with me to Phalaborwa."

Makikele looked away from his uncle and nodded to acknowledge what he had heard.

"I know, Uncle. I knew even before you arrived, and have already packed my things."

"Oh? How is this possible?"

"A few days ago, after I returned from Dzata, I had a dream. In my dream I heard the sweet soothing tones of a flute."

"A magic flute?"

The shamans and other keepers of magic lore in Phalaborwa, possessed many different kinds of magic, but one unique to them was the use of a magic flute to communicate with people in distant places, to announce a death, or to warn people during times of war. These flutes were ordinarily made from reed and bone, magically treated with ostrich feathers attached to the front tip of the flute so that, when the flute was played, air passed over the feathers in the direction of those being contacted.

"Yes; my mother contacted me using a magic flute. I did not hear her voice, but the message of the melody of the flute was unmistakable. It said, 'My son, there is trouble in Kgopolwe. Your father is not well, and your brothers squabble over the succession. You must return from Venda and be counted among your father's sons.'"

Phatladi did not seem surprised. "Many things are happening in Kgopolwe," he said. "With her new status as principal wife, your mother has also assumed the role of keeper of the king's magic, but her powers are limited because of the dissent in the royal family. Ramatladi still holds *Tlanka*, and Setakgale refuses to give up the rain medicines."

"Do not worry, Uncle. The song of the flute also told me that the medicines I have learned about here in Venda will be used to enhance those of my mother and the king. Together we will be a powerful force that Ramatladi and Setakgale and their supporters will not be able to stand against."

Makikele remained silent as his uncle continued speaking.

"These changes in the royal household did not please everyone. In particular, Ramatladi, his mother, and her family are worried. They fear the king will send them away from Kgopolwe."

Makikele briefly studied his uncle's face, and then averted his eyes once more. "Why should my brother be concerned? He has helped the king, and his people are respected."

"As you well know, they come from a different Mathipa branch than our people. They had been powerful when Mosholwane was king, and even before that, when Kgashane had ruled and they had insisted that your father, Meele, inherit the widow Setakgale when Mosholwane died. This was so that Meele might father a ghost son for Mosholwane by Setakgale. But she was of a more distant branch of the family, making her a junior sister to those in our Mathipa branch. Mokadi is senior to her in birth status, and now, as is our custom, in rank also.

"Those Mathipa that gave birth to Setakgale and Ramatladi have declined in wealth and influence over recent years. This is in part due to troubles in Pedi and Queen Modjadji's Lobedu territories, where they have trade links. But I think the king has removed his patronage from them, and the members of the king's council no longer listen to them. He prefers the counsel of the family of his wife, Mokadi, and those who are allied with them. Many of her family, including myself, have been generously treated by *Kgoshi* Meele. Many members of Mokadi's extended family are now appointed headmen of the larger wealthy trade villages. The king has also generously given livestock. And we, in turn, are generous to our followers. Because of this friendship, our voice now carries much weight.

"So you can see that Ramatladi's prestige in decision-making circles, unchallenged in earlier days, is being overshadowed by that of Mokadi's family. Her uncles, brothers, and nephews now speak loudest in the king's council. We now receive the lion's share of the king's generosity. We have become strong, whereas Ramatladi's people go without. I praise the king for his wisdom and decisions in these matters.

"In the matter of the marriage of your mother, it is not unheard of that a younger wife be shown favor by a king and her sons elevated in rank, having gained the trust of the father."

Phatladi was careful not to mention the king's death and succession, a forbidden topic that would offend Makikele.

"The king's decision in this matter is, however, resented by some of the old noble families and by some who guard the royal burials at Sealene and Modimolle Hills. They fear losing influence now that their own families have lost ground, and now that our family is favored. This is partly because of self-interest, but . . ." He paused for a moment to appraise the prince's interest. ". . .there are also those who worry about changes in the king's ritual life and those who now determine and participate in those sacred rites."

Makikele had for many years observed the priestly functions of his family at Kgopolwe and Sealene Hill, and at Modimolle Hill, the lower, rounder companion hill to towering Sealene where royal women were interred. He knew how vital these rituals were to the well-being of the land and all of Phalaborwa. And he knew that only those recognized as legitimate in the realm of the sacred could perform such ceremonies and cause them to have effect. Makikele considered the implications of Ramatladi's gradual usurpation of these sacred functions and listened to his uncle's careful analysis of Phalaborwa's political and religious controversy.

"It is essential that planting and harvest ceremonies should be done correctly by the right people, and the exact time when first plowing starts must be carefully determined by the king's shamans and diviners. There is great concern at Kgopolwe, and, may I say, in every village, about who holds the rain regalia and medicines. People are talking about the king, and there is dispute about Ramatladi's use of power. Setakgale is looked upon with suspicion. The rains came very late this year, and crops failed in some places. People must trade or eat roots.In the past, most of these rituals were a shared activity. Quite a few of the royal women from both Ramatladi's and Meele's households, and others, took part."

Makikele recalled his mother's active ritual life as wife of the king. He vividly remembered seeing her processing with his grandmother and the wives and aunts of the royal enclosure during the planting harvest, crossing the royal fields and ceremonially casting magically treated seed from flat winnowing baskets, so that all in the land could begin seeding their fields.

"This is all changing,"said Phatladi. "There is conflict about who should possess the medicines, under which roof the rain pot and medicines should be kept, and where the rain drum will be housed and cared for in drought. It is quite distressing."

"I agree, Uncle. This should not be so. It bodes ill for my father and the well-being of our people."

"Setakgale's house, which sits apart from the king's near Ramatladi's compound, holds the rain pot and the powerful drum, *Tlanka*. She will not put it with the larger ones, with *Boretsho*, *Botlolo*, and the others. Mokadi and the king's sister complain that *Tlanka* must be removed to the regalia house so it abides with the others in the king's compound. Some fear it will lose power if it is permanently removed from the king's ritual quarters.

"Setakgale keeps silent about the drum, but her family members guard it. It is said that the king will not allow the matter to be reviewed by the council of royal advisors. If they pronounce that it be taken away from Setakgale, there will be fighting. The situation is quite tense. At the planting rituals,

Queen Mokadi and the king's mother walked together with the king's aunts to throw out the first seed from winnowing baskets. Setakgale only attended at a distance, refusing to follow along with them. People watch the rainclouds and wonder if the disagreement will inhibit rainfall. Some whisper that Setakgale's hatred of Mokadi has led to witchcraft, and that both women consult with Tsonga witches from Sekgopo to protect themselves."

Makikele's guttural sounds of disapproval increased with each troubling detail his uncle related, until eventually he interrupted the discourse abruptly, asking, "Can the council not order that the rain magic be guarded by the king? And then, if need be, send members to take it?"

Seeing the prince's impatience, Phatladi softened his tone. "You must understand, my prince, that many fear these arguments will disturb the sleep of the dead at Sealene, and even anger the royal women buried at Modimolle. Some even say that *Kgoshi* Mosholwane may be disturbed if Ramatladi is dishonored. Some say the king fears Mosholwane's ghost."

"Why should they think that?" Makikele shook his head, impatient at the idea that his father might be at odds with recently dead royals. "Mosholwane was properly buried, and is well respected and carefully remembered in our prayers and fed with libations. Many animals have been killed for him, and his name is called out upon the hill."

"What you say is true, my prince." Phatladi nodded and spoke in a voice intended to soothe his nephew. "However, the queen mother Ntlabede's presence at the first seed rite this year was commented on by some." He watched his nephew's eyes lift and stare while he continued. "It is said she receives messengers when groups cross the Lepelle River and approach Kgopolwe.

They say she does this even though the king relies only on his own spokesmen to make contact and give trade permission. He does not want any Swazi or other foreigners near the capital, or to see the mines at Lolwe. He forbids this."

Makikele rose from the log stool where he had sat opposite his uncle and stood. In a shocking breach of etiquette he pointed at the old man and shouted, "It is Ramatladi and Setakgale who speak out against my grandmother. This must be stopped. My *gogo* has protected the family and the tribe faithfully. She loves Phalaborwa. No one must doubt her. There are many foreign queens asleep at Modimolle Hill, from here in Venda, from Lobedu, and from across the Lepelle. Many."

His voice softened as he thought of his *gogo* and how she had pampered him as a boy, the special foods saved for his visits, the animated storytelling during cold nights by the fire in her house, or in the cooking hut. He smiled as he remembered how he would bring her guinea hens to cook, shot with bow and arrow while herding with other boys. Mostly he recalled her dignity when appearing before councils and while performing official duties.

"What you say is correct, kind nephew." Phatladi chose a familiar term to calm his young kinsman, who remained standing over him, his right hand fingering his copper neck plate, resplendent in the morning sun against the youthful naked chest.

Makikele's courtyard, on the outskirts of Pulani's village, received the early morning sun, and the two men had removed their shoulder blankets as the compound warmed.

"Why do they attack Queen Mother Ntlabidi?" Makikele asked, his voice softening out of respect for his elder.

Phatladi carefully selected the words for his answer, not wishing to anger his nephew, but needing to be truthful about sympathies current at his father's home.

"This may bring bad fortune to the land. The rains were late this year in Phalaborwa, especially in the western farm villages. They worry about hunger and the need to trade for food in Pedi and Lobedu. Some see this as a bad sign that changes may cause harm, might disrupt the spiritual harmony enjoyed under the protection of the ancestors at Sealene. A breach in succession might be offensive to those intermediaries with the powerful forces enabling Phalaborwa to prosper."

As the morning progressed, Phatladi explained to his nephew that Ramatladi retained for the present a position of power at Kgopolwe but that Mokadi had displaced his brother's mother, Setakgale, as arbiter of royal rituals, those which were personified by the king. In addition, the king's senior sister and his several surviving aunts, powerful arbiters of royal ritual, also favored Mokadi and her son over the claims of others. He assured his nephew that his return to Phalaborwa would help resolve the dissent dividing the country.

The day following their discussion, Phatladi met with the Venda king's younger brother, a chief councilor and spokesman for the local ruler, and with the queen mother. Presenting gifts from Meele to Makikele's host royal family, Phatladi requested permission to take the much-admired prince back to his home in Phalaborwa. Explaining also the complicated succession issues, he requested the Venda leader's endorsement of Makikele's right to rule when the time came for him to assert his claim.

The queen mother was firm in her response. "Please assure *Kgoshi* Meele that a marriage tie between our two families will be seen with favor, as is also the succession claim of Prince Makikele."

Shortly afterward, she appointed a trusted servant to be her *motseta*, her go-between, to discuss marriage with Phalaborwa's aged queen mother and Queen Mokadi.

Following several weeks of farewell events, meetings among friends at Pulani's village, and in the royal enclosure, the much-respected young Malatji prince, now widely spoken about as a formidable medicine man, one infused with a sorcerer's spirit and believed by many to have learned powerful secrets to make rain and war magic, left Venda for his home in Phalaborwa.

He and his uncle joined a trade group from Shona country which was on its way to the coast. A detachment of young Venda warriors and porters and several retainers accompanied them to Ngome's border. It was a happy return trip home for Makikele in the company of Phatladi, his favorite *malome*.

CHAPTER SEVENTEEN

Cannibals

Makikele's return to Kgopolwe was received with much feast-ing and celebration. His wife, Lesibe, had also recently returned to Kgopolwe with their two-year-old son and was waiting for him in the house of his mother, Mokadi. Their reunion was one of great joy and pride for Makikele. He had departed for Venda as a newly-married man, a strong warrior, but otherwise uninitiated in the role of leadership. He returned as a mature man and a father, ready to be a strong leader and a powerful unifying force in Phalaborwa.

Lesibe was accompanied by her younger sister, Seakati, who had recently completed her *bjale* and was betrothed to Makikele's brother, Masetla. She had come to Kgopolwe, just as Lesibe had done three years earlier, to stay in her future mother-in-law's house to do chores that would demonstrate that she would be a diligent and submissive wife for Masetla. Later, when formal bridewealth negotiations and nuptial ritu-als had been completed, she would join Lesibe as a royal wife, where they would live together as co-wives and co-mothers to the offspring of the royal family.

Makikele's reputation as a sorcerer and witchdoctor, trained in the magic of northern rainmaking and warfare, had preceded him to his homeland. Travelers from Venda had regularly discussed his prowess and his high regard in Venda royal circles, and stories of the prince's exploits in Venda had reached all ears in the kingdom.

Many of the noble families who traced their ancestry to northern origins, as did the ruling Malatji, marveled about the story of his journey to the sacred hill, Dzata, and the part he played in the sacrifice to royal ancestors. Some heard these stories and associated them with legends of the ruling family's founding and migration from the north. Makikele personified the tie between Phalaborwa and its ancient origins.

His grandmother, the now-ancient queen mother Ntlabede, and his mother, Mokadi, together with the medicine man, Masalani, had woven this image of the young prince which had taken hold around the men's meeting fires and women's kitchen hearths and beer pots. Occult mysteries of Venda magic were intertwined with stories of the prince's death and rebirth in Ngome's sacred lake, and of the secrets transmitted to him by an eternal serpent spirit. These and other feats attributed to his person were now everyday knowledge, and many hoped that he would return to revitalize and strengthen ancestral rites at Sealene Hill. It was thought that the ancestral spirits—those determining the success of hunting, metalworking, farming, livestock increase, and the population's health and prosperity—would approve.

He was also widely reputed to have supernormal powers derived from the sacred waters of Venda and to possess knowledge of powerful forces that would keep his people safe and strong.

Before long, within the rules of protocol for a young man, he was accorded a voice in discussions with leaders from the many Phalaborwa regional centers and with delegations from other kingdoms.

He soon demonstrated a superior knowledge of politics and diplomacy. This was derived from familiarity with Venda language and ritual life, from growing ties with his Tsonga-connected family at their eastern Sekgopo Hill stronghold, and also with the Lobedu, where his mother had once lived. Her family maintained trading links as well as cattle interests with the Lobedu, not just as a result of the substantial marriage goods which transferred at the time she married, but dating back much earlier to older marriages with her family and lineage.

Those meeting Makikele spoke of a charisma, of a power in his words and bearing that commanded respect and even awe. It was said that he had an affinity with and knowledge of the ancients exceeding that of his elders, and that he had even spoken with the powerful spirits resting among the ruins at Dzata Mountain.

Makikele's father also recognized and valued these qualities in his son. *Kgoshi* Meele observed with satisfaction how Makikele's circumcision brothers rallied behind him and sought his presence and counsel. Following his son's return from Venda, Meele also noted how he soon began to overshadow Ramatladi and most of his brothers. Within months of his arrival, he became a key liaison between the king and Phalaborwa's elders and leaders, who knew that the changing times required strong leadership to keep Meele's hard-won realm strong and united. Increasingly they saw this quality in Makikele, and they discussed him as one promising candidate to succeed the king should he die.

The fact that Ramatladi remained a major arbiter of royal decision-making was a cause for concern in many quarters.

While steeped in formal Phalaborwa traditions and accorded the prerogatives of a prince candidate for the throne, Ramatladi was not regarded by many as a strong leader like Meele. Many did not see him as capable of galvanizing the many segments of Phalaborwa's dispersed and diverse population to face challenges from outside enemies, or able to control the forces of nature.

Makikele's status was further strengthened by the arrival of his second wife, Mosale, this one with strong *malome* ties as the daughter of his mother's brother, Phatladi Mathipa. It was from this wife of higher status that a potential royal heir might later be born.

Shortly after Makikele's second marriage, a great sorrow began to darken the land. A drought ruined the always-fragile millet and maize crops and reduced their supplies of other arable food sources. The resulting famine, called *Tlala ya makgekgetwane*, which means "the hunger when people ate lizards and roots," brought suffering and illness to all the villages. This necessitated an increase in hunting and gathering in the bush, and trade delegations were sent for food to neighboring kingdoms. Food was imported from Venda to the north, and east among the Tsonga tribes, but most of it came from Modjadji's kingdom on the western border, which continued to have abundant rain and a surplus of food. Arrangements to trade for food in times of drought were long-standing and well-established with the Lobedu rain queen.

As conditions grew worse and village prayers and sacrifices to local ancestral spirits brought no relief, all looked to the royal family and to the powerful burial ground at Sealene Hill to bring succor to those suffering.

When royal rain making ceremonies and repeated prayers on the holy mount produced no results, people feared that Ramatladi and his mother, who controlled the king's rainmaking medicines, were ineffective and that the nature of his rise to power while the king yet lived had displeased and angered the ancestors. There were even whispers that *Kgoshi* Meele had been bewitched by Setakgale and her son and that this was the cause of drought. Conflict in Meele's capital between factions within the royal family was widely discussed.

As this feuding intensified, Masalani, the king's magician and rainmaker, summoned by Meele to return to Phalaborwa soon after Makikele's arrival, suddenly fell sick and died. Although he was an old man, witchcraft was rumored as the cause of his death. Many in Phalaborwa feared that the king was also vulnerable to evil forces conjured by his enemies.

In the midst of this unsettling atmosphere, the land was then subjected to a new evil. Small groups of refugees from an equally devastating famine in nearby Pedi lands began crossing the Lepelle River into Phalaborwa. Hiding in the dense bushland, these wandering groups began abducting isolated individuals, taking them to their campsites deep in the bush, and eating them.

Details of cannibalism were first reported to the headman of Nagome Hill. A hunting party of six men had smelled roasting meat while following a game trail leading to the Lepelle River. Keeping in the shadows of the trees, they approached the site of the fire, where they heard Pedi language being spoken and the sounds of a woman groaning. Through the thick cover of bush, they could see that the woman's right leg was tied to a tree trunk close to the ground, and her right arm was attached to a rope suspended from an overhead branch. They could also see that she was pregnant. Hanging from the same tree was the limp body of a badly injured man. When the six men moved closer, they saw that this motionless form also hung by a rope from the tree. The poor man was missing both left leg and arm, that side of his body caked with dried blood at the points were the amputations had been made.

They watched with horror as two of the Pedi approached the wretched, bloodied form and began chopping at his right thigh with knives and the blade of a spear. The badly mutilated victim of their butchery regained consciousness with the renewed attack and screamed out, jerking his remaining leg in a feeble effort to resist the assault. His attackers quickly severed the leg and carried it to the cooking fire. While they discussed their grizzly accomplishment, one of them laughed and mimicked the dying man's pathetic cry. The others, amused by his joking, joined in the laughter, one slapping his thighs with pleasure while jeering at the bloody carcass.

The captive woman began to scream, pleading to be set free. The hidden observers knew from her speech that she was a local woman, and they were spurred on to do something to help her before they were detected and attacked by the distracted enemy. One of them motioned to the others to prepare their bows. At his signal, they fired on the eight Pedi cannibals with hunting arrows released with full force. Six of the Pedi were killed outright. The remaining two attempted to run away into the bush, but they too were executed with a second release of arrows, their bodies speared and left for scavengers to devour at nightfall.

The hunters cut the woman and the dying man loose from the tree. The woman fell at the feet of her liberators and cried hysterically as she attempted to tell her story. The poor man collapsed in a heap and did not move. They applied a few drops of water to his parched lips, but he died in their arms.

The woman sobbed as she told them what had happened. "He is my husband," she said. "We are from a Pilusa family living in a small village not far from the river. We left the village late yesterday evening to search for three stray goats. We were still close to home when the Pedi attacked us. My husband tried to fight them off, but there were too many of them. They took us to their campsite, where they attacked my husband again and tied him to the tree. They . . ." She burst into tears again before resuming her story, interspersed with sobs of grief. "They cut off his arm. Later they cut off his leg. We begged the Pedi to release us, but they took no notice. They left him to cry out in pain until he lost consciousness."

She then wept uncontrollably for several seconds before finding the strength to continue her story. "You can imagine how horrified I was when I watched them roast my husband's leg on their fire. I begged them to stop, but they beat me and took away my clothing and ornaments. One of them threw a rock at me and told me to shut up. It hit me in the thigh; you can see the wound." She pointed to a lesion on her left leg and began to sob loudly again.

"They saw that I am heavily pregnant and were afraid they would poison their blood by having more intimate contact with me, otherwise I would have been further harmed. Instead they left me to hang all night. During the night, my husband's groaning stopped and he became very quiet. I thought he had died. Then a jackal, attracted by the blood, ran out from the bush and attacked the stump of his leg. He screamed. I was afraid it would eat me as well, and I began screaming too, until the Pedi threw fire and frightened the animal away. Still I feared it would return, or some other animal would come out of the bush and attack me. I believe my mother's spirit protected me from them. I was afraid I would attract more animals, so I kept quiet. The Pedi intended to kill me and then eat me later, after my husband had rotted and was thrown to the hyenas and other scavengers or left for vultures."

The hunters, carrying the remains of the dead and mutilated man, escorted the woman back to her village, where she was reunited with her family. Some villagers looked in horror at their desecrated kinsman's body; others wailed and screamed, their worst fears for the couple having proved even more horrifying than they had imagined. With much mourning and crying, the man was buried shortly afterwards.

Over the course of the next few months, more and more stories of cannibalism reached the ears of the king. A fear of these *Bakema*, the human-eaters, spread to every village. Foreign visitors, especially those from the Pedi regions, were treated with distrust and threatened when arriving at Phalaborwa village gates.

This first report of cannibalism was followed by other incidents. Armed village search parties, looking for missing persons, found deserted *Bakema* camp sites with human bones and remains. It became clear that these were not isolated cases, and numerous *Bakema* had entered Meele's domain. Phalaborwa, weakened by famine and hunger, was now also beset by an invasion of cannibals. Word of the horrific remains of cannibalism, and the names of those found killed or missing, circulated everywhere. Fear grew, and all became vigilant and full of trepidation. A crisis was unfolding that required a united response.

Kgoshi Meele called a nationwide meeting. Attended by his nearest kinsmen from the capital and *ntona* and spokesmen from the Pedi border villages, he listened to accounts of the *Bakema*. Ramatladi, as court spokesman, led the questioning.

Makikele sat in on the meeting, listening and observing. A number of his age group from royal and noble lineages also attended. They gravitated toward Makikele and his growing following at court. Many were now established leaders in their home villages. Others, in the case of those from Nagome, Sekgopo, and some of the southern centers, belonged to resettled families and segments of lineages, shifted by the king following the recent succession feud that had driven Paane and his supporters into exile. They had been moved by the king to ensure loyalty in the once-rebellious villages. Many of these transplanted men and their families knew Makikele from the great initiation *Koma* he had attended. Many had hunted and feasted with him during royal visits.

Ramatladi was the first to speak. "Reports have reached Kgopolwe of a clear pattern of invasion along the several Lepelle River ford areas. From these points, the *Bakema* menace appears to be spreading out into the southern hunting regions where there are smaller isolated villages, mostly farm settlements and livestock and hunting camps. The larger population centers appear to remain unmolested, suggesting that the threat consists of small unconnected groups. Some link the *Bakema* with the Swazi or Zulu, who are known to have invaded and now occupy much of Pedi, but the weapons and personal items taken from those *Bakema* killed indicate they are from Pedi itself."

"They are people like us," exclaimed Mashale Selepe, the headman of a small farming and cattle-holding village located along the Lepelle River along one of the trade routes. "This is the way many Swazi traders travel to come here, but these are not Swazi." His words were affirmed with a general sound of approval. "They come here because the Zulu have destroyed many villages and crops and taken all their livestock. Even now, they take the women of the Pedi, the Shai, the Kgatla, and the others. The men have nowhere to go. Some join the Zulu regiments when they are defeated, but some try to run away. Where can they hide from the Zulu? They come here to Phalaborwa."

Prince Ramatladi acknowledged the headman's testimony and waited for silence as the account continued to be discussed by many. Several large beer pots had been positioned in the meeting place, and women from surrounding households brought warm beer to replenish the dwindling volume while the men drank and discussed.

Finally, sensing that the king was impatient to hear more testimony, Ramatladi held both hands up and spoke above the uproar. "Pishani Mathipa, headman of Pjeni village, please step forward and add your observations to the discussion."

A younger half-brother of Ramatladi's mother, the speaker had been appointed *ntona* of Pjeni, a prosperous fortified hill settlement where iron was forged and sold. He had been close to the king for many years and had provided a wife to his nephew, resulting in a close tie with the king as father-in-law to the prince.

"All of the people in my village and the surrounding smaller places are frightened by these *Bakema*. Women and children now stay close to the village palisades, and men do not leave the village without their weapons."

On hearing these words, one of the serving women made a loud sound expressing her disgust and horror at what she was hearing. This added to the gravity of Pishani's story.

"We killed two *Bakema*,"he said in a threatening tone, suggesting revenge. "They were camping south of our settlement. They had built a shelter in a cluster of rocks hidden deep within the bush. We took one of them captive, but he was wounded and died at our place. He was just a boy."

Pishani threw a number of items onto the ground, spears, knives, iron objects, and a distinctive Pedi-style beaded neck ring. He picked up the circular beaded ornament and held it high so all could observe it, and then he continued, "These were their possessions, taken after we had killed them. They are all Pedi objects."

The men nodded at this evidence. "Some of those items were traded to them from Phalaborwa," one man said. "That smaller pointed spear blade, used for hunting, is popular in Pedi and sometimes imported by them from our local forges."

"I agree," said Pishani before he continued with his story. "The boy told us they had become separated from a larger group that had run away when King Sekwati's cattle were taken by the Zulu. He said that all the people were starving in Sekwati's place. The boy said they had killed and eaten people along the river before and after they crossed."

There was silence when he explained what the witness had told him. "We found bones in their fire. Several of our people are missing, but we do not know who was eaten. The missing may all have been killed, since there are many *Bakema*, but we only killed this one group. The boy could not identify our people among the remains of those killed and he died before he could tell us more. He was not circumcised, but was mature enough for initiation. No one in our village could identify these *Bakema* or had any idea who the boy was."

Many other leaders from the afflicted region shared similar stories of fear and insecurity, and of abducted and missing people.

Ramatladi brought the meeting to a close with the following words: "The king has asked that the council assess the state of these developments and decide how to address the crisis. *Kgoshi* Meele and his close advisors will then approve a course of action."

After much deliberation and drink from replenished beer pots, which helped curb hunger until meat and other foods were prepared, Ramatladi appointed spokesmen on behalf of the king to recommend action.

While the council ate that evening with the king, various groups met to discuss the *Bakema* threat.

In the morning, when additional fires had been lit in the king's cattle enclosure, the men gathered for their final deliberation.

Pishani Mathipa gravely addressed the king and gathered leaders, speaking with the authority of years of service to the king and to Ramatladi. "I address the council as one leader whose village has been affected by the *Bakema* marauders. My counsel comes from discussions we have had throughout the night. Many of those who have participated in the talks are from the affected villages, the villages from which people have been stolen and killed by these cannibals and eaten. We recommend establishing a high state of alert in each village and mobilizing members of the active warrior regiments residing in each village, making them a vigilante force to pursue *Bakema* when they are reported. These guards will then hunt them down and kill them."

This mention of hunting down and killing the cannibals met with the approval of many. He noted that those from younger warrior age groups remained stolid and silent, and he was aware of a younger faction, mostly of Makikele's age set, now in the mix.

Pishani continued with his recommendation. "Should *Bakema* be discovered in the vicinity of smaller villages, I urge them to select teams of runners to seek help from the bigger villages nearby. Larger defense forces would then be brought together to pursue the bands of cannibals."

When Pishani concluded, Phatladi Mathipa stepped forward and addressed the council. The trusted counselor and brother-in-law of the king outlined a more aggressive and organized strategy to defend and drive away the *Bakem*a.

"The southern border region along the Lepelle and elsewhere is already alarmed and on the alert. The stories we have heard show that the number of marauding *Bakema* bands hiding in the bush is increasing. The names of those found killed and eaten are known, and their numbers are increasing. Fear is growing, and a bigger effort must be made than that already suggested to you by Pishani Mathipa. The active regiments must be called together from everywhere in Phalaborwa and sent to the area. The danger increases. It grows. It is now time for war."

With the mention of war, the councilmen stomped their feet and shouted approval.

One young nobleman, a warrior only recently married, stood up to praise the king and added the name of Makikele to his chant. The praise included the widely discussed belief that Makikele controlled powerful war magic that could be used to strengthen the army. With this the young men, mostly now standing on the periphery of the council meeting, began to sing one of the popular war chants. To it they added the words, "Makikele brings the war medicines, the little drum of the king, *Tlanka*. His Venda magic will rally Phalaborwa's warriors. The drum will defeat them. We will mutilate the cannibals. Death to the *Bakema*!"

The chant "Death to the *Bakema*!" was then picked up by the entire assembly and shouted repeatedly.

The aging king noted that the loudest approval came from the younger warriors and Phatladi's supporters. He observed with pleasure that Makikele remained emotionless, a decorum befitting a prince standing before his people. *Kgoshi* Meele also noted that Prince Ramatladi appeared vexed by the dissention among council members, a sign of weakness in a leader expected to speak for the king in tribal open forums such as this one.

Phatladi allowed ample time for the excited reaction to reach a peak, and then raised his hands to speak again. "As you well know, much of Phalaborwa is weakened by famine and hunger. These villages cannot defend themselves. How can they send runners from village to village in this state of danger? These runners will be killed and eaten by the *Bakema*. My kinsman, Pishani, and his nephew, Ramatladi, are proposing to feed these *Bakema*, not to kill them."

Several in the gathering gasped with surprise at this mockery of the powerful Prince Ramatladi and his influential uncle. The majority, however, stomped with approval, and a number laughed at the open rebuke, which was a breach of court etiquette.

A small crowd had gathered outside the reed and wooden fence, which partially blocked the view of the king's meeting place and his sacred fire. This crowd consisted mainly of women, children, and a number of royal visitors staying nearby. This assembly increased in number when they heard the singing and shouting. These observers, initially silent, now joined in chanting the well-known Malatji family praises. They too loudly shouted out Makikele's name: "Makikele the war-maker! Makikele of the snake spirit!"

Phatladi shouted, raising his voice to be heard above the cacophony. "The plan presented by Pishani, who is my kinsman and of the same Mathipa lineage, will not stop the *Bakema*, the cannibals who eat the people of Phalaborwa. It is a weak plan conceived by weak men."

The group became silent as the aged counselor publically belittled a senior advisor to the king. More disturbing was the negative reflection it had on Ramatladi's role as spokesman of the king. All knew of his power as the "voice of the king" and that he expected one day to rule.

Kgoshi Meele, not wishing for such a public display, spoke in private with those near him and then retired to his quarters, followed by both Pishani and Phatladi, his sons, and other men of his immediate family. As they departed, many of the remaining assembly and onlookers shouted, "Makikele will kill the *Bakema*. He is the lion of his people, the strong porcupine of the Malatji."

During the following eighteen months, a fighting force was mobilized, made up mostly of the youngest men, those still unmarried and willing to travel the countryside to fight. With this force, commanded by Makikele's brothers and high-ranking age-mates, much of the eastern border region came under active surveillance. The different parts of the territory were linked by a message system involving hilltop sentinels, drumming signals, and runners.

Makikele and others in the capital had concerns about laxity of surveillance along these areas regularly trafficked by outside groups seeking permission to trade or to pass through the kingdom to other areas. This renewed system of lookouts proved quite effective in the existing state of emergency and was made law by royal decree. There were heavy penalties imposed on headmen and *ntona* discovered neglecting village security.

The accommodation of mobile bands of warriors in the villages of the eastern regions required a redistribution of livestock and grain from royal holdings dispersed throughout the kingdom. This was another innovation that came out of the necessity to feed large numbers of men housed in or near villages already struggling to feed themselves in the drought, which persisted throughout the first year of the *Bakema* wars.

Quantities of millet and maize were imported from both Lobedu and Venda. The former had good rains that year, while Venda had not been affected by drought and had grain to trade. But the cost was dear, requiring continuous smelting and forging of metals brought in to barter. At that time, Swazi-style short stabbing spears used in battle were lucrative trading items, traded with the ruling Dlamini clan of the Swazi in their mountain villages south of the Sabie River.

The Hlame, the members of a specialized trade family of great antiquity in Phalaborwa, were based at Sekgopo Hill, from which they maintained established trade links to and into Swazi territory and among increasingly Zulu-dominated Tsonga. These provided grain for *Kgoshi* Meele's army, and also cattle, brought into the kingdom in drives that ran east of the tsetse zone, and then through the tsetse-infested regions, traveling by night when the fly did not attack livestock.

The Swazi demand for Phalaborwa iron, and especially for their distinctive war spear, had increased due to encroachment on their land by hostile expansionist Zulu. The superior-grade iron from Lolwe, and Phalaborwa craftsmanship, were much desired by warriors in the fighting regiments.

During the year, by royal dictate and public demand, both war and rainmaking rituals were intensified under the supervision of Makikele and his mother. The *Bakema* were hunted down and killed along the Lepelle, both by strategically deployed and mobile regiment detachments, and also by villagers themselves. They were emboldened now, and feeling more aggressive due to the presence of the king's army and the use of war magic sent from the capital to ward off lurking bands of cannibals.

With early rains the following year, the drought began to lift. By this time the land was mostly rid of the *Bakema*, and the river lands were green with what promised to be an abundant season for crops. As the rains brought by Makikele's powers replenished Phalaborwa, the *Bakema* crisis lessened, and then mostly disappeared. *Tlanka*, the war drum, was returned to the king's regalia house to join its sister drums, to be used for more peaceful pursuits.

CHAPTER EIGHTEEN

Succession

Two sisters sat side by side, pounding marula nuts and leaning against the decorated mud wall linking their two houses. They were co-wives of Sefiti Pilusa, an ironworker living near Lolwe Hill. They sat on reed mats, legs outstretched, enjoying the shade of an ancient marula tree.

"I tell you, this feeling of well-being we have in Phalaborwa is an illusion. I sense that things are soon going to get difficult," said the elder of the two sisters. Senyoke was a tall, fair-skinned matron, inclined to be talkative, with a sense of humor that kept the women of her domicile and neighborhood laughing—so her serious tone was a concern to her companion.

Senyoke continued her monologue on the current state of the kingdom. Her sister encouraged this flow as they kept up a ritual pace of pounding marula nuts open, extracting the nut meat, and placing it in convenient pots by their legs. They then would brush away shell fragments from the flat stones used as a working surface. They smashed open the hard marula shells with smooth river stones used as hammers, picking out the flesh with a thin polished iron point, the *modukulo*. Every Phalaborwa woman carried one or more of these useful tools attached to braided cords suspended from the neck.

"The health of the king has worsened since the *Bakema* were chased away. I still have frightening dreams about the terrible things they did to their poor victims. I think about helpless captives being butchered alive, arms and legs cooking on fires. Goats are not treated so painfully when butchered. Their throats are cut and they die first, and then they are cut up for the pot. Even here near the king's center, I felt in danger from those *Bakema*. I sleep soundly only now, knowing that Makikele used his powers to kill those *Bakema*."

Both women quietly patted their hands together in a gesture of propitiation to the ancestors, while they discussed their uncomfortable memories of the frightening *Bakema* times.

"Last year *Kgoshi* Meele's health began to weaken, and concern grows that a failing king brings ill fortune to Phalaborwa. Many fear that the rains will not come in time for planting because the power of the king is now so weak. Some say he will soon be killed by Ramatladi and his brothers, so that new rain medicines can be made."

The other woman, Kabila, spoke for the first time with a sharp warning. "Silence, sister," she said. "It is dangerous to mention such things about the king. Don't talk about the king. Ngwako is returning from her Hlame relatives at Kgopolwe very soon with her children. If these Hlame hear of your talk, it will anger people and our husband will be fined—all of us will be. If Ramatladi hears that he is being talked about and that it comes from the village of Sefiti Pilusa, his mother, Setakgale, will curse us. You frighten me when you mention forbidden things."

The elder sister assumed a chastened look, but lowered her voice and leaned closer to Kabila to whisper more gossip she had heard from the king's village. Disapprovingly, her sister closed her eyes, shook her head, and chuckled quietly, a hand masking the smile on her mouth.

Senyoke shook her head again and focused on using her *modukulo* to sift through marula shells.

The *modukulo*, a carefully forged flattened iron pick, was a defining feature of every Ba-Phalaborwa woman's neck accoutrements. A handy multipurpose tool, it was useful in both the kitchen and garden, and variously used by women while gathering food in the bush. It could serve as a scraper or a tool to probe into wood or clay, and could also be used to gut mopane worms or other insects that became seasonally available for the cook pot. It might prove handy as an incising tool when decorating a pot or even function as a toothpick. In fact, the tool was so useful and popular, it was being adopted by women of other regions where the marula did not grow, and was carried by traders for barter both as a household tool and as an item of decoration.

The flesh of the marula nut was a most favored condiment in local recipes, one that visitors from other areas requested when visiting Phalaborwa, and it could be easily stored dry for year-round eating. The rains that year had revitalized the marula tree, which had produced an abundant fruit and nut harvest.

The succulent sweet and sour juices of the small yellow fruit were fermented into a potent cider, which everyone consumed during its harvest season. When the cider was strained into a semi-clear liquid, the women and girls particularly enjoyed eating the crushed pulp, which they removed by hand from the brewing pots. Marula cider-making was a happy occasion in the middle of the harvest season, when families and friends gathered to drink together and people traveled from one village to another enjoying each other's hospitality.

But the marula season was long past, and even the millet harvest was over. This hottest part of the year made everyone tired, and the two sisters slowly, meticulously pounded nuts, stockpiling the easily dried and stored marula meat for use throughout the year.

Senyoke's younger sister had followed her to Lolwe a year after her bridewealth had been paid, to become Sefiti Pilusa's second wife. The village was located near Lolwe Hill where copper ore, the source of their livelihood, was mined. It was a comfortable place to live, close to a stream bed which was easily excavated for fresh water all year round. They enjoyed a harmonious partnership together, rarely quarreling while working side by side in their gardens, sharing domestic tasks, and rearing Pilusa's children together.

This domestic unit included a third junior wife, a Kgatla girl called Ngwako. She had been purchased as a baby by a group of Hlame traders returning from the Ba-Sekwati in Pedi during a famine. When she was a girl, she had lived in the Hlame village near Kgopolwe. After she had reached maturity and completed her *bjale* initiation, Pilusa had purchased her in exchange for several of his forged iron stabbing spears produced for the Hlame to sell to the Swazi. Although certain metal products, such as spears, hoes, and particularly copper *serale* ingots, were of great value and he paid dearly for Ngwako, the fact that no livestock had changed hands for her meant that she was subordinate to her co-wives, as were her children also subordinate to theirs.

That evening, when the fires were being lit and food prepared, Ngwako arrived with her three children from Kgopolwe. She and the oldest child, a girl of nine years, carried large leather sacks of dried game meat and marula nuts, gifts from her adopted Hlame family.

She also brought the startling news that the king had been found dead. Word had been announced in the royal *kgoro* just as she and the travelers she would accompany were leaving. In her haste to reach home before sundown, she had hurried away with only some of the information. By the time she had reached home and lit the fire to begin cooking her evening meal, word of the king's death had spread throughout the villages around Lolwe.

It was Kabila's turn to prepare food in her house for her husband. When he had eaten, he summoned Ngwako and Senyoke and others of his village into his compound.

"Ngwako, you have just returned from Kgopolwe," he said. "Tell us what you know of *Kgoshi* Meele's death. Everyone knows that the king had been ill and in seclusion for some time. However, I heard rumors that Meele died last week and that his body was being used by the women of his family to make medicines. It is not unusual for the announcement of a king's death to be postponed, but I am interested to learn what you heard while staying with my Hlame in-laws at Kgopolwe."

"There was a great silence surrounding the royal enclosure," Ngwako replied to her husband. "The king's compound was being guarded by Prince Makikele's age regiment, who would only allow women of the family to go and come with food and water. One of my Hlame uncles described hearing arguing at the barricaded gates when Setakgale and Ramatladi, and some of his brothers and uncles, attempted to enter Meele's enclosure.

"I watched in silence with my step-mother and other family members while women of the royal household carried water from the river. No one dared ask them for details. We feared that he was dead, but we could not inquire about it and only waited for the official word. There were reports of the arrival of herbalists, believed to have entered the enclosure to treat the king, so some still hoped that the king would somehow recover. There was no sound or sign of mourning or grief until just before I departed, when I heard shouts and the beating of *Boretho*, the great drum. We all awaited the announcement of the king's demise.

"Even at the time I left with the children to return here, I had not heard officially that Meele had died," she continued. "But, my step-father, Lukoba Hlame, confirmed that a king could have been dead many days before *Boretho* would have been sounded."

After the family meeting, Pilusa left home to visit Selepe, the coppersmith, in his nearby village. They were drinking partners, good friends, and intended to exchange daughters one day as they found wives for their sons.

At the home of Selepe, a group of men from the neighborhood joined them to discuss the situation. Uppermost in their thoughts was the issue of royal succession and who would likely emerge to claim the Copper Throne of Phalaborwa.

"I am worried that there will be fighting among the rivals," said Pilusa, "and if there is, I fear that violence can spread to the villages."

"I don't think we need to worry about that," said Selepe. "*Kgoshi* Meele has worked hard to build alliances with prominent families throughout Phalaborwa, and has created a sense of unity and solidarity among the various families claiming common royal descent as Malatji people of the porcupine totem. Once Meele had consolidated his power at Kgopolwe by eliminating his rivals, he established ties with each section of Phalaborwa, building alliances which were often strengthened through marriage unions in each region."

"He is not praised as 'the *kgoshi* of gifts' for nothing," said one of the other men with a laugh.

"Yes," said Selepe, "his gifts have ensured his extensive patronage to allied villages. Meele's efforts to stabilize the region have made it more prosperous, with wealth concentrated at the *mashate* and then distributed to enrich and strengthen loyal followers."

"And then there was the *Bakema* war," said Pilusa, "when the kingdom was united more than ever, thanks to the efforts of Prince Makikele and his supporters."

"So, are you saying Makikele should be king?"

"Not necessarily. *Kgoshi* Meele has many sons from his *malome* wives, but four of them have had a strong claim—Paane, Mokgoropong, Ramatladi, and Makikele. Well, Mokgoropong is dead, so we can rule him out and the others in his line."

"Paane is the son of the first of his Mathipa marriages," interjected one of the others, "and he has the support of the people of Nagome Hill."

"Yes, but Paane's mother is no longer the great wife," said Selepe.

"Nor is Setakgale, yet her son Ramatladi still wields power at Kgopolwe," said Pilusa. "He has been acting as regent for many months. He has taken over many of the king's responsibilities while he has been ill and, until recent years, has enjoyed a special place of honor, with his mother, at the king's court."

"What you say is true; however, that all changed when Meele made Mokadi his great wife a few months after Mokgoropong was killed. That surprised many people."

"You are right, Selepe," said Pilusa. "And what is more, Makikele has obviously been Meele's favored son in his old age. He clearly chooses him over his brother princes. For one thing, he is well known throughout the kingdom, and when he speaks, people listen. This is particularly so when he joins in discussions between royal councilors and leaders of regional centers, or with delegations from other kingdoms."

"Yes, he has a superior knowledge of politics and diplomacy. He has close ties with his Tsonga-related family on the eastern border country, and also with the Lobedu to the west."

"And do not forget his stay in Venda. He is conversant in the language of Venda, and knows about the magic they use in the north."

"That is where his real power comes from. In Venda, he trained in the magic of rain and warfare. Some say he had a magical experience with a serpent under the waters of their sacred lake, and another with the spirit of a leopard on their royal burial mountain."

"Most importantly," said Pilusa, "he is widely admired. The people like him. His popularity with the people is something his father has recognized and valued in recent times, when strong leadership is necessary to keep the people united. Meele has worked hard to build and maintain strong ties. Continuing these relationships will be vital to protect Phalaborwa's borders, and the trade which keeps us alive and makes us prosper. Yes, Meele expected Makikele to succeed him."

"But the king is dead, and Makikele can no longer rely on his father for support. Powerful competing interest groups will vie to occupy the vacant Copper Throne. Do not underestimate Paane or Ramatladi yet; each has a powerful following. Each man's family will support his claim to rule Phalaborwa."

While Pilusa and the men of Lolwe discussed the implications of Meele's death, Notsi, one of *Kgoshi* Meele's slaves, said good-bye to his wife and children and returned to the dead king's enclosure where he was needed.

Notsi had no memory of his early childhood before being brought to Phalaborwa as a small boy. He had been captured during a cattle raid in Tsonga country. Brought to Kgopolwe as tribute, he had been given first to the queen, Ntlabidi, and then to her son, Meele, when *Kgoshi* Mosholwane died. Notsi had been well cared for and remained at Kgopolwe, eventually becoming Meele's personal servant. Their lives had been intertwined during the many years of Meele's reign. Meele had been kind and generous to the boy and had provided him with the bridewealth to marry, and therefore Notsi had been a loyal and trusted attendant. Indeed, after many intimate years together, affection developed between the two.

Although a Tsonga slave, Notsi was a man respected in Meele's capital. He was an intimate player in the royal household, a part of every daily routine, and always a quiet presence. His daily access to the king's private domain and attendance at all important meetings and ritual events, even though in a subordinate role, made him special in the eyes of many who would wish to have the ear of the king. The wives of *Kgoshi* Meele regularly approached him for information about their husband as they went about their daily activities, with questions such as "How long will he be hunting?"; "Is he feeling better?"; "Did he enjoy the food I sent him?"; or "When should I approach him with a personal matter?"

Notsi lived near the entrance to the king's cattle enclosure with his wife, Mulewane, and his two surviving children, a young boy aged seven and a daughter who would soon attend *bjale*. Other children, all girls, had died in infancy. The son was called Patshani, which meant 'the tick.' It was an ugly name, chosen to fool any evil spirits intent on bringing harm to the boy into believing he was undesirable. Mulewane's many stillborn births and miscarriages were attributed to evil spirits. Therefore, Notsi had taken every precaution to protect this last child from evil. Notsi was happy to have a son after fathering so many girls. He hoped the boy would grow up to be strong, and that his sister would bring cattle to her marriage so Patshani in turn could marry well. Although Notsi would remain a Tsonga slave, his son, once initiated at *Koma* into manhood, would be accorded full status as a local tribesman and warrior.

But Notsi could not foresee, nor did any inquiries made of witchdoctor's divining stones and bones foretell, what the future had in store for him and his son.

CHAPTER NINETEEN

Royal Death

The death of a king or a member of his immediate family is a carefully guarded and protected time. Because of this, when Meele was close to death, the slave Notsi no longer traveled daily back and forth from the heavily guarded *mashate* to his house by the *kgoro*. He stayed instead within earshot of *Kgoshi* Meele while his master lay dying. Most of the time he sat on a stool beside the king's elevated sleeping platform, only leaving the dark smoky thatched house to relieve himself, fetch things, or locate someone requested by others in the king's immediate household.

The family entourage keeping deathwatch consisted of Meele's principal wife, Mokadi; her sons and daughter; Meele's closest male relatives; and his surviving sisters. Also present were their attendants, of whom Notsi ranked highest. All others, including the king's other wives, remained outside the enclosure.

As death approached, even Notsi was barred from access to Meele's house, although he remained within the confines of the walled royal enclave. From the small hut where he slept and ate, he watched the queen mother, Prince Makikele, and several of Meele's brothers, assisted by a group of witch doctors, performing rituals to protect the death house.

During the following week, royal counselors and the closest members of the king's lineage were summoned to the *mashate,* told that the king requested their presence. Numerous members of Makikele's regiment also began arriving at Kgopolwe, summoned by Prince Masetla, Makikele's army general. Kgopolwe became an armed military camp, while Meele's abode high up on the hill stood in silent secrecy.

King Meele's death remained unannounced to the people of Kgopolwe while his family members and witch doctors performed the many rituals required to prepare the dead king's body for burial.

His body lay decomposing for more than a week on a raised platform inside the house. A fire was kept burning, the flames fed with herbs, to fill the house with sweet-smelling smoke that seeped through the thatch into the compound and pervaded the surrounding atmosphere. Fluids oozed through incisions made in the king's skin and dripped slowly into pots placed beneath the catafalque. These fluids, along with vital organs and sections of skin dissected from the royal body, would be used as essential ingredients in rain and planting medicines and war magic.

As the royal mortuary procedures continued, Makikele met with a small group of trusted leaders in Mokadi's enclosed compound a short distance from the king's house. The group included two of Meele's younger brothers, Ramasaba and Leshoro, and the heads of principal royal villages near the capital and of other loyal villages. They gathered to discuss plans for announcing the king's death and the succession. Conspicuously absent were Ramatladi and Paane, both claiming primacy to the copper throne as elder paramount sons of Meele.

"The first task will be to select one of our number to serve as 'holder of the chair,'" said Makikele. "The one chosen will be custodian of the royal enclosure and the king's regalia during the interregnum between our father's burial and the seating of a new king."

"Would not Ramatladi fit this role?" said one. "He has acted as regent at times during the king's illness."

"Our brother Ramatladi is ineligible," said Masetla. "He may be entitled to fill this role, but he is excluded because of his claim to the succession."

They all knew that both Ramatladi and Paane, older sons of Meele, had supporters who would challenge Makikele, but few expected either brother could successfully overwhelm Makikele's kingdom-wide alliances, popular appeal and support.

"Ramasaba?" suggested another.

"I think it should be one of the younger members of the council," said Ramasaba. "I propose my younger brother, Leshoro. We must make every effort to prevent any disruption of Makikele's smooth transition to the kingship. I think Leshoro is the one most fitting to perform that role. He possesses many of the same qualities as our late king."

Leshoro Malatji was one of Meele's younger brothers and a trusted advisor.

"I agree," said Makikele. "Is there any dissent?"

There was silence. None dared to challenge the prince's decision.

"Then our uncle, Leshoro, is chosen," he said.

While they sipped beer that had been prepared for the meeting, the men laid out a plan to prevent rival forces from undermining Makikele's assumption of his father's throne once the king was buried.

Masetla spoke once again. "In assuring the people that Makikele is the rightful and designated successor to our father, it is vital that we retain control of the sacred rituals of kingship. For this reason, we must summon the village *kgoro* heads and the king's *ntona* from throughout Phalaborwa, and they must arrive here within the next few days."

By the middle of the week, when all the village *kgoro* heads were assembled, a pure black bull was slaughtered outside Meele's door. The skin, carefully peeled from its carcass, was used to enshroud the king's body. While lying in state inside the house, all doors and windows were sealed to await the next king's arrival and the ritual of the "opening-of-the-door." The heir to the throne, the one approved by the king's spirit and his ancestors, would only be recognized as king if he were able to force open the door and take possession of the house. They all recalled stories of Prince Lepane, brother of the late *Kgoshi* Kgashane, who failed to gain entry to their father's house and was excluded from the throne.

Until the next king was identified and acclaimed, everyone knew that the vital ritual link with the line of royal ancestors at Sealene was broken, leaving no avenue for propitiation and intercession. They were all aware of the threatening and dangerous times a succession dispute could bring to the people of Phalaborwa. Past succession wars had caused destruction of villages, famine, and enemy invasion. Until the sacred bond with the all-protecting ancestors and with *Kgobeane*, the creator of all, was restored, the people would quickly sense their vulnerability to evil forces and become afraid.

When *Kgoshi* Meele's body had been placed in the bull hide and his brothers had sealed it in the mortuary house, Makikele was summoned by the elders who would witness the ceremony of the "opening-of-the-door." Everyone waited and watched as the prince entered the open courtyard with his mother and siblings. Although the stripped carcass of the ritual bull had been removed, blood stained the pounded clay floor of the courtyard where it had been butchered. Its smell and that of rotting flesh, no longer masked by the aroma of herbal incense, reached Makikele's nostrils. But he did not think about the stench or hesitate in his resolve. There would be time to feel grief after he had finished the task at hand. Removing the baboon-skin cloak and hood he had worn, similar to those worn by the witch doctors who had assisted him in preparing the dead king's body, he approached the solid log door to Meele's house.

The wooden barrier, warm from the late afternoon sun, gave no sign of movement when Makikele prodded the solid left plank opposite its leather hinges. All eyes centered on the tall figure of the prince as he braced his shoulder and knee to attempt to force open the door blocking his way to kingship. It took two strenuous efforts before the pegs, hammered into the dirt floor to seal the door, began to give way. With one more heave, he managed to swing the door open and entered his father's final abode.

Once inside, Makikele called out to the men of his family to enter and prepare to carry his father to Sealene for burial. His command silenced the excited talk of those gathered outside.

Before the funeral procession began, many details had to be finalized. Makikele turned to his brother, Masetla, and gave his orders.

"Send word of our father's death to all village leaders. Establish the role of our uncle, Leshoro, as regent during the period of mourning, and announce my succession as king. Deploy segments of the royal regiment to potentially troublesome locations to discourage any dissent. Arrange a large contingent of my age-grade regiment to leave immediately for Nagome Hill where our brother Paane rules as *ntona*, and send a smaller escort to nearby Kgotwani Hill where Ramatladi and his family were resettled by our father."

While the king's body was removed from his house for the procession to Sealene, Makikele conferred with his uncles and several venerable councilors about the final details for the king's burial that evening. He entrusted his uncle, Ramasaba, with one special task.

"Instruct my father's faithful servant, Notsi, to follow you. You and the advanced party of royal men must proceed to the burial hill with this slave. Send a messenger to Mulewane, Notsi's wife, telling her to have his son, Patshani, join him."

The barely perceptible moon and dark night made the winding pathway to Sealene's royal burial terraces difficult to navigate, and required many torches. The dark night was seen as a good omen, since no shadow from moonlight would be cast by the dead man, indicating his spirit had joined those of his ancestors.

The late king's oldest surviving sister, the *Rakgadi* Mohlaba, who was popularly known as Mmamokobi, a derivative of her son Kobi's name, led the line of royal women. Makikele and his full brothers headed the long line of mourners and royal men bearing the body of the king. He would begin digging the king's grave, followed by his full brothers, and then other royal males based on their rank and birth order. This was an essential protocol because it ritually defined a new order of power headed by Makikele's line of descent.

The grave had been made deeper than the customary shallow hole, so as to accommodate two additional burials. These were interred without question or discussion along with the dead king. The first body was that of a child, encased in a black goat skin and placed beneath where the king's head would rest. This was the boy, Patshani, who would serve as the eternal pillow of the king. The other, shrouded in two black goat skins, was the body of Notsi, which was placed behind the king and positioned to face north. Both had been quietly suffocated and brought secretly to the graveyard. They would continue to serve Meele in the spirit world. Word that they had been taken by lions would be sent to his widow Mulewane and her daughter, who would become wards of the royal family.

Seven days after the burial, while all of Phalaborwa observed strict mourning for the late king, Makikele was installed as successor to Meele at Kgopolwe in the royal cattle enclosure. It was the largest ceremony in memory. The new king's regimental age-mates, and portions of subsequent warrior age grades, poured into the settlement in full ceremonial dress carrying shields and spears. Although Makikele's claim to his father's throne was accepted by the majority of lineages and villages, his popularity with the youthful, active regiments, many now seasoned fighters, made it clear that the new ruler ascended the throne in a position of unprecedented power.

However, some of the nobles and elite guests attending the ceremony were surprised by the large numbers of virile, self-assured, and in some cases arrogant younger men who soon populated the royal village. Independent of their village and lineage delegations, they sought pleasure and companionship with comrades and initiation brothers from throughout the kingdom.

A new force was coming into its own in the land of Phalaborwa, a unified fighting force capable of wielding power and taking control. The aged councilors and representatives from every village and the nobles and leaders of friendly neighboring tribes invited to attend sensed that Makikele's tenure on the copper throne would be strong and prosperous. The omens for this were good.

Early in the morning, while *Boretho's* booming thud sounded from lofty Kgopolwe Hill, a fully-armed regiment escorted Makikele and the royal family to Sealene. The early-morning mist encompassing the sacred hill had vanished with the first rays of sun, adding a fresh smell to the still, cool air. Reaching the new stone cairn marking the fresh grave, all watched as the new heir to the throne offered morning prayers and libations to the spirit of his father, and to the many other ancestors dwelling on the sacred hill.

Later, clad in the baboon-skin regalia of a senior tribal witch doctor and surrounded by his father's court, he joined the tumultuous gathering in and around Kgopolwe's royal cattle enclosure.

Members of his family attending included his multiple wives, among whom Lesibe remained his favorite. Here he would receive the late king's regalia from his uncle, Leshoro, regent guardian of the symbols of royal power.

Leshoro Malatji was a full brother of the late king. The two brothers bore a close physical resemblance, and his appearance, standing at the *kgoro* entrance in the full regalia of a Malatji prince, surprised many. He held the dead king's staff, a ceremonial crescent-shaped ax of great antiquity. The new king would carry this symbol of authority during all major tribal ceremonies, and most importantly during the initiation of new warrior regiments.

The now-silent crowd waited for Leshoro's permission to enter the *kgoro*. In a deep voice heard by everyone, Makikele addressed his uncle.

"*Rangwane*," he called. By using the diminutive title, which means "young uncle," to address the regent, he was establishing his own rank as heir to the senior male line. "I have come from our ancestors, from Sealene. All has been done properly; our customs have been observed."

"*Trobela, Kgoshi*," said Leshoro, formally greeting his nephew in a loud voice, and addressing him for the first time as king. He then bowed to the new king and handed him the ceremonial ax. The multitudes crowded tightly together outside the *kgoro* entrance cheered. Some shouted out Makikele's name as king. More whistled, ululated shrilly, and pounded spear shafts on the ground and against shields until a deafening pitch was reached. Amid this acclamation, Leshoro escorted Makikele to the ornately carved four-legged stool, now resting on a carpet of leopard skins.

Makikele removed the garb of witch doctor and sat upon the ceremonial stool to be consecrated king in full view of the gathered leaders and all who could crowd into the *kgoro* or look onto it from the surrounding fences. The late king's weapons, shield, spears, war club, and favorite elephant gun were placed on the carpet at the new king's feet. Leshoro's oldest son, Senganga, stepped forward, bowed to the king, and presented a carved wooden staff of office which was brightly decorated with ostrich feathers and tufts of animal hair. This man would serve as the new king's *mohlanka*, the chief servant of his royal household. It was a position of high honor and responsibility. Senganga would carry the carved staff and lead the king into official court assemblies and ceremonies.

Beaded necklaces made of colored glass, ceramic, ostrich shell, and copper were then placed around Makikele's neck and waist and across his chest.

This beadwork contained powerful magic. Carefully guarded at all times, it was brought out in the open only for a king's installation. The elegant and ornately crafted jewelry was otherwise reserved for ritual purposes within the king's living quarters. Some of the strands, particularly those incorporating the numerous heirloom blue and red beads, were said to date back to the time of the earliest settlement of Kgopolwe. One white and black strand, incorporated into a braided cincture resting across the king's loins, had been brought to Phalaborwa at the time of his grandmother, part of her wealth as an Nguni noblewoman. Others had been gifted to previous kings by friendly rulers in surrounding areas.

Makikele was then robed in a long cape of soft leopard skins worn over the left shoulder. Seated on the ceremonial stool and holding the crescent-shaped ax in his right hand, he awaited the long line of dignitaries who would address him. The ax was a lightweight iron weapon hafted in a delicate carved shaft and designed solely for ritual purposes. Like the ornately carved drums displayed to the right of his throne, this ax was of northern origin, similar to one he had seen in the Ngome royal household when he had lived in the Venda kingdom.

Once the king was vested and again seated, poets and praise-makers approached the throne to sing and chant tributes to the new king and royal family now gathered around him on mats and low stools. These much-loved orators, encouraged by cheers and laughter from onlookers, recited the Malatji royal genealogy, a long list of Phalaborwa rulers. This litany extolled each name with praises and sung historical commentary about warriors, legendary events, and prominent names from the past.

A loud gunshot blast followed by the blare of antelope-horn trumpets concluded the recitations and praise singing and drew every eye back to the late king's brother, Prince Leshoro. As he approached Makikele, he was joined by counselors and representatives of every major lineage and the larger villages. One by one, this prestigious assembly approached the throne with gravity and deep respect to solemnly instruct on what the people expected of a good and just king.

Following these orations, Leshoro lowered himself to the ground prostrate before Makikele and all became silent. Then rising to his feet, Leshoro turned to the assembly and loudly announced, "Behold, Phalaborwa has a new king."

The long, solemn installation concluded with loud and happy shouting, cheering, and ululations.

As flutes and drums played, and dancing began, and jesters in baboon skins brought smiles to faces, the leaders of every Phalaborwa village and lineage approached the king in a long line to present gifts of livestock, ivory, iron and copper objects, cloth, and grain. Each gift, a reverent sign of acceptance of Makikele's kingship, was accompanied with words of praise for the king and his royal bloodline.

More than ten head of cattle, and twice as many goats and sheep, were slaughtered and roasted for the installation feast, which lasted into the following day. Beer was brewed in countless drinking sites, and cooking pots on numerous fires fed the throngs of visitors wandering Kgopolwe's pathways and courtyards.

While gifts were being given and praise-makers from every corner of the kingdom attempted to outdo those who went before them in the lineup of well-wishers, Prince Masetla made note of those villages and branches of the royal family not represented. Most conspicuously missing were delegations from Nagome Hill, Prince Paane's stronghold, and from Prince Ramatladi's well-known allies, and the Seale who occupied the farmland and lower reaches of the nearby royal burial hill. The king intended to deal decisively with these disloyal elements in his realm.

That evening, in the quieter secluded royal quarters on the hillside beyond the *kgoro*, Makikele and his council met with regimental leaders to organize the elimination of dissident groups that could pose a threat to him and become a security risk to Phalaborwa.

CHAPTER TWENTY

Power Defined

During the first year of Makikele's long rule, he made Sealene Hill his residence. Here he built a new settlement with a large livestock enclosure. From then onwards, the royal family and its entourage lived and governed from Sealene in close proximity to the ultimate source of their power, the sacred ancestral burial grounds crowning the hill.

The latter part of Meele's reign and the early years of Makikele's rule were a time of great disruption in Southern Africa. This period in the 1820s and 1830s was known as the *Difaqane*.

These decades coincided with the rise to power of a number of Zulu chiefs—Mzilikazi, Shoshangan, Manukosi, and others—who broke away from the influence of the great Zulu king, Shaka. Mzilikazi moved north from Zululand with his army, invading Pedi, Lobedu, Venda, and Tsonga, and formed his own kingdom north of the Limpopo in Matabeleland. Shoshangan in turn conquered the coastal Tsonga-speaking peoples, establishing himself as ruler of the Gaza kingdom.

At the same time, Zulu under Manukosi and his followers invaded and conquered the Tsonga hinterland bordering Phalaborwa, pushing north to the Limpopo River valley. As they were subdued, these Tsonga fell subject to a more centralized Zulu leadership and their fighting-aged men were absorbed into Zulu warrior regiments, their *impi*. The enlarged Zulu forces then drove westward to Venda and Lobedu, some passing through Phalaborwa to the north of Sealene along an ancient salt trade route leading to Lobedu.

These Zulu *impi*, although a formidable threat, encountered fierce Phalaborwa resistance before they reached Lobedu to raid for cattle. Makikele's forces also mounted offensive raids into Zulu-occupied territories. Examples of this were raids by the Malongane, an assimilated group of Swazi origin living under Malatji rule. They conducted successful raids against the Zulu in Tsonga country, bringing back captured cattle to Phalaborwa, and were rewarded by Makikele with the spoils of their raiding. These forays and the trophies of war became immortalized in Malongane praises and in regimental war songs.

One factor enabling Makikele's success in thwarting Zulu attack and keeping them at bay was the enemy's respect for Phalaborwa's reputation in the occult science of metallurgy. This bordered on reverence and fear. Because of Makikele's reputed metal-making powers and the widely held belief that he was a sorcerer and conjurer of war magic, the Zulu avoided Sealene and Lolwe and, by extension, much of Makikele's domain as a place of taboo and danger. The ruler of Lolwe Hill, therefore, was given wide leverage and avoidance by these Nguni-speaking invaders. For this reason, unlike the Tsonga and many others, Phalaborwa was not conquered and made a vassal kingdom of the Zulu.

Makikele's ability to establish himself as a prominent regional leader was tied as well to the decisive way in which he dealt with, and eliminated, internal factions who opposed his kingship.

Over the months following his ascent to the throne, Makikele's rival brothers, Paane and Ramatladi, and their families were exiled to Mapulaneng in the south and to Lobedu where both had kinship ties, trade connections, and allies. Their former villages were dispersed, and new families settled where they had lived.

The new king also acted decisively in his dealings with the Seale people, who had sided with rival groups when he made his bid for kingship.

The Seale, who resided at the base of Sealene Hill, were an indigenous group who retained guardianship of the sacred mountain. Their early status as one-time owners of the hill, before the ruling Malatji had arrived, was evident to all by the privilege they retained to bury their dead at the foot of the hill, even though many generations of Malatji royals were interred in its higher terraces and cliffs.

Sensing a threat and continuing challenge from this lineage, still zealously guarding its prerogative as custodian of the sacred hill, and bitter about its refusal to accept his legitimacy as King Meele's heir, Makikele decided to act decisively and to expel them. Otherwise, he reasoned, they remained a poisonous snake in his house.

Their expulsion gave Makikele exclusive control of Sealene, this symbol of power, prestige, and fear. With the Seale gone, he had sole access to the sacred domain of the all-powerful ancestral spirits. He and his sister, Maboyana, and those they appointed became the only ones able to act as intercessors and intermediaries with the spirits of past rulers who dwelt on the mountain and who determined the fate of the land and its peoples.His control of Sealene was both symbolic and politically strategic.

Thus, at the same time as many of both Paane's and Ramatladi's people were exiled, Makikele forcefully removed the Seale from their village, expelling those most vocal against him from the kingdom. Those not expelled were relocated to more distant Phalaborwa villages. Ceremonial poles from Kgopolwe were then placed at each *kgoro* entrance in the new Seale settlements to mark their ritual subordination and clientage to their king.

The village surrounding Sealene Hill was fortified, as were nearby Kgopolwe and Lolwe Hills. By doing this, the new king set up a more defensible Royal Triangle, with Sealene as his residence and ritual center; Kgopolwe remaining the political center, housing a warrior garrison and accommodating the royal *kgoro*; and Lolwe, with its copper mines and iron sources carefully controlled and protected.

A short distance to the south of this fortified triangle was the large village surrounding Nagome Hill. Similarly fortified and repopulated with young warriors and their families, it was placed under the leadership of Mabu, one of Makikele's brothers, who was appointed royal *ntona*. This became a buffer village, a bulwark, defending access to the capital from the southern route into Phalaborwa by way of the Lepelle River.

Serving as a stronghold for the king and royal family, the triangle also became an extended smelting and forging site, using Lolwe's ore. Nagome Hill and the network of hillside villages spreading out around the trade center at Phetole, located twenty miles west of the royal triangle, became large specialized metal-producing districts as well. Iron- and copper-working families were resettled in these locations, smelting and forging zones were expanded, and metal production increased.

During these warlike years, Makikele became steeled to the realities of open hostility from outside his borders and to continuing internal divisions which might weaken defenses. His age-grade armies were trained to use Zulu and Swazi tactics in warfare, and the young warriors of Phalaborwa became a standing army, vigilant for any signs of danger.

Like the rapidly expanding Zulu and like his father had before him, Makikele learned the importance of negotiating with groups entering his lands, and he was able to absorb displaced groups, forming alliances through the exchange of women to create marriage ties and the patronage of goods and livestock. These groups quickly assimilated into Ba-Phalaborwa culture, adopting Sotho language and beliefs and submitting their boys and young men to induction into Makikele's age regiments. He allowed groups to peacefully settle in his territory under local *ntona*, and provided them with protection against attack. Men of incoming groups were incorporated into his army regiments and dispersed where needed in the kingdom. These groups became loyal to Makikele, preferring his lordship to uncertainties elsewhere. Like other residents, new arrivals joined the indigenous peoples in looking to Kgopolwe and Sealene for military and spiritual protection.

One group in particular, the Ba-Shai of Sanaskei in the Pedi highlands, was totally displaced first by Mzilikazi's Zulu *impi* and then later by Swazi invaders. They became clients of Makikele, who allowed them to live in his domain at Tsubia

Hill. Other highland groups, such as the Ngwane, Mojela, Malongane, Monyaela, and Nareng, also came to Phalaborwa under duress. They were absorbed as client groups to the ruling Malatji and formed marriage alliances with the older resident population.

However, one part of Phalaborwa remained a thorn in the lion's paw. The Eastern Province wavered in its loyalty. Sekgopo Hill, hub of the king's ivory trade, and Makwibidung to its north were home to supporters of his brother Paane and continued to be troublesome.

The eastern border region stretched many miles to the north and south of Sekgopo Hill, encompassing hilly terrain and grasslands that extended to the Lebombo mountain range, which served as a buffer to the Tsonga. Several influential families controlled this chain of Phalaborwa settlements and controlled the wealth found there. Most prestigious were the Mathipa, the king's maternal relatives, and their many lineal offshoots. The powerful group once ruled the region until subordinated to the Malatji generations before Makikele became king. They, however, remained a wealthy and influential wife-giving family to the Malatji, one from which kingship might derive.

Other important eastern families were the Pilusa, who were ironsmiths to the Mathipa as well as renowned rainmakers, and the Hlame, an extended lineage group that became wealthy and powerful in the early days of Malatji ascendency. They served as middlemen in trade with the Tsonga and peoples from the coast, and with the highland Swazi with whom they traded spears and other weaponry.

These more powerful older families maintained kinship ties with the Nguni-speaking tribes, although they were of Sotho culture and primarily linked with Kgopolwe. Meele had relied on them to maintain control in the east, and it was an alliance with the Hlame that later proved valuable in solidifying Makikele's power base.

It was in the Sekgopo region that Paane, Makikele's elder half-brother, retained a foothold of influence, and it was from here that he continued to assert his own claim to Phalaborwa kingship.

CHAPTER TWENTY-ONE

Jiwawa's War

Paane Malatji, Makikele's half-brother and a rival at the time of his succession to kingship, was now a renegade. He had returned from exile in Mapulaneng to live on the eastern border in the Makwibidung area, a cluster of villages spreading north from Sekgopo Hill. With him were his maternal relatives, his brothers, and their followers. A growing number of Tsonga, living along Phalaborwa's borders, also joined him. The king was angered by reports he received of Paane's growing association with foreigners and the belligerence being shown to the king's representatives and officials.

Toward the end of 1840, Makikele's maternal uncle, Phatladi Mathipa, brought a report from Sekgopo Hill that was very disturbing.

Makikele listened to his uncle's account, presented by the old man to the intimate circle of royal counselors sitting beside the fire in the king's private courtyard. Among the gathering of more than twenty men were Makikele's younger brothers, Masetla, who served as his war general, and Mapiti, who had developed a competence in divination and had an incisive mind on which the king depended. Mabu, the king's half-brother, who served the king as *ntona* at Nagome, sat among the senior men of the tribe, as did Kaetla Mojela, *ntona* of Namagale; Sefiti Pilusa, the king's weapons specialist who lived near the iron ore deposits at Lolwe Hill; and Ramakabe Mathipa, a brother-in-law of the exiled Prince Ramatladi. Ramakabe had sat on the late *Kgoshi* Meele's advisory council and had accepted Makikele's investiture as legitimate, refusing to follow Ramatladi into exile. He remained an advisor at the king's request.

The king had also requested that his sister, Maboyana, join him for the meeting, and to serve beer brewed that morning for the occasion. His real reason to have Maboyana present at the discussions was so that she could provide valued counsel in private at a later time. She played a little-known role as advisor to the king, as well as performing her duties as priestess for family rituals and prayer.

"I have posted watchmen to prevent eavesdropping," said Masetla. "There is a continual flow of visitors staying with family members in the royal village. Members of the royal household, and most particularly their attendants, have ears. Gossip and rumor can easily spread beyond these walls. At times, it seems that even the walls themselves can hear."

Makikele nodded his approval. "Security must be carefully maintained as we discuss the fate of my brother, Paane. Now, Uncle Phatladi, brief me on these troubles along our eastern borders."

"There is much to tell, but I will try to be brief. First, there are the Zulus. Manukosi continues to invade Tsonga lands, has again attacked villages on the eastern frontier of Phalaborwa, and has crossed along our northern territory by way of that trade route to attack Lobedu. He has defied the might of Queen Modjadji and stolen large numbers of Lobedu cattle."

"That is troubling news, Uncle, and these are dangerous times. Has the defiance of my brother Paane made us vulnerable to these intruders?"

"I am not sure if the Zulu are a real threat to us," said Mapiti, interrupting his uncle. This interruption of an elder, a breach of etiquette, caused a stir among the more senior men on the council.

Phatladi raised his hand to silence the murmurs and continued. "The Zulu and other Nguni people fear and respect us for our metalwork and the magic we possess. They also fear our Phalaborwa climate, believing diseases in our lowland region will harm them and their livestock. And it is true, they do not know how to avoid tsetse-infected areas, and their young men, their *impi*, seem to contract fever and sicken if they stay here. Because of this, we have kept relatively safe from marauding enemy regiments, unlike many of our neighbors.

"However, as you all know, there have been past incidences of attack from southern tribes. Any sign of weakness might invite acts of aggression," said Phatladi, turning toward the king to regain attention. "Our main concern is your half-brother, Paane."

"Go on."

"As we all know, there is a long-standing rift among some of the Sekgopo people. This can be traced back to the feud between your father, *Kgoshi* Meele—may his spirit protect us—and his brother Manabe, then *ntona* of Sekgopo, who challenged his right to rule."

Prince Mabu, selected by Makikele to replace Paane as *ntona* of Nagome, with a gesture of consent, stood to join the old man and continued with the story. "Yes, our uncle Phatladi is correct: Manabe sought the backing of the Sekgopo people, but only some villages followed him. Most remained loyal to

Sealene and Meele. He was an earlier example, like Paane, of a disillusioned brother challenging the succession to the throne."

"But Manabe was weak, and was defeated," said Phatladi. "Most of the villages and people in the east, including my own Mathipa family, were loyal to *Kgoshi* Meele. The majority did not take up with Manabe. He was a fool to defy tradition and to stage a revolt. The loyalty of the Mathipa and others is affirmed in our continued marriage ties with the Malatji. Only those married to Paane support him, and not even all of them."

"Paane presents a more serious challenge," added Mabu. "He turned to violence in putting forth his false claim for kingship. Now again, since being allowed to return with his people to live at Makwibidung—and remember, this was only allowed because of the king's desire to make peace with him—he is once more causing trouble. We hear he attracts a following, even some from the younger *Koma* regiments. These young men are foolish to follow him. The dissent is growing and he is saying hateful things about Sealene."

"You are right, uncle," said Masetla, bowing to the old man and to his brother as he stood to comment. "Our father fought to end this separatist attitude prevalent among enemy groups in the eastern region. He fought to consolidate his hold on power, to prevent such opposition, and to control foreign influence and interests, particularly coming from the Tsonga. So, let this be a warning to the council: do not let Paane get out of control, and remember Manabe's evil attacks. Old wounds are a source of wisdom; we should learn from past misfortunes."

Phatladi looked weary and frail as he continued, "We know from some at Makwibidung that Paane is accepting tribute from certain Tsonga leaders crossing into our land to trade in the north." The council became angry at this news, and the old man again raised his hands for quiet so he could continue. "As all know, such tribute must come only to the king, and only the king's official representatives can issue such pass-through permits and collect tribute."

Masetla interrupted his uncle, again bowing in deference and receiving the old man's nod to speak for him. "Paane has not only formed an alliance with the Shangaan-Tsonga, but also with a Portuguese hunter and trader they call Jiwawa. This white man is related by marriage to the Magwambwa Shangaan living in the south along the Sabie River. Paane has allowed them to hunt and trade in Phalaborwa. It is a dangerous situation."

"What do we know of this man, Jiwawa?" Makikele asked his uncle.

"Masetla is correct; the arrival of Jiwawa complicates the situation as we deal with Paane. He has established a trade depot on the Sabie River in the territory of Magashula, the Shangaan. Magashula's village is his base for elephant hunting forays into our eastern territory and surrounding tribal areas. From this base, he and his growing following of hunters track elephant along the Lebombo Mountains and onto the open grasslands of our borderlands. Can our nephew Mabu add any detail to what I have said?" The old man turned to the king's brother and then sat down among his fellow counselors.

"This Jiwawa has hunted in Phalaborwa several times now, entering along the trade route that follows the Lebombo Hills to the Limpopo River. He brings the Magwambwa. They hunt mostly for ivory and have acknowledged Paane as *kgoshi*, giving him the tribute due only to Sealene. During millet-planting time, these Magwambwa chased away our Sekgopo elephant hunters, and stole their ivory and a large stock of hides they were bringing to the *ntona*'s village. They are welcomed at

Makwibidung and acknowledge Paane as ruler. He has encouraged this, and keeps the king's tribute. I am told that none of it reaches the Sekgopo *ntona* as royal tribute."

The counselors again began to grumble loudly, making sounds of disgust at mention of the presence of Tsonga poachers being allowed to trespass.

Mabu continued, "Along with the loss of the king's ivory, Paane's alliance with Jiwawa has hurt our ivory trade with the coast. He threatens our prosperity. I believe the whole kingdom, and not just the east, is in danger of being fragmented at a time when there is the risk of invasion. Yes, I say Paane's behavior seriously undermines our unity and weakens us."

Prince Mapiti, the king's younger brother, was the next to speak. "With outside threats and division among our own people, there is a real danger that these Magwambwa will set a bad precedent if they are allowed to continue. The word will soon spread that we are weak and divided. We must put an end to Paane's betrayal and teach this Jiwawa a lesson. This may be the only way to hold onto our trade with the coast." He raised his voice as he concluded, "We must demonstrate the power of Sealene and remove this tick from the great Malatji elephant's back."

"We must also keep our armies mobile and controlled," said Masetla, addressing the king directly as well as the council. "It is clear that greater challenges await us from a growing Nguni presence in surrounding areas faced with invasion and raiding. To be safe, the royal family must remain united. When a Malatji prince, even this foolish brother Paane, does bad things openly, others will attempt the same. It is a precedent which will threaten the greater good of the people."

On hearing these words, the assembly grew agitated and loudly discussed the issues among themselves.

Old Phatladi seemed to gain vigor from the council's heated response. He waited for a consensus to grow among the men before citing a well-known proverb. "'Lions who do not work together are gored by the buffalo,'" he said. Then he pronounced, "We must put an end to this transgression of the king's authority. Paane must be punished; we must fight him, and chase away the Magwambwa and Jiwawa."

"This alliance between Jiwawa and Paane could prove very dangerous," said the king. "Paane has given Jiwawa hospitality and allowed him to continue his hunting expeditions. There is no room in the cattle enclosure for two bulls. Paane has challenged us, and we will fight him."

"The king speaks to us with wisdom," said Phatladi. "Paane, as we all know, was one of those who revolted and challenged rightful succession by attempting to overthrow the king. Having failed in this, he and his family were chased away to stay in the east, abandoning Nagome Hill, where he was *ntona*." Several of those listening shouted their approval of this detail in the account.

"I have heard that Paane uses witchcraft and black magic." The speaker was one of Phatladi's sons, a close friend and age-mate of Masetla.

Some members of the council feigned shock at this statement. Makikele remained unmoved, watching how the council members interacted and looking for any signs of disagreement. He noticed that Ramatladi's brother-in-law, Ramakabe, who was also related to the king by marriage, sat in silence, glancing at the ground between his knees. Some of this in-law's family had sided with Paane and had been expelled with him. The king suspected that Ramakabe sympathized with Paane, even though he had benefited from living at Nagome and being a counselor.

Old Phatladi continued his briefing. "I remind you all that Nagome has been resettled by people loyal to *Kgoshi* Makikele. That is why Mabu is now royal *ntona*, living there with his large family. The family of Mabu is loyal and reliable, and the fortified hill is now strong."

He pointed to Mabu who sat with his older brother to the left of the king. The gathered leaders voiced their approval while Mabu stared impassively, as was correct etiquette when being praised in the presence of the king.

"Nagome is now the holding point for incoming trade groups seeking business with the capital," said Phatladi.

All present knew that entry to the Royal Triangle—Sealene, Kgopolwe, and the mining center at Lolwe—was forbidden without royal permission. This made Nagome the gateway for tribute required of all foreign parties seeking to enter or pass through Phalaborwa. The patronage Mabu received as *ntona* from Makikele was dispersed among his own followers, making the residents of Nagome prosperous and giving Mabu command over many followers on behalf of the king's service.

"Since the time of your father's burial," the uncle explained, "Paane and his people have refused to acknowledge the power of Sealene or respect the king."

"He should have been killed and the others driven out when he first broke with the king," called out Masetla, who now stood in the background near the doorway opposite the courtyard gate. His outburst received several cries of dismay that he would interrupt comments of an elder and openly advocate the assassination of a royal.

Phatladi dismissed the comment, but his gesture toward Masetla with outstretched palms suggested tacit approval. "I know there may be those who agree with Prince Masetla that

Paane's fate should have been the same as that of Mokgoro-pong, or that of Ramatladi and his people. He should have been driven permanently across the Lepelle into the highlands, or to Lobedu. Instead, we are now plagued with this secretary bird in our land, running about attracting the jackal Shangaan and their Zulu overlords. Paane has truly eaten a puff adder and betrayed his circumcision brothers by his actions. This plague must be ended and driven out."

There was loud acknowledgment of his words, and then silence to hear him finish.

"Now, this annoying tick on our back, this Paane who disgraces the Malatji and is unworthy to be of the porcupine totem, brings Jiwawa here. He has traded guns to Paane, and now Magwambwa walk freely in our villages; they even hunt as they wish near Sekgopo itself. What they give Paane is only a small tribute, not the 'tusk for tusk,' as is the law. He keeps most for himself. Nothing reaches Sekgopo for the king. He must be punished for this."

Cheered on, Phatladi and several other senior leaders, summoned by Makikele, conferred quietly with the king and his brothers. Meanwhile the others talked among themselves, drinking beer passed around in gourd cups.

The king, his sister, and his brothers then left the assembly to perform divination and confer with a trusted oracle.

When the king emerged after these meetings, he joined a small group of close family advisors for further discussion. Following this, Masetla stepped forward to announce the king's decision to the waiting war council and elders.

"It has been determined that Paane must be stopped. If he is not willing to submit and accept heavy fines, then he must be driven away. Our uncle, Phatladi, will summon his family and those others who are loyal at Sekgopo to join forces with a detachment of warriors from Sealene. I, Masetla Malatji, will lead a contingent of the king's army to Sekgopo and, together with my uncle, will meet with Paane.

"His options will be made clear: he must swear allegiance to the king, desist all alliance with the Magwambwa, and accept no further tribute that is due the king. He must then make reparation for tribute taken illegally. If he refuses, he will be banished again. If he dares to disobey, he will be executed. It is not that the king desires his brother's death; however, it may be the only recourse to end the division, to reestablish unity, and to control our ivory trade. By restoring these prerogatives of the king, we will be stronger. When we are strong, we can better resist other threats from the surrounding regions."

Mabu then announced to Masetla and the council that he would bring men from Nagome to join the punitive force. Kaetla Mojela stood up and announced that he too would send men from Namagale to join Masetla. This prompted others from different regions to step forward and declare their support, and a sizeable fighting force was committed.

Pilusa, the king's weapons-maker, assured the assembly that war materials would be forged in abundance. It was his crafts-men who produced the most acclaimed spears, those coveted by the Swazi for generations.

"I do not need to tell you," said Masetla, "that you are all sworn to secrecy."

Before they dispersed, the members of the assembly were served final communal gourds of beer. The king's sister,

Maboyana, entered the men's gathering with an attendant bearing a clay pot on her head. The beer was treated with a medicinal powder poured into the beer pot by Maboyana, who stirred the liquid ceremoniously with an ornate gourd serving ladle. Then, in a kneeling position appropriate to women serving men, the king's sister handed the first cup to her uncle, Phatladi. All watched him drink it down. She then passed cups around until everyone had been served, and each of them had drunk the potion in silence. Following this communion, the council members departed, each instructed by the king to prepare in secret for the offensive against the renegade prince.

Two weeks later, a royal delegation from Sealene, surrounded by their armed warrior guard, sat under shade trees near Sekgopo's cattle enclosure. They awaited the return of messengers sent to summon Paane from his village at Makwibidung. The warrior prince, Masetla, and his uncle, Phatladi, had been received with deep respect and deference by their Sekgopo relatives, but the atmosphere was tense.

Makwibidung was located a short distance from Sekgopo, near a riverbank containing a rich deposit of red ochre that the local people had mined and traded for generations. Trade of this valuable medicinal and decorative mineral was the king's prerogative. He had granted its use to Paane and his family when they returned from exile. Tribute resulting from the profitable trade was due the king.

Makwibidung had doubled its population with the arrival of Jiwawa's Magwambwa hunters, making it appear more like a warrior garrison than a domestic trade enclave.

When the two messengers sent by Masetla to summon Paane arrived, they smelled the pungent odor of drying elephant flesh recently hunted and now strung out to cure throughout the village. Out of sight in a walled enclosure, more than fifty elephant tusks were stored, ready to be carried off by Jiwawa's porters when he arrived from Magashula's territory in the south.

The king's messengers were treated belligerently, left waiting without courtesy. As they sat outside the prince's walled compound, they watched Magwambwa drinking in groups, served by local women, and moving freely about the village, even entering the prince's cattle enclosure. Shocked at the foreigner's access to a prince's private quarters, the two patiently waited for an audience with Paane.

The younger of the two messengers, while returning from relieving himself in the nearby bush, was approached by a local woman who warned him to leave as quickly as he could. "They will kill you," she said nervously. "These Magwambwa want to fight you; they are ready for war. When you leave, they will soon follow you."

Prince Paane kept the messengers waiting in the heat for most of the day. It was not until dusk approached that he sent a servant to tell them that he would not meet the delegation in Sekgopo. With this rejection, they quickly prepared to leave to avoid traveling at night. However, they found their exit was blocked by a group of agitated Magwambwa, cursing them in their guttural Tsonga tongue.

One drunken youth began pushing the older of the two messengers, laughing and touching his skin cape and headgear. The jeering continued until the old man held up an amulet made of woven grasses attached to a snake vertebrae neck ring. He manipulated it calmly, and then looked directly into the youth's eyes. The young man froze in fear. All knew the reputation of Phalaborwa witchcraft. The group of Magwambwa abruptly stepped aside to give the old man leave, some muttering curses at the two men as they made their exit and a hasty return to Sekgopo.

On returning to Sekgopo, they reported Paane's rebuff to Masetla and his uncle.

"The Magwambwa were very aggressive toward us," said the older messenger. "Some of the villagers told us that Jiwawa is expected to return soon with additional warriors, that his men plan to invade Sekgopo and then go after the king at Sealene. They also reported that quantities of poached ivory awaited Jiwawa somewhere in the village."

Masetla was angered by this news. "We must attack tomorrow," he said.

"Prince Masetla, forgive my disrespect for interrupting," said the older messenger, "but our numbers are too small. There are already many armed Magwambwa with Paane, and Jiwawa is expected to arrive at any time with more. A hasty predator gets only a small goat, while a careful one gets a cow," he warned. By this he meant that they would gain more by carefully considering their options before staging an attack.

Masetla's uncle also cautioned him, saying, "One must not follow a snake to its hole. To approach Paane's village with armed men will force him to defend his home. This will lead to serious fighting, and we will be outnumbered."

Weighing up the elders' warnings, Masetla decided to leave Sekgopo and return to Sealene to warn them and prepare a defense. "The king will decide whether we should mobilize all our fighters and drive Paane and his friends out of Phalaborwa."

The king did approve such a plan, and he ordered all surrounding warrior regiments to gather the next day at the capital. Masetla would lead the fighting force as the Royal Triangle prepared for a Magwambwa assault.

However, the war council's deliberations were interrupted when a runner arrived with two fleet-footed companions, bringing news of the imminent danger of attack. He reported that Paane and Jiwawa were already advancing. They had bypassed Sekgopo, intending to directly attack the king. Foreign aggressors, allied with Paane, one of their own princes, would soon reach the heart of Phalaborwa, Makikele's capital in the Royal Triangle.

"Jiwawa arrived in Makwibidung yesterday," said the frightened messenger, "and it seems that he has persuaded Paane to join with him in an assault on Sealene."

"How large is their army?" Masetla asked the exhausted young runner.

"I'm not sure how many men Jiwawa has brought with him, but Paane has the support of about one hundred from around Makwibidung."

Masetla smiled. "We will defeat them," he said. He then turned to the king. "How many guns do we have?"

"There are about twenty functioning guns in my armory, mostly locally made, and I have a few foreign made guns as well with better range and accuracy."

"Excellent. I propose that most of the guns be positioned to defend Sealene Hill, but a few of them must be held back to defend Kgopolwe should they approach the king's center from the north. My warriors, armed with arrows and stabbing spears, and a selection of gunmen will engage the enemy in the bush east of both villages. This will present a barrier to their reaching either of the king's centers.

Masetla turned again to the messenger. "What weapons do they have?"

"They also have guns, mostly four- and six-pound elephant guns. We have all seen them carrying them. They are powerful weapons. But I do not know how many they have. Most will be armed with small-bladed Tsonga throwing spears. Paane's men may include some archers."

Masetla became even more excited. "Those throwing spears are less efficient in close hand-to-hand combat. With our greater numbers, the advantage will be ours. I will send an advance guard toward Sekgopo. They will cut bush and build breaks at intervals along the trail from Sekgopo to Sealene. We will hide behind the breaks and fire on the enemy from ambush as they come into range. They will be an easy target for our bowmen and gunmen, and they do not know the lay of the land or suspect ambush. When they get closer, our men will attack the enemy in shoulder-to-shoulder formation. Bowmen will give cover so we can engage the enemy using our more offensive stabbing spears and buffalo-hide shields for protection.

Makikele gave his approval to the plan, ordering Masetla to mobilize his men. With this, he left the council for his residence, instructing his mother, Mokadi, and his sister, Maboyana, to join him and to bring war medicines held in their care. They were to assist him and his team of witchdoctors and other specialists in preparing the magic necessary to assure victory.

Women, children, and those men past the age of combat made their way from surrounding villages with their livestock to climb to the higher levels of Kgopolwe and Sealene. There they could remain in safety, their herds held in fortified pens, guarded while the war against Jiwawa occupied Makikele's regiments. A few of the king's gunmen took up positions on the hills, ready to add firepower should the lower defenses be breached. Most would accompany the advanced forces, intending to prevent Jiwawa from ever reaching the capital.

The wait was not long. Realizing that the element of surprise had been lost, Paane and Jiwawa ordered an immediate attack on Sealene Hill. Jiwawa assured Paane that he would be king of Phalaborwa before the end of the day.

They had traveled a half day from Makwibidung on their trek to Sealene when they were engaged by Masetla's advance forces hiding behind ambush breaks. The leader of the advance guard, one of Masetla's trusted regiment age-mates, signaled his warriors to prepare their bows. A rain of hunting arrows, with razor-sharp iron points dipped in poison, fell silently onto the first column of Paane's men. Several fell wounded and dead, while Masetla's bush fighters vanished into the heavy undergrowth to reconnoiter further back and attack again with deadly effectiveness. Meanwhile, Masetla's main force of defenders was positioned closer to Sealene and Kgopolwe, his armed gunmen and archers strategically placed, waiting in readiness.

When the men from Makwibidung came into sight, Masetla ordered his warriors to advance. They trotted forward, shoulder to shoulder, each with leather shield and stabbing spear in hand. The pounding rhythms of the royal drums, the great carved *Boretho* and the small and most sacred *Tlanka*, drove his men forward into fierce combat.

Paane and Jiwawa led a less-disciplined army, trained more for the elephant hunt than to engage in pitched combat with Masetla's regiments. Distracted by the lethal fall of arrows and the cries of those struck by the deadly projectiles, the enemy faltered and checked its forward momentum. Without warning, while entering a boulder-strewn hillside pass, they were confronted by a solid wall of leather shields and Masetla's men, tense and poised for attack. Shots from gunmen, positioned in hidden breaks and concealed behind rock, took a heavy toll on the enemy's front line as the two armies collided in a fierce struggle to the death.

The close-knit line of spearmen paid a bloody toll when Jiwawa's elephant guns returned fire. As Masetla's men scattered into the bush to regroup for another attack, the Magwambwa began to shoot randomly and slowed down to reload their guns. When Masetla launched a new wave of spearmen and archers, Jiwawa's spearmen unleashed their weapons before being given the order to do so. Masetla's warriors, protected by a wall of shields, plunged forward to stop and rout the enemy.

Masetla then ordered his men to stop the advance and to retreat to a backup position to assess the injuries and deaths sustained among his men. There were a number of casualties, but most emerged from this assault unscathed.

As war chief, it was Masetla's job to keep his men from scattering and to maintain the discipline of his practiced line of defense. Anger, hatred, and tension set in as the defenders observed fellow combatants, relatives, and initiation brothers injured and killed. Shouting viciously, they advanced again, charging the enemy and maintaining their tested battle formation.

Fiercely pounded, sharpened metal thrust into sweating flesh, nostrils and throats choked with dust from the skirmish; the struggling men were deaf to a new war cry. Spear- and ax-wielding men charged into the battle from surrounding villages, summoned by the angry *boom, boom, boom* of *Boretho* and blasts of war trumpets. In a frenzy of hatred, they joined the charge to defend their land and their homes.

When word of the Magwambwa attack spread, all able-bodied men of the region rushed to the fray, bent on revenge against the hated poachers from Tsonga. Men from Nagome, armed and running at full trot, attacked the enemy's flanks, causing many casualties. Simultaneously, Kaetla Mojela, a seasoned fighter and hunter, arrived leading a force from Namagale Hill to join the ranks of Masetla's men. To observers high up on Sealene Hill, it seemed as if the surrounding bush swarmed with spear-wielding men attacking from every direction.

Jiwawa and Paane, seeing the flood of new combatants, ordered a retreat. Their men quickly scattered, turning tail toward Makwibidung. As the exhausted Magwambwa passed near Sekgopo, pursued by a combined force from Nagome, Namagale and Masetla's gunmen, angry local residents, alerted by the gunshots, left their walled villages to hunt down the scattered, fleeing invaders.

Jiwawa's war had ended with a devastating Magwambwa defeat. The attempted invasion of Phalaborwa by the Magwambwa caused widespread hatred and thirst for revenge, but Masetla called a halt to any further advance when Sekgopo was reached.

Following their retreat, Paane and Jiwawa argued over the ivory stored at Makwibidung. Jiwawa's men demanded the ivory, claiming their battle losses made it theirs. Paane was accused of misinforming them about the risks of attacking Sealene, and of cowardice because many of his men were unwilling to attack Sealene's defenders who were their kinsmen. A belligerent Jiwawa and his armed men then carried away all the ivory stockpiled in Makwibidung, leaving nothing for Paane.

Jiwawa and the Magwambwa assessed their losses after quickly burying their dead, then fled Makikele's domain. They took some of their wounded with them, leaving those too seriously injured to travel in the care of local villagers.

Makikele waited several days before ordering his regiments to enter Makwibidung. This was to give both sides time to bury their dead, and to allow Paane and his followers time to leave the area. None could forget Paane's betrayal, which had now led to much suffering. Many demanded that he be hunted down and killed. However, the king wished to avoid further bloodshed, which would achieve little and only add to the grief felt over so many injured and dead. Messengers were exchanged between Paane and the king, who demanded submission. Paane and his followers were once again sent into exile.

Paane quickly left Phalaborwa, traveling with his family and a core of followers, to settle in Mapulaneng among the highland Pedi. There he obtained protection and refuge with friends and long-standing family connections. In time, many others implicated in the war or believed to have been sympathetic with Paane were also forced to leave Phalaborwa. It was not a time of tolerance for those disloyal to the king.

Makwibidung and other villages occupied by Paane's family near Sekgopo were resettled with families loyal to the king. Trade of Makwibidung's red oxide ore and its equally valuable salt was transferred to trustworthy branches of the royal family and to noble families loyal to Sealene.

With Paane defeated and Jiwawa driven away, Makikele was praised as the defender of his people. War stories and accounts of Masetla's bravery and the power of Sealene magic spread outward from Phalaborwa to surrounding peoples.

Incoming trade parties brought greetings to the king from other tribal lands. Makikele's credentials as legitimate heir and ruler of Sealene and his reputation as a powerful sorcerer-king found wide acceptance, and he was able to further consolidate his kingdom at a time when more threatening forces than those of Jiwawa and the Magwambwa were beginning to challenge Phalaborwa.

News from the southern highlands and the eastern regions, where Zulu and Swazi continued to penetrate Sotho and Tsonga lands, was not auspicious, nor was news from the north, where Zulu and their growing amalgam of conquered peoples were expanding along the Limpopo and into Venda.

Shortly after their defeat, Jiwawa and his Magwambwa followers moved from Magashula's trade crossing to Ohrigstad, a Dutch Boer settlement in the Pedi Highlands. From there, they again moved, this time into Venda tribal territory, where they formed an alliance with Boer settlers also entering the region. It was not the last Makikele would see of them.

The High Price of Independence

Dark clouds of war were engulfing the southern regions bordering Makikele's kingdom. They were omens of trouble that would soon reach his land between the Lepelle and Letaba rivers. Queen Mother Mokadi, after a series of troubling dreams in which her house caught fire and then became inundated with snakes, sought the use of divination to discover the cause. Divining dice portended danger and the need to be vigilant. The warning she sent her son was received with gravity and concern. He knew that the now-aged and much-revered queen's dream messages must be heeded.

Since the *Tlala ya makgekgetwane* famine, which had led to the *Bakema* war, conditions along Phalaborwa's borders had become ominous. The war against Jiwawa two years earlier necessitated continual vigilance and a strengthening of the eastern borders near Sekgopo Hill. This state of alert had hardened Makikele's regiments into a formidable fighting force, comparable to that of the Swazi and Zulu now causing trouble in surrounding lands.

People longed for the peaceful days they had enjoyed in the closing years of Meele's kingship. They hoped that Makikele would keep Phalaborwa free of fighting. However, apprehension was building as word of invasion and burning of villages reached local ears from highland refugees seeking the king's protection. Troublesome stores circulated around the night fires at men's gathering places and by the cooking hearths. Many remembered the disturbing tales of earlier violent Swazi encounters in the days of *Kgoshi* Kgashane, and then again when Mosholwane was king. It was feared that history would soon be repeated and the land invaded.

When Bangeni Malatji, *ntona* of Phetole Hill, sent news to Sealene that the Swazi were infiltrating into villages in the western part of the kingdom, Makikele wished to avoid conflict at all cost. He decided not to antagonize the Swazi, opting instead to establish friendly ties and a flow of gifts to Swazi headmen in occupied Pedi villages. It was more prudent, he thought, to try diplomacy and to placate the Swazi. To confront them or take offensive action might jeopardize the security of his kingdom and provide an excuse for a Swazi attack. As a consequence, trade envoys were sent with gifts from Sealene to Swazi leaders positioned in surrounding Pedi tribal lands.

But when reports of growing Swazi encroachment on Phalaborwa continued, the king called a meeting of his war council.

Council elders remembered stories of earlier struggles with the Swazi that had scattered local residents; pillaged their cattle, grain, and possessions; and killed one of their kings.

"The people of Phalaborwa and the Swazi have lived for many years in an uneasy relationship, at times shattered by cattle raids and attacks on our border villages," said the *ntona*, Bangeni

Malatji. "However, their dependence on our carefully guarded metalworking and blacksmithing expertise and their wariness not to jeopardize their supply of weapons have accorded the Malatji a degree of autonomy not found elsewhere."

"So, what has changed, Uncle?" Makikele spoke with a grave concern for the stability of his kingdom.

Bangeni's reply did little to allay his fears. "Swazi cattle raiders and occasional forays by Zulu have penetrated Phalaborwa's borders, attacking villages on their way to the rich cattle regions in the neighboring highlands of Lobedu and Venda. Much of the Pedi area in the southern mountains has been badly disrupted by both Zulu and Swazi incursions, causing refugees to move into surrounding areas. Displaced families have crossed into Phalaborwa, bringing reports of theft, abductions, bloodshed, and the destruction of neighboring highland villages."

"I sense this spreading activity is a grave danger to our southern villages that will threaten the kingdom itself." Makikele's measured response was greeted with apprehension by the members of the council. "I will send spies into the southern Pedi territories."

After a week, the spies returned to Sealene and reported their discoveries to Makikele and the council.

Two men of the Ngwane family, who had traveled to several Kgatla tribal villages on the border, brought back ominous reports of the buildup of enemy forces.

"They plan to attack outlying Phalaborwa villages on their way to Venda to capture cattle," one of them said.

"We went under the guise of trading hoes and spear points," said the other. "We found many villages occupied by Swazi warriors, and the people are badly treated."

The first man took up the story. "In one village we requested beer to be brewed for the Swazi to loosen their tongues. When they were drunk, they revealed plans for an assault on both Sealene and Kgopolwe Hill, and their outlying cattle stations. Their plan is to capture livestock in Phalaborwa. These will either be slaughtered for food or sent back to the highlands to sustain the increased number of occupation forces. In the meantime, the main Swazi army will advance through Phalaborwa to subjugate the Venda living to the north. Their ultimate objective is to penetrate into the well-watered lands of Venda and steal from their large cattle herds."

Hearing of the danger, Makikele summoned representatives from every major nearby village. His war chiefs—his brother Masetla; Lerungi of the Malongane lineage; Maphalakanye Monyaela, a respected warrior seasoned by many battles; and other important leaders—joined the council in planning a defense of his capital and border villages. These were veterans of the war against Jiwawa's Magwambwa and their attack on Sealene and the Royal Triangle.

Over the next week, Makikele made several decisions.

"We must again prepare for war," he said at the next meeting of the war council. He turned to his brother Masetla. "The older regiments should remain close to their home villages to protect property and herds, but you must mobilize the younger fighters. Send them to the border regions. Where are we most vulnerable?"

"I anticipate an invasion from the west where Swazi traders usually ford the Lepelle River," said Masetla.

"Move the armies from eastern villages to the western borders to strengthen vulnerable positions. Send runners to all the villages and cattle stations, warning them of a state of alert. Instruct them to man lookout posts on hilltops near their homes, and to send runners reporting any suspicious activities in the western kingdom."

Makikele spoke to the whole council. "Return to your villages, alert your people, have your forges and smiths produce weapons for war. We need battle axes, spears, and arrow points. When the weapons are fashioned, distribute them to fighting-age men. Women and men must cut thornbush to strengthen fences around your villages and especially the fortified hill villages, which must be stockpiled with food and goods against attack and siege. I will also order the preparation of war medicines, including poisons for arrows, and perform divination to determine means to dissuade, delay, and destroy any hostile advance upon the capital."

During the second week of preparations, while men were being strategically positioned in the west, a trading party of Pedi and Swazi men arrived in the vicinity of Phetole village and encamped near one of Makikele's cattle posts along the Lepelle River.

As was the custom, the group expected to wait a number of days for permission from the king's *ntona* to enter the larger village. While they waited, it was also the custom for women and men of the surrounding countryside to visit them, selling food and beer and offering simple wares to barter. The local people reported back to Bangeni Malatji at Phetole that they had noticed something unusual about the trading party—no women accompanied them. The *ntona* immediately sent news to Makikele and the war council, who became suspicious and dispatched spies to the camp to investigate the situation and report back.

The group of spies included members of a local family of recent Swazi origin who were loyal to Makikele. Their presence was designed to put the strangers at ease and to build a rapport through meeting men with familiar names who knew Swazi language. The war council hoped that they would readily talk with locals able to understand their tongue. This ploy would gain information and better prepare them for possible attack.

The news the spies learned was disturbing. They reported that Swazi regiments were indeed preparing to steal cattle in Phalaborwa with intent to supply meat and booty to conquered Pedi settlements. They learned that three separate war parties were planning simultaneous attacks. Two of the war parties would advance near Phetole and follow the Selati River to launch assaults on Nagome, Kgopolwe, and possibly even Sealene. The third party would cross the wide Lepelle River further east along a well-known trading route and fording place. This group would raid smaller, less-defended villages as it advanced toward the large Sekgopo Hill settlement and its livestock.

Makikele consulted with Masetla and the other war chiefs. "I trust that Sekgopo is already adequately fortified, and that it will be able to withstand attack on its own and not require any further reinforcements from Sealene?"

"You are right," said Masetla. "If we are to expect a major Swazi penetration in the vicinity of our stronghold here, then I must caution against any deployment of its fighting force."

Makikele gave his orders, "Send runners to warn Sekgopo of this latest threat. All villages along the Selati River passage from Phetole to Kgopolwe and Sealene must be alerted and prepare for hostilities. All the eastern and western sections of the kingdom should be placed under a state of alert. War medicines will be prepared and taken to every major pathway into the kingdom, and magically doctored amulets will be placed in all villages on the kingdom's borders. All livestock must be shifted from vulnerable cattle stations to larger fortified population centers."

During the second week of these preparations, spies from the western Pedi border reported seeing Swazi in occupied villages making ready for war.

Men carried *Boretho*, the great drum of Makikele's royal enclosure, to the upper slopes of Sealene Hill where it was sounded. Its warning call was picked up in distant villages and relayed by their own drums.

Villagers now grazed their herds closer to home with armed warriors always at hand. Once alerted to danger, animals could be driven quickly back into fortified village pens. If attacked, they could be taken to higher ground inside the settlements. Weapons were made ready. Archers would be a first line of defense.

The first appearance of Swazi war parties in Phalaborwa was reported at one of Makikele's larger cattle camps along a river ford leading to Phetole. The site had been reinforced with local archers and spearmen.

Shortly after this news reached the war council at Kgopolwe, a team of runners from Nagome village, south of the capital, reported sighting a large enemy regiment crossing the Selati River, heading in their direction. By late afternoon, both settlements reported Swazi encampments south of Nagome. Shortly thereafter, runners from Phetole announced an attack on the Madeng Hill settlement, a smaller neighboring residential population.

Boretho sounded an alarm from high up in the terraces of Sealene, its deep resonance echoing for many miles, reaching villages and settlements throughout the broad, flat countryside. The heavy thudding of the great royal drum continued throughout the day and night as the royal women, in company with the king, performed prayer and climbed the upper granite reaches of towering Sealene to speak with the dead.

Sentries posted on hilltops checkering the wide grasslands of Makikele's domain waited tensely for signs of danger.

By afternoon, small groups of women and children, accompanied by elderly men, began to arrive at Nagome Hill from southern settlements. These refugees reported livestock theft, house burnings, injuries, and death. They had run away into the bush, leaving livestock and possessions behind. As well as casualties, they also reported that people had been captured and taken away toward the Lepelle and into Swazi-occupied Pedi territory.

In the late afternoon, two runners from Sekgopo Hill arrived at Kgopolwe. The messengers, young men of the Hlame lineage, had been dispatched by Makikele's uncle, Phatladi Mathipa. They had been deployed to recruit reinforcements from the king's regiment at Kgopolwe. The news they carried was startling: a large Swazi force had been sighted south of Sekgopo, and cattle had been stolen from surrounding cattle stations. Several offensive raids on the Swazi invaders had been unsuccessful in halting their advance. The runners said that they feared Swazi attack was imminent, and that this eastern citadel of Makikele's domain would soon itself be at war.

Makikele's trumpeter sounded the *phalaphala*, announcing his entry into the main cattle enclosure, where his councilors from surrounding villages and important generals of active regiments awaited him.

"The situation is dire," said King Makikele. "We must activate defensive plans previously agreed upon by the war council." He turned to Masetla. "You are to deploy seasoned fighters in the direction of Nagome to engage Swazi troops on the open savannah."

"This will be just a diversionary tactic," said Masetla, "to delay a Swazi attack on Nagome and prevent them from penetration into the Royal Triangle. But no reinforcements can be sent to Sekgopo at this time. We must keep the largest force here to protect the capital."

The following day, several skirmishes between Masetla's warriors and the Swazi occurred south of Nagome. The men of Phalaborwa were able to keep the enemy at bay, but reinforcements continued to swell the Swazi ranks, enabling them to advance on the village.

That night, there was an attack on the heavily reinforced thorn palisades surrounding the village. Flaming arrows were sent over the walls, igniting house roofs, and there were a number of casualties, including the death of a child.

Prince Masetla's men repulsed the raid, but with great difficulty, and then his spearmen and archers launched several pre-dawn forays against the enemy. Angered by these encounters, the Swazi launched a sunrise counter attack against Nagome's main gate and several secondary entrances. The enemy troops breached one of the smaller barricaded passageways and entered the outer defenses, fanning out single file along the inner periphery of the enclosure.

No sooner had they streamed into the village than they were set upon by a swarm of screaming, ax-wielding village men and the spearmen of Masetla's regiment. However, the Swazi forced the defenders back onto the terraced interior of the village where heavy timber barriers blockaded the enemy ascent. The fortified terraces afforded the defenders an advantage over the onslaught of murderous Swazi spearmen.

A rain of poisoned arrows fell from the protected heights of Nagome, killing several Swazi. Crouching defenders, both men and women, hiding under the protection of large boulders, took careful aim and catapulted stones onto those attempting to force their way up to the higher village levels, causing them to retreat. Three six-pound elephant guns, brought from the king's arsenal at Sealene, were fired on the advancing enemy vanguard as it attempted to climb a narrow passageway leading from low-lying and more open cattle pens into the heavily barricaded residential terraces. A volley from the guns and a cascade of arrows and stones took a heavy toll, bringing a halt to the Swazi advance. Corpses, and wounded crying out in pain, blocked the passageway. A flood of defenders, wielding axes and spears, descended from the hillside fortress in pursuit of the retreating Swazi, slaughtering those already felled by arrows or flying stones.

In less than an hour, the enemy advance was stopped. The retreating Swazi concentrated on collecting scattered livestock

Swazi attack at Nagome Hill

that had been left behind when the herds had been taken to higher ground. The men of Nagome pursued the Swazi at a distance, shouting insults and threats at them as they withdrew south toward their encampment across the Selati River.

Several young warriors, menacingly brandishing spears from behind leather shields, raced to engage lone retreating Swazi. Archers on the run continued releasing arrows aimed into the backs of fleeing men. For more distant enemy encounters, the silent, deadly Phalaborwa arrow was the weapon of defense and offense. Widely feared for their fatal accuracy and deadly swiftness, these poison-tipped projectiles could easily bring down a kudu, or wildebeest, and even the dangerous thick-skinned buffalo.

Masetla's regiment, sent from Kgopolwe by the king as a relief force, arrived and joined the men of Nagome in their pursuit. The battle stopped at the riverbank, where the fleeing Swazi were able to ford to safety.

But they were not all so lucky. While the rearguard of retreating Swazi waded waist-deep through the slow-moving current, a young archer took aim from the river's edge. Using the full extension of his bow, he released an arrow that swept across the water, finding its target in the lower back of a large man, who turned in shock to grasp the painful embedded projectile. As he turned, he looked toward his adversary and was struck by a second arrow, this time in the ribcage. He fell backwards, bright crimson blood adding pigment to the brown water of the Selati. The bowman and a companion who had joined him to fire the second deadly arrow screamed loudly with excitement as the lifeless body of their enemy drifted with the current away from the ford. Crocodiles rested and watched a short distance downstream, waiting for the body to float their way.

More than twenty Swazi were killed in the river. A great victory shout rose up from the defending regiments when the remaining enemy disappeared into the bush. Some of the retreating Swazi returned their shouts with angry replies, brandishing fists and weapons, a warning that the residents of Nagome had not seen the last of them.

When the victorious men returned to the village, they were greeted by loud ululations from women and children. These sounds of joy quickly dissipated, however, muffled by the wails and lamentations of mourners carrying wounded and dead along village pathways. The siege of Nagome Hill had taken a heavy toll. A dozen men and several women and children had died, and another dozen or more had been injured, some severely.

Nagome's *ntona*, fearing a renewed attack, ordered the village's livestock herded north to the larger more fortified Kgopolwe Hill village, and to settlements on and around the low-lying hills and granite outcroppings of the Lolwe mining complex. These strongholds guarded access to Makikele's royal enclosure at Sealene.

While this was being done, other villagers stripped the dead enemy of clothing, jewelry, and weapons and scavenged the bodies for whatever they might provide. An elderly woman, with hoe in hand, angrily smashed the head of a twisted body, cursing it as it lay lifeless, its open eyes staring into the sun.

Under orders of Nagome's headman, a delegation of village witchdoctors moved around the blood-splattered battlefield, inspecting carcasses. They cut away body parts, which they then placed in leather pouches to be used as ingredients for magic. These enemy remains, still warm and supple, would produce valuable medicines used to protect the village should there be another assault. Some would be incorporated into talismans, worn by those manning barricades or going out to pursue the enemy in the surrounding bush country.

The stunned people of Nagome prepared the bodies of their own dead for burial. In such a time of crisis, this had to be done quickly, using a shallow mass grave dug into the floor of the main cattle enclosure. While some performed this sad task, others quickly set about reinforcing the defenses and taking stock of their losses.

Two Swazi, captured during the final chase, were brought to the headman's enclosure for interrogation. One was young, about eighteen, the other a full warrior in his thirties. They stumbled through the narrow gauntlet, receiving beatings and being pelted with stones and feces, spat upon and screamed at by the enraged residents wanting revenge. Exhausted, terrified, and in shock, they were left in the headman's compound, bound with ropes, awaiting their fate. Word was sent to Sealene that the two had been captured.

The king was pleased that captives had been taken, and ordered the messenger to return to Nagome to make sure they were kept alive. Makikele consulted with two of his witchdoctors before sending them to follow the message runner to Nagome. One of them named Tlagisi, a wizened practitioner of ancient war sorcery, limped with old age, so they traveled at a much slower pace than the runner.

A guard of young warriors, armed with the long bladed Swazi-type stabbing spears and leather shields, accompanied old Tlagisi and his assistant. These troops were anxious to reach Nagome, where the fighting had taken place.

Tlagisi had no love for the Swazi. He was a refugee from Sanaskei in the southern highlands; his village had resisted against invading Swazi regiments, but had eventually been decimated. While some of his people remained in the highlands, accepting to live under Swazi domination, others, including the survivors of his own family, had begged for protection in Phalaborwa. Makikele gave them land at Tubatsi Hill, a sparsely populated village north of Sealene. But Tlagisi was well known for his healing skills and had a reputation for divination and black magic, so Makikele had ordered him to be brought to the capital as a resource for the royal family.

I will cut off the older captive's genitals with the king's own hunting knife given to me for the task, Tlagisi murmured to himself as he reached into his leather pouch and touched the long blade fixed to a heavy bone handle. He smiled as he thought how they would be used to strengthen war medicines to defeat the Swazi.

He removed the long, shining blade from its leather sheath. Knives similar to this one, which was of Swazi design, were now becoming popular in Phalaborwa, much as the Swazi spear blade had replaced the narrower, long-hafted spear of an earlier generation. The kudu antler handle was worn smooth and fitted comfortably into his hand. The blade had belonged to the late *Kgoshi* Meele Malatji; some claimed it dated from the days of Meele's father, Mosholwane, who had also fought the Swazi; others believed that the weapon had been a Swazi peace offering to the Malatji. It was now part of the king's war regalia, a holy relic of the ruling family reserved for special use, such as the task Tlagisi had set off to perform. The old sorcerer was honored to have it on his person.

He smiled and thought to himself, *I want to hear the Swazi scream as he watches me cut into his body and sever his testicles, and*

*then his ears, and then his nose, and finally his tongue. The louder
he calls out and squirms in pain, the more powerful the effect of the
medicine I will make.*

Tlagisi grinned as he considered the suffering he would
inflict on the cursed Swazi jackals being held by Nagome's
ntona. His hatred for the Swazi energized him. He spat bitterly on the ground when he remembered the son he had
left unburied while fleeing from his burning village in the
highlands.

When they were in sight of the fortified village and battlefield, the old man quickened his pace, and his entourage began
loudly chanting a war song announcing their arrival.

Tlagisi reached Nagome in the late afternoon. After his
arrival, he consulted with Prince Masetla about the king's
design for the captives. When news reached him of the Nagome
attack, the sorcerer had relished the opportunity of holding
captives. He planned to use these two hated sons of hyenas to
the king's advantage against the enemy. One captive would be
held hostage, while the second older man would be tortured
and executed, his body parts incorporated into defensive magic
used by Makikele to protect his capital.

Along the pathways running downhill from the village to
the Selati River ford, he could see enemy carcasses and those
of severely wounded Swazi who had been unable to escape.
All were beheaded and mutilated, the eyes, ears, tongues, and
genitals removed, leaving gaping holes of blood and torn flesh.
Sharpened poles were forced into their bodies, impaling them
for display. Swarms of black flies covered the corpses.

These gruesome displays, left to hang in the sun, were intended
to deter returning Swazi, a warning of what awaited them. The
horror of the scene was enhanced by vultures, attracted by the
smell of rotting flesh. These harbingers of death circled in the

sky above the battle scene. As their numbers increased, their wingtips touched, and some seemed to collide as they glided in the wind's currents. They descended and settled in trees or on the ground around the dead. Some lighted onto the impaled carcasses, tearing at putrefying flesh. This sent a signal to those still in flight, looping overhead. Soon the sky emptied, and the black hook-beaked followers of death competed for access to their food source. It was a morbid feast. The intensity of the vultures as they fed, and a lone scavenging jackal drawn to the scene, disturbed the swarms of flies. As the day progressed, dark buzzing clouds of insects rose and settled in endless succession as the sinister carrion-eaters fought among themselves for choice morsels of meat and internal organs. The squawking, screeching sounds of the vultures echoed to the river's edge.

Heads of the dead were impaled atop ceremonial poles and freshly cut pikes on the trail leading to the settlement, some positioned with their feathered headdresses still attached, their eyes and gaping mouths greeting passersby with macabre stares. These lifeless witnesses hung all day and throughout the night as if keeping vigil to ward off marauders. In the moonlight, hyenas and jackals competed for scraps of bone remaining on the ground, screaming and growling as they fought over fallen body parts. Two large hyenas, standing on their hind legs, tugged at a pair of stiffened legs, eventually succeeding in pulling the entire carcass down from the pole and onto the ground. Packs of nocturnal scavengers, attracted by the blood and sounds of vicious skirmishes for what remained, furiously tore at the body. Soon the African night set in and enveloped this scene of carnage in darkness, but the sounds of beasts of the night greedily feeding persisted.

Amid the darkened grasses and scrub bush, a lone lion, old and cast out from his pride, wandered about sniffing at dried blood, but was soon distracted by the scent of livestock within the fortified tightly-sealed village. As the lion circled the enclosure, his ears rotated to pick up sounds of nervous animals sensing his presence. While this feline hunter continued his prowl, wailing for Nagome's dead could be heard throughout the night and reached the ears of Swazi sentries waiting in the distant darkness.

On the far side of the Selati River, a solitary figure quietly pondered the sight, and then chanted a dirge as he retreated to report the fate of his compatriots. This was Molonyo, a Swazi general. His sister's son hung headless among the dead. The youthful, energetic boy had been felled with elephant shot while attempting to climb a barricade. Calculating his losses and the ferocity of Nagome's defenders, Molonyo deliberated to himself whether to push forward to Makikele's capital and escalate the war.

Several days passed without further enemy incursion. It was clear, however, from the reports of lookouts monitoring activity on the western side of the Selati that no retreat was planned, and that additional Swazi fighters were entering the area. Runners from Phetole village reached Sealene, reporting the destruction and pillaging of Madeng Hill and the abandonment of smaller settlements in the surrounding area. Livestock and captive women and children had been transported across the Lepelle River into Swazi-occupied Pedi tribal territory. Captured men had been executed and decapitated, their heads taken as war trophies.

The messengers also reported a shift eastward of enemy encampments, their numbers bolstered along the Selati. This did not bode well for the royal villages clustered around Sealene, Kgopolwe, and Lolwe, those situated just a few miles north of Nagome Hill. When tortured, the Swazi captives revealed that the attack they had participated in was intended only to steal cattle to feed a larger Swazi army on the march through Phalaborwa on its way to capture Venda cattle in the northern highlands.

The Queen mother's ominous dreams and troubling messages from her divining dice persisted following the Swazi battle at Nagome. She urged greater vigilance and readiness. Makikele trusted his mother's intuition and wove a careful plan to protect his capital from any security breach.

CHAPTER TWENTY-THREE

Witchcraft and Sorcery

The day following the Nagome Hill battle, a Pedi spy married to a woman from Kgopolwe arrived at the capital and reported troubling news to Makikele's war council. At the same time as the spoils from the first Swazi raids in Phalaborwa were being sent back to the Pedi Highlands, a large enemy force was amassing beyond the Selati. The Swazi intended to capture livestock from the larger population centers. The Pedi's report confirmed information obtained from the tortured Swazi captives. Word quickly spread throughout the capital, causing panic among the populace, who feared another bloodletting.

Such a threat called for extreme measures, both defensive and magical, to protect the royal enclave. Forges at Lolwe and on the slopes of Nagome and Kgopolwe burned brightly, stoked by bellows operators, working in shifts to produce molten iron ore to be hammered into weapons. In the king's armory house, elephant guns were cleaned and inspected in preparation for an attack. Some of the guns were newly forged or traded, others were of great vintage.

In his residence, close to the foot of Sealene's lofty granite megalith, Makikele sat surrounded by a team of witchdoctors, his court sorcerer, and his three uncles, all trusted advisors. Experienced guardians of tradition and seasoned warriors, they understood that war magic played an important role in the preparations for a battle. Working swiftly, they combined ingredients from an assortment of containers stored in the royal residence. Some included enemy body parts from the recent attack on Nagome. Other components of the formulary had been gathered with great care over time and preserved for this purpose. All were blended together into war medicines of immense power to be used against the enemy waiting on the opposite banks of the Selati River.

Mobilized for attack only a short distance beyond the fortified gates of Kgopolwe, Molonyo's forces, embittered by humiliating losses, sharpened their spears and axes to exact revenge and a bloody end to the Malatji dynasty.

Makikele's mother, Mokadi, now elderly and bent with arthritis, sat on a woven reed mat, her extended legs lavishly adorned with countless copper rings and beaded bands. She studied her prized possession, a bracelet of copper and red beads; one ancient large glass bead, the central stone of the piece, had been brought by Makikele from Dzata. She rubbed her fingers over the old glass cylinder, turning it over repeatedly on its cotton string, talking to it and the ancient ones who had once held it between their fingers as she now did.

"Protect us, shadowy spirits, from the past in this time of danger," she said. "Destroy these Swazi lice afflicting us and threatening my son."

While the entire kingdom prayed and waited, Mokadi was the guardian of these powerful medicines now being blended in secret. They had been entrusted to her at the time of the death of her husband, *Kgoshi* Meele, when she and her sister-in-law and the now-dead uncle, Leshoro Malatji, prepared his body for burial.

As she kept vigil over these royal relics, it was the king's witchdoctors, specialists in occult matters, now huddled in shadowy secrecy, who would correctly formulate the ingredients to release their power. The magic, placed in animal-horn containers, would be distributed throughout the royal centers to guard the capital. Exact placement of these ingredients would be carefully decided through divination.

Mokadi chanted her dead husband's praises in a soft, gravelly voice, invoking the late king and her own ancestral spirits to fortify her son for the serious work now undertaken to protect their land.

Four women huddled close together on mats in a different recess of the king's private abode. Two wizened figures sat with legs outstretched, resting their backs against the clay wall. Another ancient hag, her grey head covered by a fitted hyrax-skin cap, lay curled up on a mat facing the others, her dark eyes occasionally reflecting flames from the nearby hearth fire fueled by the king's slave. The fourth figure, a younger woman, Maboyana, the king's eldest sister, conducted the meeting with her paternal aunts. She had long ago returned to Sealene to serve as queen sister, the royal *rakgadi*, and as chief priestess for the king and her people.

She performed her sacred functions under the watchful eyes of these old aunts, who collectively embodied the kingdom's ritual traditions, sacred knowledge, and experience. They were all widowed, and lived near the royal compound; it was they who performed the many complex rites believed important to everyday life. Their sacred functions assured harmony between the living and the ever-present and continually demanding spirit world, resting high up on Sealene and on nearby Modimolle Hill. It was on Modimolle that royal women were interred, and they were not to be neglected. Through meticulous maintenance of ancestral rituals, these royal women, and in particular the *rakgadi*, Maboyana, ensured the safety of the royal family and the entire kingdom. The combined efforts of these powerful women would determine the outcome of the coming crisis.

Maboyana lived in Sealene's extensive royal compound, in a cluster of houses with several of her younger children. The houses of the queen mother, Mokadi, the many royal wives of Makikele, and a cadre of royal dependents, ritual specialists, court retainers, and slaves were situated nearby. Maboyana had returned to Kgopolwe after many years living in distant Setsoge, the village of her dead husband. While she studied and prayed with the others assembled around her, she wondered if the Swazi raids had extended as far west as the home of her husband's people. If so, had the family fled? Had cattle been stolen? The herd belonged in part to her, issue from her bridewealth and royal gifts to her husband's family, repeatedly exchanged and distributed over years in numerous contractual agreements.

She cleared these distracting thoughts from her mind and returned to planning the climb they would make up to the royal graves on Sealene's mortuary terraces. From Sealene they would walk the short distance to Modimolle Hill, to recite archaic prayer formulas and pour libations on the graves of the queens. Her eldest aunt, who was too old and frail to walk, had insisted on accompanying the other royal women on this vital mission, and would be carried by porters.

Maboyana and two of the aunts, sisters of the late *Kgoshi* Meele, moved across the room to sit close to Makikele, where they would finalize preparations for these propitiatory rites.

The ritual was enacted in the stone-terraced cemetery where Makikele's father and grandfather rested close to each other, and among the graves of other royal men of their generations. At the foot of the hill, animals were being ritually killed, butchered, roasted, and eaten. Included were a large bull, entirely black, and a young black goat from a herd specially bred for sacrifice. Other livestock were butchered, cooked, doctored with war medicines, and eaten throughout the villages of the Royal Triangle; in particular, the young men of the defending regiments were fed well so they could fight bravely.

After the sacrificial animals were slaughtered, court diviners studied portions of the entrails for signs from the spirit world. Following this, young runners were sent out to the borders of the capital, with animal horns infused with the protective medicines produced from the royal women's alchemy. These horns were pounded into the ground at village boundaries and along pathways where the war magic could work its effect. In every location, village magicians, headmen, and dignitaries joined the runners and added their prayers to strengthen this protective web of supernatural defense against the feared Swazi.

The gravity of the situation required intercession from the four most senior women of the ruling Malatji line. They sought spiritual protection for country and family, calling out for wisdom, courage, and decisiveness for Makikele, his advisors, and warrior generals in the critical hours ahead. The king accompanied them up the mortuary hill. However, his was a lesser role, observing and affirming their solicitation of *Kgobeane*, the creator of all humankind, and those important spirits from the dead who mediated on their behalf with the ambiguous and sometimes fickle forces of fate and creation.

Maboyana spent much of the evening in the company of several sorcerers and diviners, some of great repute throughout Phalaborwa. While these specialists practiced their science, Queen Mokadi summoned a trusted Tsonga sorcerer, known for her divination skills. This woman once lived at Sekgopo and knew Mokadi's family. She was asked to bring her regalia and divining bones, and they met secretly, following the return of the party from the grave terraces after midnight.

Mokadi and the sorcerer met in the queen's secluded compound. They were joined by Maboyana and the king's great wife, Mosale. They hoped this Tsonga woman, who used spirit possession in her interpretations, would help them discern the ambiguous and confusing messages coming from their earlier divination efforts. Mokadi was troubled that a clear message had not emerged from her own efforts. Time was of the essence as her son prepared for war.

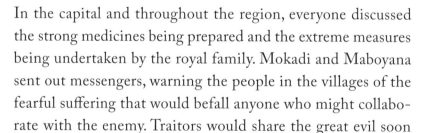

In the capital and throughout the region, everyone discussed the strong medicines being prepared and the extreme measures being undertaken by the royal family. Mokadi and Maboyana sent out messengers, warning the people in the villages of the fearful suffering that would befall anyone who might collaborate with the enemy. Traitors would share the great evil soon to befall the Swazi.

That evening, the captured Swazi youth was released from Nagome and sent back across the Selati. Fearful of the curse Makikele had placed on the land, he hastily made his way to Molonyo's encampment, and reported what he had learned.

Molonyo returned to his regiment's camp and retired to his quarters in an abandoned hut, meeting with his diviner and the ironsmith who accompanied his regiment. Both were trusted advisors. Here he also met with his war counselors to discuss conditions among the regiment and raiding tactics.

That night, however, he intended to probe the supernatural realm for answers to troubling signs he had observed during the previous week's events. He was distressed by the death of his young nephew, especially because the body of the youth could never be retrieved for proper burial at his father's village in Swaziland.

He had taken the boy under his wing and brought him to his headquarters in the conquered Pedi territory. He had hoped that the cattle captured during these expeditions might benefit his family when presented for distribution by the Dlamini princes whom he served. His elder brother, father of the dead boy, had been favored in court and had received patronage with gifts of cattle. Molonyo expected that his entire lineage might advance in court following the current great expedition to Venda.

His failure to subdue Nagome village, the death of his nephew, and the casualties sustained in the battle had all presented unexpected setbacks to his plans. Although he had a large fighting force, he began to wonder if an attack on the sorcerer king's stronghold might prove to be a mistake. While his regiments, angered by their defeat and losses, pressed to launch a new offensive and wreak revenge, word of powerful magic housed at Sealene weighed heavily on his mind.

After many months spent pillaging villages as they descended from the highlands and crossed the Lepelle River and onto the low, dry grasslands, the Nagome assault had been the first setback for Molonyo and his Swazi forces. Could this be an omen? Was this secretive metalworking kingdom cursed and to be avoided?

He was grieved that his nephew had died unmarried and without children. It distressed him that the boy's body would not receive a proper burial. News of the death would greatly upset his family. He had gathered together the youth's few personal belongings. These would be taken back to his father. One day, he thought, the family would need to perform a reintegration ritual, returning the youth's spirit to his Swaziland home.

They would need to perform mourning rites for all their dead that evening. With the assistance of his diviner, Molonyo set about selecting a sacrificial animal from the captured herd. Entering the cattle enclosure, he loudly praised his ancestors and those of the great Swazi ruling house, the Dlamini. Then quietly, almost inaudibly, he reported to them which animal he would give them that evening.

He chose a large black bull, a prized specimen, and then ordered the animal thrown to the ground and stabbed with a sacrificial spear he carried with him for such occasions. When the beast bellowed, Molonyo responded loudly so everyone could hear, "Cry out, bull of the ancestors."

Then, in a barely audible whisper, he pronounced the name of his nephew, followed by the others killed in battle. The sacrificed animal was then skinned, care being taken not to spill the blood or contents of the entrails on the ground. A segment of the fourth stomach was removed and burned with a certain yellow bush herb as incense to the dead spirits. A second portion of the same stomach section was then placed in a hidden location for the ancestral spirits to lick during the night.

The remainder of the sacrificial beast, and two others selected from the herd, were then doctored with herbs by Molonyo's diviner to purify all of the blood that had been shed in battle. The meat was roasted, and then distributed to everyone in the camp to be eaten that night. All remnants of bone and skin were burned so that nothing remained. While the meat was eaten and washed down with warm millet beer, they recalled the names of those killed and details of the battle. While they consumed the death-ritual meal, all felt a union with those who had died.

Molonyo then retired to sleep, taking a draught administered by the diviner, who was also an accomplished herbalist. The drug induced a deep dream-sleep, which transported Molonyo back to his father's village.

In the dream, Molonyo walked along a familiar path leading to an abandoned hut, its thatch half fallen in, its door missing. In the sunlight of the open doorway, he discovered a small brown snake curled up asleep on the floor. As he observed the snake, it was awakened by a green lizard falling from the roof's broken rafters. The sluggish snake then pursued the lizard as it escaped through the door, but it was attacked by a green cobra hiding alongside the wall of the hut. When the lizard escaped into the bush, the cobra devoured the brown snake, and then also disappeared, following the lizard into the surrounding bush.

When Molonyo emerged from the ruined house in his dream, his path was blocked by another cobra. This large black snake stood partially upright before him, its hood flared as if ready to strike. Fearing the deadly poisonous viper, Molonyo retreated in haste along a different path, the warning hiss of the cobra ringing in his ears.

When Molonyo awoke, memory of the vivid dream involving snakes, played on his mind. He summoned his diviner to interpret the dream.

Squatting beside the fire in the moonlight, the diviner sought out details from Molonyo's account that might help him interpret the dream as it might relate to their situation in this foreign place. Molonyo softly clapped his hands, as was the custom in such exchanges, to indicate agreement with the diviner's skillful, quiet questions.

"Was the house you dreamed of abandoned?" his earnest interrogator asked.

Molonyo softly clapped, and said, "I did see this."

"Was it a burial house?"

"I did not see this."

The questions continued. "Was the cobra green in color? Was the falling lizard also green? Were other animals, people, or objects involved?"

When the diviner felt satisfied that he had sufficient information to work with, the questioning ended. He then reached for his divining pieces: four differently shaped carved ivory cubes, several sea shells, and small animal joint bones. Removing them from a leather bag, he recited praises to the various pieces, blowing over them and then spitting on them before throwing them on a skin mat placed between the two men.

He carefully examined the configuration of the pieces as they fell onto the matting. In particular, he studied how the variously shaped objects aligned with a principal large ivory die carved with lines on each side. After throwing the pieces several times, supported by continued questioning, the diviner presented his conclusions to Molonyo.

"The brown snake is one of your ancestors attempting to send you a message of warning. The green cobra appears to be a more powerful force, possibly that of these local Malatji who pose a threat to your undertaking against them. The lizard represents a strong female force allied with the cobra. The appearance of a threatening black cobra blocking your path is difficult to tie in with the other players in your dream. I think it could indicate repercussions for or from our own Dlamini rulers. The black snake, in this case, outranks the green, and must signify our superior Dlamini princes. The black snake gravely compounds the situation in your revelation, and must be avoided. Look for a tangible sign as you deliberate your next step concerning the iron-making king's stronghold. You must follow your instinct when it is revealed to you."

Both men deliberated over the meaning of the black cobra in Molonyo's dream revelation. They recalled accounts they had heard of the powerful magic being spread throughout the local villages by Makikele, who was reputed to be a sorcerer as well as a warrior. It was also rumored that the queen mother possessed additional powers bequeathed to her by the mother of the late king, a Swazi noblewoman sent by the Dlamini as an alliance bride, and that she knew the magic of Molonyo's people.

While Molonyo and his diviner continued to discuss these omens and signs, the great drum of Sealene sounded a warning call that war magic was being disseminated throughout the land, with a powerful curse on all who challenged Makikele's precinct. The deep resonance of the repetitive pounding of the drum continued unbroken across the land throughout that dark night.

Accompanying the sound of the drum, but audible only to those close to Makikele on Sealene Hill, was the sound of another instrument, that of a magic porcupine quill flute. Several years earlier, Mokadi had used a magic flute to communicate with Makikele when she summoned him back from Venda to Phalaborwa. But the use of the flute on this occasion was different. This time, Makikele used the flute to warn the people of Phalaborwa of the planned Swazi attack, but also to forewarn them that he would use magic to defeat the Swazi, and that they should do nothing until they received his signal.

When the many *ntona* and village headmen throughout Phalaborwa slept that night, each of them received a dream-vision of a great storm, of floods, of screaming Swazi being dragged away in a rushing torrent, and of others running in retreat. The vision was accompanied by the deep boom of *Boretho* and a cacophony of other noises, which started with the deep resonance of cattle lowing, followed by claps of thunder and the sound of rushing water, and finally by the clamor of shrill croaking.

In the early predawn hours, a small herd of cattle was released from Kgopolwe and driven into Molonyo's camp. Rumor spread that these animals were of Swazi derivation, descendants of cattle exchanged in previous generations, gifted to maintain peace and accord, remnants of an old marriage tie between the Malatji and the Dlamini. The arrival of this livestock was confusing. Could it be seen as a peace offering to ward away attack? Or did it signify an act of defiance, a rejection of what was Swazi?

As Molonyo stepped away from his fire to inspect the cattle, he was startled by a snake that appeared alongside his path. The brown serpent quickly disappeared from sight, leaving Molonyo to ponder the sign from his dream.

Long before daybreak, the Swazi silently broke camp to take up positions for their pre-dawn attack on Makikele's capital. They stealthily found their way through the dark bush to organize themselves into battle formation, taking care to avoid detection of their intended surprise assault. As they did so, the great drum of the enemy king abruptly ceased its night-long droning thud.

Suddenly the sky darkened, the momentary silence yielded by the drum now replaced by the growling sounds of thunder. Within minutes, a great roaring wind swept down from the northern Venda highlands and across the open bush savannah. The screaming wind brought heavy rain and a frightening lightning and thunder, which struck and pounded the ground. The terrified regiments, crouching and positioned ready to attack, were engulfed by the storm, their wet bodies glistening as lightening struck the ground near them.

The impact of the storm forced Molonyo's army to take shelter beneath trees and their cowhide shields. Within minutes the Selati River burst its banks, and smaller water courses quickly filled with runoff from the surrounding hills and dry gullies. The land and the entire Swazi regiment, including Molonyo and his war chiefs, were soon drenched by the pelting rain. The surprise deluge reduced the important markers of regimental rank, squadron, and lineage identity, the feathered headdresses and war regalia, to clumps of limp, soggy, meaningless matter clinging to soaked skin. Facial and body war paint, meticulously applied during the night while the army feasted, was obliterated. The once fierce-looking soldiers were transformed into nondescript caricatures, which might have been laughable but for their deadly intent.

When the storm subsided almost as quickly as it had begun, the piercing sound of tree frogs filled the air. At first there were only a few of them, then hundreds began screaming, and then thousands joined in, creating a deafening high-pitched din.

With first dawn light, the granite towers crowning Kgopolwe and Sealene Hills remained invisible, shrouded by a heavy mist, and all the land appeared to be submerged beneath water. Molonyo and his warrior chiefs, perplexed by this sudden transformation and low visibility, moved forward to the banks of the Selati, only to discover it impassable. The shallows of the much-used ford were engulfed by a swift current able to carry away even the strongest swimmer.

While Molonyo waded through wet grass and pools of water along the riverbank, a green mamba raised its head and struck at his leg, hissing a warning; it raised its flared head, and its menacing eyes defied the unwelcome intruder. Seeing the reality of this sign from his dream, he ordered his generals to withdraw from the water's edge and canceled plans for the assault.

Within an hour, the Swazi invading force abandoned its campsites and began the long march north to Venda. Makikele's herd of Swazi cattle, left behind by the retreating army, roamed among the extinguished campfires and dampened detritus of the now-departed invaders. By mid-morning, when the fog burned away in a hot sun, the towering hills of Makikele's capital once again came into view on the horizon. With the appearance of sunshine, the frogs abruptly ceased their screeching. Their sounds were replaced by those of villagers emerging from their homes to assess the state of their situation and inspect the ruined enemy campsites.

Runners were sent out to villages as far as the eastern stronghold at Sekgopo Hill and west to Phetole to announce the departure of the Swazi. These messengers also conveyed the story of Makikele's powerful sorcery, and how his war and rain and lightning magic had transformed the region from dry land into a marsh, frightening the Swazi invaders into a retreat without a single arrow being fired. Not even a milch goat had been stolen or killed.

CHAPTER TWENTY-FOUR

Bloody Waters

Several months after the attempted Swazi invasion and their retreat north, a runner arrived in Sealene, sent by the Venda ruler of Ngome. Makikele knew that the northern principality of his youthful days had been raided by the Swazi following their departure from Phalaborwa. But, reports from the Venda north had been sporadic. Itinerant trading groups had ceased going north because of reported hostilities making information sparse. He was pleased at long last to hear directly from Ngome.

The man was a cousin of the Venda prince and had been entrusted to deliver an important message to the people of Phalaborwa.

After resting and eating, he sought an audience with Makikele and senior members of his council. They met at the king's cattle enclosure.

"*Trobela*, *Kgoshi* Makikele, great Malatji, king of Phalaborwa, son of the porcupine totem," the man said, greeting him by bowing low and performing the ritual handclapping required when addressing royalty. "*Trobela*, great witchdoctor, the one who knows Venda magic." The Venda messenger bowed profoundly a second time to the king and his counselors.

Makikele, having spent two years in Venda studying under the herbalist Pulani and as a guest of the local royal family and now an in-law to the Ngome ruler through marriage to his cousin, was familiar with the *losha* and understood its importance in Venda custom. He acknowledged and returned the greeting, speaking in the Venda language. "*Trobela*, cousin of the Venda prince, the great ruler of Ngome and descendant of Thovhele and Thohoyandou," he said. "You are welcome in the cattle enclosures of the Ba-Phalaborwa."

When everyone was seated around the fire, Makikele ordered his servant to bring beer, and then invited the man to speak. "What news do you bring from Ngome?"

"The news I bring is not good. The Swazi have crossed our lands without permission or the payment of tribute. They have invaded our villages, pillaged our possessions, and stolen our cattle. Even our millet crop is decimated. They now prepare to leave Venda and travel south once more."

Prince Masetla, seated near Makikele with other counselors, disgusted by the messenger's report, shouted out, "The Swazi! They are a curse upon the people of this region. We chased them from Phalaborwa and made them humble in their defeat. When we saw them traveling toward the north and further away from their homeland, we feared they were up to no good."

Makikele was greatly troubled by the news, but managed to control his anger. "Which route do they take?" he asked.

"They follow the old trade route from Dzata to Phalaborwa. They are on their way to the Pedi highlands and must travel through, or circle around, Phalaborwa. But their progress is slow. They are taking great care herding the stolen cattle to avoid where the tsetse fly hide. They hope to reach the steep tsetse-free hill country on the far side of the Lepelle, which their people now control. They try to do this without losing cattle to the fly."

Makikele thought for a moment, making some mental calculations. "How many days before they reach the ford where the Lepelle and Selati Rivers merge?"

"Perhaps five or six days."

Makikele turned to his brother Masetla, the war chief. "We cannot allow the Swazi to reach safety in the highlands. Our friends, the people of Venda, have suffered great loss and humiliation, but they will not be the last. Who will be next? Lobedu? Kgatla? Ba-Nareng? You must summon my warriors from all parts of the kingdom. The time has come for the regiments of Phalaborwa to take revenge."

"We will need weapons," said Masetla.

"Do our warriors not have enough spears, bows, and poisoned arrows?"

"Yes, we have these, but we need guns."

"Guns?"

"Yes, the Swazi will not be so easily defeated again. We will need guns if we are to prove stronger in another war."

Makikele looked across at the man from Venda. He felt pity for the people who had befriended him in his youth, and felt a need to avenge for their loss. But more importantly, he could not allow the Swazi to pass unhindered through his realm once more.

"You can have your guns," he said. "Take what you need from my arsenal, but leave enough for the defense of Sealene. If the Swazi should reach Phalaborwa unscathed, then they may try to attack me here."

Masetla was not convinced that they would be able to drive off the Swazi again, even with guns. "Our men are not enough. We will need others to join us."

"I will also send word to surrounding kingdoms and chieftaincies and ask them to join us. Pedi, Kgatla, Lobedu, Thabina, Mapulaneng—they will want to wash their spears in Swazi blood. None of them want the Swazi plundering and traveling unchecked across their lands. A large force of neighboring groups will pose a strong defense against the common enemy."

Makikele turned to the messenger from Venda. "When we have defeated these Swazi, we will, of course, return stolen cattle to the people of Venda."

"My cousin and others in Venda will richly repay your kindness," he said.

"Is there anything else your prince might wish of us?"

"*Kgoshi* Makikele, your name is known throughout our kingdom, and stories of the wonders you beheld in our sacred lake near Ngome are well remembered in Venda. My prince asks you to employ the power of the spirit lake against the Swazi."

"I did so once before, and I will do so again. Have no doubt that the Swazi shall be defeated. The waters of the Selati will run red with their blood."

Over the next few days, men began to arrive from all the villages of Phalaborwa, and Makikele's fighting forces were once again melded into a great army. While the king's age-mate regiment was no longer young and some of them had died or been killed, there were many younger warrior age-sets now dedicated to Makikele's service. The united Phalaborwa, made strong by his father, *Kgoshi* Meele, and through the later battles against invasion, was still a powerful cohesive force, and its warriors were ready to defend their king and land.

Masetla sent messengers from his brother to surrounding tribal and village leaders with a call to arms. Furious about the years of Swazi incursions, warfare, killings, and displacement, they rallied to Makikele's summons.

Two days later, word arrived that the Swazi were approaching Phalaborwa. They brought with them the stolen cattle and captives, taken from Venda.

Masetla and leaders from other tribes instructed their warriors on tactics for the impending battle. Under Masetla's command, one section of the King's regiment waited in ambush on the north bank. A second group, under the command of Lerungi, a war leader in the recent Swazi battles, hid at Lolwe Hill. His army would follow the Swazi and cut off their line of retreat to the north. Warriors from Pedi, Kgatla, and other neighboring chieftaincies assembled south of the Lepelle.

When Masetla took up his position that hot evening on the north bank of the wide Lepelle River, there were still a few hippopotamuses wallowing in the muddy waters and several crocodiles gliding silently across the shallows. Toward the south, he noticed a herd of buffalo heading toward the Lebombo Mountains, leaving a cloud of dust in their wake.

Makikele's mother, Mokadi, was at this time extremely ill and crippled with arthritis. For several weeks she had been weakened by high fevers, followed by chills, and had not been able to eat without vomiting. Her liver, diagnosed as swollen, was being treated with herbal teas and medicines specifically addressing bad blood in the infected organ. Yet she continued to weaken and to lose weight, drifting in and out of consciousness.

Bedridden, she lay motionless beneath a blanket of soft skins and woven cloths. Several family members, women from the surrounding village, and a young slave girl, who slept in the house with her, attended to her daily hygienic needs and attempted to keep her comfortable and free of pain. In her deteriorating physical and mental state, she was unable to assist with the preparation of needed war medicines, one of the many roles she had guarded and directed for decades. Nevertheless, Makikele sought her counsel before performing the ritual tasks required in times of war.

"My son," she said in a frail voice, "you are a strong leader of the people. I am so proud. *Kgoshi* Meele, may his spirit protect you always, is pleased as well that you keep Phalaborwa strong. You are a great king, the greatest Phalaborwa has ever seen. You will defeat these Swazi vermin. I curse them all."

Mokadi fell silent for a moment, lowering herself back onto her couch of furs. Then, with much effort, she raised her body and spoke once more to her son. "Now go. Do not delay. Release the powers of our war magic. As best I can from this place, I will pray to those who await me on Modimolle, and to your father. Your exploits will be told and retold in the *direto* of our people until the sun no longer rises."

When Mokadi raised a hand in blessing and gave a nod releasing her son to depart, Makikele slowly backed away toward the door, and the eyes of mother and son fixed on one another. As the king stooped to exit through the doorway, lifting the cowhide covering, and emerged into the sunlight from her darkened abode, tears fell from his eyes. He sensed he might never again see his mother alive.

Makikele, together with his sister, Maboyana, and the witch-doctors began preparing the magic necessary to assure victory. His great wife, Mosale, was also there, but only to observe and learn the royal crafts. Makikele did not consider her proficient enough yet to participate fully and take the place of his mother.

They used the medicines previously prepared from body parts of the Swazi captured during the assault on Nagome. These ingredients, together with other medicinal components gathered from the bush, were combined with secret ingredients in the hoard of royal medicines and sacred objects known only to the queen mother and a few women of the king's immediate family. Queen Mokadi had carefully stored these medicines, some passed down to her from earlier royal guardians of tribal secrets, for just such an event as this one.

Some of the war medicine was incorporated into talismans, which Masetla distributed to his chief warriors. The talismans would give them protection against the enemy.

Meanwhile, Molonyo, the Swazi war general, was making his own plans as he led his forces toward Phalaborwa. He knew that it would be difficult to move the long lines of cattle through Makikele's lands undetected, and decided to push his men and drive the stolen Venda cattle both day and night until they crossed the Lepelle to safety in the highlands. To avoid passing close to the Royal Triangle and a greater probability of confrontation, he directed his troops to skirt this western part of the kingdom and then cut eastward to the river. He had valuable booty to deliver to his homeland, and traveling slowly through hostile territory was a risky matter.

On the final night of their passage through Phalaborwa, a quarter moon afforded them some light but was not light enough to leave them too exposed. However, it was an impossible task to keep their movement quiet with several large herds of cattle on the move. The vanguard of the Swazi party was approaching the Lepelle River when the gentle lowing and hoof beats of the cattle was drowned out by the eerie sound of many horns blown from atop Sealene Hill. At the same moment, a fork of lightning struck the river, followed by a deafening crack of thunder.

"This Phalaborwa witchdoctor they call their *kgoshi* is using magic against us again," said Molonyo. He had only just completed his sentence when lightning struck a second time, only a short distance ahead of their intended path.

The lightning was so bright that it reflected from the white fur of a vervet monkey troop hiding in an acacia tree grove. Disturbed by the storm, they screamed wildly as they frantically jumped among the branches in the flashing light.

As the storm set in on them, the cattle became harder to manage and Molonyo's men had to chase after strays, bringing them back to the main herd. Suddenly, a stampeding herd of migratory wildebeest appeared from the darkness and broke into the cattle drive, crossing its path at right angles. Several lead cattle already disturbed by the storm became even more agitated, broke away, and scattered in different directions. It took the Swazi valuable time and much effort to recapture them and bring the herds under control.

After an hour had passed, the storm subsided, and Molonyo decided to move his men and cattle forward in an attempt to ford a crossing at a place where the Lepelle and Selati Rivers merged.

He gave his orders. "Drive the cattle at speed through the bush and then across the river," he said. "Then we will make a run for it to safety in the highlands."

It was too late for them to hide their presence, so the Swazi whipped the cattle into action, shouting at them as they began the difficult drive across the river. The first cattle were halfway across the water, and the last were being driven to the river's edge, when lightning flashed again, illuminating and exposing the Swazi warriors. In their haste and distracted by the struggling cattle, they neither expected nor were prepared for what was about to happen.

Masetla gave a sign to his bowmen. A swarm of arrows instantly whistled through the air and felled many of the unsuspecting Swazi warriors who were already in the water. Lerungi and his forces from Lolwe Hill, who had silently shadowed the Swazi as they approached the river crossing, then threw a stream of long-shafted spears into the backs of those trying to flee the deadly rain of arrows. Explosions from a dozen elephant guns in the hands of marksmen hunters added to the mayhem, felling a swathe of enemy who had abandoned the cattle and were attempting to wade as fast as they could across the river.

Those Swazi who had not yet entered the water, a well-disciplined rearguard of spearmen, quickly arranged themselves in war formation and prepared their spears and shields for hand-to hand battle.

At that moment, the deep thudding sound of great *Boretho* and the higher-pitched *Thakna* called out a threatening rhythm from atop Sealene Hill.

Taking heart from the steady drum beat, the warriors of Phalaborwa marched forward with confidence to engage the enemy.

A hand-to-hand battle, spears and war clubs sinking into bone and flesh, ensued between the two enemy forces. Both armies used the short stabbing spear more suited to close encounters in combat. Aided by further firepower from Makikele's bowmen and those with guns, the Swazi were soon overpowered. Many fell on the northern bank of the river. Others were shot as they tried to escape across the river to the southern bank.

Some Swazi clung onto cattle as they plunged across the river, terrified by the sound of guns and shouting. A number of them reached the far bank, out of range of the arrows and gunfire. Here, they regrouped and prepared their weapons, intent on inflicting fatal revenge on their shadowy enemy.

"These Ba-Phalaborwa devils have used magic and cowardly tactics to shoot our people in the backs," said Molonyo. "We will teach them what it means to defy the Swazi!" As he commanded a counterattack, he shouted the name of the royal clan, Nkosi, and that of their king, Mswazi. "Who is with me, men of the Nkosi, brave Swazi warriors?"

His men shouted "Nkosi!" and "Mswazi!" and rallied behind their leader, splashing into the water once more with spears, ready for attack, and their guns, primed to fire and held high above their heads. The cattle, lunging through the water and scrambling up the riverbank to dry land, were forgotten as the men focused on targets for their weapons. Many of the beasts raced away in panic across the swampy bush that stretched from the southern bank of the river toward the distant hills.

The Swazi had no sooner entered the water when the allied forces hiding on the south bank launched a rain of long throwing spears. They sailed through the air in arcs, many finding their targets in the backs of the enemy. Molonyo was one of the first to be hit. A spear passed cleanly though his lower back and out his abdomen, and he fell face forward into the water. As he took his last breaths, the screams of his fellow warriors rung in his ears. Then all was silent, except for the sound of the hiss of a cobra. When his face hit the water, Molonyo had a vision of a green lizard and a green cobra and remembered his dream from several months earlier.

Then, a large black cobra with close-set eyes emerged from the water and towered over him, its hood flared, ready to strike. Molonyo's final thought was that the water into which he was falling was no longer a muddy brown color, but was instead a bright scarlet red.

The men of Phalaborwa and their allies had won a great victory. In the stories later passed down from generation to generation this battle became known as "The Battle of *Tsolle Meetse*," which means "The Battle of Bloody Waters."

When daylight dawned, surrounding villagers, accustomed to using the river for their drinking water and for bathing, were astounded by the carnage that they found. Their water source was polluted with mutilated bodies of men and cattle. Some had been carried off by crocodiles that waited for corpses to float downstream. Vultures, jackals, wild dogs, and even the nocturnal hyena had moved in to gorge themselves on the remains.

Most of the bodies discovered were Swazi, but some belonged to their own relatives—fathers, brothers, cousins and sons—cut down by Swazi spears or guns. People cried in anguish when they recognized the faces or distinguishing marks of their loved ones fallen in battle. They sent the carrion-eating animals scurrying away from the riverbank with well-aimed stones and raced into the water to scare away the vultures. The bodies of their fallen heroes were retrieved and each buried according to tradition, either beneath the cattle kraal shared by his lineage or in the yard near his house.

The battle marked a shift in Swazi domination of the region. Many retreated away from Phalaborwa to highland strongholds controlled by their powerful Dlamini royal clan. It was a turning point that ended their threat to the lowlands.

More importantly for Phalaborwa, Makikele's reputation as a king, witchdoctor, and sorcerer became legend and he was praised as the savior of his people. Word of his deeds spread as well throughout the neighboring kingdoms, and would-be invaders henceforth chose peaceful approaches in dealing with the iron and copper king rather than war.

A few days after the battle, Makikele was called to his mother's side. She was dying.

Mokadi Mathipa, the favorite wife of *Kgoshi* Meele, had been elevated by him to become his great wife. After Meele's death, when her son, Makikele, was recognized as king, she became the most powerful woman in the kingdom of Phalaborwa and addressed as "Mother of the Great Elephant of the Nation." Much later, at the height of her son's military and leadership

The Battle of Bloody Waters

prowess, she was praised widely as "Mother of the Land" in recognition of her ritual role during planting, harvest, and in bringing rain. She would be remembered as a powerful arbitrator of things sacred to the nation.

Mokadi lived to see her firstborn established king of Phalaborwa; another, Masetla, commanded the king's armies throughout the long and embattled era of Zulu and Swazi warfare and expansion. Her daughter Maboyana returned as a widow to her home at Sealene Hill to be queen sister and family priestess. A younger son, Mapiti, renowned for his incisiveness and political acumen, became a respected counselor to Phalaborwa kings.

Mokadi was laid to rest on Modimolle Hill amid an outpouring of grief rarely seen in the land of Phalaborwa.

CHAPTER TWENTY-FIVE

Again Magwambwa

Continued activity in the region by Jiwawa, the Portuguese trader and elephant hunter, again became a problem for Makikele in the latter years of his reign as copper king of Phalaborwa. When earlier driven out of Phalaborwa and barred from trading in the kingdom, Jiwawa moved from Magashula's village on the Sabie River to Ohrigstad, a new Dutch Boer settlement in the eastern highlands. Here he built a trading business, linking the highlands with the Portuguese port town at Delagoa Bay.

In 1853, he and his Magwambwa hunters again relocated, this time north of the Letaba River in southern Venda, where he built a stronghold called Goedewensch. This new fortified trading post was positioned near the growing Boer settlement of Schoemansdal, providing it with commodities imported from the coast. In addition to trade and hunting, Jiwawa opened a postal route, operated by porters, which followed an old Limpopo River trail and the Lebombo Mountains in Phalaborwa's borderlands. Before long, the Magwambwa were again entering the hunting grounds belonging to Makikele, competing for ivory and challenging his authority.

Jiwawa was appointed Native Superintendent by the Transvaal Republic in 1859, made responsible for policing the surrounding tribal region and authorized to introduce and collect a poll tax. In the same year, he and a combined army of Magwambwa and Pedi attacked Queen Modjadji's stronghold in Lobedu, stealing her cattle to pay the poll tax and capturing four hundred Lobedu children to be sold as slaves. At the same time, the settlers at Schoemansdal were engaged in warfare with the Venda, a conflict resulting in their abandoning the fortified settlement and fleeing the region, which had become a hostile war zone.

Almost twenty years after the First Jiwawa War, Phalaborwa was once more faced with the threat of gun-wielding Magwambwa Shangaan hunters in the employ of Jiwawa. However, the times were different. Makikele's power and control of trade and access to the surrounding region was absolute. Jiwawa, on the other hand, considered Makikele a stumbling block to his expanding hold on the area. The two powerful leaders were destined to lock horns.

Overhunting with guns and continual warfare along the upper reaches of the Limpopo and in the broader region surrounding Phalaborwa had depleted the elephant populations. However, Makikele's eastern borderlands, a vast stretch of hilly river courses sloping toward the Limpopo, continued to maintain large elephant herds and a lucrative hunting ground. At the same time, expanding Portuguese trade linking Delagoa Bay with Arabia, Asia, and Europe increased demand for ivory.

Hunting and the exportation of ivory continued to bring wealth to Sealene. Demand for ivory remained high, and the coastal tusk trade became more valuable as supply became more difficult. Jiwawa saw Makikele's restrictions on access to his elephants as an impediment to exploiting the region's game for his own profit. Having to skirt Phalaborwa's borders added distance and delay for his caravans and the monthly postal service between Goedewensch and Delagoa Bay. To circumvent Makikele's costly tariffs for crossing his lands, Jiwawa once again negotiated a secret alliance with Paane Malatji. He saw a lucrative advantage if he could oust Makikele and replace him with a more compliant local ruler.

Paane and his family had recently returned again from exile to eastern Phalaborwa, where he was permitted to govern a border area as royal *ntona*. This was with Makikele's permission after paying heavy fines for his earlier transgressions. But Paane was not happy. Memories of his humiliation by Makikele, and the latter's rise to kingship at his expense, still weighed on his mind. So, when Jiwawa approached him with a plan to displace Makikele in his favor, Paane accepted.

When Magwambwa again entered Phalaborwa, news of their unlawful presence in the kingdom reached Makikele's ears. A confrontation was inevitable, as Magwambwa hunters sought to disregard law and custom and violate the king's territorial rights.

At this time, Jiwawa was in a far stronger position to attempt to usurp control of Phalaborwa hunting lands than during the earlier invasion launched when he was a younger man. Paane as well was now more mature and determined to reestablish his authority and claim to kingship. He had bitter memories of his earlier unsuccessful attempt to take control of Makikele's eastern province. With the help of the Magwambwa, he thought, he might this time succeed where earlier he had failed.

Magwambwa invaders had the advantage of surprise and, although less in number, they were better armed than during their earlier assaults on Phalaborwa villages. Little resistance was encountered as they launched their attack from the eastern border. Along the way to the Royal Triangle, along the much-used salt trail, they overran the villages of Pjeni, Vudogwe, and Kgotwani, leaving many dead. Women, children, and the elderly, who were unable to run away, were shot or captured to be enslaved.

When word reached Sealene, Makikele assembled his war council. His brow furrowed and his eyes flashed as he made his introductory remarks. "This is the fourth time my borders have been crossed by belligerent foreigners since I have been king. We have dispatched these Magwambwa before, and shall do so again, but why do they think they can get away with it? Even the Swazi were no match for the warriors of Phalaborwa."

"And no match for your war magic," added Masetla. "It seems that Jiwawa is again behind the attack. He is angry that he and his Magwambwa followers are not permitted to hunt elephant in Phalaborwa, and seeks to replace you as king so they can take the ivory from us."

Makikele's son, Lepato, was the next to speak. "Is it true that my uncle, Paane, also supports this invasion?"

"Yes," replied Masetla, "He would once again make his claim to the Copper Throne, and threatens the legitimate heirs of *Kgoshi* Makikele."

"Then we must make sure that he never again has the opportunity to meddle with succession," said Lepato, who was surreptitiously making known his own claim to be the next king without actually stating it out loud in the presence of Makikele.

Makikele chose to ignore what was considered an impetuous comment by his young son about succession and instead spoke directly to Masetla. "Send word immediately to sound the war alert. A message must go out to summon fighters from all nearby villages. Once again our men must prepare for another armed battle."

"My regiments are still stoked like iron in the forge from the Battle of *Tsolle Meetse*," said Masetla. "They are ready for war. But should we meet the enemy in open battle near Sekgopo, or wait for them to approach Kgopolwe and Sealene?"

"We do not have much time," replied the king. "They are already in Phalaborwa. I will make haste to prepare war magic. We will fight them from our hill strongholds. Send word to Nagome also to prepare for an attack."

"And," said Masetla with a smile, "when they have surrounded the hill, we will defend ourselves with a counterattack from within, but the large force summoned from the western villages will surround them. They will not be able to fight us on both fronts."

"You, my brother, must leave at once to take command of the village warriors," said Makikele. "Lepato, my son, you will command Sealene's defenses."

Makikele's great wife, Mosale, was now well practiced in the preparation of war magic, and joined her sister-in-law,

Maboyana, and the witchdoctors in assisting Makikele. Once again, they combined components extracted from body parts preserved from previous battles with other freshly collected botanical and occult ingredients. With these meticulously brought together, the preparation for battle was complete.

By this time, the Magwambwa had arrived at Nareng, a hillside village not far from Nagome. They found the village deserted. All the young men had already left to join Masetla's army, and the women, children, and aged men had taken shelter at Nagome. The leader of the Magwambwa, a man known as Ngumabangi, had heard the hilltop drums sounding, but did not realize they were a call to arms to the young men from throughout Phalaborwa. He was a stranger to the interior of Makikele's kingdom, but had heard of the Swazi defeat at the Battle of *Tsolle Meetse*, and so he moved cautiously northward into the guarded precincts of the Royal Triangle.

"We will bypass Lolwe and Nagome and go straight to the capital," he said to Paane. "Our first objective is to kill this upstart king who sits illegally on your throne."

"Do not underestimate my brother," said Paane. "My father, *Kgoshi* Meele, unified the land of Phalaborwa. Every village, with the exception of those in the east close to Sekgopo, supports the king. He is also proficient in the use of war magic. He can control the weather. He used magic to call up a storm to defeat the Swazi."

"He is but a man," said Ngumabangi. "I do not believe these tales, that he is able to control the weather. It was just chance that the storm aided in the defeat of the Swazi. Once he is dead, his people will realize that he has no special powers. Then they will unite under a new king, who is you, Paane Malatji."

When Ngumabangi's men arrived at Sealene, they took up positions in the surrounding bush using trees for cover. They planned to shoot down those guarding the heavily barricaded entrance to the hill, and then storm the citadel. At Ngumabangi's order, elephant guns were aimed. The first round of shots penetrated the gate of thornbush and poles and killed several of Lepato's men. The Magwambwa cheered as they heard the cries of the wounded and shouted taunts at those defending the fortress as they began their charge and assault.

But their victory was short-lived. Three things happened almost simultaneously. The drum, *Boretho*, began a deep, hostile thud, sounding a warning from atop the hill. Its deep resonance sent a chill through Ngumabangi's body, but he did not have time to take this in before the earth began to rumble beneath his feet. Like a drunken man, he struggled to keep his balance and to remain on his feet, but he was thrown with a heavy jolt onto the rock-hard ground.

At the same time, there was a shout of warning from Paane. "We are surrounded," he called out.

As Ngumabangi stood to regain his balance, an arrow entered his chest, piercing his heart. The Magwambwa became disorientated from the effects of the earthquake. Many were thrown to the ground or forced to take shelter. None had time to reload their guns. The heavy firing arms were abandoned to grab hold of spears for immanent hand-to-hand battle with an onslaught of Masetla's men.

Gunfire from Sealene felled several of the Magwambwa. This was followed by another jolt from the seismic activity brought on by Makikele's magic. Masetla's men, unaffected by the earthquake, then rushed forward with stabbing spears. Within minutes, many of the terrified Magwambwa invaders were dead, though some managed to escape and ran away. Among those surviving were Paane and a few of his followers from Sekgopo.

Sealene was not without its casualties. The first rounds from Magwambwa elephant guns had done great damage to the perimeter fence, and some of Lepato's men lay dead or severely wounded. The victory over the Magwambwa had been a costly one.

Paane and those who remained loyal to him were driven into exile once more. This time he moved east into Tsonga country. He was warned by Makikele to keep out of Phalaborwa or he would be hunted down and killed.

Paane nonetheless continued to defy Makikele and regularly entered his borderlands to hunt elephant. This defiance eventually led to his death. When word that he had died reached Sealene, it was widely said that he had been killed by witchcraft and elephant magic. According to one popularly accepted account, Makikele created a magic elephant formed from mud and had it placed near where women went to collect water in a village frequented by Paane while he hunted. When the women arrived with their water pots, they saw the elephant drinking and began shouting. Paane arrived at the site and shot the elephant with a gun but was charged and crushed to death. It was generally agreed that the use of elephant magic and this manner of death was a just penalty for Paane's betrayal and poaching.

Elephant hunted near Sekgopo Hill

During the 1850s, the period between the Battle of Bloody Waters and the Second Jiwawa War, Makikele was at the height of his power as King of Phalaborwa. He had continued the work of his father to unite the kingdom, and with the death of his renegade brother Paane, even the hostile factions resident in the Sekgopo region accepted his authority.

Makikele had married many wives, as was expected of a powerful king. His earliest marriage was to Lesibe, and she remained his favorite although she was from a lesser Mathipa lineage and of lower rank among the king's royal wives. Wives were secured over time through alliances with powerful local families throughout the kingdom and with neighbouring rulers such as Queen Modjadji of Lobedu, and Pedi king Sekwati, and with his former host family in Venda, which his grandmother, Ntlabidi, had arranged. It was from these marriages and many others and their offspring that the seed for future succession disputes were planted.

During his declining years in the 1860s, competition among his sons for the copper throne began to gain momentum. The primary rivalry for succession lay with two sons from two of his more prestigious marriages. One was Majaji, his son from an alliance marriage with the powerful Hlame trading family at Sekgopo. The other was Lepato, son of Makikele's great wife, Mosale, his uncle Phatladi's daughter. This was a union chosen by the royal family's council of elders because she had the right background to produce the next heir. Just as *Kgoshi* Meele had done in the case of his wife Mokadi, Makikele had ritually established his great wife as the "heir maker" through a tribal-wide bridewealth tax required of all villages, and then through performing the fire ritual by which the queen's hearth fire rekindled all those of the nation.

Yet Lesibe was Makikele's great love during his youthful days and remained his favorite while he was in his prime years as king, and then into his old age. Theirs was a deep friendship that had evolved into an emotional dependence far greater that that found in his other marital relationships. Although his love for his many wives was abundant, and the bonds of affection many and varied, it was Lesibe whom he treasured most.

When they were both old, he would often come and sit for long spells in her compound. She would gather the younger grandchildren around him, and they would rest together by the fire to reminisce about their earlier days together. As the years passed, Lesibe noticed that Makikele often became troubled by events unfolding around him. Although Phalaborwa was strong, its borders secure, and the turbulent days of the *Difaqane* had passed, Makikele sensed that greater challenges were on the horizon for his people.

"Things have changed so much during my lifetime," said Makikele. He was now thin and bent over, and his forehead, once crowned with thick dark hair, was now balding and streaked with grey. The sharp, aquiline features of his face, once feared by those who displeased him, had softened, darkened, and become wrinkled.

"When I was young, we safeguarded our borders against the Swazi, and the Zulu, and the Magwambwa. Today, new groups enter Phalaborwa in growing numbers and threaten our way of life. They are the white men who come across the great ocean and down from the highlands to hunt our wildlife and take our ivory and copper. This is why I have forbidden them from looking at Lolwe Hill and visiting its mine shafts. They ask to see the hill, but I will not allow this. We must guard our sources of wealth and limit access to our lands."

"Yes, you have made the right decision," affirmed Lesibe. She too was stooped with age, and her beautiful youthful features had disappeared, though she maintained a bearing befitting the wife of a great king. "We can understand the Swazi, or even the Pedi *Bakema* who killed our people and stole from us. They were hungry and had no other way to find food. We can understand them because they are like us, and we would probably have done the same if we had been starving. These white men are different. They have many strange customs and do not respect ours. They just want to steal our cattle and our elephants, and the products of our many forges and smelters."

"I knew when the white hunter, Jiwawa, the leader of those Magwambwa, who scar their noses to be fierce-looking, came to hunt in my lands that he would bring more trouble to our borders. All these others who now approach me for access are no different. Others will follow them. Their numbers will grow."

"That Jiwawa is an evil man." Lesibe made a hand gesture in disgust and spat juices from the pipe she smoked into the hearth fire. "Look what he has done in Queen Modjadji's lands. Not only has he stolen cattle; even worse, he has taken away hundreds of children. We have always heard stories of whites stealing children from the villages and trading them away as slaves, but never so many as captured by this Jiwawa. Even some of the family of your mother in Lobedu have lost their children and grieve that they will never see them again." She spat for a second time in anger. "Yes, you are right to keep these white men at a distance."

"I have had a good life," said Makikele, changing the topic to reminisce with his much-trusted wife and friend. "In my youth, shortly after *Kgoshi* Meele sent cattle to your family and they brought you to the house of my mother as a bride, I went away to live in Venda, and traveled widely meeting people of many tribes. It was in those days that I learned about war and rain magic and many other secrets to help my people. Most important to me at that time was a visit I made to Dzata, the place of my ancestors, those ancient Malatji of the baboon totem. They lived there before they came to Phalaborwa, and before we became people of the porcupine totem. These ancestors protected me while I lived there. There were many dangers at the time, and they kept me from harm."

At her husband's mention of ancestral spirits, Lesibe poured a small libation of beer from her gourd cup, looked upward toward Sealene's summit, and whispered a prayer. She had seen many wonders brought by these protective forces, and nodded in agreement to what her husband had said.

"I have many wives, children, and grandchildren. I have served my people well and led them through many wars. Yes, we have had a good life, all of us, thanks to those who look after us here on the hill. Phalaborwa has prospered and held strong, even though some tried to break us apart and weaken this kingdom."

"You are respected and feared because you embody the magic and the many other secrets of this place. And all the people love you. That is why you remain strong. Yes, my husband, you are the link for the people with the powerful spiritual forces here. This is why they follow you, and your young regiments remain strong and defend us. You are respected and you are also feared."

"Yes, my Lesibe, *gogo* to so many grandchildren. Yet things are no longer the same as they once were. The elephants have begun to leave our hunting lands. Fewer tusks arrive at our trading villages and here in the *mashate*. I worry for the future."

"Why do you worry so, my husband? What do you think will happen?" his wife asked in a quiet, sympathetic voice, sensing that he was troubled and in one of his frequent deeply reflective moods. She worried about the king's growing inclination to prefer seclusion and signs of increasing physical discomfort. Having secretly consulted the divining bones of a trusted court witchdoctor, she knew her husband would soon die.

"This is what I see happening," said Makikele. "I see a stream of European hunters and prospectors entering my territory. Those who pass through now are merely the point of a spear that will soon pierce this land. I hear of the Boers fighting in Venda and Pedi. Some Pedi groups have even joined with the white intruders, the Boers, to attack Modjadji, and the Magwambwa also now join with the Boers against the Venda, who return their fire to drive them from their lands. Like a swarm of locusts, they begin to circle around us here in Phalaborwa."

"My heart tells me this unity we have in Phalaborwa is very fragile. In truth, it has always been so. I fear that when my time comes and I am buried on the hill, the kingdom will begin to split apart. It will become weak and vulnerable. When this happens, these outside forces will pull us apart. This is what concerns me most. Just as my brothers and I fought over who should be successor to my father, Meele, so I see my sons Lepato and Majaji, and even others, fighting over the throne when I am gone. I still have hope, but I fear the unity we have now will not last."

"But you have worked so hard all your life to maintain that unity and to keep this land for ourselves. All the people know this is why we remain strong," she assured him.

"Maybe I have angered the ancestral spirits. My late mother now at rest on Modimolle Hill, my great wife, all of the royal family, including myself—especially myself—have done the right things, followed closely what is appropriate custom over the many difficult years. But this current animosity and arguing between Lepato and Majaji troubles me. Those on the hill will be angered by this dissension. I can feel this even now as I look up at the big rocks above us."

Lesibe ladled more millet beer into her husband's cup, and placed it between his still-firm and strong hands. "You must not trouble yourself like this. You have not angered the ancestors. You have done the things required of you."

Makikele tasted the warmed beer, nodded in approval to his wife, and smiled at her. "I tell you, Lesibe, the old patterns of rivalry threaten to divide Phalaborwa once again. The ancient cleavage between east and west, between Sekgopo and Sealene— that is where the trouble lies. It is surfacing again. Lepato, who has his home here at Kgopolwe, and Majaji at Sekgopo do not cease bickering. It endangers our unity as a people. Many have become angry and are lining up to take sides. The Tsonga and some Venda strengthen ties with Majaji, and Lepato builds friendships with those we know in Pedi, Lobedu, and even in the north with our relatives in Venda. Because of this anger, Lepato has now left to go to the highlands to work in the white men's mines. These are far deeper than my Lolwe mines, or so I am told by others who have gone there. It is a dangerous life. When he returns, if he is not killed by the whites in that place, there will be trouble here again. The counselors and *ntona* openly talk about trouble brewing."

"Lepato will return. He is the right one to succeed you and to rule here. As was the case in your own youth, his travel and what he learns will make him stronger. Mosale, his mother, has protected him with magic, and he carries medicines she has carefully prepared with the herbalists. She asks the spirits of the hill to guide him. Even yesterday, I heard her pouring a prayer libation at the shrine she keeps by the door to her house. You will see; he will return well and strong."

"Yes, but I see now that Majaji and his followers will remain in control of Sekgopo, much the same as Paane attempted before him. No, Lesibe, the kingdom will be divided once more. And with this will come new threats from outside—I mean the whites who have followed Jiwawa, and the ones who take samples of our ore and climb the hilltops to study the lay of our lands. They take what they learn with them, and will return in greater force, perhaps greater than the Swazi and Zulu. If the Malatji become fragmented when I am gone, much may be lost.

"Yes, you are right, Lesibe, I have had a good life. But soon I will sleep forever on the hill. I do not fear going. I welcome going to my place there, and to be with those who keep eternal watch over the land."

CHAPTER TWENTY-SIX

Hovering Spirit

The death of *Kgoshi* Makikele came quite suddenly. He had been weak and frail for several months, and when he died peacefully in his sleep, the omens were good for a smooth transition of power.

As was the custom, the death of the king was kept secret from the general population until his family members could be summoned, and witchdoctors had performed all rituals required to prepare the body of the king for burial. Royal counselors and the closest members of the king's lineage were summoned to Sealene. Runners were sent to bring Lepato back from the highlands to participate in the death and burial rites.

Following the same traditions observed after the death of *Kgoshi* Meele, the king's body was left to decompose over a period of many days. It rested in the house of death, bodily fluids exuding from imposed incisions and collected in pots to use in medicines for the well-being of tribe and land.

As predicted, a dispute for succession began when two rival groups met during the king's mortuary rites, each to stake their

353

claim. One group consisted of the supporters for Lepato and were mainly members of the king's council and *ntona* from the villages in the west and center of Phalaborwa. The other group, from the Sekgopo area, asserted that Majaji was the rightful heir.

Both groups recognized the need for agreement on important matters relating to the succession process and burial arrangements, so their uncle, Prince Masetla, was chosen as the "holder of the chair," the custodian of the royal enclosure and the king's sacred regalia until a new king was recognized and acclaimed.

When village leaders from around the kingdom had arrived and it was time for the royal burial, a pure black bull was killed and its skin placed around the corpse. The house was then sealed off to await the ritual of the "opening-of-the-door," which would identify a new king and successor to Makikele's Copper Throne.

What occurred next shocked the traditionalists of Sealene who were guarding the king's body and overseeing his funeral. In the middle of the night, without notifying these venerable council members or Masetla, the holder of the chair, Prince Majaji entered the compound with a group of followers. They aimed to foil any attempt by his brother, Lepato, to gain the throne by being the first to walk through the dead king's doorway and thus demonstrate his right to rule.

The prince crept through the open courtyard until he stood in front of his father's door. Removing his skin cloak and headgear, he set to the task of opening the door. Pushing gently at first, in expectation that the aged gray planks would budge a little, he was surprised to find the barrier immovable. So he tried pushing a little harder. Still nothing moved. The door remained solidly closed. The prince was renowned for his physical strength and prowess in battle and as a hunter, so he was sure he could force his way in. He braced his shoulder against the door and used every ounce of his strength. Sweat poured from his lean and tense body as he strained to force open the door, but it was no use.

"The spirit of the king and those of his ancestors do not approve," whispered one of those attending.

"He is excluded, just like the *direto* tell us happened to Prince Lepane back in the time of *Kgoshi* Kgashane," said another.

Prince Majaji's face contorted into a dark scowl. He took a few paces back and charged at the door, using his right shoulder as a battering ram. When he met the full force of the resistance of the door, he howled with pain and fell, dejected, onto the ground. As this happened, he heard the sound of a flute and turned to see his brother, Lepato, entering Makikele's courtyard with his mother and brothers and other family members.

"Enough, brother," said Prince Lepato, while blowing a high-pitched note on the flute and pointing its feathered tip at his brother.

"You . . . where did you come from? How did you know . . . ?" Majaji rose to his feet, stunned by the jolt to his shoulder, and approached his brother.

"Our father spoke to me in a dream and told me that you would be here. He said that the ancestors were angry with you, and that you would not succeed in opening the door. It would be best for you if you left Sealene immediately." As he said this, more men carrying torches entered the compound. Some wielded spears and clubs, and gathered behind Lepato.

Majaji snatched the flute from his brother's mouth, blew a loud note back in Lepato's face, and then threw it to the ground, crushing it under his foot. This show of defiance and insult to his brother stunned the growing mass of onlookers who feared the power of Lepato's medicated flute. The observers stared in silence as Majaji arrogantly and mockingly laughed, then walked from the courtyard with his companions.

As he crossed beneath the lintel supporting the gateway to the royal compound, Majaji turned back and glared at his brother. Their eyes met in anger. Spitting on the ground, he pointed at Sealene's towering granite outcropping. "You call this a strong mountain, but I will one day make it a ruin. I will destroy it, and I will drive you away." With this he strode away, joined by family members and allies to return to Sekgopo.

Later, when Lepato's mother, Mosale, entered Makikele's regalia hut, she discovered that the small war drum, *Tlanka,* was missing. Ngwanaphura, Majaji's mother, had managed to secretly remove and take it with her to Sekgopo. The drum was of great antiquity and power, and Mosale knew that its theft and efforts to retrieve it or replace it, would cause problems for the people of Sealene and all the Ba-Phalaborwa.

Without wasting a moment following his brother's departure, Lepato called his supporters, including his mother and brothers and senior family members, to come close. When they were all assembled, he pushed hard against the door of his father's house. At first it did not move, and some thought Lepato might also fail in this critical ritual test. But, with several more strenuous attempts, the door opened slowly, and then swung wide as he was able to dislodge the pegs, driven deep into the floor, that held it immobile.

He entered the house of the dead king and looked with satisfaction toward his father's body, recognizing that he was the blessed one, chosen by those spirits inhabiting the rocky tombs of Sealene to be the next king.

Men of the family followed him inside and prepared Makikele's body for the journey to Sealene and burial in his final resting place.

News of Makikele's death and the succession quickly spread among the villages, as did word of Majaji's humiliation and Lepato's triumph.

The procession to Sealene and the burial followed much the same pattern as that of previous kings and men of the royal family over the centuries. Lepato and his full brothers headed the long line of mourners and royal men bearing the king's body, and the late king's sister, Maboyana, led the line of royal women.

A bright full moon emerged from a cloudy night sky as Maboyana crossed Sealene's royal burial terraces to determine where the hole should be dug to place her brother. After marking the interment site by shoveling away soil with a ceremonial iron hoe, she signaled the funeral cortege of royal men to bring the hide-enshrouded body onto the terrace.

As they approached, balancing their burden on bare shoulders, steadying it with many hands, the wizened royal sister stood silent, surveying a hillside now no longer hidden in clouded darkness. She looked for signs. Her ears and nose were attuned for sounds or odors that might portend a message from the dead, those cherished and nurtured spirits living among the rocks and retaining walls. But there was no sign. All remained silent. Only the muffled sound of hundreds of bare feet ascending the stony pathway leading up the granite hill could be detected.

Adhering strictly to protocol, Lepato, as successor to his father, began digging the king's grave, followed by his full brothers, and then other royal males based on their rank and birth order. Digging continued until the hole was large enough to accommodate the body and the grave offerings to be included in the royal entombment.

Maboyana was troubled by the brightness of the moon. So clear was the night, in fact, that torches carried by the royal mourners were of little need. *Herein lies a problem*, she thought in silence. She watched the dark shadow cast by the large bull hide shroud containing the dead king as it was placed close by the pit being dug. *To cast a shadow on such an occasion,* her cautious mind told her, *could portend trouble for Phalaborwa. It was something to be feared.*

Maboyana knew that shadows during such nocturnal rites indicated the dead person's spirit was disturbed, and might not stay reposed in the grave; might even fail to enter the grave, preferring instead to roam the land. She waited and watched, hoping a stray cloud might block the moon and any phantom shadow before Makikele was buried.

The king's shadow lingered as his remains were lifted on high, and then lowered into the hole now hidden from view by royal men, concluding the complex interment rituals.

Maboyana watched the shadow of her brother ascend and then descend across the gray stone surfaces marking the western borders of the burial amphitheater. For a brief moment her eye detected movement in a distant higher recess of the dominant granite pillars, and then whatever had caught her eye seemed to dart downward and beyond. The sign she sought was now clear. It was not auspicious. The brother she knew and loved would not rest contentedly or passively under stone and earth. His spirit would roam the land, requiring attention. But Maboyana would keep her countenance. She knew that Makikele Malatji, son of Meele and the much-praised sorcerer-king of Phalaborwa, would continue to watch over his people from the stones of Sealene and elsewhere when needed.

Makikele is buried at Sealene Hill

Makikele was mourned with all due ceremony, and his bones rest on Sealene today.

It was only a few weeks later that Makikele's great love, Lesibe, also took her last breath. She was laid to rest on Modimolle Hill beside the bones of Mokadi, and Ntlabede, and all the other royal women who make up the cast of characters in early Phalaborwa history. Both Modimolle and Sealene Hill would continue to be spiritual beacons, guarding the land of Phalaborwa and the Ba-Phalaborwa people.

One son of Makikele was conspicuously absent at these sacred mortuary rites. Prince Majaji had returned to Sekgopo Hill, where he would hold political sway, declare himself *kgoshi*, and ally himself with eastern interests and with Umzila, a neighboring Tsonga king. He would later seek assistance from Makikele's hated enemy, Jiwawa, and attack Lepato at Sealene. This action would bitterly divide and weaken the Ba-Phalaborwa, causing continued schisms and feuds between the two branches of the royal Malatji family that would last for generations.

It is said that to this very day, Makikele's restless spirit roams the lofty heights of Sealene Hill waiting for the time when his land and people will again be united. Some believe that only then will he rest content.

Author's Notes

It was cold and windy when I first met with elders of the Ba-Phalaborwa tribe. A fire had been built in a windbreak at the home of an aged counselor to the tribe's ruler. Old Maboyane Malatji was one of the few remaining royal praise singers responsible for transmitting carefully memorized tribal oral history. It was a cheerful, hospitable group that sat together with me on my first day in the poor, overpopulated Makhushane tribal reservation. This was a small parcel of parched land set aside near the town of Phalaborwa for the indigenous Sotho-speaking people by the white-controlled administration then governing the vast northeastern lowland bush country in modern-day Limpopo Province.

The group of men included several of the king's advisors, and sons and grandsons of my host. We huddled close together, seated on wooden stools and benches, partly to keep warm and partly to hear clearly what the frail-voiced octogenarian knew of his people's past.

Accustomed to an audience, the diminutive grey-headed bard proudly recited a genealogy of the royal family, which extended back more than twenty generations. He then praised the accomplishments of each ruler in his inventory of royal names. This lengthy and erudite saga was the first of many testaments given to me in multiple versions and expanded detail during the course of my stay in Phalaborwa. It told an amazing story, never before documented and mostly unknown outside of the tribal reserves of the region.

I believe this story of Makikele Malatji of Phalaborwa, which is partially derived from oral traditions collected in the 1970s and partially from ethnographic reconstruction, has an important place in Southern African history. It is the story of a talented man of unusual political acumen and cunning, someone who fashioned his people's survival, sustainability, and destiny during one of the most volatile periods of regional history. It is also clear that ancient internal cleavages, running along kinship lines and caused by political and trading rivalries, were a countervailing force held in check by Makikele, but ultimately divided the kingdom, making it vulnerable to outside forces following his death.

Makikele's name, often numbered as the twenty-first ruler, or *kgoshi*, of Phalaborwa, is the most praised of those in an extensive and carefully preserved Ba-Phalaborwa oral history. From this we know that he was a remarkable man. It is said by knowledgeable tribal elders that the era of Makikele was a turbulent time in pre-European and early colonial history.

Elderly locals identify Makikele as a hero to his people, praised for his wisdom and strong leadership in dangerous times. Many believe that without his courage and fortitude, the land of Phalaborwa would have been conquered by neighboring tribes, and the Ba-Phalaborwa people would have vanished, absorbed by others, their land taken away from them.

As epilogue to the story, it may be helpful for the reader to know that *Kgoshi* Meele's dream of a united Phalaborwa, brought to fruition during the reign of his son and heir, Makikele, ended with the latter's death. When Makikele's kingdom was divided among various branches of the Malatji royal lineage and allied groups, the schism that developed between his sons, Lepato of Sealene and Majaji of Sekgopo, was enduring.

Makikele's prediction to his wife, Lesibe, that outside influences would cause the ruin of the kingdom became a reality in the decades following his death. As the kingdom divided, a series of other factors came to bear which brought about dispossession from the land and economic decline.

The first of these was an increase in the number of European settlers entering the region. Earlier white traders, hunters, and other travelers, crisscrossing Phalaborwa for centuries, had respected local customs and authority, paid tribute when required, and observed rules of hospitality. Although rogue opportunists such as Joao "Jiwawa" Albasini stirred up trouble and breached custom in pursuit of their own interests, encounters with visitors had for the most part been peaceful and beneficial. The factors that brought about change and disruption in the later nineteenth century were typical of European colonialism throughout the world: greed, exploitation, and disregard of local customs and rights.

In 1887, gold was discovered in a range of hills running just west of Phalaborwa's boundary with Lobedu. White prospectors and traders flocked to the area, which became known as the Selati Goldfields. Mining and prospecting activity continued for a decade, giving rise to new makeshift white settlements, the largest being Leydsdorp, founded in 1890. This influx of white prospectors was accompanied by the introduction of cheap manufactured goods, which quickly undermined Phalaborwa's traditional metal production. However, gold mining proved unprofitable and, after about a decade, the Selati Goldfields were abandoned. By 1913, Leydsdorp had become a virtual ghost town.

Simultaneous with these developments, a major ecological change was occurring in the region. In 1896, rinderpest, an infectious viral disease, entered Phalaborwa and became widespread, killing most native livestock and decimating the large herds of wild herbivores.

The consequences of this disease were twofold, one unfavorable and the other beneficial. Initially, it proved disruptive to the Ba-Phalaborwa, causing abandonment of villages and famine. The decimation caused by rinderpest, however, had a longer-term beneficial effect not immediately perceived. The epidemic, by killing off most of the grazing species in the region, also wiped out the endemic tsetse fly, which was unable to survive without the animals it fed on. In just a few years, Phalaborwa became tsetse-free, making it more hospitable to animal husbandry and hunting, as herds returned.

While proving beneficial to the local population, the disappearance of tsetse brought about another change, a demographic change which would have a lasting impact on the indigenous population. With the elimination of tsetse fly, Europeans, who previously avoided the region as unhealthy for settlement, found Phalaborwa attractive for the first time. Seeing this, the South African Republic (Zuid-Afrikaansche Republiek, or ZAR) was quick to enact proscriptive laws giving opportunities in the region to white interests at the expense of those of the native Ba-Phalaborwa people.

The process had in fact already begun earlier, before the rinderpest epidemic, as white interest groups sought dominance over local owners of the land. This process was made official through a series of ZAR parliamentary enactments and laws favoring white settlers, to the detriment of the local indigenous residents.

Unbeknownst to the Ba-Phalaborwa, a ZAR proclamation in 1887 declared much of their traditional tribal homeland to be public land available for outside investors to prospect, mine, and farm. This was followed, again unbeknownst to the Ba-Phalaborwa, by a precious metal act passed in 1892, placing large tracts of land north of the Lepelle River in government hands to be sold or issued for use by outsiders. Under this new law, the indigenous populations were to be restricted to small native locations, called 'kafferlocaties,' leaving the majority of the land open for outside development and settlement.

These enactments excluded the tribal population from all legal regress, except within the four small reservations allotted to them under the new laws.

In 1909, Phalaborwa's revitalized and repopulated hunting territories were declared Crown Hunting Land to be administered by the Province of the Transvaal, and supervised by game rangers.

In 1914, all of the land between the Lepelle and Letaba Rivers, the traditional boundaries of Makikele's kingdom, were declared part of the Sabie Game Reserve, making it illegal for local people to hunt.

Until the 1920s, however, little had changed in the day-to-day way of life of the people of Phalaborwa. The new laws remained on paper, with little effort at enforcement. Meanwhile, the Ba-Phalaborwa had recovered from their losses during the rinderpest epidemic, and were again farming, herding, and hunting throughout their traditional tribal lands. The land remained unsurveyed, and the government kept its distance. At the time, few suspected or understood that this might change.

Change came about in 1926, when all of the Ba-Phalaborwa hunting lands were joined with surrounding tracts and formed into a larger Kruger National Park. With the establishment of the Kruger Park, physical dispossession and relocation of the native populations began. Officials of the Department of Native Affairs, wardens, and rangers of the National Parks Service, together with armed police, began arriving at farmsteads and villages, confiscating guns and weapons and chasing people from their homes. They were forced to live on four small reserves in the vicinity of what later became the white mining town of Phalaborwa.

Beginning in the 1920s, a small number of white farmers began entering the region, attracted by cheap land rentals from the government. However, little acreage was actually farmed by these settlers. Instead, most was used by absentee owners for hunting in the winter months.

In time, a small number of English and Dutch Boer farmers settled permanently on private and government-owned land tracts. Many lived as neighbors of Ba-Phalaborwa families who, in the early days, still remained on their farms. Some of these new arrivals were poor single men involved, like their African counterparts, in marginal farming, cattle ranching, and hunting. In a number of well-known instances, the new settlers intermarried with local African residents, establishing kinship bonds and partnerships with their Ba-Phalaborwa neighbors. Sometimes these unions followed local African tradition, involving bridewealth transactions and ongoing gift-giving relationships. However, due to the country's expanding racial segregation laws known as Apartheid, children and descendants of these interracial unions often moved to the tribal locations with their maternal families.

Phalaborwa's twentieth-century tribal leaders followed Makikele's example and resisted threats to the integrity of their homeland by powerful, and sometimes unscrupulous, external interests during the dark times of the Apartheid regime. Disbarred from legal action outside of the restricted government appointed tribal locations, this took place through protests at tribal authority offices, and through verbal denunciations when they perceived their rights being further eroded.

Repeated protests about the displacement, and petitions to the government by tribal leaders demanding the return of their land, were ignored. By the 1950s, the Ba-Phalaborwa found themselves dispossessed of their land, without compensation, and barred by South African law from taking legal action.

During this breach of Ba-Phalaborwa civil rights and displacement, white men, protected by the various government enactments, started exploiting the area's resources on an ever-increasing scale. In 1931, the South African Phosphate Company began mining operations in the vicinity of the royal family's Lolwe Hill mines and metalworks. This was followed by the Transvaal Ore Company's mining of vermiculite near Lolwe Hill in 1939. The following year, the Phalaborwa Phosphate Company also began mining operations near the ancient mine works.

In the 1950s, new and larger companies, Foskor and The Palabora Mining Company, expanded the earlier industries into large-scale modern operations, which eventually obliterated Lolwe Hill with what is today one of the largest open-pit copper mines in the world. In less than two decades, the site of Makikele's Royal Triangle was transformed into a major mining complex with state-of-the-art technology and communications. What had been a relatively obscure area in the early twentieth century was emerging as a mining hub on the border of one of Africa's most populous and diverse game reserves and tourist attractions.

The modern town of Phalaborwa grew up around these industrial sites to accommodate white miners and their families, while indigenous tribal people and a growing African migrant labor force lived in surrounding designated "Bantu" zones.

A 1993 notarized affidavit from *Kgoshi* Lepato Brown Malatji, leader of the Makhushane tribal location, on behalf of all of the Ba-Phalaborwa, gives a poignant and detailed history of the tribe's uncompensated displacement. It documents their continued and consistent demand for the return of their lands and natural resources. In this official tribal writ, the honorable leader protests renewed South African government threats of further dispersal of their land to outside interest groups and settlers.

With the 1994 election of Nelson Mandela as the first president of a multi-racial South African democracy, new laws were enacted for the restitution of lands taken without compensation from native peoples as the result of Apartheid laws. Shortly following this new enactment, the four hereditary rulers of the Ba-Phalaborwa people, representing their tribal locations of Makhushane, Selwane, Maseke, and Mashishimale, lodged a united claim for the return of their traditional lands and mineral rights in their entirety, as they existed in the time of *Kgoshi* Makikele Malatji.

In 2010, the Ba-Phalaborwa land and mineral rights claim was recognized by the courts and declared undisputed by the South African government. This positive pronouncement by the courts in favor of the tribe's united community litigation brings hope that a new era of reconciliation and prosperity has begun.

Today's strongly held Ba-Phalaborwa values concerning rights to the land and its resources, and the distinctive pride of culture preserved in the lowlands between the Lepelle and Letaba Rivers, are Makikele's legacy passed down to later generations and descendants. This land continues to be regarded by the Ba-Phalaborwa as "a land better than the South," where "the ring of the forger's hammer continues to echo," at least metaphorically, in the modern mining establishments still extracting wealth from an ore source that was Makikele's Lolwe Hill mine.

A few words about how I came to work in Phalaborwa. In 1970, as a graduate anthropology student at Binghamton University, New York, I joined a team of archaeologists from several American and South African universities conducting Iron Age research in Phalaborwa and in the nearby Kruger National Park game reserve. Phalaborwa had by that time become a modern copper mining center with a burgeoning migrant African labor force. The team's survey work included exploring numerous geological outcroppings, both inside and outside the game reserve. These locations were thought to have been early settlement sites of the metalworking peoples we sought to identify and document.

I was asked to be the team's ethnographer. An ethnographer is a social anthropologist who studies the people living in or near a research location. Ethnography includes such things as observing and asking people about the way they live and how they understand the world around them. In the case of the Phalaborwa Iron Age research project, my job involved asking local residents about the way people lived long ago. This included recording and analyzing oral traditions about the past that might shed light on the area's unrecorded history.

While I conducted my research in the modern tribal locations, the archaeological team set about locating, mapping, excavating, and dating Iron Age ruins throughout the region. At times, the two approaches overlapped nicely. Local oral traditions often pointed out the location of archaeological sites, while materials exhumed from the sites provided dates and cultural artifacts verifying the tribe's extensive and ancient presence.

Collectively, the team uncovered information documenting a local metal-producing culture dating back to at least the eighth century. Excavated village sites near the ancient Lolwe Hill copper mine shafts provided evidence that Phalaborwa's Iron Age culture was continuous from the tenth century until the early 1900s. Analysis of traditions, passed down by word of mouth to modern day, confirmed the importance of Lolwe and the many other hill sites in Phalaborwa's Iron Age history.

The story of Makikele Malatji, while framed as an historical fiction, is a compendium of many stories and historical explanations shared by Phalaborwa area residents. I have taken considerable literary license in portraying the characters, many of whom survive in local tradition only as names on recited lists or points of reference in historical narrative. While much of the drama and dynamic in the story is fiction, the chronicle of events around which it is structured are vivid components of an oral tradition remembered with pride by locals and sometimes substantiated in accounts from early travelers to Phalaborwa and in the ethnographic studies published about surrounding peoples.

My work with the Ba-Phalaborwa people was made possible through the generous hospitality and cooperation of the late

Chief Lepato Brown Malatji, who was *kgoshi* of the Makhushane Tribal Location, and by his counterparts in the Maseke, Madume, Mashishimale, and Selwane Tribal Locations.

This story would not have come about without the enthusiastic involvement of the people of Phalaborwa who shared their rich oral history passed down through the generations.

At the time I lived in Phalaborwa, *Kgoshi* Malatji was a member of the Lebowa Northern Sotho Parliament and served as its Minister of Forestry. He saw the research as an opportunity to better document and tell the story of his Ba-Phalaborwa people's proud history and long tenure as indigenous owners of the land.

I am also indebted to the late Dr. Eileen J. Krige, who shared unpublished field notes on Phalaborwa royal genealogy, which she collected in the 1930s coincident to her ethnographic study of the neighboring Lobedu tribe and its legendary rain queen. Also helpful in reconstructing details of eighteenth- and nineteenth-century Phalaborwa and its neighboring peoples and cultures were the writings of Henri A. Junod, Charles E. More, H.O. Moninig, J. D. Omer-Cooper, H.A. Stayt, Nikolaas J. van der Merwe, Nikolaas J. van Warmelo, and Monica Wilson. The latter also graciously lent me her University of Cape Town, Rondebosch (UCT) office for two months in 1975 during my stint as a guest lecturer.

The project was funded by a United States National Science Foundation (NSF) grant and was sponsored by UCT. Professor Nikolaas J. van der Merwe, of Binghamton University, was the team's leader. We were joined from time to time by students and professors from the then Sotho-speaking University of the North at Turfloop, and the Universities of Pretoria, Witwatersrand, and UNISA. There was much interest at the time to learn more about this little-known part of Africa. Following the first season of fieldwork, the project's ethnographic component continued for an additional two years (1974–1976) and helped answer many of the questions raised in the initial investigation.

In preparing this publication, the author wishes to thank the many who helped. Particular thanks to Les Bill Gates of Edi+addition, Tokoroa, New Zealand, for proofreading and editing book revisions. Chris Freeman of Freeman Art, Lincolnshire, UK provided illustrations. Bill Bray and Bowen Craig of Bilbo Books Publishing, Athens, Georgia, provided encouragement and comments on story outlines and early drafts. My wife Jennifer Lee Landman Scully, as always, provided the best, wisest advice and encouragement and did the final read-through. Their many talents helped bring the book to publication.

Robert T.K. Scully

The author and research assistant, Isaac Mabelane, Makhushane tribal location, Phalaborwa 1970

Ba-Phalaborwa Rulers

Official list of Ba-Phalaborwa rulers printed in 1990 by the Makhushane Tribal Authority, with additional detail by the author in parentheses.

MALATJI I

(Lived north of the Limpopo River in "Bokgalaka", had the baboon totem.)

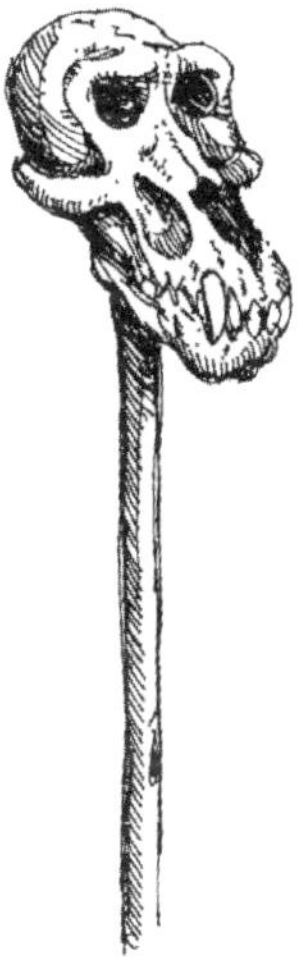

MMAKAU

MALATJI II

(Adopted the porcupine as his totem.)

SELEMATSELA

RANTSHANA

SESETLAMABU

RAMOKGONWANE

LESIKAPITSI

SEYALEMABU

TSHEHLE

MOTHATEWALEOPENG

SEKHUTUSEMMOTO

LEPANA

MOKGOROPONG

KGOTHWANE

PAANE

MASALENI

MOTHUPI

KGASHANE

MOSHOLWANE

MEELE

MAKIKELE

(died circa 1869)

LEPATO I

(died in 1894)

MATOME PAI PAI MAKHUSHANE I

(died in 1925)

MOGALE JULY MAKHUSHANE II

(died in 1964)

LEPATO II BROWN MALATJI

(died in 1997)

ANDREAS MAKATIKELE MALATJI

(Current "Kgoshi" of Makhushane Tribal Authority, Phalaborwa)

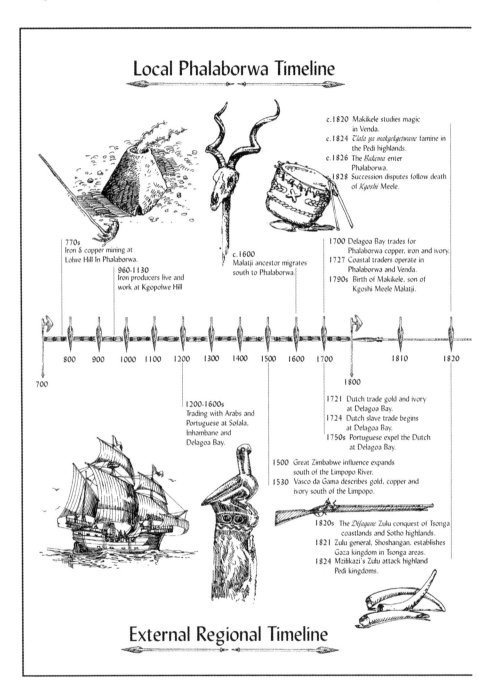

Local Phalaborwa Timeline

c.1820 Makikele studies magic
in Venda.
c.1824 *Tlala ya makgekgetwane* famine in
the Pedi highlands.
c.1826 The *Bakena* enter
Phalaborwa.
1828 Succession disputes follow death
of *Kgoshi* Meele.

770s
Iron & copper mining at
Lolwe Hill In Phalaborwa.

960-1130
Iron producers live and
work at Kgopolwe Hill

c.1600
Malatji ancestor migrates
south to Phalaborwa.

1700 Delagoa Bay trades for
Phalaborwa copper, iron and ivory.
1727 Coastal traders operate in
Phalaborwa and Venda.
1790s Birth of Makikele, son of
Kgoshi Meele Malatji.

800 900 1000 1100 1200 1300 1400 1500 1600 1700 1810 1820

700 1800

1200-1600s
Trading with Arabs and
Portuguese at Sofala,
Inhambane and
Delagoa Bay.

1721 Dutch trade gold and ivory
at Delagoa Bay.
1724 Dutch slave trade begins
at Delagoa Bay.
1750s Portuguese expel the Dutch
at Delagoa Bay.

1500 Great Zimbabwe influence expands
south of the Limpopo River.
1530 Vasco da Gama describes gold, copper and
ivory south of the Limpopo.

1820s The *Difaqane* Zulu conquest of Tsonga
coastlands and Sotho highlands.
1821 Zulu general, Shoshangan, establishes
Gaza kingdom in Tsonga areas.
1824 Mzilikazi's Zulu attack highland
Pedi kingdoms.

External Regional Timeline

374

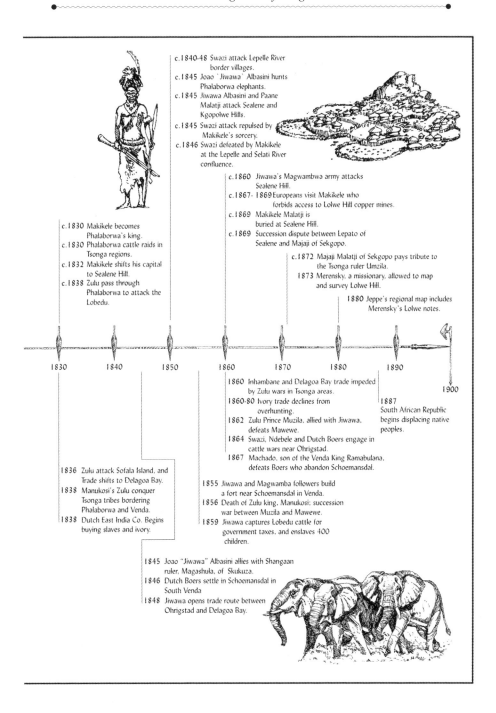

c.1840-48 Swazi attack Lepelle River
border villages.
c.1845 Joao 'Jiwawa' Albasini hunts
Phalaborwa elephants.
c.1845 Jiwawa Albasini and Paane
Malatji attack Sealene and
Kgopolwe Hills.
c.1845 Swazi attack repulsed by
Makikele's sorcery.
c.1846 Swazi defeated by Makikele
at the Lepelle and Selati River
confluence.

c.1860 Jiwawa's Magwambwa army attacks
Sealene Hill.
c.1867-1869 Europeans visit Makikele who
forbids access to Lolwe Hill copper mines.
c.1869 Makikele Malatji is
buried at Sealene Hill.
c.1869 Succession dispute between Lepato of
Sealene and Majaji of Sekgopo.

c.1830 Makikele becomes
Phalaborwa's king.
c.1830 Phalaborwa cattle raids in
Tsonga regions.
c.1832 Makikele shifts his capital
to Sealene Hill.
c.1838 Zulu pass through
Phalaborwa to attack the
Lobedu.

c.1872 Majaji Malatji of Sekgopo pays tribute to
the Tsonga ruler Umzila.
1873 Merensky, a missionary, allowed to map
and survey Lolwe Hill.

1880 Jeppe's regional map includes
Merensky's Lolwe notes.

1830   1840   1850   1860   1870   1880   1890

1900

1860 Inhambane and Delagoa Bay trade impeded
by Zulu wars in Tsonga areas.
1860-80 Ivory trade declines from
overhunting.
1862 Zulu Prince Muzila, allied with Jiwawa,
defeats Mawewe.
1864 Swazi, Ndebele and Dutch Boers engage in
cattle wars near Ohrigstad.
1867 Machado, son of the Venda King Ramabulana,
defeats Boers who abandon Schoemansdal.

1887
South African Republic
begins displacing native
peoples.

1836 Zulu attack Sofala Island, and
Trade shifts to Delagoa Bay.
1838 Manukosi's Zulu conquer
Tsonga tribes bordering
Phalaborwa and Venda.
1838 Dutch East India Co. Begins
buying slaves and ivory.

1855 Jiwawa and Magwamba followers build
a fort near Schoemansdal in Venda.
1856 Death of Zulu king, Manukosi; succession
war between Muzila and Mawewe.
1859 Jiwawa captures Lobedu cattle for
government taxes, and enslaves 400
children.

1845 Joao "Jiwawa" Albasini allies with Shangaan
ruler, Magashula, of Skukuza.
1846 Dutch Boers settle in Schoemansdal in
South Venda
1848 Jiwawa opens trade route between
Ohrigstad and Delagoa Bay.

Glossary of Northern-Sotho Words

Ba-: Prefix to a group name indicating "the people of," as in Ba-Phalaborwa

Badimu: Ancestral spirits

Bakema: Cannibals

Bjale: Female coming-of-age ceremony

Difaqane: Widespread regional upheaval caused by Zulu expansion, 1820s to 1840s

Dikomathuku: Ritual marking the return of a newly initiated male regiment

Dingaka: Medicine men

Direto (pl.), *Sereto* (sing.): Traditional praise poems and songs containing oral history

Gogo: Grandmother

Kgobeane: The creator God

Kgoro: Headman's cattle enclosure and meeting place

Kgoshi: Hereditary ruler or king of a tribal group or region

Koma: Male circumcision and initiation rite

Lepelle: Oliphant River

Losha: Ritual bowing to show respect and deference

Malome: Mother's brother

Maloti: Drakensberg Mountains

Marale (sing.), *Serale* (pl.): Copper ingot used for trade and gift exchange

Mashate: King's residence usually including a *kgoro*

Motseta: Go-between messenger who helps arrange marriages

Motheko: Goods exchanged in marriage transactions

Noko: Porcupine, Malatji lineage's totem animal

Nkwe: Leopard

Ntona: King's representative sent to administer a village or region

Phalaphala: Sable antelope horn trumpet

Rakgadi: Older sister

Rangwane: Diminutive title, meaning "young uncle"

Trobela: Greeting used in Phalaborwa and surrounding areas

For Further Reading

Berger, Iris. 2009. South Africa in World History. New York: Oxford University Press.

Hall, Martin. 1990. Farmers, Kings, and Traders, The People of Southern Africa 200-1860. Chicago: University of Chicago Press.

Hammond-Tooke, W.D. (ed.) 1974. The Bantu-Speaking Peoples of Southern Africa. London and Boston: Routledge & Kegan Paul.

Krige, E.J. 1965. The Realm of a Rain-Queen. London: Oxford University Press.

Monnig, H.O. 1967. The Pedi. Pretoria: J.L. Van Schaik Limited.

Omer-Cooper. 1974. The Zulu Aftermath, A Nineteenth-Century Revolution in Bantu Africa. London: Longman Group Ltd.

Scully, R.T.K. 1979. The Lists of Phalaborwa Rulers, a comparison of variant 'fixed' sources. History In Africa Vol. 6: 211-223.

Van der Merwe, N.J. and Scully, R.T.K. 1971. The Phalaborwa Story: archaeological and ethnographic investigation of a South African Iron Age group. World Archaeology 3(2):177-196.

Wilson, Monica and Leonard Thompson (eds.) 1969. The Oxford History of South Africa, Volume 1. London: Oxford University Press.

About the Author

Robert T. K. Scully was born and educated in New York State, where he earned a PhD in Anthropology at Binghamton University. He served in the United States Peace Corps in western Kenya and conducted ethnographic research in Phalaborwa, South Africa. Retired from the international health field and university administration, he lives in Sandy Springs, Georgia. This is his first historical novel.